One Day at a Time

One Day at a Time

Tessa Alexandra

Copyright © 2023 Tessa Alexandra

All rights reserved

The characters and events portrayed in this book are fictitious. Any similarity to real persons, living or dead, is coincidental and not intended by the author.

The poems of Ranata Suzuki have been used in this book. Per author's webpage, "Sharing and reusing of material is permitted as long as it is clearly stated as being written by Ranata Suzuki."

No part of this book may be reproduced, or stored in a retrieval system, or transmitted in any form or by any means, electronic, mechanical, photocopying, recording, or otherwise, without express written permission of the publisher.

Cover design by: Tessa Alexandra

ASIN: B0C9JQK78G (ebook)
ISBN: 9798399978963 (paperback)
ISBN: 9798850090951 (hardcover)

Contents

Prologue 1

Part 1: The Rhodeses 9

Part 2: Viola Rhodes 51

Part 3: Bartholomew 87

Part 4: June Pearson 133

Part 5: Owen Hart 167

Part 6: August Pearson 231

Part 7: Henry McCoy 275

Part 8: Eric Shaffer 295

Part 9: Emilia Rhodes 333

Part 10: The Shaffers 367

Prologue

The road before Emilia stretched, rising and falling with the hills until it disappeared from view. But the more she drove, the more of it she saw, like catching a glimpse of her future seconds before she arrived there. How far had they gone? She checked the clock and tried to do the math in her head, but gave up quickly. The road behind her didn't matter. All that mattered was what lay ahead.

It took her several minutes to notice the cassette tape had ended. That the only sounds were the whirr of the car's engine, the whoosh of the highway racing by, and the fuzzy noise that meant it was time to turn the tape. Well, those and the clamor of thoughts in her head.

She jammed the eject button and fumbled with the cassette, turning it over and trying to push it back into the slot. The car swerved.

"Hey! Eyes on the road. I've got that." August took the cassette from her and fed it into the tape player. The next moment, "Uptown Girl" began playing in her car.

Emilia sighed and turned down the volume. She could feel August's eyes on her. He was probably wondering why she was frantic to get the car to play music she didn't even want to listen to. She followed his instructions and kept her gaze on the dark highway in front of her. His hand appeared on her leg next, squeezing her thigh in a way that would have tickled her, if she hadn't been so upset.

"I'm worried about him," she sighed. "I'm worried he's going to do something really stupid."

"Your dad?"

"No, not my dad," Emilia snapped. "I don't care what he

does. I'm talking about Eric."

"Oh, right. Eric. Of course." There was an edge to his tone, but she didn't have the patience to try to dull it.

"He doesn't need to be there! He's always doing this—allowing himself to get sucked up in all their drama, convincing himself he's the only one who can fix it—but he can't fix everyone. He needs to let it go."

"That's just Eric though, isn't it?" August shrugged out of the corner of her eye and stretched his long legs out in front of him, though there wasn't much space for them in the small car. "My mom said he's like that little boy from the story with the dam. You know the one who puts his finger in the hole?"

"Yeah," she nodded. "To plug the leak and save his town from flooding or whatever."

"Yeah, that one. My mom said she thinks Eric's mom probably told him something like, 'take care of the family' before she died, and he took it to heart. So the first time a problem came up, he stuck his finger in the hole. He's been doing that for years, another finger, then another. Maybe a toe. A whole damn hand at some point.

"Before long, he's standing there in front of a dam that's about to blow and we all see it—it's fruitless what he's trying to do, he needs to get the hell out of there—but he's just doing his best to protect his town—or family, or—you get it."

Her eyes stung with tears as she pictured Eric standing in front of a crumbling dam, trying in vain to keep it from collapsing. "I like that analogy. Your mom's right. And he doesn't see it."

"No, I don't think he does," August agreed, voice low. She turned and saw him running his fingers through his hair like he did when he was feeling nervous. Or guilty. She wondered which one it was.

They were quiet for a while and Emilia sang along to the faint music under her breath. As the song changed, she exhaled heavily, then adjusted in her seat. "If he adopts Henry—"

"He won't," August cut in.

"I just wish he were here. So I could make sure he wasn't doing anything stupid."

August placed a hand on her leg again. "You're where you need to be. Or, you will be tomorrow. Try to think about something else."

Another silence stretched between them. Emilia listened to the entirety of "Christie Lee," which she'd never liked very much. Why was this the only tape in her car? Because she'd left in such a rush, that's why. She sighed again.

"I hate his sister," she announced when the song was over. "Leaving her son behind like that. Actually, she probably learned it from their dad. I hate him too. Running off and leaving Eric to pick up all the pieces."

"In his defense, he'd just lost his wife."

"That's not a good defense! He practically abandoned three kids. That's illegal, by the way, leaving them alone as much as he did and—ugh!" She hit the steering wheel. "A man screwing his family over like that—it's so cliché."

"Are we talking about Eric's dad, or your dad?"

Emilia fixed him with a stern glare, but he was unphased. He held her gaze until she finally looked back at the road.

"Maybe you're focusing so hard on Eric to keep from focusing on yourself," August said gently.

"I'm fine."

"Is that why you're grinding your teeth? I can actually hear it. And you're—shit! Can you slow down? You're going 80!"

"Oh, crap." Emilia eased her foot off the pedal and forced

herself to take several deep breaths. August was right, of course. He knew her better than anyone, except perhaps Eric. She took another deep breath, then placed a hand on top of August's.

"I'm fine, really. Thank you, by the way, for coming with me. For missing Thanksgiving; your favorite holiday. I just—it means a lot. Really."

August turned his palm up and linked their fingers together. "Of course I'm here. I'm an excellent boyfriend. Remember that in a few weeks when you're shopping for Christmas gifts," he added with a grin.

She turned to smile at him, but he was looking out the window. "Hey, Em? That was the exit."

"I know. We're driving straight through."

"What? No. I'm exhausted. Last night was a nightmare."

"Yeah? What happened?" she asked, hoping to distract him from the missed exit.

"I had a post op patient who was complaining about pain, but he wouldn't take the morphine the chief ordered, since apparently morphine is for dying people. I wasn't about to bother the chief about that—I'm just a med student, you know? So anyway, I was stuck in this back and forth with the idiot all night—it was awful. I can't wait until Eric gets to his clerkship so he can experience these joys along with me."

Emilia was exhausted too, but she didn't say so, since she knew it wouldn't help her case. She'd taken extra shifts at the legal clinic so she could take the rest of the week off. She was supposed to be spending the next few days relaxing at August's parents' house, but instead she was here, responding to her sister's distress call.

"I can't drive anymore," August was saying, shoving his thumb and forefinger into his eyes.

"You don't have to."

"Let's just stop."

"You didn't hear her, August. Viola's never upset. But she was crying. She's the most even-keeled person I know, and she never cries. Even as a baby she never cried."

"Do you remember?" he asked doubtfully.

"Sure I do. I was four. Children can form memories as early as three."

"I don't remember anything before, like, nine. But, whatever. Is getting there eight hours quicker really going to change anything? You're going to be dead tired. You'll just go straight to sleep once we're there, so—"

"I'll be fine. I'll drink coffee," she said firmly.

"Em, you're not—"

"I don't want to talk about this."

"You're being sort of crazy, and we should discuss it. If you really want to be a lawyer, you're going to need to develop better arguments than, 'I don't want to talk about it'."

Emilia gave him a large eye roll. "I don't need a lecture about what it takes to be a lawyer. Especially not from you, someone who doesn't know the first thing about it."

"Just talk to me," he said through clenched teeth.

"No. I need to focus on driving."

August groaned and dropped his head into his hands. She kept her eyes forward, trying her best to ignore him. She was glad he was here; really, she was. But her family was in crisis, something August, whose family history did not include sisters who abandoned their kids or dads who took up with bank tellers, would never understand.

"I wish Eric were here too," August said, pulling Emilia out of her thoughts. Her brow crinkled as she turned toward him, confused by the abrupt change of topic.

"He'd be able to talk some sense into you," August explained when he saw her looking at him.

Emilia rolled her eyes again. "You're just tired and it's making you grumpy. Sleep, okay? I don't need help driving."

"Fine," he grumbled, then proceeded to shift his tall, lanky frame around, folding and unfolding his limbs several times before finally going still. Before long, she heard him snoring softly.

Emilia sighed and turned the music back up, then blinked hard, willing her eyes to stay open.

She needed to turn the cassette over. The car had been playing static for several minutes now. She reached for the eject button, then blinked twice at the clock. 1:23

She could have sworn it was 12:31 when she'd first noticed the static. Had she really been listening to that for almost an hour? Or maybe she'd just read the time wrong? Damn, she needed to wake up.

Emilia blasted the air conditioning and flipped on the radio, but had no luck finding a station and turned it back off a few minutes later. Her thoughts drifted to Viola and her mom, who were probably holding each other and crying over her stupid dad and the damn bank teller. An affair with a bank teller?! Emilia was going to strangle him.

Her foot pressed a little harder on the gas. She forced herself to take a deep breath when she noticed she was white-knuckling the steering wheel. She needed to think about something else. Her mind went to Eric next, but she pushed it elsewhere, settling on August and his post op patient.

Morphine is for dying people. Where did that patient get that? Maybe he'd watched too many war movies. She wondered how old he was. She'd have to ask August later.

She jolted and blinked rapidly, looking at the time. 1:47

Damn she was freezing. She reached for the AC knob and jumped at the sound of a horn blaring. She screamed as headlights flooded the car. August shouted. She threw her weight at the brakes.

CRASH!

Pain.

Then nothing.

Part 1: The Rhodeses
Try your best not to worry about them. They're okay

* 1 *

When Emilia woke up, her first thought was *August!*

She jumped out of bed. "August?! August!"

She looked around frantically, but she was alone in the room. And she was ... standing? Shouldn't she be injured? Where was she?

She wasn't in the guest room at her parents' house. Nor was she in a hospital room or a motel. She walked to the window and peered through a gap in the curtains. Mountains. She knew those mountains.

Emilia looked down and patted her body, expecting to find some sort of injury, or at least discomfort (hadn't she just been in a car accident?), but she was fine. And she was back in Aspen Grove.

But *where* in Aspen Grove? This wasn't her apartment. For one, it was way too nice. The crisp white molding lining the floor and ceiling, the high quality furniture, the new carpet, and the amazing view. No, she couldn't afford a place like this. But some of the things in this room were hers.

The lamp on the nightstand, that was hers. But the nightstand itself and the large bed, as well as the sheets and comforter, were not. There was a desk and bookshelf along the wall that were also foreign, but she recognized the books and knick-knacks that filled their shelves as her own.

Did she live here? It seemed like it. When had she moved? How did she not remember that?

She shook her head. She could get to the bottom of this later. She needed to find August and—

Emilia stopped when she spotted a letter on the nightstand,

folded like a tent and begging to be noticed. She approached it carefully. Her name was written on the outside in her own handwriting. She snatched it up and flipped it open. As she scanned its contents, her eyes filled with tears.

She crouched next to the nightstand and peered at the date on the alarm clock, wondering in the back of her mind how she'd known there would be a date there. Her old alarm clock hadn't displayed a date.

The clock read: FEB 01 87

"No," she whispered. Was this a joke? She pressed several buttons on the clock, determined to change the date back. It wasn't hard to change the date on these things. But even as she thought it, she knew it wasn't a trick. This was real. It was 1987.

Her knees buckled and she managed to lower herself onto the bed before she fainted. She took deep breaths as she clutched the letter in her hand. She looked back at the lines written in her handwriting, but all the words were blurry. She squeezed her eyes shut, tried her best to clear her mind, then started reading again, slowly this time.

Emilia,

In November 1984, you and August were driving to Nebraska, on your way to see your family, when you got into a car accident. First off, August is okay. He broke an arm, but recovered quickly. The truck driver is also okay—barely got a scratch. You were injured the most.

In the accident, your brain was damaged and ever since, you haven't been able to create memories that last longer than a day. You were in the hospital for months and attracted the attention of experts from all around the country, but nothing they tried worked. The part of your mind that stores longer-term memories is broken and will likely never be fixed. Every night when you sleep, your memory resets.

If you're still doubting whether or not this is real, look at your scars. There's one on your neck, one at the base of your skull, one on your right elbow, and one cutting across your ribs.

Emilia paused her reading and looked down at her right elbow. Sure enough, there was a scar. An old scar. Jesus Christ! That was more convincing than the date on the alarm clock. Dammit! She looked back at the letter.

Breathe, Emilia. Inhale ... exhale. Inhale ... exhale. Don't panic. It's not as bad as it sounds. You could have died in that crash, but you're here. You're alive and you have systems in place to make things manageable.

At first, you tried writing everything down and would study it the next day, determined to remember everything. After several months, it was too much. You'd spend hours each day studying a past you couldn't remember instead of just living your life. The system now sounds a little complicated, but it works.

You still take time to study all the notes you've taken about the time you lost, but not every day. You do that once a month now. It takes a long time and is always a painful process. You read the history you've written for yourself, filling in the gaps from November 1984 to the present. You review the details of everything that happened over the past month and you edit your history and this letter as needed.

Then, at the beginning of every month, you start fresh. There are summaries about all the important people in your life on the desk. Read those every day. At the end of each day, update any summaries that changed (e.g., new job, girlfriend, etc.) and write down anything notable that happened that you want to remember. Also, make notes for yourself for the next day. There's a calendar where you can keep track of plans, things you'd like to continue working on, or a conversation you want to follow up on.

I know this is a lot. But you can do this. I know it's scary to march into each day without a plan, with no idea what you're walking into, but remember, you're not alone. Breathe one more time, read the summaries, and enjoy your day as best you can. If it's bad, oh well, there's always tomorrow.

-Emilia

By the end of the letter, Emilia's heart was in her throat and her vision was blurred by tears. She pulled at her shirt, at the spot just over the tightness in her chest. Was it like this every morning? How did she bear this?

She placed the letter back on the nightstand and took several breaths, as instructed. Then she carefully crossed the room and took a seat at the desk. There was a large calendar on top for the month of February 1987. In the middle of the calendar was a stack of papers with the word *Summaries* scribbled across the top.

Emilia scooted her chair in and bent over the pages. She flipped through the pile and saw there was a page for each of her loved ones: Viola, Eric, August, June ... ending with a summary for her parents. She read that one first.

The Rhodeses

Martha Rhodes still lives in Kearney, Nebraska while her ex-husband, Paul Rhodes, moved to Omaha at the beginning of 1986. Despite the fact that they're divorced (and no, Paul did not end up with the bank teller) they have managed to find some peace and mostly get along these days.

Emilia leaned back and swiped at her bottom lashes. It was so detached. Had her past self thought that would make it easier to read? If so, she was wrong.

You call them on the first Friday of every month and visit them once a year, usually in the fall. It's always a hard visit. Be sure to bring someone with you. It's hard on them to see you this way, since they blame themselves for the accident. And it's hard for you to witness them behaving so differently around you. But they're happy! Try to keep that in mind.

They are better apart then they ever were together, and even though things are strained between you and them, they could be so much worse. You're here, for one. And you're not without family. Viola lives just a mile away. Try your best not to worry about them. They're okay.

Emilia placed the paper down and sighed. They were okay. Happy, apparently. But divorced. She wasn't sure how to feel about that. And they were distant.

But honestly, they'd been distant before. Ever since she'd left Nebraska and never looked back, visiting home only once a year for Christmas and even then, for just a few days. The thought made her feel hollow. She rubbed the ache over her heart, then flipped back to the beginning of the notes. She began to read about Viola and her friends.

The summaries didn't fill in all the gaps. For example, August's summary said they weren't dating anymore, but not why. But she had enough information about her friends to understand the general state of affairs.

She lived with Eric in the house where he'd grown up. Eric worked "in the medical field", a description Emilia found unpleasantly vague. August was in Boise, doing his first year of residency. Her sister Viola was living here, which was weird. She was supposed to be in New York.

August's sister June still skied professionally but wasn't dating Eric anymore. She was dating a girl on the ski team named Ruby. Owen still lived near Camp Ouray and was working on a degree in agriculture. Henry, Eric's nephew, was three years old and stayed over at the house two nights a week. At least Eric hadn't adopted him. All that worrying for nothing.

It was a lot to take in, in a short amount of time. Emilia spotted a glass of water on the nightstand. She sipped on it as she read the summaries a second time. She was hoping for a sense of familiarity or déjà-vu. She'd read these pages hundreds of times, but everything felt new. She tried to shake the disappointment that had settled in her gut.

When Emilia was finished, she stacked the pages back into a pile, straightened them, and moved them to the edge of the desk. It was time to study the calendar. The only problem was, it was blank. Was that normal? The letter made it seem like there should be information here.

She leaned over and studied the large piece of paper further. She noticed smudges all around the page, like the calendar had held information that had been erased. Then she saw a line scribbled across the top. It was also in her handwriting, but the scrawl was a lot messier than normal.

New challenge for February 1987: Take things one day at a time

Emilia frowned and pushed back from the desk. Was this a joke? Didn't she always take things one day at a time? Wasn't that her curse?

She rose to her feet and walked into the hall, but stopped, unsure where she was going. That's when she saw a page taped to the wall. It read, *Your Bathroom,* with an arrow pointing to the right. Her heart jolted at the familiar handwriting. Eric.

She suddenly had an urge to see him. She looked around the hall. Where would he be? There was only one door to the right, which she knew now was the bathroom. Then, to the left, two more closed doors. Was he behind one of those? Before she could investigate, she heard movement below.

Emilia ran down the stairs, following the sound to a kitchen at the end of the hall. She stopped short. Was she ready for this? She patted her hair. It was probably a mess, but who cared? This was Eric. He'd seen her looking worse.

Should she read his summary again? She tried to recall what she'd read.

You've been living at Aspen Grove with Eric since September 1985 ... He works in the medical field ... He insists on teaching you how to ski, despite countless protestations ... He blames himself for not being there to prevent your accident (classic Eric).

Emilia smiled to herself and took a breath. This was Eric. She knew him almost better than she knew herself. They'd been best friends for six years, ever since that first day she'd met him at Camp Ouray.

That was eight years ago, a voice corrected in her mind.

She turned away from the painful thought and back toward the memory of meeting Eric. Her first task as a new counselor had been to start a fire for the campers to roast marshmallows on their first night. She'd been struggling with the matches, trying and failing to get the wood to catch as she questioned her decision to take a job that required so much time in the wilderness, a place she knew nothing about. That's when Eric walked up.

He grinned down at the pile of matches she'd gone through and introduced himself, then asked if she wanted to see how the locals started fires. She nodded and watched him grab a bottle of lighter fluid, coat the wood in the liquid, then toss a match on the pile. The fire started instantly.

She'd laughed, and they'd been friends ever since. He was an expert around the camp, as he'd been spending his summers there since he was ten, and was more than happy to show her around. But before long he grew from being a guide, to a dear friend. He was the first person she could really talk to since, well, ever. And it seemed to be the same for him.

While lying under the stars after lights out, she told him

about her plans for the future. She told him how she never felt like she was doing enough. She tried to explain her burning desire to do more, to help, to right so many of the world's wrongs. How she wanted to be a lawyer so she could fight for change, but how there were so many issues, she didn't know where to start.

He told her about his family. About his mom, and how he had to watch her die of cancer over the course of a long, painful seven years. How he was going to dedicate his life to researching the disease to ensure no one else had to die like that. How his dad was absent, and his sisters were a mess, and he didn't know how to keep his family together.

After the summer ended, they'd gone back to Aspen Grove, where they were both attending the same college, though on opposite sides of the campus. Eric introduced her to his best friend, August, who he said was the only other person he'd met who wanted to be a doctor as badly as he did. August was one of those people who was impossible not to like, so she became friends with him easily, and the three were inseparable from that point on.

She took a deep breath. How different could things be? Well, she wasn't with August anymore, for one. And Eric and June weren't together, for two. For three…

Emilia turned off that line of thinking. She was overcomplicating this. It was Eric. Her best friend. And it was his birthday, wasn't it? At least, yesterday had been, if the date on her clock was correct. That was one thing that hadn't changed. She would tell him Happy Birthday and give him a hug and it would all be fine. She took two steps forward but stopped again in the doorway. He was there, staring into the open refrigerator.

The kitchen, like the rest of the house, was very nice—new

appliances, clean lines, and crisp white cabinets. This was new. She'd visited this house a handful of times before the accident and remembered the kitchen differently. She wondered how long it had taken Eric to renovate it. Had she helped? She hoped she had, since she doubted she was paying rent. It's not like she could hold down a job with her condition.

Damn, that was a depressing thought

Eric was completely still and she got the sense he'd been standing there for a long time. She cleared her throat and spoke a tentative, "Hi."

He jumped and turned, closing the door of the refrigerator behind him. She took in his altered appearance as he slowly crossed the room. The most notable difference was that he had facial hair. She'd describe it as closer to long stubble than a short beard, reminiscent of a few times during the summers when he'd forgo shaving for a while, but tidier.

His hair was different too. It was shorter on the sides and the top looked just as long and wavy as she remembered, but was styled up and out of his face. So he'd finally learned how to tame it. She smiled at that. And he had new glasses. That purchase had been long overdue.

Eric, who had stopped just in front of her, was looking at her strangely. Before she could question her actions, she lifted her hand and ran it along the hair on his jaw. Then she pushed a few brown locks that had fallen onto his forehead back in place. The whole time, Eric continued to stare at her.

Emilia pulled her hand back. "Sorry," she muttered, suddenly embarrassed.

This must be weird for him. He'd seen her just yesterday. Did she do this every morning? She couldn't help herself. Now that she was with Eric—looking slightly different, but still undeniably her best friend—the emptiness that had begun to grow in her chest finally started to shrink back to a manageable size.

He was still staring at her intently. She thought he was trying to tell her something with his eyes, but she didn't understand. After a few more moments of silence, she altered her original assessment. He wasn't trying to tell her something; he was trying to read something. But she didn't have the answer like she usually did. Surely, he knew that.

"I—uh—I don't remember anything." She stumbled through her words. "I don't know, um, is there something I'm supposed to be doing? Something I missed? I didn't forget your birthday, did I?"

"No, you didn't," he said, still staring at her.

What are you looking for from me? she added in her mind.

Eric's gaze softened. "You write yourself notes for the day. What you want to do, plans you've made, books you want to keep reading. Sometimes ... things you want to say ..." Eric placed a hand on her arm and added gently, "Did you miss those this morning?"

Emilia shook her head. "Um ... are you talking about the calendar? It was, uh, blank. It looked like it had been erased."

Eric frowned and dropped his hand.

"I thought it was weird," she added in a rush, "and I guess you're confirming it. There was one note—something about a personal challenge to take things one day at a time for the next month."

"One day at a time?"

"Uh ... yes?"

Eric laughed darkly and dipped his head. He took off his glasses and pinched the bridge of his nose.

"I don't know the joke," Emilia said slowly. She reached

around in her mind for something, anything to explain Eric's behavior, but it was blank. What was he looking for from her? What had she done?

"I don't see how living one day at a time is a personal challenge," he said bitterly, putting his glasses back on. "You've been living that way with me for a while now."

"Was there some sort of ... catalyst?"

Eric exhaled softly. "Catalyst? Sure. Last summer. Check your notes."

"Oh." Emilia looked down at the floor, embarrassed again. He'd thought she was asking why she lived one day at a time with him. That was something she'd have to look into. What notes was he talking about? The ones she was only supposed to review once a month?

"I meant a catalyst for the challenge; the reason my calendar is blank," she clarified.

Eric's jaw tightened and the deep pools of blue in his eyes turned to ice. "I don't know, Emilia." He placed a hand on her shoulder and breathed heavily, clearly trying to keep his anger in check. "I have to go. I—" He paused to exhale again. "Have a good day."

He brushed past her. From somewhere deep in her chest, something stretched out to touch him. An extra sense, something beyond the usual five, that reflexively reached for Eric's hand as he passed.

But her arms, which were suddenly much heavier than usual, stayed rigid by her sides. As he thrust his arms through the sleeves of his coat, she felt an icy chill spread from somewhere near her heart, its cold stretching down her veins until it covered the surface of her skin. She stayed frozen in place, a statue carved in ice, unable to do anything but watch as he stomped out the door.

The echoing bang of Eric's exit shook the walls, the windows, the crystalline glaze that had become her skin. She felt tiny cracks spread through her as she stared after him, still and silent, motionless except for the slow trail of tears melting their way down her face.

* 2 *

Emilia managed to keep herself whole. Just barely. She stood in the hall for several moments, hugging herself as Eric's face flashed across her mind, twisted in anguish—an anguish she was sure she'd caused, though she had no idea how.

This was so awful—not knowing how to help one of her closest friends—knowing she needed to apologize, but not knowing for what. She had always known what was going on with Eric. But now … she didn't know anything. How did she live like this?

Emilia decided to take a long bath; that always made her feel better. She stood naked in front of the mirror for a long time, inspecting her new appearance. Her thick, dark hair was the same. She usually grew it out until it was midway down her back, then cut it shoulder-length and started again.

She seemed to be about halfway through that process. Her face was the same as she remembered it. Same large brown eyes, framed by thick eyebrows. Same olive skin with faint freckles sprinkled across her cheeks. Same full mouth, same oval face.

She inspected the new scars, glad to note they were small. She'd been expecting to look like Frankenstein, but it seemed to be just her brain that was marred beyond recognition. She would have preferred it the other way around.

Emilia sighed and lowered herself into the warm water, then willed herself to relax and be happy she was alive. To push the thoughts of Eric to the side.

It didn't work.

Once she was clean and dressed, she felt just as bad as before. She sighed and began to explore the house, starting upstairs. She already knew what was in the two doors at the end of the hall, her bathroom and bedroom. She tried the other two doors.

The one at the opposite end of the hall led to the master bedroom, which she assumed belonged to Eric. The bed in this room looked identical to the one in her room but unlike hers, was unmade. Drawn forward by large windows showcasing a gorgeous view of the mountains, Emilia almost walked inside when she stopped herself. The cold expression in Eric's eyes from earlier came to mind, and she decided not to invade his privacy.

The other bedroom on the floor was a kids' room, with dragons painted on the walls. She wondered if her sister had painted them. It looked a bit like her work. This must be where Eric's nephew, Henry, slept when he stayed over. She spotted a photo on the nightstand and crouched down to look at it. Her heart jumped when she saw herself in the picture.

She and Eric sat at an outdoor table with Henry, eating ice cream cones. Henry, who had a chubby face and the same wavy brown hair as Eric, happily licked his cone as half of it melted, dripping down his hand to his elbow.

The Emilia in the photo was grinning at Eric, who was in the middle of a laugh. She could picture the sparkle of his deep blue eyes that must have accompanied the action, even though the photo hadn't captured it.

She smiled to herself. This proved that Eric didn't completely hate her. She closed her eyes and willed herself to recall this moment. In the photo she could tell she'd ordered a chocolate ice cream cone. She tried to imagine the taste of the ice cream, how Eric must have made fun of her for picking such a boring flavor, like he always did. How she'd probably quipped that at least she hadn't picked vanilla.

There was nothing there. The moment was gone. She wiped her eyes as she rose to her feet and resumed her search of the house, heading to the main floor next.

The first room she encountered looked like a small library. There was a comfy-looking beige sofa in the middle of the room and two plush green chairs next to it. One of the walls was lined with bookshelves. Emilia almost stopped to investigate but kept going. She'd come back later. Once she sat down next to all those books, she'd never leave.

There was a family room next to the library, furnished with a TV, another sofa, a plush armchair, and some side tables. There was also a large stone fireplace on the side of the room, framed by windows that showed off more of that lovely mountain view.

The stone around the fireplace was different than she remembered it, and the windows looked new. Eric had renovated the house since she'd last visited and done a good job. It was a lot lighter, friendlier, almost. It made her think of home, even though it was nothing like the house where she'd grown up.

A small office came next, most of which was filled with a light oak desk. On the desk stood a computer, surrounded by papers containing Eric's handwriting. She was about to leave when she spotted a photo at the edge of the desk. She picked it up and smiled when she recognized it, relieved to finally find something she remembered.

August, Emilia, Eric, and June were standing in front of one of the bars in town, smiling excessively for the camera. Emilia had just turned 25 and had planned a progressive dinner through town to celebrate. But after appetizers at their first stop, they'd given up on eating and just ordered drinks at every bar they could find. The Emilia in the photo was having trouble standing upright, with her arms draped over Eric's and August's shoulders.

She smiled and placed the photo back on the desk. "If you only knew what was going to happen the next month," she whispered.

It occurred to her then that she'd hardly seen any photos on her tour. Just a photo of Eric's family on the stairs, which showed a teenage Eric, his two sisters, and his parents. She knew from Eric's age, and by how thin and weak his mom looked, that it was taken shortly before her death.

But there were no recent pictures. Just that one in Henry's room. Was that for her benefit? Did she find it hard to see photos of events she couldn't remember? Just as she thought it, she spotted one more photo, tucked behind a stack of books.

The scene featured her, Eric, and August standing in front of a lake in their swimsuits. The scar on Emilia's neck was visible. Eric looked about the same as he had this morning and August looked a little different from how she remembered him. He didn't have facial hair like Eric, but his dirty blond hair was shorter and styled similarly.

Their poses surprised her. They were all standing at the edge of a lake Emilia didn't recognize. Emilia was on Eric's back with her arms around his neck and her legs wrapped tightly around his middle. August was standing slightly apart, but had leaned in to smile for the photo.

Emilia touched her fingertips to the glass and couldn't help but smile. They were all having fun. That much was obvious. But it was odd seeing Eric picking her up so casually and not August.

She and August weren't together.

She kept having to remind herself of this fact. She expected it to hurt more, but it wasn't so bad. Honestly, she'd never expected to end up with August. And now, with August off in Boise working on his residency, she'd become closer to Eric. It made sense, as he was the roommate she saw every day.

And forgot every night

Her eyes stung and she began blinking quickly, forcing

herself to focus on the smiling version of herself in the photo. It was strange to think that this scene had started just like today, with her remembering nothing and reading a letter she'd written to herself.

This was proof that not all her days were bad, wasn't it? Or maybe days like the one at the lake were rare. Maybe that's why Eric had this photo on his desk, to remember one of the few good days they'd all spent together since her accident. Emilia sighed and set the photo down, then continued the tour.

She popped her head into the kitchen, which she'd seen earlier, then looked around the entryway, where she found several of her coats and jackets stuffed into a small closet. She found a door to the basement, but it looked unfinished, so she skipped it.

Just then, her stomach growled and she made her way back to the kitchen. After eating some leftovers, then wondering if it was okay that she'd eaten them and if this was just something else Eric would be angry about, she walked back to the library.

It took her a little while to figure out the organization system for the books but once she did, she couldn't help but compliment her cleverness. The first section contained books she'd read before her accident. These were all books she could pick up and start reading from any point.

The next section held books she'd finished reading since her accident. At each chapter, there was a short summary of the book up to that spot. So she didn't have to just read the beginning of every book and could start reading from any chapter.

The last section contained the books that were in progress. There was a stack of paper and a pen on the shelf for her to write summaries as she read.

Emilia didn't feel like reading and settled back on the sofa.

That's when she spotted the book on the bottom shelf. She'd originally thought the shelf was empty, but saw a large book with lots of pieces of paper sticking out of it. She picked it up and brought it to the couch. There was a note stuck on the front: *Only read when you're in a good mood! I mean it, Emilia!*

Well, she was certainly NOT in a good mood, but was too curious to just put it away. The first page said simply: *Emilia's search for the meaning of life*

She teared up and nearly closed the book, but something made her continue. She opened it to a random page.

Theory Five: To seek wisdom and knowledge

Relevant philosophies:

Platonism—the whole meaning of life is to attain the highest form of knowledge

Legalism—only practical knowledge is valuable

Sikhism—seek to balance moral and spiritual values with a quest for knowledge

Emilia flipped back to the beginning of the book and saw she'd written out a description of all the major philosophies she'd studied. She'd also boiled down her research to six main theories about the meaning of life.

Theory One: To realize one's true potential

Theory Two: To love and improve the lives of others

Theory Three: To leave the world better than you found it

Theory Four: To enjoy the act of living

Theory Five: To seek wisdom and knowledge

Theory Six: Life has no meaning

Emilia turned back to the section about Theory Five. On the page following the initial description, she'd listed out her classes from law school. Next to each one she'd either written *credit achieved*, followed by a date or, *not possible with current condition*.

She was disappointed, but also a little impressed that she'd managed to complete any of her classes. Maybe her professors had gone easy on her because they felt bad. Where was the harm in giving the poor brain-damaged girl credit for a few classes? It's not like she'd ever pass the bar, which was all that really mattered. Even people with working brains struggled to do that.

Emilia sighed and closed the book. So much for seeking wisdom and knowledge. How was she supposed to do that if she couldn't remember anything? Hopefully her research didn't conclude that that was the true meaning of life.

She should have heeded her own warning and never opened that damned book. She put it back on the shelf and stuffed it near the back so it would be hard to find again.

She sat back on the sofa and looked out the window. So … this was it. This was her life. It felt … foreign … empty … lonely. Her mind kept drifting back to her cryptic conversation with Eric. She figured it went there so easily since there weren't any other memories taking up space in her brain.

Emilia considered going to her room to check the desk for whatever notes he'd been referring to, but she couldn't find the energy to get up. Fatigue, listlessness, sadness. These were all signs of depression. She remembered reading that somewhere. It wasn't surprising. Of course she was depressed; this was the saddest life she could imagine.

She had to leave notes for herself just so she could remember her friends. One of the theories she'd just read was, "improving the lives of others." She couldn't remember the lives of others, so how could she possibly improve them?

She thought of Eric again and his pained expression, which she was 100% sure by now she'd caused. Why was he upset? What had she done?

Remember, Emilia! Remember! Eric needs you to remember!
Nothing.

"Remember!" This time she shouted the word aloud, but her mind stayed stubbornly blank.

Emilia thought back to the letter from earlier, the one she'd written herself at some unknown point in time.

I know it's scary to march into each day without a plan, with no idea what you're walking into, but remember, you're not alone.

"Bullshit."

She *was* alone.

She was totally and completely alone.

* 3 *

Emilia didn't move from that spot for the rest of the day. She watched the sky make the thrilling transformation from cerulean, to azure, to navy as she thought about her current life. When that got too depressing, she started listing all the presidents, just for something to do.

She could remember each one, in order, including how many years they'd served, but not what she'd eaten for dinner the night before. She didn't even know if Reagan, who had just been re-elected before her accident, was still in office. What sort of person didn't know the current president?

Several hours later, she heard a door open and close. Eric. He was back. She wasn't in the mood to see him. He stomped upstairs and after several moments, she heard the sound of the shower. She could disappear into her room. Go to sleep and forget all about this terrible day.

Then repeat it again tomorrow

She stayed in place. Partly because she didn't have the energy to get up, partly because she wanted to talk to another person, and partly because she wanted to see if he'd come for her.

He did. She knew he would.

"Emilia?"

She stayed quiet. Her face was wet since she'd been leaking tears for hours, something she'd just noticed. How embarrassing. She turned her head so she was facing the bookshelf. Now that he was here, she was rethinking her decision to stay.

He came to sit on the sofa next to her. "Why are you sitting here in the dark?"

She shrugged. It wasn't completely dark. There was still a dull light filtering in through the window.

"The craft room is in the basement," Eric continued. "Did you see?"

"No."

"Oh, shit. You don't know. You told me your calendar was blank, but I didn't put it together. I'm sorry. You usually knit blankets on Sundays and donate them to the homeless shelter. There are instructions and supplies in the craft room downstairs, but I guess you didn't know to look for them."

"I don't know how to knit." Emilia's voice was rough from disuse.

"You learned. Your mind can handle motor learning, or, uh, muscle memory."

"Oh. That's ... cool," she said slowly, trying to keep her voice from shaking.

Emilia was overcome by a fresh rush of despair. She was supposed to be a bar-certified attorney by now, working her way up in a law firm. She was supposed to be fighting to change laws that would help thousands, maybe even millions of people, but instead she was knitting blankets to keep a handful of hobos slightly warmer. A new leak sprang at the corner of her eye.

Eric shifted closer to her and grabbed one of her hands. "Emilia," he said gently. "How long have you been sitting here?"

She shrugged, keeping her gaze down on their clasped hands. "I've been in here for most of the day. It's a lovely room, by the way. I don't remember it from before."

Eric squeezed her hand. "It was a formal living room, stuffy and never used. We converted it to a library together. You designed everything and we renovated it over the course of several weeks."

Emilia looked up and finally turned to face Eric. His eyes were sad and swimming with concern. "How many times have you told me that?"

"More than once."

Emilia started crying in earnest. She tried to remove her hand from Eric's so she could hide her face in her palms, but he kept a firm grip on it. He wrapped his arms around her and she rested her head on his shoulder and cried.

"You're okay," he murmured, threading his fingers into her hair. "I promise, you're fine. I know it seems like a lot, but you're going to be okay."

When she regained control of herself, she leaned back and began wiping her face with her hands. Eric stood and grabbed a box of tissues from the table behind the couch. She nodded and took a tissue, then patted her eyes.

She hadn't noticed the box of tissues before. Why was it here? For times she didn't heed the warning on that book? Or maybe for times she thought about her condition for too long. Perhaps there was a box of tissues in every room. She'd never been much of a crier, before. Was she a crier now? That made sense. The list of things to cry about these days was endless.

"I shouldn't have left you like that this morning," said Eric as he resumed his seat. "The first few hours of the day are critical. They make the difference between a good, productive day and one where you're depressed and feeling sorry for yourself. I'm sorry. I was just upset."

"You were upset with me. With something I did."

Eric sighed and leaned his head back against the couch. He rubbed his hand along his jaw as he looked up at the ceiling. "Yeah," he admitted after a while. "We—uh—had a disagreement last night."

"And instead of making notes about the fight and facing it this morning, I let myself forget. No wonder you were angry. That's a pretty shitty way to leave an argument. I'm sorry."

Eric nodded, then turned his head to look at her. "I forgive you."

"You're too forgiving."

"Maybe," he said as he got up and clicked on a lamp on the other side of the room, turning the switch a few times until it was on the lowest setting before returning to the sofa.

"What did we fight about yesterday?"

Eric shook his head. "I promised myself I wouldn't tell you things you chose to hide from yourself."

"Is that why you told me to check my notes? Where are they? In my room somewhere?"

Eric nodded, then moved to change the subject. "Are you hungry? I ate on my way home, but I brought something back for you."

"Where were you?"

"Skiing."

"Oh, right. I should have guessed." They shared a smile and the tightness in her chest eased.

"Do you want to eat?" he pressed.

"No. I'm not hungry, but thanks. That reminds me, I ate some leftovers for lunch. Is that okay? Were you saving those or—"

"Of course it's okay," he cut in. "This is your house; help yourself to anything. I'll write that out for you. Anyway, we need to cheer you up. Let's go watch TV."

Eric stood but Emilia stayed sitting on the couch. Were they really okay? Just like that? It seemed too easy.

He looked down at her and grinned. "Come on. You clearly need this. I'll carry you over there if I have to," he added challengingly.

Emilia's mind flashed to the photo she'd seen of them on his desk. The one where he'd been casually holding her on his back while they were both half naked. And because she wanted to feel someone's arms around her after the lonely day she'd had, she stuck out her lip and crossed her arms in defiance.

Eric rolled his eyes, then bent down and scooped her up in his arms. "You're so difficult," he grumbled. She crossed her arms tighter over her chest and tried to maintain her pout, but could feel her smile breaking through. Before long she unfolded her arms and wrapped them around his neck. She didn't want to be dropped.

Then again, maybe getting hit on the head would improve her condition. Had they tried that? Probably. The letter said they'd tried everything.

Once in the hall, Emilia caught a whiff of Eric's scent and was overcome with an intense feeling of familiarity. She leaned closer and tried to smell him again, as discreetly as possible. She knew this. She knew *him*. And this wasn't from before her accident. The smell was some new mixture of soap, the outdoors, and something male that she couldn't quite define. It gave her an overwhelming sense of security.

Eric, being the observant person he was, noticed her smelling him. After he sat her down on the sofa, he smirked at her. "You love my very masculine, musky scent," he teased. "Can't get enough of it."

She blushed and opened her mouth to protest, but he waved his hand dismissively as he took a seat on the other end of the sofa. Her legs were stretched out in front of her, and before she could move them out of his way, he lifted them up, sat down, and pulled them onto his lap.

"You recognize it, yeah?" he asked.

Emilia nodded absently. She'd momentarily lost the string of the conversation, distracted by the way they were sitting with her legs on his lap. Why hadn't he taken a seat on the armchair? Or let her move her legs out of the way?

"It's fine. I get it," Eric continued. "You don't have to be embarrassed."

She blushed again. "The recognition," she explained. "It was a lovely feeling. Is that—uh—common? Me remembering things from after the accident?"

Eric nodded as he pulled the blanket off the back of the couch and tossed it to her. "Yes and no. You were unconscious for over a month after the accident. You suffered a traumatic subarachnoid hemorrhage, but it was small, and it didn't explain how severely encephalopathic you were. So you were transferred to a place called Craig Hospital that deals with traumatic brain injury.

"All sorts of experts got involved in your case. Neurologists from all over the country were consulted… no one had ever seen anything like it. You even got the first MRI ever performed in the state of Colorado. You were diagnosed with diffuse axonal injury, and—"

Emilia was listening, but the words didn't make any sense. Except "traumatic brain injury." She knew what that meant and supposed it was all that mattered. She felt the sting in the corners of her eyes, the one that was rapidly becoming familiar.

"Sorry," said Eric softly. "I spent a lot of time researching what happened to you. I get a little wrapped up in the details sometimes, but they don't really matter. I'm sorry, I—"

"Don't apologize," she said, taking a shaky breath. "I … I want to understand."

Eric nodded. His face turned thoughtful. "Think of it like this … you know those pumpkin pies that August loves so much?"

"With the entire carton of whip cream on top?" she said with a small smile. Thanksgiving was August's favorite holiday, and pumpkin pie was his favorite thing about it.

"Yeah, those. Now imagine you've got one of them in your lap while you're driving down the highway. Suddenly, you stop. What happens?"

"Umm … the whip cream goes flying off?"

"Exactly. The heavy part, the pie, stays still, while the lighter part keeps going."

"Okay…"

"Something like that happened to your brain. Different parts of the brain have different densities. Diffuse axonal injury, the thing that you had, is when you're going fast and you suddenly stop. The different parts of the brain change speed differently, and the connections between them can get damaged."

"What happens to people who have that?"

"It varies." Eric's face darkened. "Some people are unconscious for a little while, then they're fine. Others … die. We were told that you might not survive, and that you'd probably never walk or talk again. The neurologists thought you'd have severe brain damage."

"They were right, weren't they?" Emilia muttered.

"They were wrong." Eric's eyes captured hers, the brilliant blue boring into her. "You woke up. At first you couldn't talk, and you could barely move. But slowly, it started coming back. I was sitting with you when you said your first words after the accident." Eric smiled, his grin lopsided. "I told them they'd underestimated you. And I was right."

"But … my memory … does that mean it might come back?"

"I … I don't know, Emilia. We all hoped it would, at first. You were doing so much better than your doctors thought possible. But you've had all sorts of tests, and exams, and detailed assessments. There's been no change for almost two years now. It seems like the connections between your frontal lobes, where you think and reason and make decisions, and your hippocampus, where memories are processed, are permanently damaged."

"But I can remember some things?" Emilia pressed. Eric's scent still tugged at her nose, and she was sure it was something she didn't recall from before her accident.

"Your neurologists said no."

There was more to that statement, Emilia was sure of it. "But?"

"I don't agree. I've done a lot of research on memory in the past two and a half years. There's more than one way to make them. Our sensory cortex processes things like smells. Our cerebellum processes motor skills. The amygdala handles visceral emotions ... anger, that sort of thing. They all have their own pathways to the hippocampus, and I think those pathways have recovered."

"So you, Eric Shaeffer, know better than the best neurology specialists in the country?"

"I know you," he said softly. "And besides, the evidence is on my side."

"What evidence?"

"You learned to knit. And ski. And juggle."

"Juggle? Did I consider joining a circus for a while? A lame attempt to liven up this farce of a life I'm living?"

"Sorry to disappoint, but you're not good enough for the circus," he teased. Eric grabbed the remote and pointed it at the TV. "There's this sitcom with a really annoying song that you can usually hum along to. Let me see if I can find it."

As Eric flipped through the channels, Emilia spread the

blanket over her. Eric had one arm draped over her shins and when she pushed the blanket down, he lifted his arm and pulled the blanket over her feet before resting his arm back on her, all while focusing on the channels flipping by.

They were close, she concluded. That wasn't surprising. She used to hug him often and would occasionally hold his hand or lay her head on his shoulder. This closeness just seemed weird because her most recent memories were of dating August and of Eric dating June. Once that had happened, she and Eric had stopped touching each other so much.

Eric wasn't able to find the show he was looking for so put on another sitcom that he said they both loved to hate. Emilia nodded. It was strange, having him list off all these truths about her. And it was even stranger that she just took them at face value. But what other option did she have?

Besides, this was Eric. He wouldn't lie to her. It was good she had someone like this in her life. Someone she had trusted so implicitly before the accident. She couldn't see this working any other way.

They joked about the stupid antics of the characters during the commercials. While the show was playing, and Eric was focused back on the TV, Emilia snuck looks at him. Whenever he saw her watching him, he lifted his eyebrows in question. After the third time this happened, he muted the show and turned to her.

"You're looking at me weird. Why?"

"I don't know. You're smiling at me. I like it. I spent most of the day convinced you hated me."

Eric's face fell. "I really am sorry for starting your day so terribly."

She nudged his leg with her foot. "I'm sure you had a good reason."

Eric shrugged. He lifted the remote but instead of turning the volume back up, he turned the TV off. He pushed Emilia's legs off his lap and stood up. "Come on. Let's go upstairs." When she didn't move, he added, "Are you going to make me carry you again?"

Emilia shook her head and followed him upstairs. He led the way to her room, flipped on the lights, and went to stand by the desk. "May I?" he asked, motioning toward the calendar and pile of summaries.

"Sure." It's not like there was much to see. The calendar was still blank.

Eric bent over to study the calendar as Emilia went to his side and watched him. He was biting his lip and she wondered what he was looking at, since there was only one line written on the page. As if in answer, Eric placed his hand on the paper. When he lifted it, she noticed a few water spots in the place he'd touched. Tears. She'd missed that before.

So, she'd been crying when she wrote that note about the "personal challenge" and erased whatever used to be written here. And she would bet Eric knew why.

"Where—?" He started to ask a question but cut off.

"What? Where what?"

Eric shook his head, then took a deep breath and sat down at the desk. As he picked up her pencil he announced, "I'm acknowledging this personal challenge you've set for yourself, but as it applies to you and not me, I'm going to break it a little bit. Okay?"

"Um, okay."

She watched him write on the spot for February 2nd, *Eric's making chocolate chip pancakes (get excited!)*

On the following day he wrote, *Visiting the farm with Viola*

"What farm? The one she works at?" Emilia asked as she read over his shoulder.

"Yeah, that one. She'll explain further, but all you need to know now is that you go there every other Tuesday. There. You have two things to look forward to. There are more plans you've already setup, but I guess we can leave those for later."

"Sure." Emilia was still thinking about Viola as Eric stood. "So, I spend every other Tuesday with Viola and I assume our other friends have recurring spots on the calendar too? And you're stuck with mornings, it seems. It's like a babysitting rotation. Who keeps the master schedule? You?"

Eric sighed and shook his head. He put his hands on her shoulders and said seriously, "No, Emilia. It's nothing like babysitting." His tone was sad and he sounded slightly exasperated, like he'd said this many times before. How did he stand living with her? The repetition would drive her crazy.

Eric pulled Emilia into a hug. "I know you had a shitty day, which was primarily my fault. This is one of those times when it's good to know you're going to forget it."

When he pulled away, he looked thoughtful. He opened his mouth, then seemed to decide against whatever he was going to say and turned back to the door.

"I'm sorry for whatever I did," she blurted.

"You're fine. Really. I'll leave you to this." Eric motioned toward her desk.

Emilia shifted in place. He was leaving and she felt like he was taking a large part of her with him. She hadn't felt like herself until the end of the day, when they'd been joking and watching TV, and now she was going to be alone again.

"Are you okay?" he asked when he reached the hall.

"Uh, yeah. I just—um—what do I do?" She pointed to the desk.

"Write down things you want to remember about today in your—" He cut off and walked back into the room, looking at her desk curiously. Eric's eyes scanned a shelf above her desk that was lined with books. Emilia hadn't looked through those and made a note to do so later. Eric finally spotted what he was looking for and pulled down a black, leatherbound notebook. He flipped through it quickly before putting it on her desk.

"Usually you write down thoughts from the day in this notebook. I'm not sure how that fits into your one day at a time thing, or if there's a reason you ripped out half the pages of this and tucked it away. You left yourself absolutely no instructions for how to go about this challenge—" He cut off and sighed heavily.

Emilia could tell he was trying to keep the bitterness out of his tone, but she could hear it right at the edge of his words.

"I recommend going ahead and writing about what happened today. You can rip the pages out and toss them in the box if you don't want to remember what you wrote."

This made no sense to Emilia, but she nodded along anyway. "Okay. Thanks. You mentioned my notes earlier. Should I check those? Where are those?"

Eric dropped his head and pinched the bridge of his nose under his glasses. "You don't check your notes until the end of the month. I'm sure you saw that in the letter. Like I said, I was upset, you can ignore all that. That's what that box is for." He pointed to a miniature trunk on her bookshelf with a lock. "But you—you should probably leave it alone until the end of the month. It's a good system, honestly. Your past self developed it for a reason."

Emilia chewed on the inside of her cheek, trying to keep Eric from seeing how lost she was. She hated the feeling of not knowing, which was a feeling that had dominated her entire day. It had probably dominated the past two years.

Eric seemed to pick up on her unease and walked back into the room. He grabbed her hand and asked softly, "Would you like me to stay? I can keep you company while you work and sit with you until you fall asleep."

YES! she almost shouted. The last thing she wanted was for the one person making her feel sane to leave the vicinity. But Eric had his own life. He'd been away from the house all day. Perhaps he wanted to watch more TV, read, call a friend.

She shook her head as she looked at his hand, holding hers. She couldn't have him lie in bed and rub her back until she fell asleep. She was a grown woman and she needed to take care of herself.

Emilia squeezed his hand and dropped it. "I'm okay. Thanks."

He looked like he didn't believe her, but still nodded and went back to the door.

"How do you stand it?" she blurted when he'd reached the hall. He looked back at her confused. "The repetition, constantly answering the same questions, tiptoeing around topics from the gap in time that might upset me. This has to be driving you insane."

Eric came back into the room and stopped in front of her. "You're my best friend and I have a lot of fun with you. Is it repetitive? Yes, sometimes. Sometimes we'll have a really great moment and later, when I get to live it again, I feel lucky, *not* irritated, or exhausted, or like I'm going insane."

Emilia could tell from his eyes he was sincere. The weight on her chest felt lighter.

He smiled and added conspiratorially, "It's a good answer, isn't it? Kills every time."

She laughed. Of course she'd brought this up before. And yes, his response was perfect. Eric reached up and stroked her cheek. "Tomorrow will be better. I promise. Pancakes!" he added in an excited whisper.

Emilia nodded and forced a smile on her face as she watched him leave, taking some of the brightness from the room as he closed the door softly behind him.

* 4 *

Once Eric left the room, Emilia took a seat at her desk. She looked at the tear stains on the calendar again. Eric had spotted those so quickly. Had he been looking for them? She sighed and placed her palms flat on the desk as she looked at the items in front of her. There was the large blank calendar, the stack of summaries she'd read this morning, and the notebook Eric had found on her shelf.

Were there any other items missing that were usually here? Why had she ripped out the pages from her notebook? Why had she started this "personal challenge?" Why had she and Eric argued?

Emilia hated the endless questions and was slightly relieved that in a few hours, they'd be erased from her mind. But then she'd just spend the next day forming them again. How depressing. She straightened in her chair and grabbed the leatherbound notebook. She was relieved to find a few lines of instructions on the inside cover.

Every night, record anything you'd like to remember. If you want to see the items throughout the month, leave the page in here. Otherwise, rip the page out and put it in the small trunk on the shelf. You'll review those at the end of the month. There aren't any strict criteria for what to put where, just trust your judgment.

Huh. So that's what Eric meant when he'd said she could tear out whatever she wrote. Emilia turned to the first page, scribbled the date on the top, and began writing.

Eric was angry about an argument we had last night but won't say what it was about.

Eric mentioned something that happened between us last summer; he seems sad about it.

I recognized Eric's smell. I know it sounds weird, but it was an incredible feeling.

We watched TV tonight and it felt like old times, so it seems like Eric has forgiven me for whatever I did yesterday.

Emilia stopped writing. That was a lot about Eric. But he was the only person she'd seen today. She chewed her lip, then added:

I took a long tour of the house. It's nice; definitely the nicest place I've ever lived (that I remember).

Heed the warning on the large book on the bottom shelf in the library. I read it today and it was really depressing.

Emilia leaned back from the desk and reviewed the page. Was this the sort of thing she was supposed to be writing? She had no idea. She closed the notebook and put it on top of the pile of summaries.

Emilia looked down at the calendar. Next to her note about the personal challenge she added: *Try to figure out how this came about, but don't ask Eric.* She had no idea how she was going to do that, but thought it was a good goal.

She smiled. Okay, that felt good. Tomorrow would already start out better than today had. Eric was making pancakes in the morning, and she could start to investigate this personal challenge mystery. She had a purpose.

Now, it was time to do a little digging. She started with the box on the shelf. It looked like a miniature trunk, between the size of a bread box and a microwave, with a lock on the outside and a small slot just big enough for a letter. That was the slot where she was supposed to put pages from the notebook she didn't want to read until the end of the month. But how was she supposed to know how to unlock this thing? Perhaps it was the sort of puzzle she could solve if she put her mind to it.

She had a sudden urge to break in and started scanning the

shelves for clues. Her whole history was in here. The mystery behind whatever was going on between her and Eric. How could she just leave it alone? She picked it up and set it on her desk. A book and a few picture frames that had been leaning against it fell over, but she ignored them as she sat and stared at the trunk.

"Okay. Where's the key?"

As she looked around, she spotted a note taped to the top of the trunk.

You're only supposed to open this at the end of the month. You'll be tempted to do so earlier, but try your best to refrain. This is a system YOU set up and it's imperative that you trust yourself, now more than ever.

She sighed and pushed back from the desk. Stupid past Emilia. But she was right. She must have had a good reason for limiting her forays into the box to just once a month. She also probably had a good reason for that damned challenge, even though it would have been nice if she'd left more instruction behind. She needed to trust herself, even though it sucked.

Emilia grabbed the leatherbound notebook again. She took the page she'd written on and ripped it out, then shoved it into the slot of the trunk. There. It was gone.

"Happy?" she grumbled. "I'm following your stupid challenge, though I have no idea why…"

She was about to return the trunk to the shelf when she noticed the book and picture frames that had fallen. She picked them up and glanced through them. These were old photos from before her accident, so not very interesting. One was of her, August, and June making snow angels somewhere, all smiles and ruddy cheeks.

The other was of her and Eric at Camp Ouray. They were sitting on the dock, leaning toward each other and wearing smiles so contagious, they snuck through the glass of the frame and infected her, causing her lips to curve as she propped the photos on the desk.

She was left holding a thin book of poems by Ranata Suzuki. Huh. She had never heard of her (that she remembered). There was a section at the beginning that seemed well worn, titled, *Letters to the Sun from the Dark Side of the Moon.*

Emilia began to read.

To my dearest love, my brilliant Sun, the world has decided we can no longer be one. So you take the day and I'll take the night, you with your warm, happy glow, me with my cold, lonely night...

Emilia stopped reading. Her heart was beating quickly and it felt like the hairs on her arms were standing on end. She knew this. But ... had she read this book of poems before the accident? She flipped to the front and checked the publishing date. No. This book was published last year. What she was "remembering" was something recent.

She flipped to the next page.

And as they said goodbye, the Sun said to the Moon—'Don't ever change. Stay just as you are and always shine for me.' He'd never understood that she couldn't. That she only ever reflected his light. That without him ... she could not shine.

Emilia felt like someone was holding her heart in her hand and squeezing it painfully. The poems seemed to be awakening something in her; a deep, heartbreaking pain. But still, she kept reading, because even though it hurt, she was *remembering.* Finally!

Like all things that surround you, I was once caught in your gravity. Even now, I am inexplicably drawn to you in a way that time and distance cannot seem to stop. But I stay here, where I am ... away from you. Not because I want to ... but because I know it would lead to nothing but destruction.

Emilia slammed the book shut. She was crying and wiped her eyes quickly. No. Whatever pain she'd associated with these poems was too much. She'd rather not know. She put her hand over her heart and took several deep breaths, trying to release the tension there.

But even with the book closed, the lines were floating through her mind.

The world has decided we can no longer be one.
Without him ... she could not shine.
But I stay here, where I am ... away from you. Not because I want to ...

"Stop!" she cried, dropping her head into her hands. Emilia stood up and scanned the bookshelf. Her eyes landed on a legal textbook she remembered from school. Perfect, the opposite of poetry.

She placed the trunk back on the shelf, then shoved the book of poems into the space next to the locked box and went to her bed where she lay on her stomach and began to read about constitutional law. But the feelings the poems had incited were still reverberating through her, and the lines wouldn't stop echoing in her mind.

Emilia sighed and looked around for another distraction. There, on the shelf, three tennis balls. Eric said she could juggle. Why not give it a try?

She grabbed the balls and tried tossing them in the air. It was a disaster. They bounced all around the room, ricocheting off the walls and furniture. In a huff, she collected the tennis balls and was about to return them to the shelf when she remembered the proud way Eric had said, *"I told them they'd underestimated you. And I was right."*

Emilia took a deep breath and collected the balls again. Since this was a new skill, one she'd learned after the accident, so she had to try to perform it instinctively. In theory, it made sense, but in practice, she had no idea how to go about it.

After closing her eyes, she focused on her breathing and cleared her mind (at least, as well as she could, how did people not think?). She opened her eyes and tried again, letting her body take over. The balls moved in a circle. Her hands seemed to know what to do. Oh God! She was juggling!

"I'm doing it!"

The balls dropped, one right after the other. She didn't care. She'd learned a skill! That was good, right? It meant she wasn't completely useless. The last ball bounced off the edge of the bed and hit the lamp. Emilia dove, trying to keep the lamp from falling, but ended up tripping over one of the other tennis balls and sending the lamp she'd been trying to save into the wall. "Shit!"

She hit the floor with a thud.

She was groaning on the floor, rubbing a bruise on her hip, when Eric burst into the room. "What happened?! Are you okay? Where are you?"

"Here." She waved so he'd see she was behind the bed.

He appeared above her the next moment, holding a plastic yellow bat. "What happened?" he asked as he helped her up.

"I—uh—juggled, then knocked over a lamp. But I still did it!" she added proudly.

Eric smirked as he put the lamp back on the nightstand. "I already told you you could juggle. Didn't believe me?"

"I did. I just—well, yeah, I didn't believe you."

Eric shrugged and walked back to the hall, tapping his shoulder with the plastic bat. "Okay. Well, I'm glad you're not being murdered. Good night."

"Is that a toy bat?"

Eric looked at the bright yellow bat and colored slightly. "I grabbed it from Henry's room on my way to save you."

"My hero," she quipped.

Eric rolled his eyes, then turned to leave.

"Tomorrow's going to be better!" she called after him.

"I think that was my line."

She smiled widely, still elated from having done something new. It was small. And dumb. And had virtually no real-world application, especially since she didn't seem particularly good at it, but it was something she hadn't known before, and she was determined to be happy about it.

"Oh, and Happy Birthday!" she added as Eric was shutting the door. "I know I said it earlier, but I wanted to say it again, since it sounds like I screwed up yesterday and maybe that was part of it … I don't know."

He forced a smile, though it came out looking more like a grimace. She'd stumbled onto something, an obstacle she'd been blind to, since she was blind to every damn thing in her life.

"It wasn't about that," Eric said softly, the earlier unease already hidden away. He nodded and made to close the door again, but she couldn't leave it there.

"Today was awful," she said in a rush, "then I managed to turn it around, all thanks to you. I'd be lost without you, Eric."

He paused for several seconds. When he finally spoke, there was sadness wedged between each word. "That goes both ways, Emilia. Good night."

Part 2: Viola Rhodes

She hates when you apologize for ruining her dreams, so don't.

❊ 5 ❊

The next morning, Emilia sat at her desk, running through everything she'd learned so far. She'd damaged her mind, her most valuable asset, the thing she'd always drawn her self-worth from, and now it seemed impossible to imagine—

Stop! Don't be overly dramatic. That's not helping anyone

She took a deep breath and thought of her friends. At least they were all continuing with their lives. Meanwhile, Emilia stayed stagnant. Unable to move forward. Lacking the ability to—

Seriously, stop

It was hard not to be frustrated when she was going about life—how had she put it?—"one day at a time." This was a pretty twisted application of the common phrase. She sighed and looked at the note Eric had written on the calendar for today: *Eric's making chocolate chip pancakes (get excited!)*

"Fine, Eric. Why not?"

Emilia pulled her hair into a bun, then stood and went to find Eric. Unsurprisingly, she found him at the stove in the kitchen, cooking pancakes. It was a small thing, but seeing him doing what the note at her desk had said he'd be doing was comforting. A small oasis of certainty in a vast desert filled with doubt.

Emilia stayed standing in the doorway, watching him cook as she took in his altered appearance. He looked different. Not very different, but still different from how she remembered. Would other things about him be different? Would he sound differently? Act differently? Interact with her differently? Bring up things she didn't remember? She had no idea what she was walking into.

That was a line in the letter, wasn't it?

I know it's scary to march into each day without a plan, with no idea what you're walking into, but remember, you're not alone.

But she *was* alone. Because even though she had friends around her, none of them really *knew* what she was going through. She herself barely knew because as soon as she figured it out, her mind reset. Her eyes filled with tears at that thought, then Eric said something, drawing her attention back to the present.

He was looking at her over his shoulder. "I'm sure you're thinking to yourself, 'So, this guy *does* know how to cook? That would have been helpful back at camp, when we snuck into the kitchens after hours and he made *me* prepare our late-night meals.'"

He smiled and Emilia's heart leapt. He didn't sound different. Not at all. He was joking in the same way he always had. Everything this morning had felt foreign but Eric—Eric she knew. She crossed the room and wound her arms around his middle.

He placed one hand over her wrists, which she'd linked across his stomach, as he used his other hand to flip one of the pancakes. "Good morning to you, too," he said warmly.

Emilia's face burned, but she didn't let go. "I know I should let go, but I'm threatening to spiral into a deep depression as I continue to think through the ramifications of my accident and this hug is the only thing anchoring me to sanity."

She felt Eric chuckle under her firm grip. "Wow. I didn't realize how critical this hug was."

"Yes. It's of the utmost importance," she mumbled into his back.

Eric laughed again. "Okay. Well, hug away. But I should warn you that after these last two pancakes are finished, I'm going to need to start moving around."

She lifted her head and looked around him at the pancakes in the pan. They looked like they needed another few minutes. "I think I'll be good after these two pancakes."

They were quiet and the only sound was the sizzling of the pan. Eric ran his hand along her arm as he watched the stove, causing goosebumps to rise there. When he felt them, he rubbed her arm more vigorously. He probably thought she was cold, but she decided against correcting him.

He grabbed the pan and slid the pancakes onto the plate and Emilia reluctantly unwrapped her arms and took a step back.

He turned to face her. "You're okay, Emilia. Your life is good. I promise."

"Really?"

"Really."

"How do I keep from being severely depressed all the time? This situation is awful."

"Yeah. It's pretty bad," he allowed, "but there are worse fates than memory loss. You almost died." His voice caught on the last word.

"Yeah, I know," she said, looking down at the floor. "You're right."

Eric lifted her chin. "Honestly, you do spend some days sitting around feeling sorry for yourself. Yesterday was one of those days. You holed yourself away in the library and didn't move for most of the day. But you can't do that all the time. That's what I'm here for."

"There's a library?" Emilia asked hopefully. She'd visited this house before, back in college, when Eric's younger sister, Claire, had still been in High School, but she didn't remember a library.

Eric let out a laugh and turned to grab the plate of pancakes. "Yes, there's a library. But first, pancakes."

As they ate at the table, Emilia saw Eric working on some sort of calendar. She leaned forward and saw he'd made a spot for every day of the week and was listing out different meals for lunch and dinner.

"You used to have a lot more notes on your desk," he explained. "General notes about the house, a chore chart, meal plan—" he tapped the paper he was writing on, "—and a schedule with recurring events—like how you're supposed to knit on Sundays and spend the day with Viola every other Tuesday."

"I knit?"

He nodded as he wrote *Spaghetti* in the spot for *Friday Dinner*.

Weird. She'd follow up on that later. "What happened to those notes? They sound helpful."

"They were, but it appears you hid them as part of your personal challenge to live one day at a time. But some of those were practical, like this. I'll stick it on the fridge and hopefully it won't interfere with your challenge too much."

She could tell Eric was irked by her "one day at a time" challenge and before she recalled the note on her calendar that warned her not to ask him about it, she blurted, "How did this challenge come about?"

Eric's expression darkened but he recovered quickly. He got up to tape the meal plan on the refrigerator and when he sat back down, his face was blank. "I don't know. You decided that one on your own."

She was about to apologize for whatever unknown offense she'd caused when he waved her off. "It's fine, Emilia. It's important that you trust yourself. So, if some past version of you thought it would be a good idea to erase all the little tools helping you stay sane, well, I guess we should trust her. Right?"

She had no idea what to say to that, so she just shrugged. Desperate to change the subject, she looked over at the meal plan. "Was I making the same thing over and over? All my favorite meals? Is that why we needed a meal plan?"

Eric gave her a sad smile before gathering her empty plate. "No," he said quickly, turning for the sink. "You were making my favorite meals."

"Oh." Emilia wondered why that made him sad. Maybe because she asked this every day and he was sick of answering the same questions over and over. "How many times have I asked that?"

Eric set the dishes in the sink before joining her back at the table. "The most repetitive conversation we have is this one, about repetitive conversations. It's the thing you're most self-conscious about and I tell you every time that I don't mind. Honestly, we don't repeat things as often as you'd think."

Emilia nodded to herself. She wondered if the reason they didn't repeat things was because she was so self-conscious about it. She could see herself steering clear of questions about the past—figuring those had been covered—and focusing more on the present and future to spare Eric from the monotony.

He nudged her arm to get her attention. "Hey. Are you up to coming to work with me today?"

"At the lab?"

"No. I'm not in school anymore," he replied, tone clipped. "That should be in your notes."

Shit. She'd almost forgotten. *He's not on a path to become a doctor anymore. He says he prefers the calmer, more flexible career path he's chosen, but clearly doesn't like to talk about it.*

"No, that's right. You're working in the medical field," she recited. "Sounds … um … neat."

"Yeah. I work for a medical device company near the city, helping with clinical trials."

"Oh. And you want me to come with you?"

"Yep."

"But ... what will I do?"

"You'll use your comprehensive knowledge of legal documents, excellent writing skills, and unmatched attention to detail to review reports and submissions for the regulatory team. They love you, actually."

Emilia's forehead crinkled. She knew nothing about the regulations surrounding clinical trials. "And I've done this before?"

"Yes. The work can be a bit tedious, but you're great at it and never seem to mind."

"No, I don't mind," she said in a rush. She was excited at the prospect of getting to do something productive. "I should get dressed." Emilia took in Eric's outfit, black slacks and a button-down shirt, and resolved to match that dress code.

Once she was in the bathroom upstairs, she saw that Eric had taped a piece of paper on the mirror and written in bright blue marker: *This house is yours too, help yourself to anything*

Emilia smiled, then leaned forward and assessed her hair critically in the mirror. She investigated the roots and combed her fingers through it. If she had to guess, she'd washed it yesterday, or maybe the day before. She didn't need to wash it now. As Emilia took a quick shower, she thought that a small calendar in the bathroom to record the last time she'd washed her hair and when her period was coming would be useful.

According to Eric, she'd had little notes like this for herself but got rid of them and hadn't left any explanations as to why. That's probably why there was that instruction on the calendar to try to find out how the challenge to live one day at a time had come about. How odd. It didn't sound like something she'd do. She always liked to know what was going on. Why leave herself in such disarray? Wasn't the memory loss already bad enough?

Emilia tried to push it out of her mind. There wasn't anything to be done for it now. She got dressed and went downstairs to meet Eric, who was reading the newspaper in the kitchen.

They passed the drive to Eric's office in silence. Emilia started feeling uneasy as soon as they reached the highway. She was grabbing her knees tightly, something she didn't even realize until Eric placed a hand on one of hers. He turned the radio to a news program which did a good job of distracting her for the rest of the trip.

Once they arrived at his work, he showed her to the cubicle she'd be working in for the day, a few spots down from his. She tried not to be depressed by the fact that Eric worked in such a mundane place. What happened to curing cancer?

"You've written yourself notes on what to do," he was saying, holding a folder. He leaned past her and placed it next to the computer. He was so close. She could see every shade of blue in his eyes. "These should be enough to keep you busy all day," he continued, unphased by their proximity in the cramped cubicle. "If not, I showed you where I sit."

Emilia just nodded dumbly. God, she hated feeling so out of her depth. She resisted the urge to cry. She would *not* cry at work. Well, this was Eric's work, but still.

"I need to go; I have a meeting." He squeezed her shoulder. "I'll come check on you after."

"You don't have to. I can take care of myself."

"I want to." He gave her shoulder a final squeeze before leaving her alone with the computer, folder, and stack of reports.

She took a few deep breaths before sitting down and investigating the folder. There wasn't much to it. The regulations only took an hour to read through. All she had to do after that was make sure the documents she reviewed complied, then edit where she could to make them more clear and concise—easy for a layperson to understand. She was a layperson now, wasn't she? She pushed that depressing thought to the back of her mind, which was getting a little crowded.

The work was boring, just like Eric said it would be, but it was nice using her brain, even though she wasn't working it particularly hard. At least she was being somewhat useful. It was better than sitting at Eric's house, doing nothing.

She wondered how many strings Eric had had to pull to get his company to let her work here. Then, she wondered if she was like a charity case for them. Maybe they gave her random stacks of paper to keep her busy for a day, then tossed out her notes. It's not like it mattered, since she wouldn't remember anyway. Maybe she'd been through this exact stack of reports hundreds of times already.

Even before the conspiracy finished forming in her mind, she knew it wasn't true. Eric would never betray her like that. This was real. They would use her edits. He said she had to trust herself, but that extended to him, too. Damn, it would be so easy for him to take advantage of her. The thought made her a little sick. She was so dependent on him.

But … it wasn't just some random person she was dependent on. It was Eric. Trusting him was easy. She took a deep breath. She was fine. No one was taking advantage of her. This was … fine. Okay, even. She was helping. Things could be much worse.

* * *

"It's easier for me to collect the money for the work you do, but I keep a separate account for you. And I promise I don't skim any off the top, though I guess you're just going to have to trust me."

They had just got in the car and Eric was pulling out of the parking space while delivering this cryptic message.

Emilia's eyes widened when she finally put it together. "I got *paid* for that?!"

"For doing a full day's work that not many people can do? Of course you got paid."

"But I—it was—okay … how much?"

"$17.35 an hour. So something like $140 for the day."

If she'd been drinking something, she would have spit it out. "What?! But—but minimum wage is like—like $4 an hour."

"That wasn't minimum wage work. Besides, out in the real world, people get paid in more than class credit. Pretty cool, yeah?"

Is that why you quit school? Did you need the money? Thankfully, she caught the words before they were out of her mouth, remembering the note on Eric's summary about how he didn't like talking about why he left halfway through his MD-PhD program.

Also, unless his dad had stopped delivering those large sums of money he sent in place of love, she doubted he needed the money. Mr. Shaffer was a dick, but she couldn't see him cutting off his son. Besides, Eric wouldn't be living in such a beautiful house if he was lacking money. He'd left school for some other reason, something big, and she had a sinking suspicion it had to do with her.

Eric asked her how her day was, and she told him, thanking him profusely for finding work she could do. After that, she spent most of the drive deciding how to delicately address the topic of him abandoning his dream to become a doctor to work in a boring row of cubes, at a boring company, that made boring pacemakers. She landed on, "What do you like about your job?"

He considered her question for a while. "What does your summary on me say about it?"

"That you're not on path to be a doctor anymore, that you prefer your calmer, more flexible job, and that you don't like to talk about it," she recited.

He was quiet for several moments. As she watched the road and other cars zip by, she wondered if she should have answered that differently. She was drawn out of her thoughts by a large sigh.

"I like it, Emilia, I do. I'm working on clinical trials and while the current one I'm on is pretty dull, I'm still learning a lot. How they work, the balance between what's important to physicians, patients, regulators, and the company. It's something I can see myself getting really good at and soon enough, I'll have my pick of trials to support. I'm helping improve people's quality of life. Maybe not as directly as I wanted to, but I'm still a part of it."

He turned to look at her, blue eyes intense. "Plans change, and it's okay. And yes, the more flexible aspect of my work is nice, so you got that right. Gives me plenty of time to hang out with Henry." He sighed again and turned back toward the road.

"That was a good answer. I should add it to my summary."

His lips turned up. "You should."

Eric turned on the radio and they were quiet the rest of the way home. As they were walking into the house, she turned to him and said in a rush, "Was it me? Just tell me. Did you quit because of me?"

He closed the door behind him before answering her. "No, Emilia. I did it for me."

She could see the truth of the statement in his eyes and let out a breath she hadn't realized she'd been holding. "I'm sorry," she whispered.

"You're a bad listener," he teased. "I just said—"

"Not for that. For the accident. It was stupid. I should have stopped. I knew I was tired. I knew it was a bad idea, but I just *had* to get there. Then I made this whole mess—"

"No," he said, grabbing her arms. "Don't apologize. I understand. Really, I do."

"Yeah. I guess you would."

"Thanks for not dying."

"Anytime."

Eric smiled, then leaned forward and kissed the top of her head. "Let's go for a walk."

"A walk? It's freezing."

"That's what coats are for. Besides, it's nice, and the sidewalks are clear."

Emilia shook her head as she grabbed a scarf and hat from the hook near the door. It was comforting to know that while so many things were different, some things, like Eric's obsession with being active and outside as much as possible, were exactly the same. His body probably had some internal alarm that had gone off because he'd been sitting for too long.

"Thank you for being the same," she said when they reached the sidewalk.

"Anytime." He nudged her side, then reached into his pockets and pulled out a pair of gloves. "Oh, here."

"Thanks."

As Emilia pulled the gloves on, she considered how attentive he'd been to her all day. It was unnerving. She'd never had anyone pay her that much mind since—well—since she'd been a kid living at home. It was usually Emilia who was floating around, trying to keep Eric and August happy but now, their roles had switched. If she was being honest, she hated it.

"I was thinking leftovers for dinner," he announced. "I brought some back from a restaurant last night. It's this stew you like. You've had it before. And we can make garlic bread to go with it."

"Sure. Sounds good." She frowned down at the ground.

Eric leaned into her. "What's wrong?"

"How did you get the job as my handler?"

"Ah. I applied and beat out all the applicants. It was a very rigorous selection process with multiple stages." He was smiling, but the hard look in his eyes was clear. He didn't want to talk about this. He wanted her to let it go.

Emilia forced a laugh, ready to drop the topic. She supposed she owed him that much. That much and more. So much more than she'd ever be able to repay. The $140 she'd earned today wouldn't come close.

"Hey." Eric stopped on the sidewalk and grabbed her arm, turning her toward him. "Being your friend isn't work, Emilia. You need to write that down and read it every day. If things were reversed, you'd be there for me. I know it."

She nodded. He was right. She'd be there for him every day, no questions asked. And she'd probably get annoyed if he kept complaining about it. But this was different. Because she was the one who needed help. And it wasn't a temporary thing, like helping Eric through a recent conflict with his sister. This was going to go on forever. She would always need someone to help her, and she didn't know what to do with that.

"But if it *were* a job," he said with a grin, "I would have definitely applied."

"And won," she added, forcing a lightness in her tone she wasn't feeling.

"Obviously." His smile widened as the light from the setting sun glinted off the pools of blue in his eyes. She couldn't help but beam back at him, her smile real this time. He was right; it was nice outside.

* 6 *

The next morning, Emilia was sitting at her desk, reading Viola's summary a second time, since she'd seen on her calendar that she was supposed to be spending the day with her sister.

Viola lives in Aspen Grove now. She moved shortly after you gave up trying to live in Nebraska with mom and decided to return to the only place that ever truly felt like home.

She's still pursuing her art, but it looks different now. She showcases it at farmers markets and outdoor art shows, instead of swanky New York City galleries. She says she prefers it though, and that her art is better presented in nature. She hates when you apologize for ruining her dreams, so don't.

Viola lives near Red Plate Diner, but she doesn't like their pancakes and says Eric's are better (insanity, I know).

She finally realized she can't make enough money off her art to live. But you know her, she bounced back from the crushing realization that her dreams were shattered in the time it took to drive to Anna's Creamery and buy a milkshake. Now she works at an equine therapy farm, which suits her. She's always loved animals and has finally fulfilled that desire to learn horseback riding. I guess she replaced one dream with another.

She's angry with mom and dad for splitting up, for causing the accident, and for not supporting you enough afterward. It's weird, seeing anger on her, but it's her way of coping. You try your best to stay out of it. Because while it's about you, it's not really about you at all.

Emilia pushed back and reviewed the other items on her desk. There were two photos from before her accident, a large calendar that was mostly blank, a leatherbound notebook she was supposed to write in at the end of the day that had half its pages torn out, and a letter she'd written herself the night before concerning her challenge for the month: to live one day at a time.

The letter explained that before the challenge she'd left a lot more practical notes for herself but had suddenly decided to ditch them, to Eric's confusion and irritation. The letter also said that on February 1st, she'd set a secondary challenge for herself to figure out how the first challenge had come about, but warned that Eric shouldn't be asked about it, since it seemed to make him sad.

It was all very confusing, but it was sort of like a puzzle and Emilia loved puzzles. Maybe she could ask Viola about this challenge while they were at the farm. She also considered ignoring the notes about Eric and asking him, since he must know something about it. Maybe she could glean more from him than her past self had.

Ultimately, Emilia decided against this plan and resolved to trust her past self. If she couldn't trust these little notes she'd left, then what could she trust in this crazy new situation she found herself?

As if in answer to that question, there was a knock on her door followed by Eric's voice. "Emilia?"

Emilia jumped, then rushed to her feet. She checked her reflection in the mirror above the dresser, but that just confirmed that her hair looked terrible. She pulled it back into a ponytail but that wasn't much of an improvement.

"Emilia? Are you okay?"

"Uh, yeah."

Relax, Emilia. It's Eric. He doesn't care that your hair is a mess

Once she opened the door, Eric stepped back into the hall and gave her a chance to take in his altered appearance. When she hadn't said anything for several minutes he asked tentatively, "How about a hug?"

She nodded and nearly threw herself into his arms.

"Are you feeling okay?" he whispered into her hair.

Emilia nodded into his chest. This felt perfect. She sort of wished she had started her day like this, with a giant hug from Eric, before reading all the letters from herself.

"I know it's scary, but you're okay," Eric was saying. His soothing voice was warming her up, like slipping into a bath on a snowy day. "You're surrounded by people who love you, me more than anyone, and you always enjoy your days with Viola."

He stepped back and moved his hands to her arms. Emilia almost pulled him back into a hug. She hadn't been ready for that to end.

"I'm sorry to come barging up here but I have to be at work early today. I just wanted to check on you and let you know that Viola will pick you up at 8:30. You'll be outside for most of the day, so dress warmly. The boots you usually wear are in the garage. And the keys for the house are on a hook in the kitchen. Don't forget to grab those and lock up, since Viola might. You know how forgetful she is."

Emilia nodded.

Eric was searching her face. "Did you get all that? Do you want me to repeat it or write it down?"

She smiled and Eric visibly relaxed. "I got it, thanks. 8:30, warm clothes, boots are in the garage, and don't forget the keys, because Viola might." Emilia smiled again and added, "I'm sure we make quite a pair, with her tendency to get distracted and me not knowing what the hell is going on in the first place."

"You do alright together." Eric was still studying her and Emilia suddenly felt self-conscious.

"What is it?" she asked, raising her hands to pat down her flyaway hairs.

"Nothing."

"Tell me. Otherwise I'm just going to think the worst."

Eric sighed. "You're so manipulative."

She tried to push him but he caught her wrist, expecting the attack.

"I was just thinking that I love days like today when you're smiling and joking this early in the morning. It usually takes longer. Anyway—" he paused to look down at his watch, "—I do need to go. I'm glad you're in a good mood and I hope you have a great day. I'll see you later."

"Eric!" Emilia called when he'd nearly reached the stairs. He stopped and turned around to face her. "Um, it's really good to see you," she said in a rush. "I know I just saw you like—several hours ago but—uh—"

"I get it. It's good to see you, too."

Once he had disappeared down the stairs, Emilia followed a sign in the hall to the bathroom. She saw two notes from Eric written on the mirror. The first one said simply: *This house is yours too, help yourself to anything.*

There was a second, longer note underneath that said: *Being your friend isn't work, babysitting, a chore, boring, or repetitive. I love having you in my life and would be lost without you.*

For some reason, that second note made Emilia tear up. Perhaps because she'd just been wondering how awful her condition must be for her friends, and Eric, in particular. She committed the lines to memory as she brushed her teeth. Well, she'd have them memorized for today, at least. Then tomorrow, she'd memorize them all over again.

* * *

Viola looked exactly like Emilia remembered. She had always been a hipper, more willowy version of her older sister, and still was. With long dark hair and stylish-looking bangs, which Emilia would never be able to pull off. She had Emilia's same large, inquisitive eyes, but they were lined in expertly applied eyeliner, which looked incredible on Viola, but made Emilia look like she had two black eyes any time she mimicked the look.

Viola was wearing an outfit that made Emilia think of what a cool hippy would wear if they were going skiing. With fashionably mismatched pants, sweater, and jacket, topped with a frayed scarf with a Native American pattern. Emilia's outfit was much more boring, just a matching blue snow pants and jacket set she'd found in the closet. Judging by the quality and how well it fit her, she guessed August's sister June had been the one to pick it out, and that Eric had been the one to pay for it.

"Hey, Em! How are you? Ready to go?"

Emilia looked down at her clothes. "Uh, I think so. I just need to put my boots on. Is this outfit good?"

"Sure. Come on."

On the drive, Viola chattered on about a date she'd been on the previous weekend, apparently picking up from a conversation she'd had with Emilia the last time they'd seen each other. She barely acknowledged Emilia's condition, which Emilia found both unsurprising and refreshing.

"So anyway, when we get there, we're going to have to finish up in the barn, since we didn't do the whole stall last time. But if we're quick we may be able to fit a ride in. How does that sound?"

"Um, good?" she replied warily, then admitted, "I have no idea what you're talking about."

Viola waved her away. "That's fine."

"I also don't know how to ride horses."

"Sure you do," Viola said dismissively.

Emilia just nodded, knowing better than to argue with her sister. After a while, Emilia said, "I didn't know you could ride horses in the winter."

"Of course you can ride horses in the winter. They don't hibernate. Besides, we're not riding outside, though you can, as long as there's not too much snow. There's an indoor arena. We don't want to deprive people of therapy during the winter months." She looked over at Emilia. "I assume you're wearing leggings and a sweater under those?"

Emilia looked down at her outfit, which was getting a little hot in the warm car. "Yeah. Good guess."

Viola shrugged. "You wear the same thing every time. Anyway, you'll want the jacket and pants in the barn, since it's pretty cold, but once we get inside you can take them off."

Emilia felt like this was something they should have worked out before leaving the house, but didn't say so. "Okay … anything else I should know?"

Viola chewed her lip as she considered, then said airily, "Nah. You'll figure the rest out."

Emilia resisted the urge to laugh. If she were with Eric, he'd launch into a detailed explanation of everything that was about to happen, maybe even hand her an hour-by-hour itinerary, so she'd know exactly what to expect. But Viola certainly wasn't Eric.

Emilia turned up the volume on the radio and settled back in her seat, trying to get in touch with those "go with the flow" Rhodes genes that must be swirling around in her body somewhere. The ones Viola had been gifted in abundance, but which Emilia could only find with careful concentration.

* * *

The work in the barn Viola had referred to on the drive

ended up being a replacement of one of the horse's stalls. By hand. Emilia was surprised to learn that last week, she and Viola had designed and measured the new stall, cut all the wood for it themselves, and managed to replace about a quarter of the enclosure before running out of time.

Emilia was prying one of the old boards off with a crowbar as a large, light brown horse stood a few feet away, watching her. "Should the horse be in here while we do this?"

"I told you, her name is Eleanor," Viola replied, taking a break from nailing one of the new boards in place. "Besides, why wouldn't she be here?"

"I don't know, because half her stall is missing. You're not worried she'll escape?"

Viola motioned toward the closed barn door. "And go where? She wouldn't escape, anyway. She loves her stall. Especially today. The client she had this morning was one of our more aggressive ones, so I'm sure she's enjoying resting in a familiar place. Aren't you, Ellie?"

The horse didn't answer. Just continued to watch Emilia with a look that said, *Don't fuck this up.*

"If she's supposed to be resting, isn't all this hammering bothering her?" Emilia asked, keeping a wary eye on Eleanor as she worked. She was worried if she made a wrong move, the horse would kick her or something.

Viola straightened and rubbed Eleanor's mane. "We're not bothering you too much, are we, Ellie? You're probably excited to finally see these rotting boards replaced."

Emilia was about to ask Viola if she thought Eleanor could understand her when the large barn doors creaked open and an older man called to them. "Hey, Vi! Emilia!"

Viola waved back at him. "Hi, Ernest! How's the training going?"

"Alright," he said as he pulled a saddle down from a hook on the wall. "Do you two need anything?"

"No! We're okay. Good luck!"

Ernest gave them a final wave before leaving them alone in the barn. "Does he know about me?" Emilia asked.

"Yeah. Everyone here does. Do you want me to reintroduce you later?"

"Do I ever say yes to that question?"

Viola thought about it for a moment. "No. But sometimes I reintroduce you without asking," she added matter-of-factly. She'd just finished the section she was working on and paused to stretch and roll her shoulders. Emilia could feel her sister's eyes on her as she removed a few more boards, continuing to watch Eleanor as she worked.

"She's not gonna hurt you, Em," Viola teased.

Emilia shrugged. "I'm just being cautious. Don't want to make, um, any sudden movements."

Viola rubbed the spot between the horse's eyes. "Eleanor knows you're the one who saved her. Don't you, girl?"

Emilia looked over her shoulder at Viola. "What?"

"Yeah. If it weren't for you, we would have lost her."

Emilia set the crowbar down and turned toward Viola and the horse. "What did I do?"

"Gerry, the lady who runs this place, got in this stupid fight with her ex-husband. He came around here, demanding she give him back the horses he bought when they were together, even though he's the one who ran off almost five years ago and never showed an interest in the horses during that time.

"Gerry was about to give in and hand the horses over, which included Eleanor here. She didn't want to deal with a big legal dispute, but you intervened. You wrote up some papers, went to see the ex-husband and threatened him with all this legal stuff, and he dropped it. We were lucky we had you."

"Oh." Emilia picked up the crowbar again. "Or just lucky Gerry's ex-husband is an idiot who doesn't know a bluff when he sees one. I couldn't have done anything real to help her. I'm not certified."

"You're very pessimistic, Emilia," Viola said sternly. "This is a good thing. You should celebrate the fact that you had a big hand in saving three of our horses."

"Yeah. Okay."

Viola let out an uncharacteristic sound of exasperation. "I'm surprised you didn't read about this in that list of accomplishments Eric wrote for you."

"Wait. What? There's a list of accomplishments? You mean I did more than impersonate a lawyer to save a few horses?"

Viola looked at her oddly. "It's been more than two years since your accident, Emilia. Of course you've accomplished things. Do you think you've been sitting around doing nothing? Do you think I'd let you do that?"

Viola looked offended at the insinuation and Emilia rushed to explain. "Of course not. This missing list must be part of my personal challenge. It must go along with why my calendar is blank, as is the notebook I'm supposed to write in at night."

"Blank? Your entire calendar?"

Emilia nodded.

"And the photo album and all the other notes. Are those gone, too?"

"Yes. There's some challenge I set for myself; to live one day at a time, but I have no idea why."

"Dammit, Emilia. That wasn't the intent of the challenge—to completely erase everything. But I see how you would do that.

You're very all or nothing."

"Wait. You know something about this?"

"Yes. It was my idea," Viola said proudly.

"What?" Emilia couldn't believe her luck. She thought she'd be working on this mystery all month, adding to that initial letter any new information she discovered each day. But it was just the third day of the month and she'd already found the person who had invented it. "Can you tell me how it came about?"

Viola thought about it for a second. "Yeah. I can do that."

Just then, Eleanor nudged Viola's side. Viola looked at the horse and cocked her head. "What do you need?"

Emilia bit her tongue. She wanted to know about this challenge, but Viola was busy talking to a horse. *Horses can't talk!* she wanted to shout. *Just give her a damn apple and tell me about the challenge!*

"You look tired," Viola was saying. "Do you want a little break? We can work on the door somewhere else and come back and attach it later."

Eleanor must have said yes, since Viola proceeded to gather up several boards and motion for Emilia to do the same. After following Viola to the side of the barn, Emilia turned and looked at her sister expectantly. It took Viola a moment to catch on. "Oh, right. One day at a time."

"Yes. What happened?"

"A few days ago, Saturday, to be exact, you were doing your end of month review where you look at your history—the notes you've slipped in the locked box, past info you haven't included in your summaries on all of us—"

"Yes, I understand the concept," Emilia cut in. "What happened?"

"You were in the library crying when I stopped by to ask

about ... what was it ...? Had I forgotten something? No, I don't think so. Maybe I needed—"

"It doesn't matter. Just tell me what happened."

"Okay," Viola continued. "You tried to send me away, but I could tell you were crying and demanded you let me in. You were spiraling, on the verge of a nervous breakdown." She said this calmly, as if this weren't that big of a deal.

"Why?"

Viola bit her lip. "Now this is tricky, because I don't think I'm supposed to say. Let's just say you were overwhelmed and, uh, having trouble picking out your true desires and feelings in a sea of confused thoughts. So, I recommended a reset."

"A reset? Is that a joke? I reset every day."

"Yeah, I know that. But you were under the impression that the large amount of notes you'd accumulated along with the photos, calendar, and all that were muddling things up. You were having trouble picking out what was truly you and what was you doing what you thought you were supposed to be doing, based on outside influences."

Emilia was thoroughly confused. "That doesn't make sense."

Viola shrugged. "I'm not sure how else to put it."

"Okay... So I threw away all these helpful notes and now I'm starting each day feeling especially disoriented. How is that a good idea?"

Viola crossed her arms in annoyance. "The idea was for you to take a pause. To remove anything from your morning routine that might bias your view of your life and just live." Viola put her hands on Emilia's arms for emphasis. "Simply live.

"Then—and this is the part you missed—you need to reflect at the end of the day. Really, truly, reflect. Ask yourself what the best part was. What the worst part was. What do you want? What are you scared of? Things like that. Then, at the end of the month, you can review all the responses and look for patterns to get a true sense of what's important to you in your life."

"I—oh. That doesn't sound completely terrible. It's like those meditation retreats people take to find their purpose and that crap."

"Sure." Viola's attention had been drawn back toward the boards they were supposed to be hammering together.

"I guess I need to add those questions to my notebook. And I should maybe list out that thing you said about pausing and removing biases. I should also add something to the letter about how things are harder than they need to be, but that it's just for a month."

"That should work," Viola said, clearly distracted now, but Emilia didn't care. She was glad to have some clarity.

"I left a note for myself to not talk to Eric about the challenge because it makes him sad and annoyed. Do you know what that's about?"

"Yes."

"Can you tell me?"

"I could, but I don't think I will."

"That is extremely frustrating," Emilia grumbled.

"I'm not surprised you think so."

"But the rest of it—it was really helpful. Thanks."

"You're welcome. Can we focus back on this? I really want to have enough time to ride today, and you'll like it too. I promise."

"Yeah, sure." Emilia crouched down and held the board in place for her.

Viola lifted her hammer, then paused to say, "You're going to be fine, Em."

Emilia smiled at her sister. It was hard to doubt her when she spoke so confidently. And honestly, she wanted to believe her.

* 7 *

Emilia was in the kitchen, reading the local newspaper, *Aspen Whispers,* when Eric returned from work. He was holding a large paper bag in his arms. Emilia guessed from the meal plan stuck on the refrigerator that it contained Mexican food.

"Hey. How was the farm?" Eric asked as he grabbed plates and utensils.

"Good. I spent the day doing manual labor and riding a horse and somehow managed to have fun."

"That sister of yours is magic."

Emilia released a small laugh. "How was work?"

She found the casualness of the conversation odd, since in her memory the last real conversation she'd had with Eric was a bad fight. Then she'd gone and almost killed herself and his best friend, and this morning she'd given him a large hug. But from his perspective, he saw her every day and had been living with her for over a year.

Eric told her a little about the clinical trial he was working on, but stopped talking when he arrived at the table holding out two plates of food. "Which one do you want?"

She bent forward and inspected both dishes. One was a plateful of orange sauce with bits of vegetables and what looked like shredded chicken mixed in. The other one was similar, but with green sauce. "What is this?"

"Mole. Pick one."

"What's mole?"

"A Mexican dish. Pick one."

"Is this some sort of test?"

"Kind of."

"I'm assuming I've had both of these before…?"

"Yeah."

Emilia smelled each dish and went for the green one, which smelled incredible, leaving Eric with the orange one. He smiled as he took a seat at the head of the table. "Did I pick right? Do you like that one? I don't mind switching."

He shook his head. "About a year ago we discovered this Mexican place on the edge of town. Apparently mole is their specialty so one night, we ordered every kind, about eight or nine dishes. We wanted to try everything at once so you wouldn't forget which was your favorite. We had leftovers for days."

Emilia laughed. "Yeah. I bet."

"Anyway, that one, mole verde, was your favorite and now, no matter what I order for myself, when I hold the two dishes up for you, you always pick it. A part of you remembers."

Emilia looked down at her plate, then took a tentative bite. It was delicious, but the rush of memories she'd expected to reappear in her mind as she ate this familiar dish didn't come. "It's very good," she said, trying to hide her disappointment. "Thanks for picking it up. What do I owe you?"

"Owe me?"

"Money."

Eric waved her off.

"Oh. I guess I don't have money, since I don't have a job." Emilia looked down at her plate, embarrassed.

"Before you start thinking you're some big charity case, let me reassure you that you *do* have money. You do a number of jobs that pay pretty well, but I would never let you give me any of it—though you've offered like a million times."

Emilia cocked her head, intrigued by his mention of jobs she did that paid money. Then she thought of the list of accomplishments Viola mentioned and scowled. Would it have been so hard to leave that one list behind? Then she wouldn't feel so useless or be surprised anytime someone mentioned her managing to be productive in this new life.

Eric, as if sensing her thoughts, said gently, "I know it's surprising to think you can get things done with your memory loss, but you're actually quite impressive. Better than most unencumbered people. I made a list of everything you've done in the past two years and I think it helped you to see it every morning, but…"

This was Emilia's opening, if there ever was one, but she was hesitant to take it. She remembered her note about Eric not liking to discuss her "one day at a time" challenge and even Viola had confirmed there was something there. But Emilia had to know. This mystery that seemed to include Eric had been eating away at her all day. And why all the secrecy? That part made no sense.

"You mean to say I had a list of accomplishments I read every morning, but now it's gone. I hid it as part of this 'one day at a time' challenge for the month of February."

Eric dropped his eyes and focused hard on his plate. "Yeah," he replied in a strained voice.

Emilia almost stopped pressing. Almost. But she needed answers. She was sick of not knowing.

"I can tell from my notes that this new challenge has been a big mystery to me for the past few days. But I learned a lot more about it today. Apparently it was Viola's idea."

Eric's head snapped up. He looked just as surprised as she had been. That was interesting. "Viola?" he asked. Emilia could see him making a mental note to talk to her later.

"Yeah. Viola."

"I thought you decided last Saturday during your month-end review, but you didn't see Viola that day."

"Apparently I did."

"When? What time?" he pressed.

Emilia shook her head. "She didn't say."

Eric frowned thoughtfully as he tapped his fork on his plate. She wished she could peek into his brain. "Eric, we must have talked that day. What do you know about all of this?"

He pushed his plate away, then leaned back in his chair with a heavy sigh. "Yeah, we talked," he said flatly, keeping his eyes on his plate. "It was my birthday and you woke up really early and made a huge breakfast." He smiled slightly at the memory.

"Then I went skiing with June and you said you were going to start your monthly review. I was back just after lunchtime and checked in on you. We—um—talked about what you'd learned. There was no mention of a challenge at that point, so I'm guessing Viola stopped by after."

Emilia shifted her chair closer to Eric. She was silently willing him to look at her, but he kept his eyes down. "Eric. Uh—was I upset when we talked? Because Viola said when she saw me, I was on the verge of a nervous breakdown."

Eric closed his eyes and pinched the bridge of his nose. "A nervous breakdown?" He nearly growled the question. "And then what? Viola swooped in and saved the day? Told you to erase everything I'd given you to make your life happier and convinced you to take on this stupid challenge?"

Emilia got the sense that whenever Eric met up with Viola to ask her about this, there was going to be a lot of yelling. That wasn't fair to her sister, since Emilia had gone more extreme with the whole thing than Viola had ever intended.

"She said I did it wrong," she explained. "I wasn't supposed to erase everything. I was just supposed to remove anything biasing me to—I don't know—act or feel a certain way. Honestly,

I'm not sure what she meant by that. But anyway, I was supposed to take time to reflect at the end of each day. It was just meant to be a sort of reset for the month."

Eric snorted. "A reset? You reset every day."

"Yeah. I said the same thing."

He pushed back from the table and grabbed their plates without even checking to see if Emilia was done. He rinsed them off and put them in the dishwasher, but he didn't return to the table. Instead, he stayed at the counter, gripping the edge of the surface tightly. Emilia went to his side and carefully placed a hand on his back.

He flinched at her touch, causing her to wince. She shouldn't have brought this up. She wished she could take it back. Knowing wasn't worth it. Not if it hurt Eric. And yet … she couldn't help herself.

"What's with all the secrecy?" she whispered. "It doesn't make sense. Just tell me what's going on so we can fix whatever's upsetting you."

Eric sighed and turned to face her. He reached out and placed a hand on her shoulder, rubbing his thumb along her collarbone. "Honestly, it wasn't always like this."

Emilia waited patiently for him to continue. When he finally looked up at her, his eyes were sad.

"You didn't remember things but when we talked about the time you'd forgotten, nothing was off limits. Then, one day, you decided there were parts of your life you wanted to hide. And—it caught me off guard. I honestly didn't know the right thing to do. Should I tell you? Was that fair? This is actually a point of contention between our friends."

"It is?"

Eric was looking back at his hand now, which was still on her shoulder. He used it to brush her hair back, then slowly trailed his fingers down her arm, stopping to grab her hand. "Viola and Owen agree with me, that we shouldn't tell you. August and June don't."

Emilia wanted him to expand on that but could tell he wasn't going to. She wondered who she would have sided with. What was she hiding? And why?

"When did this happen?" she asked.

"Last summer."

Emilia raised her eyebrows. That was longer than she had expected. Had this secret she was determined to keep from herself driven a wedge between her friends? She hoped not. But it was clearly putting a strain on Eric. That was bad enough. "And if I asked you to tell me now, would you?"

Eric pushed his thumb into her palm, and she got the feeling he was trying to tell her something with the gesture. "Are you?" He paused to take a deep breath. "Are you asking me to tell you?"

She nodded, completely caught up in the intensity of his gaze. Suddenly, Eric dropped her hand and turned back toward the sink.

"I'm not going to tell you. Of course you want to know. You're curious and can't stand not knowing the answer to every question. But when you did know everything, you didn't want to remember." Eric gave her an apologetic look. "I think I have to honor that Emilia's wishes. I'm sorry."

She reached for his hand and linked their fingers together. "How bad is it?"

"It's nothing bad," he replied, talking to their hands. "Just ... hard for you to come to terms with, I think."

Emilia could tell by the finality in Eric's tone that this conversation was over. She made a mental note to take copious notes about what he'd said tonight so she'd never have to put him through this again. They stood there for several moments, holding hands, until Emilia said, "Eric?"

"Hmm?"

"Is it always like this between us? So heavy, with me prodding you for painful secrets? How do you stand it?"

"Things are rarely this heavy between us. Don't worry." He cocked a grin at her. "Do you know what we need?"

"What?"

"Some time with the Seavers."

"That means absolutely nothing to me," she admitted.

Eric smiled knowingly. "It will in a few minutes. Come on."

He took her hand and tried to drag her out of the kitchen, but she pulled him back. "Wait. One more heavy thing. Just … I have to know, because my summary said not to ask her. Viola living here. Is that—? Did she give up that whole life in New York for me?"

Eric shook his head, but he was wearing a smile. "She—"

"You know, never mind. I'm sure you've already told me this a thousand times. It's fine."

"It'll take me two sentences to set your mind at ease. If you hadn't interrupted me, I'd be done by now."

She couldn't help but smile at that. "Okay then. Tell me."

"Yes, Viola moved here for you. Her plan was to stay for just a few months and help you get settled, then she fell in love with the place. I remember another Rhodes girl with similar plans—to just stay here for her undergrad and go back east for law school. She also fell in love with the area and never left."

"That was a lot more than two sentences," Emilia pointed out, smiling. She was thinking of Viola and how at ease she'd seemed at the farm. She belonged here, out in the country.

Maybe Eric was telling the truth. Of course he was. He'd never lie to her.

"Come on," he said, tugging on her arm. This time she let him pull her to the sitting room.

When they were on the couch, sitting next to each other, Emilia motioned toward the blanket Eric had draped over his legs. "Can I have some of that blanket?"

"Sure. Take some." He moved an inch of the blanket onto her leg.

Emilia rolled her eyes. "I thought your lifelong goal was to help people. I'm over here shivering and very sad from my memory loss condition, and all I'm asking is for you to share your blanket with me."

He rolled his eyes and made a big show of shaking out the blanket and putting a generous amount over her legs before settling back into his seat. "Better?"

Emilia nodded, and they started watching a sitcom. It was very stupid, but the entertainment came from all the heckling she and Eric did throughout the show. He was right; this was fun. She already felt better than she had earlier. But there was still a slight ache in her chest that she couldn't quite place.

During one of the commercials, Emilia sidled closer to Eric and laid her head on his shoulder. "Is this okay?" she asked.

"What?"

"Me smothering you. I just feel ... it's hard to explain. Actually, I'm sure you know why I'm feeling off. You seem to know everything about me. But I don't want you to guess."

"Okay," he said simply.

"You do know, though, don't you?"

She felt Eric turn his head to look at her, but kept her eyes forward. "Know what? Why you feel empty right now?"

Emilia nodded as tears sprung into her eyes. That was the perfect word for it. Empty.

"Hey." Eric pushed her up. "Wait here."

He left the room and returned a moment later with an envelope, which he handed to her before resuming his seat. "That arrived in the mail today. I forgot to give it to you earlier."

"What is…?" She cut off when she saw the return address at the corner. It was from the law firm she'd interned at the summer before her accident. She tore into the envelope, eyes darting to the end of the short note before reading it.

It was from Beth Larsen, the owner of the firm, and one of Emilia's favorite people. She was who Emilia wanted to be when she grew up. Or, well, had wanted to be, when she had a working brain. Her eyes darted back to the top of the letter and began to read.

Beth was thanking her for her help on a recent case. Yes, a *recent* case. Apparently Emilia had helped with the research for a big domestic violence suit. And she must have actually helped, since Beth wasn't the sort of person to give praise where it wasn't earned.

A lightness permeated through Emilia's insides as she set the letter on the coffee table. "Is this real?" she asked Eric.

"No."

Emilia suddenly felt cold and twisted her hands in the blanket, pulling it up further, but she relaxed her grip when she saw the glint of amusement in Eric's eyes.

"I make these about once a week—just replace the date to make it look current—then hand them to you when you need cheering up."

Emilia pushed him. "Smart ass."

He just grinned at her, then took back half of the blanket.

"Feel better? Less empty?"

She nodded as something tickled at the back of her throat. "I don't know what to say."

Eric picked up the remote and unmuted the TV. "You don't have to say anything. All I did was deliver a letter."

At the exact time she needed to read it. She leaned against his side and looked back at the letter. She had helped Beth Larsen. With her current condition. She had no idea how it was possible and didn't want to ruin the moment by pestering Eric for details she'd forget in a few hours. She was just content to enjoy the fact that she wasn't completely useless.

Eric wrapped his arm around her. "I actually like feeling smothered," he said softly.

She wasted no time snuggling against his side. He held her close, anchoring her to the couch, which she felt light enough to float away from. "I decided what I want to say."

"I knew the speechlessness wouldn't last long," he quipped.

She tilted her head to look at him. "Thanks," she whispered.

He looked down at her, and she noticed then how close they were. A breath away, maybe less. His proximity was comforting and unsettling, all at once. "No problem," he breathed. She thought she saw a hint of regret pass across his eyes, but it was gone before she could wonder more about it.

Part 3: Bartholomew

He always seems to be around when you're having a particularly hard day.

* 8 *

It was Saturday (FEB 07 87, according to Emilia's clock). After learning that her life was completely changed, Emilia had breakfast with Eric. Then he left for a hike, because Eric was one of those crazy outdoorsmen who weren't deterred by minor things like snow, ice, or below-freezing weather. He invited Emilia along, because he was polite, and she said no, because she was sane. That was how she found herself alone in the house, sitting on her bed and chatting with one of her oldest friends.

"You know, when I saw you had a page in my stack of summaries alongside my friends and family, I laughed out loud. Here, I'll read it, and you can let me know if anything's wrong."

Emilia picked up the stack of papers from the desk and flipped to the correct page. "Okay, here it goes."

"Bartholomew is alive and well. He still prefers the outdoors, but Eric trained him to come home each night. He sleeps in the basement and comes and goes through a flap in the door. I have no idea how Eric managed to tame the beast, but he knew you liked knowing where Bartholomew was, so he set all his energy to the task.

"I'd never considered before who would win in a contest of wills between Eric and Bartholomew, but now I know."

Emilia reached out and scratched the cat behind the ear. "Thanks for letting him think he tamed you. But we both know the truth."

Bartholomew let out a self-satisfied grunt as Emilia focused back on the summary.

"Sometimes he sleeps with you, sometimes downstairs, so he can be out bright and early. I suspect he knows about your condition and understands. He always seems to be around when you're having a particularly hard day, ready to give the bare minimum to provide

support, without overdoing it. He's as clever (and aloof) as always."

Emilia set the pages down and looked at Bartholomew. "Well? Is it accurate? Would you like me to make any changes? Maybe set the record straight about who really won that battle of wills?"

Bartholomew looked bored, then turned toward the window, which she took as a sign that the summary was just fine. She moved the stack of papers to the nightstand and lay on the bed next to him.

"I'm going to the Pearsons' anniversary party tonight. According to Eric, everyone in town will be there. What do you think? Is it going to be a disaster?"

Bartholomew let out a sound that could only be described as the cat version of *hmph*, then turned around and plopped down, presenting her with a lovely view of his backside.

"Yeah," Emilia sighed, tossing her arm over her face, "I'm not feeling great about it either."

She spent a long while just lying there, feeling sorry for herself. When she tired of that, she got started on the list of chores she'd seen posted on the fridge during breakfast. She cleaned the bathrooms, vacuumed, replaced the sheets on all the beds, and did laundry, listening to the radio as she worked.

She was surprised to find herself humming along to a few songs that she knew she hadn't heard before her accident. By lunchtime, she was on the last room, the kitchen. Eric found her scrubbing the sink when he returned from his hike.

"Hey, it looks great in here. Did you clean the whole kitchen? Because that's my—"

"I cleaned the whole house!" she said proudly, pointing to the chore chart. "I did all of those."

"We're supposed to split those. That's why there are names on the side, showing who does what."

"Yeah, I saw that. But I just thought …" She shrugged. "Why would we split chores? We're hardly contributing evenly."

Eric scoffed. "We've had this argument. We settled on splitting chores, which was one of the reasons I had *you* write the chart, so you'd see you had a part in making it."

"But it's *your* house, and I doubt I'm paying rent—"

"This is *our* house. We both live here and besides, *I'm* not even paying rent. The house is paid for."

"Okay, but what about utilities? I assume you're paying for those. And food, too. Right? And what about things like toilet paper, laundry detergent, soap, shampoo? You buy all of those, don't you? Actually, what about my clothes? Who paid for the dress I'm wearing to the party tonight?"

Eric didn't respond. He just sighed and shook his head. "Fine. Thanks for doing all the chores. But I'm making lunch."

She wanted to keep pressing. She was the sort of person who could argue for years. But Eric was clearly done. He had never been the type to dig his heels in. He was a mediator by nature, and conflict usually put him on edge.

He made them sandwiches, glowering at Emilia as she wiped down the cabinets. She was trying to entice him back into the argument, but he didn't take the bait. When they were finished eating, he rushed to grab her plate and clean up after her, sticking his tongue out over his shoulder as he washed the dishes with exaggerated motions.

"I think I'm going to make myself a note to clean all your clothes, fold them, and put them away while you're at work Monday," she said casually.

Eric presented her with another view of his tongue.

"You used to have better comebacks than this."

He tossed the dish towel over his shoulder and leaned back

against the counter. "It's possible I spend too much time with Henry."

Emilia laughed.

"I'm going to go and take care of my laundry before the party," he announced. "Just in case…"

* * *

When it was time for Emilia to get ready, she enlisted Bartholomew for help, which meant she was completely on her own. The cat watched her critically while she shimmied into a forest green satin dress. It was simply cut, with just two thin straps at her shoulders and a floor-length skirt that hung flat against her body. Then, at the top, was some added detail, she guessed to keep the dress from looking like a long slip. Sheer sleeves covered her chest and arms with a lace pattern at her wrists and along the neckline.

Emilia nodded approvingly at her reflection. It was fairly comfortable. Nothing itchy, nothing poofy, no excessive layers, and the color looked good against her olive skin. She usually hated dressing up, but this wasn't so bad.

She turned toward Bartholomew. "Well?"

The cat was busy licking his paw but paused for a moment to spare her a look of complete indifference.

"Never change, Bartholomew,"

He let out a small snort and continued cleaning his paw.

From there, Emilia went to the bathroom. Putting on a dress was easy. Now for the real work. She looked at her reflection for a while, contemplating skipping make-up altogether. But it seemed wrong to wear such a nice dress and not put on make-up. Plus, she'd look out of place, and that was the last thing she wanted.

She fumbled around with the eyeliner, cursing all the while

and wishing she had thought to call Viola to come do this for her. She kept forgetting her sister lived just a few miles away. Once she managed to line her eyes without looking like a racoon, she stopped. Best to quit while she was ahead.

She applied mascara next, trying really hard not to blink and mess it all up. There, it was on. And it kind of looked okay. She made a mental note not to rub her eyes as she put the make-up away.

Next was her hair. She just made several braids, then pulled her thick hair back into a low bun. She didn't know how to do anything more elaborate, but had learned that braids made things seem more fancy. Okay. She was done.

She watched the Emilia in the mirror for longer than was probably necessary. She retied the thin satin string around her waist, then considered doing something better with her hair. No. She forced herself to leave the bathroom. Best not to overthink it. It was just the Pearsons' thirtieth anniversary party. Not the Oscars.

Emilia met Eric in the hall. He was wearing a dark gray suit with a blue shirt and looked … dashing was the only word that came to mind. She'd called him a mountain man earlier, because he'd been wearing a flannel shirt and had facial hair, but now he looked, well, nothing like a mountain man.

"You clean up nice."

Eric just nodded as his eyes moved up and down her dress.

"I don't know why I have this," she said, looking down at the long skirt. "But you said the party was formal and this was the only long dress in the closet. Is it okay?"

"Claire's wedding." He seemed to have found his words, but not his ability to form clear sentences. He was looking at her strangely. She had to resist the urge to run back into the bathroom and check her reflection again.

"So, I've worn this before?"

"Yeah." He cleared his throat. "Sorry, but you look… I know I've seen you wearing this before … guess I forgot…"

"I believe I've rendered you speechless with my incalculable beauty," she teased.

To her surprise, he didn't laugh, but nodded solemnly. "I believe you have."

Emilia blushed and looked down at her feet, which were bare. She was hoping she had nice shoes downstairs somewhere, since she hadn't found any in her bedroom. "That was a joke," she said to the floor.

He stepped toward her and tilted her chin up. His blue eyes were almost pulsing with intensity. "Why?"

"I don't … it's me. I'm … okay, I guess."

He dropped her chin but didn't take a step back. He was so close, she had to crane her neck to see him properly. "You're a lot better than okay," he said in a low voice. "You're the most beautiful woman I've ever seen."

"What?" She let out a laugh, then took a step backward. "Have you not seen June? And what about Viola, the prettier version of me?"

Eric shook his head. "You are terrible at taking a compliment."

"Well, I—I'm not used to it. Not from you." Or anyone, she added in her mind. Sure, there was the occasional pervert at the bar or heckler on the side of the road, but she was pretty sure they did that to everyone.

Most people she met were too put off by how demanding and bossy she was to stop and consider whether or not she was pretty. It had taken August four years to notice. And Eric … she didn't think he'd ever considered her like that.

But the way he was watching her, like she was the last lemonade in the desert, as her mom would say, made it clear that something had changed. "I think it's easier to tell you things like this when I know you'll forget them," he admitted with a shy smile.

"Maybe I'll write it down."

"I'm sure you won't." The words were heavy, the weight of them drawing her forward.

She reached for him, without a thought for what she was doing. One moment, her hand was safely at her side and the next, it was resting on his chest. She was so close, she could feel his breath on her forehead.

"Eric?" she whispered.

"Yeah?"

The question she'd been meaning to ask hadn't formed fully in her mind. *What am I missing? Is this okay? Why is it that one moment, things are normal and the next, I've forgotten how to breathe?* None of those seemed okay to say out loud.

She took a step back. "Nothing. We should go."

He didn't seem ready to drop it, however. He was watching her, trying to send her a message. But no matter how intensely he looked at her, or how much use he made of every color and facet of his irises, he wasn't able to produce a message she could hear.

She should ask him to voice it. To put words to what was happening. To help her understand. But again, every question she started got lost on the way out of her mouth.

Eventually, he released a reluctant, "Okay," and pulled his eyes away from her.

* 9 *

The party was in an event hall just outside of town that resembled an oversized barn. There were Christmas lights and sheer fabric decorating the high ceilings. Where the barn doors would be, large windows and doors led to a wrap-around porch that showed off a lovely view of the snowy mountains.

Emilia vaguely remembered coming here for a wedding back in college. It was one of August's friends from class, but she couldn't remember his name. He'd moved to California shortly after that and he and August had fallen out of touch.

Speaking of August, where was—?

"August!" She spotted him at the edge of the dance floor and closed the distance between them as fast as her stupid heels would allow. Once she was close enough, she lunged at him. "You're safe! Thank God."

August wrapped his arms around her middle and twirled her around. "You greet me like this every time, and I love it every time."

He kissed her cheek before setting her down, then nodded at someone over her shoulder. She assumed it was Eric, but was too busy scanning August's face to confirm. Her letter said he was fine, and Eric had told her he was fine, but she preferred to see things for herself. He did look fine. Better than fine, actually. He looked really good. And happy.

She'd been worried things would be awkward between them, especially since she couldn't find it in herself to feel sad about their breakup, but he was looking at her like he always had, wearing that lopsided grin that managed to coax a smile out of her, no matter how low she was feeling.

August turned to Eric, who was at Emilia's side now, and the two boys exchanged one of those half-hug / half-handshake maneuvers guys loved. "Been a while," said Eric.

"Yeah. When's the last time I saw you two? New Year's?"

"I think so."

"Yeah, sorry. This last rotation kicked my ass. This month should be better, though." August turned back to Emilia. "You look incredible, by the way. Have I seen this dress? It looks familiar." This last question he'd addressed to Eric.

"Claire's wedding," Eric provided.

"Oh, that's right." August took Emilia's hand and pulled her to the dance floor. "Come on. Let's dance."

After placing her hands on August's shoulders, Emilia took a moment to study him again. His sandy blond hair was a little shorter and less messy than she remembered. Everything else about him looked the same. Same blue eyes, several shades lighter than Eric's. Same tall, lithe frame. Same easy smile, which was directed at her now.

"Well? What's the verdict?" he asked.

"Very handsome."

"Yes, I know." He winked.

She laughed. "As modest as ever, I see."

He just grinned, then turned as someone called his name, which was when she noticed the deep gash at the base of his neck, mostly hidden by his shirt. She touched her fingers to it, then followed the scar along the back of his shoulder, where it continued past her reach. That was from the car crash. She'd done that to him.

He turned back and grabbed her hand, placing a quick kiss on top before handing it back to her. "Don't cry, Em. I'm fine."

Damn, she was going to mess up her eyeliner. She blinked quickly and reminded herself that August was okay. That he'd healed. That her stupid mistake had only messed up her life, not his. He pulled her close and whispered soothingly in her ear, "It was an accident, Em. And we both made it out okay. Try to let it go."

She clutched the tops of his arms for several moments, blinking quickly and taking deep breaths, until she finally felt calm enough to step back. "Sorry," she murmured. "Did I mess up my makeup?"

He reached out and brushed away a tear that had fallen on her lower lashes. "No. Gorgeous as always, Em."

She smiled. This was familiar, August casually telling her she was beautiful, the same way he would say the weather was nice. Nothing like the intense way Eric had done it.

"Eric told me I was the most beautiful woman he'd ever seen," Emilia told him. "He must feel really sorry for me and my memory loss to throw out a pity compliment like that."

She expected August to see the joke, but his brows knit together, and his gaze shifted to something behind her. She turned to see Eric dancing with August's younger sister, April. Eric nodded when he saw them looking at him.

"I think he was telling the truth," said August.

"What's going on?"

August lifted an eyebrow. "Why don't you tell me?"

"Because I can't remember anything."

"Oh, that's right. I almost forgot."

"Hah hah," she said sarcastically. She wanted to press him further, but it was clear he was finished talking about this. Maybe they'd already discussed this a hundred times and he wanted to talk about something else for a change.

She was about to steer the conversation elsewhere, but while she was here, she couldn't help but peer down one more path before moving on to lighter topics. "We're okay, right? With being broken up? My summary said it was fine, and you seem happy, and I just—you're not angry, or annoyed, or sad, or—"

"We're fine. Better than fine. We're better as friends." He was sincere. She could see it in his eyes, which were still the same pale blue as the sky on a clear winter's day.

Emilia lifted on her toes and kissed his cheek. He smiled down at her, then pushed her out into a twirl. "How's work?" she asked when she was in front of him again. "You're a resident, right? Doesn't that mean I should be calling you Dr. Pearson?"

"You can. I'm more used to being referred to as 'the tall Intern,' or 'Gus.' One of the nurses called me that once and unfortunately it stuck. Or, as my attending lovingly refers to me, 'you.'"

"Oh. So, it's not good?"

"No, it's fine. I just don't like this rotation. You'd think emergency surgery would be interesting. It's not. It's mostly appendectomies, which are boring as hell. And I'm having to constantly switch my days and nights, so I'm always tired and never know what time it is. It's just not for me. I can't wait until I'm a cardiothoracic attending with my own interns to boss around. That'll be fun."

"How much longer until that happens?"

"Six years. Or, five and a half. But I'm five and a half years closer than I was. I try to look at it that way. Plus, if anyone in here chokes on something and yells for a doctor, I can finally raise my hand."

Emilia smiled at that. "I'm proud of you, Dr. Pearson."

He matched her smile. "I know. You yelled the loudest at my graduation. Anyway, what have you been up to?"

"No idea. I did a lot of chores today. And according to my

calendar, Eric and I went night skiing a few days ago, but I'm convinced that's just a joke, since he can't provide any proof besides a lift ticket that could belong to anyone."

"You do ski. I've seen it."

"What? I must be so bad."

"Yeah. You're pretty bad," he agreed, then turned her around again. "What else? How's Viola? Still a struggling artist?"

Emilia bit her lip as she tried to remember her summary about Viola. Part of her wanted to swat August and tell him she didn't remember a damn thing about her life, so please stop talking to her like she did. But maybe he thought this was helping? Maybe he thought ignoring her condition was what she wanted? She honestly had no idea what she wanted. Besides, once she figured it out, she'd just forget.

"Are you okay?"

"Uh, yeah. Viola's doing fine, I think. My summary said she's still an artist, and the calendar said we met at the farm she works at this past Tuesday."

"Oh yeah! I've been there. It's pretty cool, with that large indoor arena."

He did understand that since she hadn't seen the farm *today*, she didn't remember it, right? Weren't doctors supposed to be smart? She sighed and said in a clipped tone, "Yeah, I'm sure past Emilia thought it was cool."

August didn't pick up on her annoyance and just turned her around again before saying, "I heard about your challenge."

Emilia nodded. Finally, something she understood. "Yes. To live one day at a time. Did I tell you about it?"

"No. Eric did."

He glanced to the side of the room, where Eric was talking to an older man with a mustache who looked vaguely familiar.

Emilia was pretty sure he was one of the professors from his and August's medical school, but couldn't recall his name.

"Do you talk to Eric a lot?" she asked as she dragged her eyes back to August.

"Yeah," he said absently. He was still watching the conversation between Eric and the man with interest. "He calls about once a week."

"August?" He looked back at her. "Is he okay? Eric? He seems ... sad. Is it his family or ... something else?"

August shrugged and placed his hands back on Emilia's waist. "He's fine. And the family's fine. His dad is still out of the picture, as is Sarah. But his aunt has Henry and Eric likes helping out with him. Claire is married and living in San Francisco. You wore this dress to her wedding last year."

"She married the banker, right?"

"Yeah. I guess you can say Eric never kept that dam from falling, but at least he got himself to safety."

Emilia hummed as her eyes found Eric again. He was still talking to the man, who she'd finally placed. Dr. Cain, the head of the lab Eric was working in at the time of her accident. How could she have forgotten that jerk?

By the looks of it, Eric was not enjoying the conversation. His smile was forced and his eyes kept darting around the room, like he was scoping the area for exits. As she watched him, she thought of another possibility for his sadness.

"What happened to the MD-PhD program? He wanted it more than anyone and now ... nothing? My summary says not to ask him about it, but you can tell me."

"There's not much to tell. He didn't want to be stuck in a lab anymore. He wanted more time with Henry and ... and more time to ski."

August had always been an awful liar. "He left medical school so he could ski?"

"You know Eric," he shrugged. "Loves being outside."

"Yeah, I know Eric. You know what else he loves? Sacrificing himself. Have you already forgotten the hell he put himself through when Henry was a baby? If he had to give up skiing for a few years while he worked his way through the worst of medical school, he would have done it. He *was* doing it! He left for another reason and the timing is too much of a coincidence. It was me, wasn't it? He left for me."

"Em, don't worry about Eric." He placed his hands on her shoulders. "He's happy and he loves living with you. And he likes his job. Let's talk about something else. Actually," his eyes focused on something behind her, "my mom's waving us over."

"Oh." Emilia looked over her shoulder and waved back at Mrs. Pearson. "When's the last time I saw her?"

"No idea." August took her arm and pulled her toward his mom. "Come on. We'll get this out of the way, then track down some food."

* * *

"Did you see her? Emilia Rhodes?"

Emilia started at the sound of her name. She was in one of the bathroom stalls, about to leave, but stopped with her hand over the lock on the door as a second voice joined in.

"Yeah, I did. Crazy, right?"

Emilia rolled her eyes and was about to open the door and put a stop to this when she heard the first voice say, "I can't believe she lives like that. I would have killed myself by now."

Angry tears sprung into Emilia's eyes and she rushed to blink them back. She was not going to let a pair of stupid gossipy girls make her cry.

"It's not all bad," the second girl chimed in. "She's with Eric Shaffer, isn't she? He's so hot. And smart. And he lives up in Canyonview, so is probably rich, too. She certainly could have done worse than him."

"They're not together. He's, like, her keeper. I think because they were friends for so long he feels like he has to take care of her."

"Ugh. Poor Eric. Hasn't he been through enough? Now he's stuck with his crazy friend. She should go live with her parents, wherever they are. Or, doesn't her sister live here?"

"No idea. But I'd kill to get a chance to play house with Eric Shaffer. Show him the sort of woman he really deserves…"

The girls laughed while Emilia fumed, curling her hands into fists at her side. She pushed the door open and glared at the pair of girls. She didn't know them, but thought she'd seen them hanging around the Pearson twins earlier. "Hi. I'd introduce myself, but it sounds like you already know me."

The girls just stared at her in stunned shock. If she hadn't been so angry, she would have laughed. "Nothing?" she pressed. "Don't want to tell me I should kill myself? Or that I'm crazy? Or that I need to leave Eric alone?" Her voice wavered on the last line, and she had to force it to stay steady.

The taller girl, who was fairly pretty with mousy brown hair and large green eyes, found her voice. "Oh, uh, I think maybe you misunder—"

"Spare me. I have amnesia, I'm not stupid."

The other girl, who had blonde hair and a horse-ish face, blurted, "Are you going to tell Eric what we said?"

Emilia glared at her cruelly. This was the one who had said she wanted to play house with Eric. And who had said Emilia should kill herself. Emilia took a step toward her, fists still clenched, and grinned when the girl backed away.

"No, because I don't know who you are, nor do I care to find out. Besides, you're not worth Eric's time. I know Eric, and I know his type, and he wouldn't spare you a second look, so you can drop whatever candle you're holding for him."

The girl's eyes had turned to liquid, which Emilia didn't feel sorry for at all. She marched out of the bathroom, but stopped at the door and threw a final barb over her shoulder. "Maybe I don't remember things but at least I'm a caring person who tries to understand and help people more unfortunate than me. If I was as awful as the two of you, *then* I'd seriously consider killing myself."

* * *

Emilia marched out of the bathroom in a huff. She began scanning the crowd for Eric but couldn't see his wavy hair anywhere. She'd meant what she'd said to the girls, she wasn't going to tell Eric what they'd said, but there was a small (and annoyingly pathetic) part of her that needed to find him and confirm she wasn't a burden to him.

Where was he? When she didn't find him in the main area, she searched the halls, but no Eric. Maybe he was in the bathroom. After settling herself near the bar at the side of the room and facing the hall that led to the bathrooms, she saw a man with a cigarette slip outside. Oh, right. There was a patio.

She followed the man outside, pulling her arms around herself instinctively, but it wasn't that cold. There were heaters attached to the building, radiating warmth onto the balcony. The man went right while she headed left. Emilia walked along the deck until she spotted August and Eric leaning against the railing. Beyond, the mountains shone with luminescent white, ethereal giants playing silent witness to the moonlight.

She smiled to herself and closed the distance between them,

but stopped in place when she heard August say, "So ... you brought Emilia tonight."

"Shut up," Eric snapped back.

Emilia was alarmed by the harshness in his tone. What was going on here? She pressed her back up against the wall of the building and turned so she was hidden by a folded up umbrella.

"I could have brought her," August was saying. "I'm not dating anyone right now."

"It's hard for me to keep up with your endless stream of girlfriends," Eric replied bitterly.

August sighed. "I'm not going to apologize for being young and having fun like a normal guy our age. Something you could—"

"Not now," Eric cut him off. "Emilia's so worried about repetitive conversations, but the most repetitive conversation in my life is this one, with you and June."

"Why are you doing this to yourself?" August asked, his voice concerned.

Eric was quiet.

"What was Cain saying to you? Inviting you back into the program? Do you know how many people would kill for—?"

"Stop. I get enough of that wasted potential shit from everyone else. I don't need it from you too."

August sighed, but didn't say anything else.

When Eric spoke again, his voice was muffled and Emilia guessed he was covering his face with his hand. She could only make out some of his next words. "I date the ... you set me up with ... every two weeks ... we agreed ... I don't have to listen ... And the program ... you know, out of everyone ... the one who ... Fuck off."

Eric stormed away, passing right by Emilia. But she was well hidden behind the umbrella and further concealed by the low light. She watched August for a few moments as he stared at the mountains in the distance. Then, a minute later, he straightened, rubbed his face, and made his way back inside.

Emilia stayed there for a while, trying to puzzle through what she'd heard. August was upset because Eric had come with Emilia tonight. Why? He didn't seem jealous, just concerned for Eric. And Eric said he'd agreed to go on dates every few weeks. Why?

She walked back to the door, not wanting to be found outside by Eric, who would probably guess at what she'd overheard. Once inside, she was confronted by a stocky man about her age who she didn't know, but who seemed to know her. "Emilia. I've been looking for you."

"Oh. Uh. Hello..." She smiled awkwardly, hoping the man would provide his name and maybe a brief description of the role he played in her life, but he just powered on.

"I wanted to tell you that there's another case in the office you might be interested in. There's a poor woman being tried for defending herself against her husband. He's pretty well off, and well connected, and she's not from around here. She's not even white, so that'll cause a bit of bias. And without his support she can't afford a lawyer ... anyway, you know how the story goes. What do you say? Are you in? These cases are becoming a bit of a specialty of yours," he added with an encouraging smile.

Emilia had no idea what to say. This man obviously had previous interactions with her and was asking her to do some work. *Legal* work, which seemed odd, since she wasn't a lawyer. He had to know that, right? But even if she agreed now, she wouldn't remember agreeing. Certainly he knew that, too. Or had she tricked this man into thinking she was normal to get some work? Should she keep up the charade?

Just then, she felt a hand on her waist. "Hello, Martin."

Emilia let out a sigh of relief when she saw Eric. He looked down at her and winked.

"Eric. I was just telling Emilia we have another case for her."

"That's great. How about I call your office Monday and get the details?"

"Yes, of course. No work talk at a party. Lorna would smack me if she found out. You call Monday; Beth will be thrilled." He grinned at Emilia before adding, "Which for her means she may allow herself half a smile. You know Beth." He laughed at his own joke while Emilia turned this new clue around in her mind. Beth. Beth *Larsen?* Was that the office she was helping?

"Yes, we'll call Monday," said Eric. "Thank you, Martin."

Martin nodded and left Eric and Emilia alone, taking off in the direction of the bar. Eric turned to face Emilia but didn't take his hand off her waist. "Hey. Where have you been?"

"Um, around. I met June's girlfriend, then went to the bathroom then, uh, met Martin. Was he talking about Beth Larsen?"

"Yes, Martin works in Beth's office. You help them with cases sometimes. I have a pile of notes on it back at the house that I can show you from old cases you worked on. And Beth even sent you a thank you note earlier in the week. It's probably on your desk somewhere."

"Beth sent me a thank you note?" she asked, shocked.

Eric smiled. "Yes. You were thrilled when you first saw it. If you want to work on this, I can remind you Monday to call her office."

"I can make a note for myself. You don't have to do everything for me," she replied. The words came out harsher than she'd meant them to.

Eric stepped back and dropped his hand from her waist.

"Right," he said, looking a little wounded.

She was about to apologize but before she could, he held out his hand for her and bowed slightly. "Will you dance with me? You're my date, but I've barely seen you all night."

She thought of his conversation with August again. Eric looked fine, happy even. All the anger and bitterness she'd heard in his tone earlier was gone. "Of course," she said as she placed her hand in his. "Sorry about that. I didn't mean—"

"Don't worry about it."

Eric guided her to the dance floor, and they passed most of the first song in silence. Emilia's mind kept replaying his conversation with August, then the one she'd overheard in the bathroom. They all seemed to think she was holding Eric back. She wanted to ask him if she was keeping him from dating and if that was why August was upset. She wanted to know if she really was the reason behind him quitting medical school and if there was anything else she'd taken from him. But she was too afraid to hear the answers.

By the next song, she couldn't hold it in any longer. "Are you there every morning?"

Eric looked down at her, confused. "Where?"

"At the house, waiting for me. Waiting to see me and reassure me that everything is going to be okay."

"Yeah," he shrugged. "The letter is good and all, but it's also good for you to see someone you trust first thing. It starts the day off right."

"And that's why you're not in school anymore? Because the schedule didn't give you the flexibility to always be there for me?"

"Who told you that? August?"

"Just tell me. Am I keeping you back?"

Eric grinned at her. "Yeah, you're keeping both of us back.

You're very hard to move around this floor. Can you stop trying to lead?"

He was deflecting. There was her answer. She was the reason he would never become a doctor like August. So, her accident hadn't just crushed her dreams, but Eric's as well.

The truth hit her like a tidal wave. Maybe from that dam Eric had been trying to hold up. August was wrong; he hadn't escaped at all. He'd just transferred his efforts to a new hopeless cause: her.

"Emilia?"

She saw their relationship in a new lens, the way any outsider must see it. Eric killing himself day after day, trying to make everything seamless for her. While he had the same conversations, performed the same routines, put everything on hold, all for her. She was stuck in time, never able to progress, but he'd gone and stuck himself right alongside her.

Everyone else was moving on, but Eric had given everything up. No wonder August was annoyed. Why try so hard for someone who didn't even remember the effort? He could leave Emilia alone for months and she wouldn't even notice. If she were in August's position, having to watch Eric do that to himself, she'd be livid.

"Emilia? What's wrong?"

"I need air." She pulled away from him, but he caught her wrist and started to move with her. She snatched her hand back. "*Don't* follow me. Just—just take care of yourself. For once."

He stayed put as she walked away, though it clearly pained him to do so. Just one more example of Emilia keeping him frozen in place. Tears clouded her vision as she ran for the door. She had a passing thought about her makeup and how it was probably ruined for good, but it didn't matter. Nothing mattered when it would be erased from her mind in a few hours.

* 10 *

Eric didn't stay away for long, and Emilia hadn't expected him to. He seemed like an agreeable, easy-going guy to people who didn't know him well, but he could be stubborn when he wanted to be. You didn't become the sort of person who ruined their life on behalf of others without possessing a good bit of bullheadedness.

He'd brought reinforcements. She was leaning against the railing and watching the mountains glow in the moonlight when Eric and August settled in on either side of her. They were quiet for a long while, and she almost snorted. She knew what they were doing. They were trying to wait her out, and they were going to win. She'd always been the most impatient out of the three of them, and with a deadline looming for how long she had until she forgot everything, she was even more so.

"Sorry, Eric," she said with a sigh. "I shouldn't have snapped at you. Let's go back inside. It's cold out here."

She turned to leave but Eric caught her by the elbow. "Tell us what's wrong."

"I'm brain damaged and can't remember a fucking thing. And I've been meeting people all night who know me or things about me and I just—I hate it. But it's fine, because I'm just going to forget it all in a few hours and try again tomorrow."

"Em, you can't—" August began to say.

Eric cut him off. "That's not what it is. What's really the matter?"

Emilia glared at him. He glared right back at her. They were caught up in another battle of wills and again, Emilia gave in first. "Fine," she sighed, returning to her spot on the railing. "There were these stupid girls in the bathroom talking about me."

"What did they say?" August asked.

"That I'm a drain on my friends. That if they were me they'd kill themselves. And I know that part is extreme, but they aren't entirely wrong. Is a life like this really worth living?"

"Yes," they both said at the same time.

Emilia chewed her lip for several seconds, then looked over at Eric, who was frowning with his eyes trained ahead. She turned to August next and met his worried stare. "We've been through this before, Em. Of course your life is worth living. Back when you were living with me, during my clerkship, I came home with a story of this one dude who lost the use of his legs, then said he didn't want to live anymore because he wouldn't be able to hike and ski. We joked that he sounded like Eric, then you said, what was that line you used? I'm sure you know—it's probably whatever you're thinking now."

"I don't know," she said coolly.

August powered on, unphased. "It was something about how you hated how society treated damaged people like they were inherently flawed, and that they didn't deserve full lives. That it was the basis for the legal protections for disabled people. Is that ringing a bell? Anyway, we—"

"No, August! It's not ringing a fucking bell! God! Do you think this is helping?! Talking to me like I know what you're saying when you *know* I don't! I didn't even know we used to live together! I know nothing!"

August's face rearranged itself into something hard. "I tried the other way before but you bit my head off for babying you. For not treating you like normal. You're always changing your mind, always trying a new tactic, a new challenge, and it's fucking insane. You're not going to outmaneuver this one, Em. You can't be cleverer than the amnesia. You lost, and you need to accept—"

"No, man. Not now." Eric moved swiftly and took August by the shoulder, pulling him away from Emilia.

"She is—"

"—having a really hard night, okay?" Eric finished for him. "Now is not the time for this. Just go inside and get a drink. We'll meet you back in there."

August stared Eric down for a few moments, then sighed. "Fine." He fixed Emilia with one more hard look before marching across the deck toward the door. Emilia jumped at the sound of it slamming as Eric resumed his spot at her side, looping an arm around her waist and holding her close to him.

"Emilia, your life is one thousand percent worth living. You're healthy, capable, beautiful, strong, brilliant, beautiful—"

"You already said that one," she pointed out.

"Well, you look really good tonight."

She smiled. "Thanks."

"And despite what you just shouted at August, you *do* remember. Maybe not in the traditional sense—but you *know*. Believe me, I've been with you the whole time. You aren't the same person now you were six, twelve, or eighteen months ago. You're changing, growing, *living*—and it's worth it."

Emilia leaned against him and rested her head on his chest. "Thanks, Eric."

They just stood there for a while, and Emilia was surprised to find that she felt a little lighter, even though she hadn't brought up the root of her concerns.

Eric shifted away and turned so he was facing her, leaning his side against the railing. She turned toward him as he said, "But that wasn't it. You don't care what some stupid girls think about you. There's something else going on."

She was quiet. Eric had become a mind reader since her

accident. How did he do it? Did it apply to everyone or was this mysterious new ability something reserved just for her?

"You can tell me," he said softly.

Emilia shook her head. "I can't."

"You mean 'won't.'"

"Maybe."

He studied her for a moment, then stepped back and held his hand out. "Dance with me."

She cocked her head in confusion. "You want to dance out here?"

"Why not? We can still hear the music. Besides, it seems like the least you can do, since you interrupted our last one and won't even tell me why."

He had a point. She placed her hand in his, and he wasted no time pulling her close, resting a warm hand behind her waist while the other one maintained a firm grip on her fingers. They moved slowly, in time to the rhythm of the music, which was the only sound in the still, night air.

At the start of the next song, Eric whispered in her ear, and his warm breath sent shivers down her spine. "It was when I said I was there for you every morning. You were upset, because you think I've given everything up for you."

Tears filled Emilia's eyes. She shifted closer to him, so he wouldn't see.

"I quit for me," he said gently.

She hummed, not trusting herself to speak. Eric turned them around one more time, then stopped and stepped back. "Hey."

She looked up and saw his somber expression. "Has it occurred to you that maybe it was important for me to see you every morning not for your benefit, but for mine?"

Emilia shook her head.

He took her in his arms and started moving them around the patio again. "It's a long story, and I know you have it written down somewhere, so I won't rehash all of it, but you were about to leave. You were living with August, and you weren't doing well, and you were about to go to New York and live with your sister. She was convinced you'd do better with a consistent routine, and more attention, and without trying to recall everything you missed every day. She was the one who came up with the monthly review thing, by the way."

He stopped to push her out into a twirl, then continued speaking when she was back in his arms.

"I panicked when I heard you were leaving, even though I'd spent most of that year ignoring you. So I took the summer off. Dr. Cain nearly killed me, but we agreed to a part-time schedule. I spent three days up here, in the lab, and the rest of the week I spent at Camp Ouray, with you. We tried Viola's plan. You stopped studying the time you'd missed every morning and just lived. And it worked. You thrived."

"So the summer ended, and you quit so you could continue to foster that environment that made me thrive," she said. "How is that not quitting for me?"

"Hush and let me finish. You're not considering my side of things. No one ever does. They see us living together, and they see me helping you, and they see that I'm no longer in medical school, and they assume it's all for your benefit. But they never see it from my point of view.

"You weren't the only one who thrived that summer. I felt lighter than I had in years, more myself, happier. Then I'd have to go back to the lab and it was like I had a rain cloud over my head until I made it back to camp."

He spun her again and when he pulled her into his chest, he

held her so close, their faces were just inches apart. His next words were just above a whisper.

"Have you thought that perhaps, in this life that is filled with a lot of sadness as I mourn not just the loss of my mom, but the abandonment of dad and both of my sisters. Where my best friend moved away, and my girlfriend decided she didn't want me anymore. Where I still struggle to figure out what I'm supposed to be doing, and where I belong, that maybe I like starting the day with someone who's thrilled to see me every time? Who loves me for me, and not the person she thinks I am, or thinks I should be? Who has always been supportive and understood me better than anyone?"

He moved a hand to the base of her neck and began rubbing his thumb along the scar from her accident.

"I quit for me. Because I had to see you everyday, but it wasn't fair to insist you stay, then continue to ignore you while I pursued my training. Because I looked at the pros and cons of staying and leaving the program and leaving won out. It wasn't a matter of what was best for you, Emilia. I'm sure you would have done great living with your sister. I did what was best for me, and I've never regretted it."

Emilia's eyes were filled with tears by then. She dipped her head into the crook of Eric's neck as they swayed in place. Mountain air, leaves, a hint of musk, and soap. That's what he smelled like. She was overcome with a feeling of familiarity. She hadn't realized how empty she was until the sensation of knowing something, of knowing *him*, was filling her up. That feeling, mixed with his words, drew up a well of emotions, making the tears she'd been struggling to hold back finally fall.

When Eric realized she was crying, he walked her to the side of the patio, under one of the heaters. He took a few tissues out of an inside pocket of his jacket and handed them to her. He must have packed them back at the house. Oh, Eric. Why was he so wonderful?

"How do you always know the exact right thing to say to make me feel better?" she asked as she wiped away her tears.

"This is you feeling better?" he joked.

Emilia gave him a small, teary smile.

He leaned against the wall and smiled over at her. "I've had lots of practice," he said, answering her previous question. "Whenever I say the wrong things, you forget, and then I get a chance to tweak it the next time until I get it just right."

Emilia's face fell and Eric nudged her side. "That was supposed to make you laugh. I'm kidding. We've never had this conversation."

She leaned against the wall next to Eric. "I find it hard to believe I've never brought up the topic of you not being a doctor because of me."

"You've brought this up before, but I've never answered it like that."

She sighed and leaned her head back against the wall. "Oh, Eric," she whispered. "It's so much. So much to come to terms with in such a short amount of time. So many facts, but more than that, so many emotions. I can't even explain it clearly."

"You don't have to explain. I know."

Emilia kept her gaze on the sky. Maybe he thought he knew, but how could he possibly understand?

"I know what it feels like to have no control over your life," Eric continued. "For things to keep going wrong, one right after another, while you stand by with no power to stop them. To do everything right and still lose. I know how painful it is to have to come to terms with the fact that there's a tiny sliver of things you can control, and that you have to let the rest of it go. The only way I got through it was with friends who loved me unconditionally and supported me as best they could. You did it for me and now it's my turn. And I truly love doing it."

Emilia turned to look at Eric. They stood there for several moments, staring at each other as the music played faintly from inside. He reached out and took her hands. Her heart was pounding hard, and as she looked in his eyes, she could see that he *did* understand her. She hadn't felt this with August.

August was sorry for her. August loved her and wanted her to be happy. But Eric, Eric *knew*. Maybe that was why she lived with Eric and not August, and probably why she'd snapped at August earlier.

It was Eric who broke the trance. If it had been up to Emilia, they probably would have stayed there staring at each other for the next hour. Eric stepped back and dropped one of her hands. "Come on. We both need a drink," he muttered, pulling her back toward the door.

"Or ten," Emilia added as she followed him. "And I should probably apologize to August."

Eric smiled at her over his shoulder. "Yeah, you should. That was a bit much."

"I know."

They were inside and making a beeline for the bar when Eric asked, "Ten drinks? Is this going to be a repeat of your 25th birthday?"

She shrugged. "Would that be so bad? That was a fun night. I think. Honestly, I don't really remember it."

"Yeah. Me neither," he laughed, pulling her close and tucking her under his arm. She wrapped her arms around his middle and smiled up at him, determined to make the rest of their night better.

* 11 *

Emilia was *not* drunk, just pleasantly tipsy. A fact she'd just informed June of for the tenth time.

"Yeah, yeah," June muttered as she pulled Emilia out of the back seat of her car and set her carefully on the driveway. "At least you two didn't throw up in my car, so thanks for that."

"She's right, you know," said Eric, draping an arm over June's shoulders. "We're not drunk."

"The smell of your breath says otherwise. Also, the way you're putting all your weight on me, no… not drunk at all."

Emilia poked the dimple on June's cheek. "June's grumpy."

June patted the top of Emilia's head. "And Emilia's giggly. Let's get you two inside." She pulled a set of keys out of her jacket and marched toward the front door. "Ruby's on her way over here in your car, so you won't have to worry about picking it up in the morning."

"You're the best!" Eric exclaimed. "Isn't June the best?"

Emilia didn't respond. She'd run ahead of June and tucked herself out of sight, behind one of the columns on the front porch.

"Emilia?"

Emilia stayed in her hiding spot until June and Eric appeared on the doorstep. "Boo!"

She was sure she hadn't surprised either of them, but Eric still let out an elaborate, girlish scream, which caused June to roll her eyes and Emilia to laugh so hard, she nearly fell over. Luckily, she caught herself on the door before tumbling to the ground.

"It's not fun being sober when your friends are drunk," June grumbled. "Why didn't you all tell me you were planning to drink half the bar? I would have joined you!"

Eric had crossed the porch and pulled Emilia off the door. He was half holding her up but she could feel him swaying on his feet and kept a hand on the doorframe to balance both of them. "We didn't drink half the bar!" Emilia argued. "Only, like, a quarter."

She looked over at Eric and he nodded eagerly, then leaned into her and added, "Maybe a third."

Emilia burst into laughter again.

June shook her head and shooed them away so she could open the door. "Okay, you two, off to bed," she said, holding the door open for them. "Can you make it up the stairs or do I need to help you?"

"We can walk up the stairs!" Emilia countered. "We're not drunk just—"

"Pleasantly tipsy. Yes, I've heard. Go along then. Show me how well you can walk."

Emilia extricated herself from Eric, then went to the stairs and started walking up slowly, taking it one step at a time. When she was halfway, she turned to June. "See?" She raised her hands over her head. "No hands!" She went to take her next step and nearly fell, but caught the railing just in time.

June nodded and said sarcastically, "Very convincing. Let's do it with our hands this time. Okay?"

Emilia stuck her tongue out at her.

Eric had an easier time making it up the stairs. When he reached Emilia, he placed a steadying hand on her arm while also gripping the railing tightly. "I've got her. See?" he said over his shoulder.

"Okay…" June said reluctantly. "Don't do anything you're going to regret," she called after them as they continued to slowly make their way up the stairs. "And I say that to Eric, since, well,

Emilia won't remember."

Emilia thought this was exceedingly funny and began to laugh again as she took the final few steps to the top of the landing. She turned around and gave June a proud smile. "I made it!"

"Yes. You just need to make it to the end of the hall now. I'll see you two at my parents' place for lunch tomorrow. And don't forget to drink water!"

"Okay. Bye, June!"

"Bye!" Eric added.

Once June had closed the door behind her, Eric turned to Emilia and asked seriously, "Do you think you can make it to the end of the hall without hurting yourself, or do you need my assistance?"

"I definitely need assistance."

Eric picked her up abruptly, causing her to squeal, then began stumbling toward the end of the hall.

"Eric! Put me down! You're going to kill both of us."

"Worst case, we trip and fall. It's highly unlikely we'd die from that. Unless you're hiding a knife or something that we might skewer ourselves on."

"I am not concealing a knife. Well, not that I remember."

They both laughed as Eric reached the door to her room. He set her down and propped her up against the wall. "Safely delivered to your room, m'lady."

"My hero." Emilia turned and leaned with her side against the wall. Eric stood opposite her, mirroring her pose.

They watched each other for what felt like forever, until Emilia broke the silence with a soft, "Hi."

"Hi. That was fun."

"It was."

Eric reached out and grazed his hands along the skirt of her dress. "You look beautiful. Have I told you that?"

"Yeah. Several times."

"Good."

The laughter from just a few moments ago faded. She was reminded of that moment they'd shared earlier in this same hall when he'd told her she was the most beautiful person he'd ever seen. Then something had passed between them. Something she couldn't place at the time. Something that made it hard to breathe.

She had a sudden, bizarre urge to kiss him. Why was that bizarre? They were both single, weren't they? Both attracted to each other. At least she was attracted, and he kept going on about how beautiful she was, so he'd probably be okay with it. Why shouldn't they kiss?

That thought sobered her up. She straightened quickly, which caused her head to spin, making her stumble. Eric caught her arm. "Are you okay?"

"I—yeah."

Eric placed her back on the wall. As he pulled his hand away, she remembered the conversation she'd overheard him having with August. How inconvenient. She'd been drinking to forget that conversation and here it was, back in her mind.

Of course she couldn't kiss Eric. She was all wrong for him. She was damaged. She couldn't be with anyone. He needed to date and find someone better. Someone who'd remember him.

"Emilia?"

Beads of tears were collecting at the corners of her eyes. She shut them quickly, but the tears escaped. Eric was on her the next moment, pulling her against his chest. "What is it? What's wrong?"

She'd had too much wine. Her head was spinning. His familiar smell was intoxicating. She was using all of her willpower to fight back her tears, which was probably why the words she'd been trying to hold in all night came spilling out. "You don't date because of me. You're supposed to date, and you don't, and it's all wrong."

Eric released her and stepped off the wall. "What?"

"I heard you talking to August," she explained. "He was annoyed you brought me and he wants you to date. But you don't ... you don't want to."

Eric exhaled and leaned on the wall again. He rested his head against it and sighed.

"Why not?" she pressed.

"Are you really asking me this right now? Dressed like that, when I've had three—maybe four too many drinks?" He paused to give her a sad smile. "If you're not careful I might just tell you the truth."

"Tell me," Emilia whispered.

Eric closed his eyes and took a deep breath.

"I'm going to forget in a few hours," she pressed.

Eric opened his eyes, then took a step closer to her. He picked his hand up and traced his finger along her jaw.

"Are you going to tell me what that conversation with August was about?" she breathed.

"I'm telling you right now. Don't pretend you don't understand."

Eric moved his finger down her neck, along the neckline of her dress, then over to her shoulder before feathering it down her arm, pausing to rub the scar on her elbow. His touch was like fire, leaving a burning heat in its wake. Emilia's entire body lit up, pulsing with anticipation. When he reached her hand, he picked it up and placed a searing kiss on her knuckles.

"You like me," she said tentatively.

Eric raised his free hand and placed it on the side of her neck. He wound his fingers behind her head and buried them in her hair. Emilia's breath was coming out in pants now, and it took the little self-control she had remaining to keep the few inches separating their mouths intact.

"Like you?" he said softly. "I wish. I love you, Emilia."

Eric let the words hang in the air for an uncomfortable amount of time. Emilia was speechless. She had no idea what to say to that. But at the same time, she wasn't surprised by his admission. Hadn't he been telling her this all night? With every look, every touch, even his words of reassurance.

"I love you," he repeated, eyes piercing into her. "Utterly, completely, painfully. And I can't stop. Even if I could figure out how, I don't think I would. You're ... everything."

She looked down. She couldn't hold his gaze anymore. The raw emotion she saw in his eyes seemed closer to torture than love. She couldn't bear the thought that she was the cause of his pain.

Eric dropped his hands and took a step back. "That's the big secret," he said simply.

"What secret?" she asked, looking back up at him, confused.

"The dark scary truth that you forget every time you learn it. The thing that nearly drove you to a nervous breakdown and caused you to start this damn challenge."

"So, I—I've known this?" Her head was spinning. She didn't know if it was from the revelation or the alcohol.

Eric was back in front of her, holding her waist, and she immediately felt more at ease. He took his other hand and placed it over her heart. "You know it here. Come on, Emilia. You're not surprised. You never are."

She dropped her head against his sternum. His words traveled from one end of her mind to the other as the damaged organ struggled to make sense of them. She'd already known. Of course she'd already known. She'd felt it all night. He'd told her before today, and although she'd forgotten the words in her mind, the truth had settled in her heart. How many times had this happened? How many times had she forgotten?

She'd let herself forget. Over and over again.

Emilia lifted her eyes until they met his. They were a crisp blue, like the lakes in the mountains. Beautiful, but cold. That chill—that sadness—she'd been sensing it all day. Was this what it was about? Had he been continuously opening himself to her, just to have her tear him apart? No wonder August was angry. No wonder he'd been harsh with her. He must know.

"I'm not going to forget," she declared. "I don't want to forget."

"Then don't." Eric leaned forward and placed a soft kiss on her cheek. "I dare you to remember."

She could feel his warm breath on her face. She placed a hand on his cheek, the beard there familiar and new, all at once. God, she wanted more. She wanted to turn his face and capture his mouth. She wanted to know what it was like to kiss the soft lips that had just brushed her cheek. To chase the source of the heat that had lit her body aflame.

He was pulling away, taking a step back from her. "But you won't, will you?" he asked. He took another step backward, putting even more distance between them. She felt his absence like a cavern in her chest, empty and cold.

Several beats passed. It was her turn for reassurances, but she couldn't think of anything to say. All she wanted was to hug him and have him tell her this would be fine, that they'd figure it out.

But she couldn't make her body move. She'd been turned to ice. Her arms remained at her sides, heavy and stiff, and her lips were still, frozen shut, not allowing any words to pass through them.

Eric gave her a curt nod, then turned toward his room. He wasn't walking in a straight line but wasn't stumbling, either. She guessed their conversation had sobered him up as much as it had her. She watched him disappear into his bedroom, then listened to the low click of the door closing behind him.

Her arm finally thawed—several minutes too late—and she pressed her fingers to the spot where he'd kissed her. She could almost feel his lips there and was sure that tomorrow, long after the memories of the moment had disappeared, the feeling of his kiss would remain.

* 12 *

When Emilia returned to her room, Bartholomew was waiting for her on the bed. He picked his head up and cocked it at her, but she couldn't find the words to answer his unspoken question. She kicked off her shoes and collapsed into sobs on the bed. Bartholomew curled up next to her and purred loudly.

"Have we been in this position before?" Emilia asked through her tears. "How many times has Eric told me he loves me? Does it always make me cry like this?"

Bartholomew just purred in response.

After the initial onslaught of emotions had passed, she lay back on the bed and took deep breaths as she watched the ceiling spin.

"I love you… utterly, completely, painfully. And I can't stop."

That revelation had hit her like a semi-truck.

That's not funny. What is wrong with you?

Emilia sighed as Bartholomew climbed onto her stomach. She focused on the feeling of him. His comforting weight, the vibrations of his purrs, and the soft fur against her hand as she petted him.

Her mind was still spinning from all the wine she drank earlier but she resolved to lie there and wait for the spinning to stop. She was going to think through this clearly. She owed that to Eric. If she had to stay up all night until she figured everything out, she would.

An hour later, when the fog in her mind was clearer, and the ceiling had stopped spinning, she sat up to test her sobriety. Everything felt stable. Her heart was still fluttering, but she guessed that was more from Eric's declaration than from alcohol.

She took a deep breath and pulled Bartholomew into her lap.

"Eric loves me," Emilia said aloud.

It felt impossible and fitting at the same time. She knew there was no point in dwelling on the statement further. It was true. There was no denying that after tonight. The next logical question was, "Do I love him?" She spoke that aloud too.

The answer came easily. Absolutely. Definitely. One thousand percent, yes.

Emilia had always loved Eric, even before her accident. She had a crush on him from the moment she met him, which had only grown the more she got to know him. But when it became clear he didn't feel the same, she'd locked those feelings away, deep in her heart, until even she had forgotten about them.

But now they'd escaped and were running wild through her mind and body. This should be shocking, shouldn't it? Maybe, but it wasn't. Her mind was processing the information with detached acceptance. The secret must have been revealed so many times by now, the novelty had worn off.

She closed her eyes and tried to access those feelings she'd hidden away back in college. They were raw, and so much stronger than she remembered. Maybe this proved Eric's earlier claim about her growing over the years, even though she didn't remember it. Her feelings for him had certainly grown.

So, he loved her and she loved him. Then why weren't they together? Why did she always let herself forget this truth?

Eric's words echoed through her mind: *"I dare you to remember. But you won't, will you?"*

"Yes, I will," she insisted.

Emilia stood up quickly, rousing Bartholomew from his slumber. "Oops. Sorry, Bartholomew." She placed him on the foot of the bed, then sat at the desk. She wrote on the calendar:

Eric is in love with me and I'm in love with him.

There. She'd see that tomorrow. Then what? Would she question it? Without having spent the whole night with him, without experiencing his touch, without hearing his heartfelt reassurances, would she believe it? Would she be able to access the part of her heart she was feeling now? The part that deeply loved Eric in return, without all those experiences to unlock it?

Or would he have to get her to this point every day? How long would it take? Several hours? Longer? What if she didn't start loving him this fully until after lunch? Or after dinner? How was that fair to Eric?

She hated being bombarded with questions she didn't know how to answer. She searched around the desk, desperate for something, anything to help her. The notebook was useless, it was blank except for four questions she was supposed to answer each night:

What was the best part of today? What was the worst? What are you most afraid of right now? What do you want most?

Emilia snorted. The notebook hardly seemed thick enough to be able to contain the full answer to those questions. She put it aside and started scanning the shelves. She spotted the miniature trunk with a slot on the front.

That was it. That was where all the information she was supposed to review every month was stored. That was probably where she'd hidden all the extra notes and photos she typically reviewed each morning but had put away for her "one day at a time" challenge. And that box probably contained her history with Eric.

She knew she wasn't supposed to look in there, especially since it was just the seventh day of the month, but she didn't care. She *had* to know what was going on. She had to know why

Eric was so sad, why August had said what he had, why Emilia's heart felt like it was literally breaking.

Her right hand touched something when she reached for the box. It was a small, paperback book leaning unassumingly against the trunk. She pulled it out and looked at it curiously. Why was it on this shelf, away from the other books?

A Collection of Poems, by Ranata Suzuki. She didn't recognize the author or the title. She flipped through it, and the book opened naturally to a collection of poems titled: *Letters to the Sun from the Dark Side of the Moon.*

Emilia inspected the spine and saw that it was broken so the book would always open to this section. Interesting. She went back to the page and began to read.

Once upon a time, the Moon loved the Sun. Until … The End.

Emilia's heart thumped. "Yeah," she whispered back, "that was depressing." She read the next poem.

I call him my Sun because he is the center of my universe. For me, time starts and ends with him.

I call him my Sun because to me, there was a long … drawn out, almost unending stretch of nothingness before he first dawned on me… But once he did—it was as though life itself had begun.

I call him my Sun because I watched as he disappeared over the horizon one day … knowing I would never see him again…

And it's been dark ever since.

Emilia was crying now. This felt so … real … familiar … She was struggling to find the right word.

Relevant. That was it.

This was Eric and her. He was her Sun. Always had been and now, with this new life she was living, it was truer than ever before.

Her eyes scanned the next page and stopped on one line: *The only thing in this world I wanted more than you was your happiness.*

Her heart stopped. This was the answer. She didn't need to open the box. She understood exactly what had happened. Why Eric was sad, why August was angry, why hearing Eric tell her he loved her had made her cry. Why this section of the book was so well-worn. And more than anything, why she always let herself forget.

She couldn't be with Eric. What kind of life would that be for him? Having to convince his girlfriend she was in love with him every day. Reliving the same conversations over and over. What would happen if he were angry with her, asked her to do things differently, and she forgot?

And a physical relationship would be a disaster. She was a virgin. Was she going to think it was her first time every time they slept together? That would be terrible for Eric. And kids—hah!—absolutely not. Eric deserved a family of his own, one he could protect and keep together, and she couldn't give that to him.

Emilia cried as she looked down at the book of poems. The words blurred so much she could no longer read them but it didn't matter, they were etched across her heart. It probably went like this every time: a rush of hope, excitement, determination to remember. Then the questions, the searching, finding this book, reading those lines, and ultimately deciding that if she truly loved Eric and wanted the best for him, she had to let him go.

And now it was time for her to tell him. She had to get up, walk across the hall, knock on his door, and tell him why they couldn't be together. As soon as she pictured it, she knew she couldn't do it. If he fought back at all, and he would, she'd cave in a second. Then she'd be right back here tomorrow night, agonizing over all the same problems. So, she decided to do the next best thing.

She grabbed a piece of paper, folded it in half, and held her pencil above the page. How to explain? She looked up at the open book of poems and copied over the line that said it all: *The only thing in this world I wanted more than you was your happiness.*

Eric would know what it meant. He'd be hurt but one day, he'd move on. He wouldn't hold out for her forever. It sounded like August and June were already pushing him to find someone else. She just had to keep putting Eric first and then, eventually, he'd lose interest; see that a relationship with her was impossible.

When she stood up to take the letter to his room, she faltered. She wasn't sure she could trust herself to stand that close to him and not barge inside. To beg him to change her mind.

If you love him like you say you do, you need to do this. You need to let him go. He deserves more than you'll ever be able to give him

She forced herself up and out of her room, then down the hall, moving as swiftly and quietly as possible. The space under the door was dark, which probably meant he was asleep. She tried not to think about the fact that Eric was on the other side of the door. That all she had to do was turn the knob, and she'd be with him again.

She crouched down and flicked the note under the door. There. It was done. She returned to her room and took a seat at her desk. She felt empty and cold, and desperately wanted to change into her pajamas and go to sleep, to welcome the oblivion that would take over her mind tonight. But first, she had to take care of a few more things.

She erased the note she'd written on her calendar, rubbing hard with the eraser until all traces of it were gone. Bartholomew, probably sensing she needed comfort, rubbed against her legs as he purred loudly.

Emilia took a deep breath, then pulled the leatherbound

notebook forward. She read the four questions she was supposed to answer and sat there looking at them for a long time. She decided to answer the hardest one first: *What do you want most?*

She wrote: *To leave the world better than I found it,* then paused before moving onto the next question. Eventually, she picked up her pencil and continued writing as tears streamed down her face, wetting the page.

Part 4: June Pearson

She's really brave, but she doesn't like it when you say so.

* 13 *

It took Emilia a long time to wake up the next morning. She touched her left cheek, expecting to feel something there, but there was nothing. She rolled over and groaned. Her chest was tight and her heart was pounding steadily against her rib cage. She felt like it was trying to tell her something.

There was a half-remembered dream at the edges of her consciousness. But as her vision slowly came into focus, revealing more pieces of her reality: the shards of light coming in from the curtains, a bookshelf, a desk, a nightstand with a clock radio, they clouded her mind, pushing the dream out of reach.

What was it...?

There was something she was supposed to remember...

She touched her cheek again, then shot up in bed. *August!*

Emilia's eyes darted around the room. She spotted a letter on her nightstand. As she read it, tears stung her eyes. She read it again, then went to her desk and read everything she could find.

After she studied the large calendar, the summaries of her friends and family, and a letter she'd left herself on February 3rd that further explained her "personal challenge," she felt bereft. It was as if there was a question deep inside her that she'd been expecting to find an answer to in this pile of papers but had not.

She placed her hand over her heart and took several deep breaths, trying—in vain—to relieve the tension there. No matter how many breaths she took, it wouldn't go away. She stood up, got dressed, and slowly made her way downstairs.

Emilia found June in the sitting room watching cartoons. "June?"

"Oh. Hey there, sleepy head. I was starting to wonder if you were ever going to wake up."

"What are you doing here? I thought I lived with Eric." Emilia crept into the room and took a seat next to June on the sofa.

"You do. He's busy today so you're stuck with me."

"Oh," Emilia replied, trying to keep the disappointment out of her tone. Why was she disappointed? She loved June just as much as she loved Eric and August. In many ways, they were closer.

Emilia took a moment to study June's appearance. She looked very different, but Emilia had been expecting this; it was in her summary. Her blonde hair was short and stopped at her chin. She had a small stud nose-ring and a tattoo on her forearm.

Emilia thought it looked vaguely familiar and wondered if it was related to skiing. Wasn't she on a ski team? Did they have a name? Or was it just the US team? She didn't know how professional skiing worked and wasn't sure if she was allowed to ask.

"You look good," Emilia announced. "Very…"

"…cool?" June finished with a grin. "Your word, not mine."

Emilia nodded. This was so weird. How would she ever get used to this? Oh, right, she never would. That was the problem. Emilia sighed and settled back against the sofa. She looked around the room. Everything was new, including the TV. It all looked nice.

June tapped her arm with something cold and Emilia turned to see her holding a glass of water. "You probably need this. You had a lot to drink last night."

"Oh. Really? Why?" Emilia took the glass and drained it, then scanned her body. She did have a headache, but the severest pain was the tightness in her chest. That wouldn't be from alcohol.

"It was my parents' thirtieth anniversary party."

Emilia nodded as she remembered the note on her calendar. Had she gotten drunk in front of the Pearsons? How embarrassing.

"That answers where you did the drinking but not why," June was saying. "I don't know that part, since the three of you didn't let me in on it. You'll have to ask Eric or August later."

"Oh." Emilia turned back toward the TV.

She and June watched the cartoons for a few minutes before June turned to Emilia and said, "This show is incredibly stupid."

"It's for kids. It's supposed to be stupid. What's stupid is watching a show you don't like."

June shrugged, lifted the remote, and powered off the TV. She turned on the couch to face Emilia, pulling one of her legs up and wrapping her arms around it. "How are you? I don't usually see you first thing in the morning when it's all still settling in."

Emilia had no idea how to answer that. How was she? Terrible. She'd just found out her mind, the thing she valued most, was permanently damaged. And here she was hungover, suffering from a pain in her chest that seemed familiar, but that she couldn't place, and weirdly defending cartoons to June.

Emilia sighed and closed her eyes. "Tell me honestly, how bad is this?"

"What? Your memory loss?"

Emilia kept her eyes closed and nodded. She knew if she had met Eric or August first and asked this question, they would have lied and said she was fine—even if it weren't true. But she could trust June to tell her the truth.

"It's not great," June began, placing a hand on Emilia's leg. "But you have a really good life. You do all sorts of different things and still manage to work. Your friends adore you, and, um, you don't remember it. But it's still happening, and we're here to remind you. So it's not bad."

The feeling in Emilia's chest said otherwise. If her life was so good, then why did she feel like this?

"It's Sunday and my mom's making a big lunch," June said. "We're going. Everyone will be glad to see you didn't drown from all the alcohol you drank last night."

Emilia perked up. "Will Eric and August be there?"

"No. They're spending the day alone together before August has to go back to Boise."

"But you said Eric was busy."

"He's busy with August. Hanging out and stuff."

"Did they not hang out last night? At the party?"

"Is Eric not allowed a break?" June replied sharply.

Emilia leaned back, alarmed by her harsh tone. "I—what? A break from what?"

June dropped her head onto her knee and let out a long sigh. "Nothing. Ignore me. I'm in a weird mood."

Emilia was still reeling. What was wrong with Eric? Why wasn't he here? What did he need a break from? Her? It must be her. What had she done? Is that why June seemed angry?

"Come here," June said, shifting closer to Emilia. "You look like you need a hug."

Emilia stayed in place and waited for June to initiate the hug, just in case. June wrapped her arms around Emilia and gripped her firmly. "I'm sorry. I'm screwing this all up. This is why I never get morning duty."

"Who usually gets morning duty?"

"Eric. Since he lives here."

"But today ... he needs a break?"

June leaned back and put her hands on Emilia's shoulders.

Her expression was soft now. "No, Em. He's fine, really. I saw him this morning and he was hungover, like you, but otherwise fine. But you—you don't look well. Are you okay?"

Emilia thought of the pain in her chest again. Should she tell June? Or maybe she'd just unwittingly walk into another sensitive situation that would set June off. June was a great friend, but she had a terrible temper, and Emilia wasn't in the right mood to weather it today. She plastered a smile on her face. "I could use that hangover cure you invented in college."

June jumped up. "I can do that. Do you and Eric have pickle juice? Actually, you wouldn't know, would you? I'll go investigate while you take a shower. When you get back, I'll have the cure ready."

Emilia nodded and picked herself up from the couch. Getting ready seemed like a gargantuan task in her current mood but she could do it. She'd just take it one step at a time.

Is this what your life has been reduced to? A collection of lame clichés?

If you don't have anything nice to say, don't say anything at all

Emilia sighed as she stomped up the stairs.

* * *

After spending most of the day at the Pearsons', June took Emilia to dinner at a restaurant near Eric's house. June had dropped her back at home an hour ago and asked if Emilia wanted company, but Emilia said she didn't mind being alone.

She'd been surrounded by people all day and thought it would be good to get some time to herself. But a few minutes after June left, she regretted her decision and almost called her back. She didn't, though, because she was a grown woman who should be able to handle an evening by herself.

She made her way to the library she'd discovered earlier in

the day and found a large book on the bottom shelf. As she read it, her heart felt like it was being squeezed, then ripped into chunks and tossed into a messy pile on the floor. But she couldn't put it down for some reason.

The feeling from right after she'd awoken this morning was back, like there was a question she needed to find the answer to, and she thought, maybe, she'd find the answer here.

She was engrossed in her reading so didn't hear Eric until he was standing in the doorway and saying, "Hi."

Emilia jolted. She put the book down and slowly crossed the room. He looked different, but in some way, familiar. She stopped in front of him and tears welled in her eyes, but she had no idea why. She blinked them back. Why was she such an emotional wreck? Was it always like this?

"Eric. Hi."

His eyes were scanning her face, and she tried to put a smile there, but she couldn't do it this time. She seemed to have reached her acting limit for the day.

"Bad day?" he asked, though he seemed to already know the answer.

She knew it wasn't worth lying, so she ignored the question. "How was your day? How is August? Everyone missed you at lunch."

That was an understatement. It seemed like every person at the house, even the new faces she didn't know, had asked her where Eric was. By the tenth time she wanted to scream, "I don't know! I don't have a memory! Leave me alone!"

It was obvious he didn't typically skip out on visits to the Pearsons' house. And while June didn't give any further indication about why he and August so desperately needed to spend all day alone, Emilia was pretty sure it had something to do with her.

Eric cocked his head toward the sofa. "Let's sit and you can tell me…" His voice trailed off. He was looking at the large book she'd been reading. "There's a warning on that for a reason."

She didn't reply. When he picked it up and moved to close it, she caught his arm. "Wait. I wasn't done! I—um—had a question."

"Okay," he said, tone wary.

She took the book back and saw him scan her face again. What was he looking for? She dropped her eyes and resumed her seat on the couch, crossing her legs and propping the book open on her lap.

Eric took a seat next to her. "What's your question?"

Emilia bit her lip and looked down at the page that contained countless notes she had no memory of writing. "Uh. I think I need to work up to it. Tell me about your day."

He shrugged and leaned back on the sofa. "It was nothing special. I caught up with August. We spent most of the day skiing, then had dinner at that burger place at the base of the mountain. How about you? Did you have fun with the Pearsons?"

"Yeah. The twins are big. Like, real adults now. And April was sweet, like always. I apologized to August's parents for getting drunk at their party, because June had said something about it, but I guess it was a joke, because they had no idea."

Eric let out a laugh, but it was small and never reached his eyes. "You *were* drunk, all three of us were—me, you, and August—but we managed to hide it from the Pearsons. Fucking June. She's just bitter because we didn't include her."

"Is that why she was angry with me?"

He avoided her eyes, focusing on the far wall.

"Do you know why she was upset?" she pressed. "Did I do something? If so, I'm really sorry. I never meant—"

Eric placed a hand on her arm. "It's nothing. Don't worry about June. She's just stressed. She's got a race coming up and is killing herself in training. You know how she can get. It wasn't you."

Emilia could tell he was hiding something but didn't know what question to ask next to get at it. The list of things she didn't know was endless.

"Was that your big question?" he asked

She shook her head and looked down at the book. "It was about this."

He leaned forward and began reading the page upside down. "Ah. Theory four. One of your favorites."

She traced her fingers along the title at the top of the page. *Theory Four: To enjoy the act of living.* "This is a lot of research. It must have taken days, weeks even. How do I spread research across multiple days?"

"It's not as hard as you'd think. Occasionally, you'll have this urge to dive into a subject and when that happens, you'll leave a note for yourself the next morning to keep it going with a summary of what you covered the day before. It usually comes in spurts—you'll dive into researching a new topic, go hard for a few days, then burn out and take a step back."

Emilia hummed. She couldn't imagine being overcome with a desire to research all day in this dark mood.

"I know for this book in particular," he continued, "you need to be in the right mindset. Hence the warning," he added sternly.

She ignored the admonishment. "You said this one was my favorite." She glanced down at the notes at the bottom of the page, stopping on the last one, and read it aloud. "'Because of my condition, I should be better at living in the moment than most and should find it easy to simply enjoy the present. I sort of hope that out of all the theories about the meaning of life, *this* is the answer, because I think I can actually do this one.'"

She closed the book and looked up at Eric. He still had a hand on her arm and squeezed it. "Why does that make you sad?"

Tears flooded her eyes again and this time, a few drops fell down her face. Eric wiped them away quickly with the back of his hand. "Tell me what's on your mind, Emilia," he whispered.

"I woke up feeling ... sad." That was not a big enough word for it, but she didn't know how else to describe it. "And when June said we were going to spend the day at her parents' house, I went upstairs and got dressed and thought to myself in the shower: 'Okay, this is your life. You truly do live it one day at a time. Being sad isn't helping anyone, so just, be present and enjoy the day.'"

She stopped to take several deep breaths.

"That sounds reasonable," he said, his tone gentle.

Emilia looked up at him. "I tried, Eric. I tried so hard but I'm so, so ... sad doesn't really describe it. And, I don't know, I was just pretending and then I saw this and if this is how I'm supposed to live a meaningful life, if this is one of the only theories I can adhere to with my condition and I can't even manage this—then what does that mean?"

Eric took the book and placed it on the ground. "You do enjoy your life, Emilia. But you have bad days; we all do. They just seem worse to you because you can't remember the good ones."

"Maybe you just think I've been having good days. Maybe I've just been pretending this whole time while this ache in my chest gets worse and worse. Maybe years of acting is finally catching up with me and, and—" She cut off. She could no longer talk through her tears.

Eric pulled her onto his lap and wrapped his arms around her as she cried into his chest. She shook with sobs, finally releasing the tension she'd been holding in all day, while he stroked her hair.

As she fought her way back to composure, she focused on the feeling of Eric's lungs rising and falling under her head. When she was finally able to take long, deliberate breaths without shaking, she looked up at him. He stared blankly at the ceiling, his own eyes sad and wet. She sat up and climbed out of his lap. "You're sad too. Why?"

Eric took his glasses off and wiped his eyes with his thumb and forefinger. He let out a long sigh before looking back at her. "I don't like seeing you sad, especially when I know I could have prevented it by being here this morning. I just … couldn't." His dark blue eyes were pleading. "I'm sorry."

"It's okay. You can't be here every day. You're not my keeper or anything."

He sighed again and put on his glasses. "I promise you do have good days. A lot of them. Yesterday was one. We had lots of fun at the party, danced for hours, and drank way too much. I'm sure you felt the hangover all day which probably didn't help with your mood."

She was chewing her lip as she tried to puzzle through what he'd said. "You said you could have prevented it? My sadness? How?"

He shrugged. "The morning is always hard. You've learned about the accident, are trying to piece everything together, and if anything disrupts you in the first few hours—a snarky June, for example—it's hard to enjoy the rest of the day because your mind is set to wondering what you did wrong, how you could possibly be living a good life, stuff like that."

"Oh."

"But, full disclosure, me being here isn't a guarantee. You've had bad days that start with me doing everything right. Like I said, we all have bad days."

"That's fair. But have I ever managed to have a good day that didn't start with you?"

This question caught Eric off guard. He took a moment to consider, running his hand along the stubble on his jaw. "In the beginning, yes. But not lately," he said eventually.

Emilia had no idea what to do with that information, so she cataloged it away, then realized it would be gone the next day. She tried to push the depressing thought to the side and focus on last night, when she'd apparently been happy. She closed her eyes and tried to feel the carefree part of herself that had danced and laughed and drank too much. The memories were gone, but the feelings might still be there.

She couldn't find them, which just made her cry again. Eric pulled her back into his lap and wrapped his arms tightly around her.

"I'm so sorry," she said through her sobs. "I—I—there's this feeling in my chest that's been there all day and I can't get it to go away. I—I don't know, Eric. I know I'm making no sense."

"Shh, try to relax. You don't need to explain it to me. I understand." Emilia could feel his words vibrating in his chest. It was nice, being this close to him, and she tried to wring as much solace out of the gesture as she could. "Tomorrow will be better," he continued. "I'll make pancakes. That always works."

Emilia lifted her head. "Pancakes? You made those Monday. I saw it on my calendar. Was I sad then too?"

"Yeah."

"Why?"

He reached out and brushed her cheek with the back of his hand. "You're longing for something you don't think you can have because of this new life you're living. But you *can*, Emilia." He paused to stare at her, eyes bright and intense. "You're allowed to be happy. You need to stop worrying about everyone around you and let yourself be happy."

She was confused. Hadn't she just told him she wasn't able to force herself to enjoy the day? And now he was implying it was as easy as choosing happiness. But she didn't dwell on it, since it was clear there was something upsetting Eric.

"You can be happy too, Eric. You deserve that so much. That's all I ever wanted, was for you to find a way to be happy." Maybe this was why she was so sad. It wasn't because of Eric's cryptic reasoning but simply this:

Eric was sad, so she was sad.

He watched her for several beats, then said challengingly, "You didn't want *you* to be happy? Just me?"

The only thing in this world I wanted more than you was your happiness. The phrase popped into Emilia's mind, but she had no idea where she'd heard it. It caused the ache in her chest to intensify, and she began to cry again.

"Shit. Sorry. Don't cry. I'm surprised you have any tears left." Eric had his hands on her face and was wiping her cheeks with his thumbs.

"We're a mess," she declared when she managed to get her tears back under control.

"Yeah. But we've been here before. My family ... your accident. We made it through that. I think we can survive one bad day."

"Yeah." Emilia pushed back a few locks of hair that had fallen onto Eric's forehead. As soon as she realized what she was doing, she froze. This was intimate. More intimate than she ever remembered them being. But it felt completely normal.

She was sitting on Eric's lap with one arm wrapped around his neck while she fixed his hair. She tried to recall how they'd ended up in this position. He'd been the one to pull her onto his lap, hadn't he?

"Emilia?" his voice cut into her thoughts.

She shook her head and tried to remember what she'd been thinking about. Their shared melancholy. Right. She opened her mouth and almost asked if it was okay that she was sitting on him like this, but at the last moment she changed the question, not wanting to give him a chance to ask her to move away. "Why are you sad? Is there anything I can do to help?"

"You can stop looking so miserable. That would be a great help."

She gave him a sad smile. "Okay. I'll try. How about we play the game?"

Eric groaned. "The game we played thousands of times but that I never once managed to beat you at?"

She shrugged. "There's a first time for everything. And my mind is damaged so maybe now you can beat me."

His lips turned up slightly. "Dark joke."

"Funny, though."

"Fine, we can play GHOST." He sounded annoyed, but she could tell it was just a show.

She shifted in his lap and linked her hands behind his neck. Her thoughts puzzled again at the strangeness of their position, but it felt natural, and the pain in her chest was finally fading.

"Okay," she said, searching the room for inspiration for a starting word.

This spelling game had been a compromise they'd developed

during their summers together at Camp Ouray. Emilia would agree to go on hikes with him and in exchange, he'd play this spelling game with her while they walked.

She beat him every time but he'd told her once he didn't mind—that it was better than the string of swears that usually spilled from her mouth anytime she was on a trail of any sort of difficulty. Then he'd tease her, like he always did, about how she was the worst camp counselor in existence.

She looked back at him. "Actually, you start."

"Okay. A."

"C," she said quickly.

"T."

"U."

Eric stopped to think, then he rolled his eyes. "Shit. I already lost. Actuary will end on me. You were supposed to say 'I' so I could hit you with acting."

"There are other words that start with ACTU."

"Yeah. Actual. But if I say A, you're not going to say L, are you?"

"Nope," she grinned.

"Fine. I'll just take the loss. That's a G for me. You're too good at this." He tickled her side.

"Stop!" she cried as she squirmed and pushed his arm away. "You start again."

"Okay. E."

"M."

Eric stopped to think again, spelling under his breath as he counted on his fingers. "Eric?" she asked after a few moments.

"Yeah?"

"I'm sorry for whatever I did to upset you. I'm sorry you feel like you need to be here with me every morning to set me off right. I'm sorry to burden you with this, and I'm sorry— "

Eric pressed his fingers to her lips. "No. You are not a burden. You are the most important person in my life, and I would be completely lost without you." Emilia tried to protest but he cut her off again. "No arguments. Now stop trying to distract me. I."

Emilia couldn't help but smile as Eric lowered his hand from her mouth. "E M I." Her mind reached for all the words she knew that started with EMI. Damn. He'd got her.

"There are a lot of words that start with EMI," he said smugly. "We've got emission, emissary, emigrant, emigrate, eminence, emissive. All eight letters. All ending on you."

"You've trapped me like this before."

"I have. And you should see this coming by now, since it's the start of your own name."

She swatted his chest. "Shut up. I'm thinking. There has to be something else."

They were quiet for a few moments, then Eric broke the silence. "Quick question, while you think. Were you planning to climb out of my lap sometime tonight? My legs are falling asleep."

Emilia blushed and moved back to her side of the sofa. "Sorry. You know I get clingy when I'm upset."

He stretched his legs out and rubbed his thighs, then shifted to her side of the sofa and wrapped an arm around her. "You can be clingy. I just wanted the feeling in my legs back."

She laid her head on his chest. "Is this really okay?"

In answer, Eric wrapped his second arm around her and pulled her close. "E M I," he said. "Stop stalling."

"I'm thinking."

"About how you're going to lose this round?"

Emilia smiled, and, unlike all the other ones she'd worn today, this one was real.

* 14 *

According to Emilia's clock, it was FEB 12 87. And according to her calendar, she was spending today (which was a Thursday, apparently) with June, which was why she was giving June's summary a thorough review this morning.

June is still skiing professionally (much to her mom's displeasure). According to August and Eric, she's pretty good and may even have a shot at qualifying for the Olympics in 1990. She just missed making the team in 1986 and doesn't like to talk about it.

She and Eric broke-up during the summer of 1985. It turned out that a shared obsession with the outdoors was not enough to sustain a relationship. Fortunately, they are still close friends. Their breakup was mutual and there isn't any awkwardness between them.

June has a new look these days, the theme of which seems to be: "things that will most irk Mrs. Pearson." She's also bisexual (which you already knew), but she's dating a girl now, a ski jumper she met at the training camp in Denver named Ruby Reynolds.

It's one thing to tell your friends you're attracted to other women while you're dating a guy, but it's another thing entirely to bring a girl home to your very conservative mom. She's really brave, but she doesn't like it when you say so. She doesn't want people to make a big deal of her sexuality.

June lives in an apartment nearby with another cross-country skier, Alba. As you can imagine, 95% of her conversations revolve around winter sports with a bit of soccer thrown in. Luckily, you won't remember them!

Emilia smiled at the last line. It was surreal, joking about something so awful. But she figured that was probably one of the best ways to cope with her condition. She rubbed her eyes, which felt strained, yawned, then slowly began to make her way downstairs.

When she reached the stairwell, she heard two voices below. As she descended, she recognized June and Eric speaking. Emilia stopped in the hall, a few feet from the doorway to the kitchen, and hid in the shadows. She could see Eric and June inside. He was standing at the counter, making coffee, while she sat at the table, with her chair turned around so she was facing him, and her legs stretched out in front of her.

"You didn't make breakfast?" she was asking. "That's why I came over here so early."

"There's cereal." Eric motioned toward one of the cabinets. His head turned slightly and Emilia saw that he looked different. He had facial hair and his haircut seemed different too, but she couldn't be sure since his hair was a giant mess. He was wearing pajama pants and a t-shirt and seemed to have just woken up. As if on cue, he yawned.

"But I can get that at my place," June whined. She also looked different. As the summary said, she'd certainly made changes that would upset her mom. She had short hair and a small nose ring. "Do you have bacon or eggs or anything hot?"

"This is hot." Eric cocked his head toward the coffee pot. "If you want something else, get off your lazy ass and make it yourself."

June sighed, then stood up and grabbed a mug from the cabinet and held it out for Eric. "Fine. I'll take coffee."

He poured coffee for her, then himself. When he put the pot down, June grabbed his chin. "Let me look at you." Eric looked annoyed but stayed still for the examination.

"You look good," she announced.

"Yeah? Interested in getting back together? Finally finished dating women?" Eric gently kicked June on the back of the legs before going to take a seat at the table.

June crossed her arms and leaned back against the counter. "You know that's not what I meant. But if you need me to tell you you're handsome—if the fact that my younger sisters and all their friends have a giant crush on you isn't enough—then I can do that."

June grabbed her mug and turned her chair back the right way before taking a seat. "And no, I'm not finished dating women," she continued. "It's so convenient dating a teammate. There are no schedule conflicts to deal with."

"Breaking up with a teammate ... less convenient," Eric said teasingly.

"No kidding," June muttered under her breath.

The two of them sat at the table for several moments, sipping on their coffees while Emilia tried to work up the courage to join them. She was alarmed by their easy banter. It was normal for them, that part wasn't alarming, she just didn't know how she'd possibly fit into the conversation. All the information she had about them was irrelevant, two years old, stale.

Before Emilia could worry further, June said loudly, "She thinks we can't see her."

"I know. She thinks she's so sneaky." They both turned towards the hall and smiled at Emilia.

Emilia blushed and shuffled into the doorway. "Uh. Hi. Sorry. I was just—"

"You're fine." Eric stood up and crossed the room. When he reached her, he pulled her into a firm hug. "Are you hungry? I can make you eggs or bacon."

Eric turned to wink at June, who had risen from the table and was standing just behind him. June rolled her eyes and pushed Eric out of the way. "My turn," she announced before wrapping her arms tightly around Emilia. "Good morning,

Emilia. Welcome to your new life." She lowered her voice and added in a whisper, "Ask for bacon."

"Yeah. I'll have bacon," Emilia said as she pulled away from June. "But I can make it."

Eric got the pan out for Emilia as she rummaged through the fridge. When Emilia was cooking at the stove a few minutes later, sipping on a mug full of coffee, June turned to Eric and asked, "What did you two do this week?"

"Oh!" Emilia chimed in. "I know this one." She'd seen a note about it on her calendar.

Eric nodded in approval. "Okay, then. Enlighten us."

"I've been assisting with a case at Beth Larsen's firm. We're helping a young woman who's being sued by her abusive husband. She ended up hurting him while defending herself and now *he's* accusing *her* of assault, which is disgusting. I worked on researching precedent and organizing a defense strategy for most of the week and am taking a break for a few days but will start again Monday to make sure the team is ready for the hearing next Wednesday."

Emilia looked to Eric for confirmation. "Yes. But saying you worked 'for most of the week' is a bit of an understatement. It was more like all waking hours with very short bathroom breaks. Even while eating, you had your face buried in a book."

"Oh. Sorry."

"Don't be," he smiled. "It's for a good cause. I'm just glad you're taking a break today. If you hadn't agreed to this day off with June, I was tempted to write it on your calendar anyway."

Emilia nodded and turned back to the bacon, which was finished cooking. She transferred it to a plate and brought it to the table as she considered Eric's words.

"I guess you could do that," she said as she sat down. "You

could take away or alter any of the notes I leave for myself and completely change my plan for the next day. For the next week, month..." Her voice trailed off.

Eric grabbed her hand and squeezed it tightly. "I would never do that. Ever." His blue eyes bored intensely into hers. "I know how out of control you feel with this memory loss, and I know how much you rely on us to carry on your wishes each day and I would *never* abuse that trust. It was a joke, that's all."

"He's right," June added. "He's actually a bit obsessive about honoring your past self's wishes. Even when your past self is being completely—ow!" She cut off, and Emilia could tell Eric had kicked her under the table.

He was glaring at June as he moved to change the subject. "What are your plans for today, June?"

She stared at him a moment longer. They seemed to be having a silent conversation. Eventually, June shrugged and motioned toward the window. "We're going to enjoy the lovely weather."

Emilia looked to the window and saw it was a bright, clear day. "Wait. Is that code for skiing?" she asked, her stomach dropping at the thought.

"It is," June said matter-of-factly before taking a bite of bacon.

Emilia looked over at Eric, who gave her a reassuring smile. "You're actually a decent skier these days. Just trust your instincts."

Emilia's instincts were telling her not to put on a pair of skis. Her stomach turned again at the thought of being high up on the mountain, hurtling toward the bottom. She focused back on her coffee and took a big gulp.

"It'll be fun," June declared. "I need a break too. We've been training non-stop all month."

"Yeah, okay," Emilia said weakly, trying to remind herself that June wouldn't let her get hurt.

As if hearing her thoughts, June said, "I won't let you crash. Besides, it's just cross-country skiing. I'm not brave enough to take you downhill skiing without Eric there."

That last statement was confusing, but Emilia was too busy being relieved to pull at that thread. "Oh, so we'll be on level ground? And I can go slow?"

"Yep. You usually do. Ruby and I don't mind."

Ruby Reynolds. The ski jumper girlfriend. Emilia was actually pretty excited to meet her, then remembered that she probably had met her, lots of times. Damn, how embarrassing.

Eric got up and cleared their plates. "I should go get ready. You two have fun. Your skis and boots are in the garage."

"I have my own?"

"You have two sets, one for cross-country and one for downhill," June said. "You're a proper Aspen Grover now. Eric made sure of that."

Emilia looked back at Eric, who was smiling at her shyly.

"I see. So you took advantage of my memory loss to finally force me to learn to ski. Maybe told me I'd decided the day before I wanted to try or something."

Eric's smile dissolved. "I'd never. I just said I wouldn't—"

"She's kidding," June cut in. "You better tell him you're kidding, Em. You know Eric. He can't sleep at night if he hasn't killed himself to better the lives of at least three people that day." Her tone was light, but there was an edge to her words.

Emilia nodded, looking curiously between Eric and June. What was she missing? A lot. Two years' worth of information. June could be referring to anything. "Of course I was kidding. Skiing sounds, um, fun? I'm glad you taught me, Eric. And bought me the skis. And, um, I didn't mean to upset—"

"You're fine." He bent down and kissed her cheek. It was a weird gesture, but did wonders for calming the butterflies in her stomach. "Have fun. I'll see you tonight." He nodded toward June and left the kitchen, but stopped when he reached the hall. "I'm down to only needing to improve the life of one person before I can sleep," he said over his shoulder.

June choked on her coffee and spent several seconds coughing while Eric smirked at her from the hallway. "Progress," June said when she could talk again, but whether it was because she hadn't yet recovered her breath, or something else, it sounded forced.

* * *

Later that afternoon, Emilia, June, and Ruby were sitting under some trees a little ways off the path, looking out at the snowy landscape. There was a blanket of thick powder around the area with crisscrossing ski paths cut into it and an icy lake in the middle, glittering in the sun. The whole expanse was framed by large, snowy mountains. As much as Emilia liked to complain about hiking and skiing, there was no denying that the views that came at the end made all the effort almost worth it.

They'd skied for several hours and Emilia had been surprised to find she liked it. She preferred to go slow and avoid any trails with a hint of a slope, but as long as she was able to stay in control, she didn't mind skiing. It was hard, though. She had a newfound respect for June and how fast she managed to go during her races.

"I can't believe Eric's skiing lessons worked," June was saying. "When he first brought it up, we all said it was a waste of time, since you would forget anything you learned. But he insisted your body remembers, and he was right. Well, he had some big technical explanation for it, then dumbed it down for us by saying the body remembers, even though your mind may forget."

Emilia turned that idea over in her head. It kind of made sense. Not all of her brain was damaged, just parts of it. She wondered what other sort of knowledge lay in her body, beckoning to be unforgotten.

"The body remembers," Ruby repeated. "I guess he'd know better than anyone." June swatted Ruby. "Ow!"

"Not okay," June hissed at Ruby.

Emilia sat up quickly. "What? Why would he know better than anyone?"

June waved away her question. "Because he's been your roommate for months and researched your condition like crazy after the accident, so knows more about it than any of us, you included. Anyway. Let's talk about something else."

Emilia settled back against the tree, eyeing June, but she was avoiding Emilia's gaze.

"I want to continue our conversation from last week," Ruby announced.

June groaned.

"What?" Ruby asked. "She's in a good mood."

"What is it?" Emilia asked. "What was the conversation?"

"Believe me," June said, "you don't want to know."

"The conversation," Ruby continued, ignoring June, "was about the prospect of you dating someone."

"That's obviously impossible," Emilia said immediately. "No. I don't want to talk about that."

"See?" June said in a very "I told you so" sort of tone.

"Yeah, you always say that," Ruby countered, "but I was considering all your arguments from last time, and I think you can make it work."

"I don't want to talk about this," Emilia repeated.

"Fine. Then just listen to me," Ruby said. "Your first concern was that you'd find it too hard to trust someone you didn't know and trust in your previous life. You'd see this stranger and they'd tell you that they were in love with you, and that you were in love with them, and you'd immediately be suspicious."

"But she could just use an endorsement for that," June cut in, thoughtfully.

"Exactly," Ruby replied. "A letter from one of her friends. Maybe even with a picture of you all together with the new dude."

"Fine," Emilia chimed in, unable to stay quiet and listen to them talking about her. "But how could I possibly fall in love with someone new? You can't fall in love in a day."

"That's not really an issue," June said. "You love Henry and you didn't really know him before. Love seems to live in the body."

Emilia frowned and tried to access these supposed feelings for Henry. Did she love him? She didn't even know what he looked like. Maybe it was sparked when she saw him or when he hugged her. It was strange to think she could love someone whose image she couldn't even conjure in her mind.

"Okay, fine, assuming that's true, how would they fall in love with me? Someone who just repeated everything, had to be reminded of who they were every morning. Someone who didn't remember even basic details about their life. Someone who could never give them a family and a physical relationship—hah!—that would be a joke."

"I'm not so sure—" Ruby started, but June hit her.

"You hush," she hissed, then turned to Emilia. "There are plenty of men out there who don't want children. And I'm still not convinced you can't have them."

"I'm sure I can have them physically," Emilia allowed, "but

mentally and emotionally, waking up with no memory and finding myself pregnant? Or worse, with a five-year-old whose name I don't know? Being a mom to a kid whose life I don't remember? No way."

"But you wouldn't be going at it alone," June argued.

"She's right. You'd have a husband to fill in all the gaps for you," Ruby added.

"I would never do that to anyone I loved. I would never subject them to that sort of life." There was a painful tightness in Emilia's chest. She paused to take several deep breaths in an effort to alleviate it. June placed a comforting hand on her arm.

"It's a pointless conversation, anyway," Emilia concluded, "because back to my previous point—no one would put up with this. Not for me. There are tons of women out there with normal, functioning brains they could pick from who are more beautiful, and funnier, and more personable and … and all that," she finished lamely.

June rolled her eyes. "That's one thing that hasn't changed since before your accident. You still have such a flawed view of yourself. Not only are you smart and strong, but you are funny and beautiful, and any guy would be lucky to have you."

"Yeah. You're quite a catch, Emilia," Ruby added with a wink. "I wouldn't mind dating you, if you were up for it. The memory thing wouldn't bother me."

June threw a hand over her face in exasperation. "Can you not proposition my friend while I'm right here?"

"I'm clearly talking about some hypothetical situation where we've already broken up. On good terms, of course. Otherwise, I'm not sure why I'd still be hanging out with Emilia."

"This got really weird, really quickly," Emilia muttered.

"Ruby has the tendency to do that to conversations," June

explained. They all laughed.

Emilia placed a hand on her heart. The tightness was still there. "Ruby, don't bring this up again? Okay? I—just—it hurts too much."

"Sure thing, Emilia." Ruby nodded back at her, her expression sad. "I'm just trying to help."

Ruby and June moved on to talking about June's search for a new roommate. Her current one was planning to take a few months off to attend some training camp in Europe. Emilia zoned out as the girls talked but focused back on their conversation when she heard her name.

"What?"

"Would you consider living with me?" June asked.

"And leave Eric's house?"

June shrugged. "I was thinking maybe you could rotate around. It's not like you need to be in a familiar place, and then all your friends would get a turn with the whole routine."

"Oh—um, I don't know." Emilia was about to say she hadn't thought of it before, but had no idea if that were true. She certainly hadn't thought of it today.

"I mean, I do travel every so often," June was saying, "but we could figure something out on those days. And it's not like you never leave Eric's house. You used to spend a lot of nights at Camp Ouray, and you go back to Nebraska sometimes, so we know you can do it all elsewhere."

"Have we ever discussed this?"

"I haven't talked about it with you. I was talking about it with Viola and Owen recently, and they thought it might be a good idea too. Owen said he'd love to have you up at Camp Ouray over the Summer, and Viola has an extra room at her place. So, maybe you could do Summer with Owen, Spring with me, Fall with your sister, and Winter with Eric, so he can keep up with your skiing. I don't know. It's just a thought."

Emilia leaned against the tree again as the implication behind June's proposal became clear. Emilia was a burden. That made perfect sense. And June was trying to look out for Eric here, not Emilia. She wanted to give Eric some room, maybe give him a chance to date, focus on work, ski at a reasonable pace, maybe even travel. Time to just--not deal with Emilia. Would it be so bad to live somewhere else for a while? It would all be the same for her, wouldn't it?

* 15 *

Later that night, Emilia and Eric were on the sofa watching a movie. It was one she knew, set in the Regency Era. She'd insisted they watch it when she recognized it on the screen, while Eric had been flipping through the channels, but now she was regretting her decision.

The story was about a grand romance based on a foundation of witty banter, longing glances, and lingering touches. But due to some confusing circumstances about the couple's standing in society and lack of fortune, their relationship was doomed from the outset.

Emilia wanted to shout at the screen, "Just be together already! You love him, he loves you, your circumstances be damned!" But sometimes circumstances couldn't be ignored, and that thought was downright depressing.

She turned to Eric. "This movie's stupid. You can pick something else."

He looked relieved and picked up the remote and clicked the TV off, then turned and leaned back against the arm of the sofa. "Why don't you tell me about your day? I can tell it was good."

"You can? How?"

"Easy," he said simply. "You're sitting all the way over there."

"What?"

"Where you sit on the sofa is directly proportional to how sad you are. On bad days, you sidle right next to me and lay your head on my shoulder. On good days, you sit far away."

"What?" Emilia shook her head. "No."

"And on really, really bad days," he continued with a grin, "you sit right on my lap."

She kicked him. "There has never been a time I've sat on your lap."

Eric just shrugged. "Am I right? Did you have a good day?"

"I had a lot of fun. Those two are hilarious together. It's like watching a comedy routine."

Eric nodded knowingly. "I'm actually a little surprised you haven't bombarded me with questions yet. You tend to stock them up as you learn new things about the time you missed and lay them on me once you return home."

Emilia recalled her conversation with Ruby and June about dating and nearly brought it up—figuring Eric would definitely be on her side. She almost opened her mouth to ask him about it when something deep in her gut screamed at her to shut up.

It was an odd feeling. She thought of what June had said about Eric's insistence that Emilia's body remembered while her mind forgot. Is that what this was? Some intuitive part of her remembering a previous conversation she'd had with Eric about this topic that hadn't gone well?

"What?" Eric asked.

"What?"

"You were going to say something."

"Um," Emilia was reaching for something to talk about besides her doomed dating life and landed on, "I was talking to June about maybe moving in with her."

Eric went completely still. "What?"

"She said her roommate is leaving to go to some training camp, and she's going to have a free room. She asked if I wanted to stay there for a few months. We thought it might be good if I sort of ... rotated around, that way it doesn't put too much of a burden on any one person."

"No."

"What?"

"No," Eric repeated. "You're not moving."

Emilia crossed her arms over her chest. "It's not your decision. If I want to move, I can."

He narrowed his eyes at her. She could tell by the tightness in his jaw that he was trying to keep his temper in check. "So, that's what you want? To leave? We made this house up together. You picked everything in here," he motioned around the sitting room. "Not just in here, but in all the rooms. I made a library for you, and a craft room and office downstairs, and—and now you want to leave?"

"It's not that I'm not grateful. This is for your benefit. It's—"

"No!" Eric shouted. "Dammit, Emilia! Look at me and I really need you to listen this time, okay?"

He leaned forward and grabbed her arms. Emilia nodded, alarmed by the vehemence in his tone.

"You. Are. Not. A. Burden," he said slowly. He stood and began pacing the room. "Fuck!"

Emilia was stunned into silence. She'd clearly struck a nerve, but had no idea which nerve, why it was a nerve, and what to say to fix it.

"I want you here! Okay?!" he yelled, turning to face her.

She nodded again.

"I want you here, sleeping in this house every night, and I want to say hi to you every morning. I'm sick of you deciding what's best for me. I have never gone against any of your wishes but you ignore mine daily. But this ... no! I won't let you do this."

"Eric, I didn't—" Emilia started to defend herself but cut off, unsure what to say.

He stopped in front of her and crouched down so he was at her level. "If you want me to be happy—if you really want to put my needs above your own, then stay here. Be here, every day." Then he added, almost as an afterthought, "Please."

"Okay."

"Write it down."

"Okay. I will."

"Now." Eric left the room and returned with a pad of paper and pen.

"Write this," he instructed. "'No matter what happens, I'm going to keep living with Eric. I made a promise to him and I don't intend to break it.'"

She began to argue against the absoluteness of the phrase. "Eric, we don't know—"

"Write it," he snapped.

"Fine," she sighed. She wrote out the phrase on the paper, then added a date for reference.

"Tape that up at your desk. Okay?"

"Okay."

"Do you promise?" he pressed.

"I do. I promise."

He stared at her a little longer, as if to make sure she wasn't lying, then eventually resumed his seat on the sofa. He turned the TV on. The movie they were watching before was back on the screen, but neither of them were paying attention. Eric was still fuming and Emilia was trying to make sense of what had just happened.

What had he meant when he said she ignored his wishes daily? And when he'd said, *"if you really want to put my happiness ahead of your own,"* that had seemed significant, but she couldn't pinpoint why. She wanted to ask a hundred follow-up questions, but now wasn't the time. She needed to comfort him, which was more important than finding out what was going on. The problem was, she was at a complete loss for what to say.

So, instead of speaking, she crept over to his side of the couch and laid her head on his shoulder. He wrapped his arm around her, and she felt him relax against her. Emilia turned back to the TV and after a few minutes, when Eric's breathing had calmed, said, "You need to alter your theory."

He looked down at her. "What?"

"The sofa and mood theory. I'd say my proximity to you on the sofa is directly proportional to our combined sadness level, not just mine."

Eric nodded and looked back at the screen.

"Unless, um, unless you'd prefer if I left you alone."

Eric pulled her closer and propped his chin on her head. "I think I made it clear that I want you close to me."

She smiled. "Yes. That came across."

"Good."

Emilia shifted so she was facing the screen, and they both watched the movie in silence. After a while Eric asked, "Do these two ever get together?"

"No. He marries someone else and has kids. She never marries. She writes romance novels though and always gives her characters the happy ending she never had."

Eric let out a long sigh. "That's depressing."

"Yeah. That's because it's based on actual events. In real life, not everyone gets to live happily ever after." She was thinking again about the conversation with June and Ruby about her doomed dating life.

"That was dark. What happened to planning for the worst and hoping for the best? That used to be your motto."

"I don't know, Eric. I might need you to hope for me, because I don't see a future for myself where I don't end up alone, like this lady in the movie."

Eric wrapped his second arm around her and pulled her close.

"Okay. I can do that."

* * *

Later that night, after taping up the note Eric had insisted she write, Emilia answered the questions in her notebook. She realized by the fourth question that she'd only written about Eric, even though she'd spent most of the day with June and Ruby. She almost went back to correct her answer about the best part of her day to *Skiing with June and Ruby*, then decided to leave it to *Watching a movie with Eric*.

She stared at the note about living with Eric as she pondered the final question, *What do you want most?* She almost wrote, *To be happy with Eric*, but paused. That's not what she meant. She wanted both of them to be happy, not to be happy *with* him. That was impossible. She tapped her pencil on the page several times, then ended up writing, *To be happy*.

Part 5: Owen Hart

If you ever need anything, he'll drop everything to come help.

* 16 *

"Emmy."

Emilia's eyes shot open. "Wha— what's happening?"

She sat up and looked frantically around her. She was in an unfamiliar bed, in an unfamiliar room. It was dark except for a dull glow coming in from the windows. This wasn't her room in Nebraska. Nor was it a motel or hospital room. Something moved at the foot of the bed. There was a small creature trying to climb up.

She almost kicked it, but her legs froze and wouldn't do what her brain was instructing. Instead, she reached over and clicked on the lamp on the nightstand. The light revealed a small toddler with wavy brown hair. He was sitting up on his knees, clutching a stuffed dragon, and looking extremely scared. Before she could consider what she was doing, she leaned forward and pulled the child onto her lap.

The little boy melted into her. Emilia wrapped her arms around his small frame as she tried to figure out what was going on. Her mind was racing but her body was oddly calm. It was a strange juxtaposition.

"What's your name?" Emilia asked the boy. He was quiet for a long while, then he shifted and looked up at her.

"Henry."

Emilia held his gaze, unable to look away. He was staring at her with a look of such raw adoration that she couldn't shake the feeling that he knew her. But she'd never seen this boy, had she? The weight of him in her arms was eerily familiar, and the way her heart felt, full and warm... What was going on? All she knew was that sitting here with this child was calming her body while her mind ran wild, so she wasn't letting go of him anytime soon.

Henry... Henry... think, Emilia

She only knew one Henry and that was Eric's nephew, but he was a baby. Though this kid could be related to Eric. He had the same deep blue eyes, and the same hair, too...

"How old are you, Henry?"

"Free."

Emilia leaned over and checked the date on the alarm clock. FEB 13 87

"Holy..." She looked down at Henry and cut off. She checked the date again, but it was still the same. Was this real? Was it really over two years later than she last remembered? And was this child in her arms really Henry Shaffer?

"Emmy owie," Henry whined into her chest. She realized she was holding him tightly and relaxed her grip on him.

"Sorry, Henry."

She needed to get rid of Henry, then she could figure out what was going on. She stood from the bed and propped Henry on her hip as he linked his thin arms around her neck. She smiled back at him and before she could consider what she was doing, placed a soft kiss on his cheek.

The hall outside her room was dark, except for a low light coming from the only open door. She peered inside and saw a kid's room, which she assumed belonged to Henry. The light was coming from a night light near the door, and the sheets on the bed were rumpled. Okay, she'd found Henry's room, but what she really needed to find were his parents. So, Eric's sister Sarah, if this was the Henry she thought he was, or Eric. No, please don't let Eric be his parent. If he'd ended up adopting Henry, she was going to strangle him.

She looked at Henry, who was looking curiously into his room. "Hey, uh, Henry? Do you know where Eric is?"

Henry nodded vigorously, then pointed a chubby finger toward the door at the end of the hall, closest to the stairs. She slowly made her way toward the room indicated and let herself inside. After waiting a moment for her eyes to adjust to the dark, she approached the sleeping figure in the bed.

"Eric sleep," Henry said as he shifted his weight and motioned to be put down.

Was this really Eric? She couldn't tell. She looked at the nightstand and saw glasses that looked like his. Relief flowed through her. Eric. So, this *was* Henry? What was going on?

Henry had approached the bed and placed a hand on the sleeping figure's arm. "Eric," Henry said.

Eric jolted, then relaxed when he saw Henry. He groaned and turned to check the clock on the opposite wall. "It's five o'clock, Henry. Way too early to be awake. Can you go back to sleep?"

Henry nodded and started climbing into the bed. He went to the side closest to the window, and Eric tucked him in. "Please sleep for at least another hour, two would be preferred. Okay?"

Henry mumbled something, and Eric shifted back onto his side. He was laying his head back on the pillow when he spotted Emilia standing against the wall. He swore under his breath and sat up. "Shit. You scared me."

Emilia stood frozen in place, studying Eric. He looked different, which just backed up the fact that she was living in a time two years in the future. How had it happened? Why didn't she remember anything?

"Hey. Come here," he whispered, patting a spot at the edge of the bed.

She slowly crossed the room and lowered herself onto the mattress. Eric began rubbing the top of her back. "Did you read your letter?"

She shook her head. She didn't know what letter he was talking about. Eric dropped his forehead to her shoulder and let out a sigh. "You must be so scared."

She nodded as tears sprung into her eyes. Eric shifted in the bed. She saw him look down at Henry, who seemed to be fast asleep again, and move him closer to the edge. Then Eric propped up the pillows and sat against them, motioning for Emilia to sit in the spot next to him.

She shifted further onto the bed. When she reached Eric, he wrapped an arm around her and pulled her head down so it was resting on his chest. Emilia wound an arm across his middle and let herself relax against him.

"Just breathe," Eric whispered, rubbing her back lightly. "Take a few breaths, and I'll tell you what's going on."

Emilia did as instructed, then listened as Eric told her about an accident she'd had over two years ago. She listened to the steady beating of his heart as he spoke, using the *thump, thump, thump* sound to anchor her to the feeling of calm in the room that was so at odds with the turmoil in her head.

Eric's heartbeat, the soft gray light coming in from the gaps in the curtains, Henry's quiet snores, Eric's fingers ghosting along the top of her back. She focused on all of these as Eric's words tore apart every hope, dream, and desire she'd had for her life. She was crying by the time he finished his explanation.

"I know it's a lot," he whispered, "but you have a varied, full, amazing life surrounded by people who love you. You continue to accomplish things and improve the world. You've learned to ski, and knit, and even juggle. You've worked on cases for the same firm you interned with the summer before your accident. You can still make a difference in the world, Emilia. I promise."

Her tears started falling faster. "I can?"

"Yes. You are just as impressive a person now as you were before."

She let out a sigh. It was a lot to take in, but Eric had addressed all her fears, and now she just needed to let the information settle in her mind. She watched the clock tick on the wall as she continued to clutch Eric. 5:20. It was so early. They should be sleeping, but she didn't think her mind would be able to rest right now.

Eric shifted and looked down at her. "How are you?"

Emilia shrugged. "Okay. Considering. Do I do this alone every morning? You said I have a letter?"

"Yeah. You're usually alone. And I usually remind you to lock your door on the nights Henry sleeps over to prevent this. I must have forgotten."

She couldn't imagine wading through that information by herself every morning without someone she trusted like Eric there to hold her and tell her everything was going to be okay. But she understood why she did it. She couldn't barge into Eric's bedroom every day and make him repeat this spiel. Tears flooded her eyes again, and she tried to blink them back. She'd cried enough for now.

Eric pushed a lock of hair behind her ear and wiped the tears from her face with the edge of the sheet. "Do you want to sleep more?" he whispered.

"Will everything reset if I sleep? Won't you have to go through all that again?"

"It shouldn't reset after a short nap but if it does, I'll just tell you again. I don't mind."

Emilia knew she should go. She was sitting in Eric's bed, in his arms, which was wildly inappropriate. Would June burst in in a few hours and slap Emilia? Where was August? There was a toddler here, so at least that added some proprietary points to the situation. But even though she knew in her mind she should return to her room, there was no way she was going to be able to make herself go.

"I don't think I'll be able to sleep with everything you just told me, but I'd like to lie here if that's okay."

Eric nodded and pushed her to a sitting position. He moved the pillows back down, checked on Henry, then lay on his side, facing Emilia. "I might sleep," he admitted.

"Of course," she said as she lay down, mirroring his pose. "You should sleep."

He gave her a small smile and closed his eyes, but before he had a chance to fall back asleep she whispered, "Eric?"

"Hmm?"

"How weird is it that I'm in your bed right now?"

He opened his eyes again. "Very weird. And I've seen a lot of weird things in my life. I once knew a family that named all their kids after months. August, June, April. Then the mom got pregnant with twins and do you know what she called them?"

Emilia smiled. "January and May?"

"Anna and Jack."

She let out a gasp of mock surprise. "If you're going to have a theme like that, you really need to stick with it."

"I know, right? Good thing Lorna Pearson is so scary, it's not like anyone is going to call her on it."

"No. Definitely not."

"But anyway. This, you lying right there across from me, is weirder than that."

Emilia smiled back at him. "Maybe I should sleep so I can forget that lame joke."

He gave her a beaming smile, then reached over and traced

the side of her face with the back of his hand. "It's not even six, but I already know you're going to have a brilliant day."

He pulled his hand back, and she reached out and grabbed it with both of hers. They lay there for a few moments, smiling at each other. "Okay," he said. "You need to shut up now, so I can sleep."

She nodded but didn't let go of his hand.

After another few minutes, Eric cracked one eye open and asked, "Are you just going to watch me sleep?"

Emilia blushed. She had been doing just that, but not on purpose. She'd been absently watching him as she replayed what he'd told her, then tried to guess at how her friends' lives were these days. She shrugged. "Yeah. Seems like it." She waited to see if he was finally going to kick her out.

"Okay. Just making sure." He gave her one more smile before closing his eyes again, this time for good.

She did watch him sleep for over an hour and it didn't feel weird. When Henry began to stir, Emilia crept out of bed and carried him out of the room, turning off the alarm on her way out so Eric could sleep in.

* 17 *

Later that morning, Emilia was sitting at her desk with one arm wrapped around Henry, who was bouncing on her lap and waving a small flashlight she'd found in the drawer of her nightstand.

"Light! Norby light!" he repeated as the beam from the flashlight danced across the walls in her room. Emilia shifted him to her other leg as the one he was straddling began to go numb. She was pretty sure Henry would be fine if she set him down, but she liked the feeling of holding him. He was solid, unlike the unknown truths of her life.

But Emilia was learning more by the minute. She'd learned that Norbert was the name of the stuffed dragon Henry was holding, that Henry's last name had been changed to McCoy to match his great aunt and uncle's last name, and that Eric was not Henry's adoptive father (thank God). But even though Henry didn't live here full-time, Eric had a room for him because he kept his nephew two nights a week to give his aunt and uncle a break.

She'd read through all the notes on her desk and learned that it hadn't been completely inappropriate for her to lie in bed with Eric this morning, as they weren't dating August and June anymore. June was dating a girl on her ski team and August was currently "in between girlfriends," whatever that meant.

Emilia had learned that she'd made a promise to live with Eric "no matter what," that she was in the middle of some sort of personal challenge to live "one day at a time," and that at night she answered four questions about her day in a notebook, then tore out what she wrote and fed it to a locked box. She'd also learned that she usually had a lot more notes around, but had hid them for the month, as part of the challenge.

Though by using the notes scribbled across the large calendar, she'd been able to piece together a bit of what had been going on recently.

She'd visited an equine therapy farm with Viola, prepared for a hearing that would be happening next week, attended a party for the Pearsons' 30th anniversary, spent a few days with June, and had pancakes with Eric. On the calendar for the next three days, she'd written: *Camp Ouray*. That was why she was reading Owen's summary now, since she assumed she'd see him later today.

Owen lives near Camp Ouray and is working on an independent study in agriculture with one of the local farms. He's making great progress and says he'll be done in two years. Pam says it'll be just one, and that Owen should brag about himself more often.

He's not currently dating anyone and doesn't seem to care. He's completely focused on earning his degree and says he'll have plenty of time for "all that drama" later. But that hasn't kept the entire female population of Camp Ouray from having a crush on him and sending him little gifts and notes, which he hates and finds slightly creepy, since most of his admirers are underage. You and Eric tease him endlessly about it and call him "Counselor Heartthrob."

His parents are still not talking to him, though his siblings visit him occasionally. Besides Eric, he is the most understanding of your condition and believes you can live a completely normal life, despite your memory loss. If you ever need anything and Eric isn't available, reach out to Owen and he'll drop everything to come and help.

"Hi."

Emilia jumped and turned to find Eric leaning against the doorframe.

"Eric! Light! Norby light!" Henry cried.

"Oh. You've got a flashlight? Or, wait, Norbert has the

flashlight. Cool." Eric came into the room and crouched in front of Henry. "If you pretend, you can imagine this is Norbert's fire blasting out of his mouth. What do you think? Isn't it a little like fire?"

Henry nodded seriously, then held the flashlight up to Eric's face, flooding him with a beam of light.

"Okay, thanks for that," Eric laughed as he held his hands up to shield his eyes. He blinked several times, then got up and smiled down at Emilia. "Thanks for watching him this morning."

Emilia set Henry down on the ground and rose to face Eric. "Of course. Thanks for—uh—this morning."

"For letting you watch me sleep?" he teased, nudging her arm.

"Yeah. And, you know, helping me."

"Glad to. Come here." Eric pulled her into a hug. "When did he wake up?" he added as he pulled away, ending the hug much too quickly.

"Around 6:30. I took him down to the kitchen, we had some cereal, then read some books in his room until he got too squirmy. After that we came up here and he's been playing while I've been learning about my life." She motioned toward the papers spread across the desk.

"Damn. You had a whole day." Eric looked over at the alarm clock, which had just turned to 8:30. "I usually have an alarm set, sorry about that. I must not have—"

"I turned it off. I thought you should sleep."

Eric started, then a slow smile spread across his face. "I think that's the nicest thing anyone has ever done for me."

She let out a small laugh. "I really hope that's not true. Actually, I *know* that's not true. I've done nicer things for you in the past."

"True." Eric turned to Henry. "Okay, Henry. Let's leave Emilia alone. She's going to Camp Ouray today and probably wants to get ready."

"I had a question about that."

Eric nodded for her to continue.

"How do I, um, get there? Do I ... drive?"

Eric shook his head. "You don't like to drive, but you do sometimes, though you don't have your own car. Owen's going to pick you up. He'll probably be here around 9:00 or 9:30."

"Oh. That's ... nice of him."

"Owen's as nice as ever."

"So, I just... pack for three days and he'll drive me back Sunday? And do I bring all of this?" She motioned toward the papers on her desk.

"Right. I keep forgetting you don't have your standard notes. This morning, Owen will drive you up there while I get this kid back home. Then I have to rush to work which, because of your incredible gift, I'm very late for. After work, I'll drive up and spend the rest of the weekend with you. And to answer your other question, yes, you usually pack your notes. Just the letter, the summaries, and the notebook should be plenty for the weekend. I can fill in anything else. There's a duffle bag in the closet you usually use to pack those and your clothes."

"Oh, shoot! I didn't even think about your work! I've been studying that calendar all morning and it says 'Friday' right there. A work day."

Eric waved her away. "It's fine. I'll just leave a little later today. It's not a big deal. You already fed Henry, which helps. Don't worry about me."

"Are you sure? I could help with Henry or, or, make you breakfast or—"

Eric shook his head as he pulled Henry up to a standing position. "Don't mind us. Just focus on packing and getting yourself ready. We'll be fine." He took the flashlight away from Henry and handed it to Emilia. Henry looked shocked, and Emilia could tell he was working himself up to cry, when Eric picked him up and held him upside down, causing him to laugh instead.

"I'm going to take you home, okay?"

"Okay!"

Eric flipped Henry around and set him back on the ground. "How about you go pick out some clothes and bring them to my room? Pants and a long-sleeve shirt, please."

Henry nodded and bounded toward the hall, stumbling over his own feet.

"Careful!" Eric called. He turned back to Emilia. "I should jump in the shower. Do you have any questions for me? Are you okay?"

She had a million questions, obviously, but there was nothing pressing at the moment. She felt … okay … calm. "I think I'm good. Are you sure it's okay that I made you late for work?"

"It's fine. They don't care when I come in, as long as I get my work done."

"Good. That's—that's really good." Emilia sighed and took a moment to organize her thoughts into words. "I can tell from my notes and also from how I feel that you—" She stopped again. "I—what I'm trying to say is—"

She gave up. There were no words adequate enough to describe her feelings. So, instead of speaking, she stepped forward and wrapped her arms tightly around his neck.

* * *

Emilia didn't know how hard it could be to get a three-year-old out the door. It was a good thing she'd ignored Eric's insistence that he didn't need help. She got Henry dressed while

Eric was in the shower, then made Eric a quick breakfast he could eat in the car. What followed was a chaotic back and forth between the car and house as they collected all the things Henry required for his short, ten-minute trip across town.

There was Norby, who he'd left somewhere inside, but couldn't remember where. Emilia found the dragon on the floor of the bathroom, behind the toilet, and decided it was best to ignore the toy's questionable cleanliness as she handed it to Henry. Then they realized Henry was missing a shoe (just one) even though he'd been wearing them both five minutes ago.

There was a water bottle that needed finding, then filling, and lastly, a desperate search for the fuzzy black hat with kitty ears (which Emilia was surprised to learn she had knit for him), that he could suddenly not exist without

"Okay, that's going to have to be good enough," Eric said as he rushed from the house for the fourth time that morning, holding the black hat. He stopped and turned around, crossed the room in three paces, and kissed her quickly on the cheek. "Have a great day. I'll see you tonight."

"Bye!" she called as he pulled the door closed behind him, the ghost of his lips still pressed into her cheek.

Emilia sighed and flopped down on a chair. The house, which had been mayhem just moments ago while Emilia and Eric shouted across the house about their progress in finding all of Henry's misplaced things, was eerily still. There was an ache in her chest, something she hadn't noticed before. Maybe she'd been too distracted by all the excitement. Or maybe it was something that only revealed itself when she was alone.

She shook her head and cleaned up the kitchen, then went upstairs to get ready. According to Eric, Owen would be here any minute. In the bathroom, there were two notes taped to the mirror, both written in Eric's handwriting.

This house is yours too; help yourself to anything.

Being your friend isn't work, babysitting, a chore, boring, or repetitive. I love having you in my life and would be lost without you.

She smiled, then looked at herself in the mirror and watched the quirk of her lips disappear. How many times had she stood here, inspecting her reflection for differences and willing herself to remember? This was so bad. So, so bad. But the all-consuming grief she was expecting never came. There was just that ache in her chest, which had mostly subsided.

She'd had a good morning. Chaotic, yes, but good. She smiled again as she recalled whispering in bed with Eric. The peace that had come over her when she'd watched him sleep. Laughing as she listened to Henry talk to Norby, and the smiles she'd exchanged with Eric during his hectic departure.

Yeah. It was a good morning. And the day would just get better. She'd be seeing Owen soon and would spend the day at one of her favorite places, then see Eric again tonight. And yes, she wouldn't remember any of it tomorrow, but that didn't mean it hadn't happened.

All lives were a collection of moments, mosaics crafted from countless colorful tiles. Due to her condition, she could only view her mosaic one tile at a time. Though that could have some advantages. Weren't people always saying you should live in the moment? Wasn't that her whole life? And just because she couldn't view her whole mosaic at once didn't make it any less beautiful.

This accident had made her into a poet. *I must have damaged my brain very, very badly.* Emilia released a final smile before turning on the sink and washing her face. Enough metaphors. She wanted to be ready to go when Owen arrived.

✷ 18 ✷

The doorbell rang as Emilia was packing her notes in her duffle bag. She zipped the bag and tossed it over her shoulder, then went to answer the door. Owen was crouched down, petting a white cat who, she realized belatedly, was Bartholomew.

"Oh, hi! Um, both of you."

Bartholomew completely ignored her, as she wasn't offering him any rubs under the chin, while Owen smiled up at her from his crouched position. "Hey, Emilia! You look great."

"Really? Not the same as always? When did you last see me?"

Owen stood and Bartholomew grunted in protest, then began weaving through his legs, trying to catch Owen's attention again. "I dunno," he shrugged. "Three weeks, maybe? You looked great then and you still look great."

"So do you."

"Yeah?" He held his arms out and looked down at his torso.

Emilia nodded. He did look good—different from when she'd last seen him, but still unmistakably Owen. He was a little bulkier, broader around the shoulders and chest, with more weight on his face, which was good; he'd been too skinny before.

His dark hair was longer and he had a small amount of stubble around his jaw, but she guessed that unlike Eric's, which seemed purposeful, Owen's was just caused by not shaving for a few days. As he beamed at her, the smile flickered in his emerald eyes. He was good-looking, but had that endearing quality of someone who had no idea he was attractive. She could certainly see why the girls at Camp Ouray had a crush on him.

"You are very handsome, Counselor Heartthrob," she teased as she hugged him.

"Ack. Do you want a ride up north, or not?"

"Yes! Please drive me, Counselor *Hart,*" she corrected.

"CC Hart, now," he countered. Bartholomew, who had given up on them by now, darted past Emilia into the house.

"Chief Counselor? Do you run the place now?"

"Pretty much," he said, a pink tint coloring his face as he followed her into the house. "Pam just does the opening and closing meals, and the admin stuff, like hiring and getting people to sign up, but I'm in charge of the rest of it."

"Wow. That's great. And you're getting your degree too? I saw that in my summary."

"Yeah. Been working a lot on it lately, since there's not much to do around the camp or the farm in the winter. But when the spring starts up, I'll be busy at the farm again, then soon enough, it'll be summer. So I'll have to take a break from school. But yeah, it'll happen. Eventually. I'm not in a big hurry or anything." He picked up the duffle bag at the bottom of the stairs. "You ready?"

"Yeah, let's go." She went to open the door, but paused with her hand on the knob. "I should lock up, but I—I don't know where the keys are." She began scanning her brain for any mention of keys from her notes, but couldn't recall anything.

Owen placed a firm hand on her shoulder, then reached past her and opened the door. "I know where they are. Also, you're definitely going to want this." He reached into a closet behind him, pulled out a puffy blue jacket, and handed it to her.

"Oh, right. Thanks."

Now it was her turn to blush. Was she really about to charge off to Camp Ouray in the middle of winter with no coat? That place got cold even in the summertime. She'd spent every night during her first summer there wearing one of Eric's extra jackets, since it had never occurred to her to pack one.

She smiled at the memory as she pulled the coat on, then thought of Pam, who Owen said was still in charge of the hiring. Was she still hiring girls who knew next to nothing about the outdoors? Who were overly serious and uptight and could do with "gettin' up close and personal with good 'ol mother nature," as Pam had put it? Emilia hoped so.

Once in the car, Owen launched into a detailed explanation about one of his favorite classes, plant pathology. He described the common pathogens: bacteria, viruses, fungi, nematodes, and parasitic plants, and how best to battle each type.

He was clearly passionate about the topic, which wasn't a huge surprise. Back at camp, he'd always been naming all the different trees and plants—pointing out the different kinds of berries and vines, and teaching the campers how to tell which ones were poisonous.

Owen had grown up like Emilia, with a childhood completely devoid of hiking and camping and swimming in real lakes, rather than public pools. He had Pam to thank for his introduction to nature, just like she did.

When Owen was still in high school, he'd been kicked out of the house after coming out to his very religious family. That's how he'd come to live with Pam, his mom's wacky cousin who his family mostly tried to ignore. Pam had taken him in without question, given him a job at the camp, and helped him get his GED.

It was an awful situation, but had probably turned out for the best. Owen was at ease and self-assured—more so than Emilia had ever seen him—and she doubted he would have found this confidence in his parents' oppressive household.

"What?" Owen had stopped talking and was looking at her curiously.

Emilia realized she'd been staring at him. She couldn't say what she was actually thinking, *I'm glad your parents kicked you out of your house, because you seem happy and so much more grown up than I remember.* She shook her head and said instead, "Nothing. I was just wondering what we're going to do today."

"Renovating cabins. You always ask me what we do around the camp in the winter, and that's it. Fix up the indoors since everything else is covered in snow. Last time we were painting and you and Eric flicked paint at my back all day. I didn't notice until I got home and went to take my sweater off and it was as hard as plaster."

Emilia snorted, then tried to rearrange her features to look contrite. "That sounds mean. I'm sorry."

Owen shrugged. "I poured paint on your heads the next day, so I'd say we're even."

"That is not a fitting punishment! All we did was ruin a sweater!"

"Yeah. You said the same thing when I did it," he grinned. "But today, you're not going to be doing much renovating. You promised to help Pam with the waivers, or lack of waivers. One of the campers got hurt last season and there was a big stink about it, apparently made worse since she doesn't make any of the families or counselors sign safety waivers."

"Wait, what? She doesn't?! How did I not know that?"

Owen shrugged. "Because you started in college before you were all lawyery?"

"But, we signed something as counselors, didn't we? I remember signing something."

"Just a basic employment contract. Nothing about our safety, and how we promise to be smart and not go hiking on a trail we don't know, then end up getting stuck in the woods for two days, freak out, and sue the owner of the camp. That's why you agreed to help."

"Yeah, of course. But I—I didn't bring any of my books."

"We have them at the camp. You started this last time and took all these notes. I'll show you when we get there."

"Good. I couldn't draft waivers like that from memory. Well, not good ones."

"I'm sure you could, but I know how you like everything to be perfect." He nudged her arm.

Emilia smiled at him as they turned onto the main highway. She recalled driving down a darker version of this exact road with August two years ago. Cool air had been blasting in her face, the sound of static had filled the car, then those two headlights.

Terror gripped her and she squeezed her eyes shut, just as Owen reached over and covered her hand with his much larger one. "You're okay, Em. You're with me. You're safe."

Emilia clutched his hand and used his soothing reassurances to anchor herself to reality. She peeked her eyes open and saw the brightly lit highway lined with snow—so much different from that night. The pressure in her chest eased. Her breath was still coming out in pants, but she was able to make each new breath longer than the last.

"Sorry," she murmured. She loosened her death grip on his hand, but didn't release it entirely.

"You don't have to apologize."

They were quiet as Emilia took slow, deep breaths, focusing down on their clasped hands so she wouldn't have to look at the road. When she finally felt like herself again, she asked, "Do I go up to visit you and Pam a lot?"

"Yeah. About once a month. Except for summers."

"What's different about the summer?"

"You come more often and for longer stretches. One time, the summer after your accident, you were with us the whole season. You'd been living with August before then, but then you two broke up and you decided to spend the summer with us. It was great. Like old times. We'd climb up to that ridge after lights out and look at the stars, eat all the s'mores ingredients we'd stolen from the kitchens, and try to list every constellation we could remember."

"I hope I didn't fall asleep up there, like I used to."

"You did."

"I did?! Then woke up outside, completely confused?"

"No, of course not. I always took you back to your cabin—the same one you used to stay in back when you were a counselor, so it would be familiar."

Owen paused to frown. "It was a lot harder back then. It would take hours for you to come to terms with what was going on and feel well enough to start the day. Eric was always the best at it, getting you through it all in half the time I could, but he wasn't there all the time, since he was still working at his lab a few days a week. But that's all better now. You told me last time you were here that it takes you about an hour these days. Right?"

Emilia was about to say that she'd done it in twenty minutes this morning but held back. She'd been in Eric's bed, lying in his arms, so that wasn't a typical morning. And the twenty minutes hadn't included reading all the notes on her desk, so that would have added another ten or fifteen minutes. But still, that was well under an hour. She just nodded in response to Owen's question.

"Your subconscious knows," Owen said proudly. "It's learning. That's why it's easier this year than last year, and next year will be even better."

"You think so?"

"I know so. In the beginning, you were so alarmed to see me. You'd curl up in a ball and tell me to leave and get Eric or August. I wasn't offended or anything. We were friends before, but not *that* close, like we are now. But after just a few months you got used to me. Your mind was still muddling through everything, but the rest of you was more at ease. You wouldn't lean away from me and would relax when I hugged you. Anyway, all that to say that I think by next year you'll have your morning routine down to under thirty minutes."

Emilia took Owen's hand again. "Thank you so much. I had no idea you did all that for me."

"No worries. I was happy to help."

"And, um, thanks for telling me all of that," she continued. "I'm sure we've had this conversation before and—"

"Emilia," he cut in. "Even people with intact memories relive old times. I don't mind. Really. Plus, talking to someone my own age is a huge relief. I love living with Pam and all, but she and her friends are more than twice my age, and the campers and counselors are a lot younger, so I don't have any real friends. I spend most of my time talking to plants."

Emilia gave him a sad smile. She could see how it would be hard for him to make friends and even harder to date. There weren't that many men his age in the rural town where he lived, much less gay men his age. But who knew? Maybe he'd meet someone through the camp. An older counselor he hit it off with, or maybe a sibling of one of the campers. Owen was one of the most likable people she'd ever met. When he was ready to date, she was sure he'd find someone.

"That was a really fun summer," Owen said, cutting into her thoughts. "I'd thought that after you two graduated college, you were done working at the camp, so it was a nice, unexpected reunion."

"You said Eric was there but was also working at the lab? What was he doing, just driving back and forth all the time?"

"Yeah. He worked in Aspen Grove Monday through Wednesday, then would drive up Wednesday night and stay with us through the weekend, then go back into town Sunday night."

"And where was June? Had they already broken up? Or did she come up too?"

"They broke up after that summer." The way he said it, she knew there was more to that story. Was it because Eric had insisted on driving up to Camp Ouray on his days off, rather than spending them with his girlfriend?

"Do you know why?" she pressed.

Owen shook his head. "I don't know the details. I know it was her idea and at first Eric was down about it, but he got over it pretty quickly."

Emilia nodded as she considered this new piece of information. So, she'd broken up with August a few months after her accident, then June had broken up with Eric not long after. Poor Eric. But apparently he'd moved on quickly, and her summary said he and June were still friends.

"You okay?" Owen asked, turning to look at her.

"Yeah. Just piecing things together. I'm glad Eric wasn't too sad. He adored June, but you said he moved on, so that's good."

"Yeah. He moved on."

"It probably wasn't hard for Eric to find someone else. He's Eric, everyone loves him."

Owen's brow furrowed before he turned back toward the road. "Yeah, it wasn't hard. He didn't have to look far."

It was hard to imagine Eric flirting with other girls. He'd only ever been interested in June, and that relationship hadn't started until after they'd been friends for years. She wondered how he'd met whoever Owen was referring to. Was it someone he worked with in the lab? One of the counselors? Or maybe just a girl he'd met at a bar or something.

Was he still with her? What would she think if she knew Emilia had climbed into her boyfriend's bed that morning? What did she think about Emilia, in general? Pathetically feeding off of Eric's kindness. Her stomach turned. She crossed her arms over her middle and leaned forward.

"You okay?"

"Yeah," she lied. "Just a little dehydrated, I think. I'll be fine."

* * *

Later that night, Emilia was sitting at a desk in Pam's office, surrounded by legal texts, notes, and draft contracts. She was nearly finished with the new contracts and waivers for Camp Ouray, but wanted to have a real lawyer read through them before she handed them over to Pam. Maybe she could call someone at Beth Larsen's office. She'd seen some notes on her calendar indicating that she still worked with her and would be back in her office on Monday.

She pushed back from the desk and massaged her neck. Her eyes drifted up to the clock on the wall. 8:23pm. It was later than she'd thought, though not as late as it felt, which she guessed she could blame on her early morning wake-up call from Henry. She yawned as her mind drifted to Eric.

Where was he?

He said he'd drive up after work. It was only an hour drive. He said he may need to work later to make up for arriving late this morning, but working until past 7:00 seemed excessive. Then again, she didn't know where he worked. Maybe it was a long drive. Then he had to pack.

She needed to stop. He would get here when he got here.

And worrying about it was going to get her nowhere. Scenes of the highway flashed through her mind. Dark, lit only by the headlights from the cars. The indistinct shadows of the landscape racing by.

What if he was hurt? What if he was late because he'd gotten into an accident? Maybe he'd hit his head and come out if it like her, only able to remember one day at a time. She smiled, in spite of the pit that had settled in her stomach. They could hang out together, living each day to the fullest before resetting the next night.

It's not funny, a voice in her head scolded. *What if he never makes it up here? What if—?*

"Emilia?"

She jumped. "Shit! Sorry. You scared me." She pressed her hand to her racing heart as she turned to face Owen. "Hi."

"Didn't mean to sneak up on you like that. I knocked." He motioned toward the open door.

"You're fine."

"I was just checking in. Seeing if you wanted to break for the night. Maybe go back to your cabin and read or something."

She shook her head. She wouldn't be able to relax until she knew for certain Eric was fine. "I'm going to go through these one more time." She picked up a pen, but her hand was shaking, so she set it down and pressed her palm into the desk.

Owen walked into the room and placed a firm hand on her shoulder. "I'm sure he's fine. Just got held up by something. He'll be here."

She forced herself to smile. "Yeah. Of course he will." Her voice was too high, but Owen didn't comment on it. He squeezed her shoulder and returned to the door.

"I need to move some more firewood into the cabins and

lock up for the night. I'll check on you before I turn in, okay?"

"Yeah. Sounds good."

Emilia tried her best to focus on the contracts in front of her, but her mind kept being pulled away to thoughts of Eric. Watching him sleep this morning. How he'd held her while he told her about her new life. The way he'd laughed at Henry, his deep blue eyes bright with amusement. She imagined him driving in the car, racing down a dark highway. She saw headlights flood into the car, making his pupils constrict the same way they had when Henry shone the flashlight in his face. His mouth opened. He tried to scream.

No! She balled her fists. She needed to think about something else. Eric was fine. She wasn't going to lose him. He was perfectly fine. Eventually, the early morning finally caught up with her and she fell asleep on top of the draft she'd been editing.

* * *

Emilia was awoken later by the feeling of someone picking her up. Her mind felt sluggish. She forced her eyes open, but all she could see were large, blurry shapes. After several moments of trying to sort out the colors and shapes around her, with no success, she closed her eyes again. That was better.

"Can you wrap your arms around my neck?" the person holding her asked. She couldn't place the voice, but knew it was someone she trusted, so she complied.

"Sorry, Em. I lost track of time. You'll be fine, though. I just need to get you back to your cabin."

"Eric," she mumbled. Her mind was gripping onto something. Eric. She needed to know where Eric was.

"He's fine," the voice said. "I'm sure he'll be here any minute, apologizing for keeping us waiting, then scolding me for letting you fall asleep at your desk. Ah, there he is."

"She fell asleep?" a second voice asked. This one was even more familiar. Her heart thumped at the sound of it. She opened her eyes again, but still couldn't make anything out.

"I have to tell Eric," she whispered.

There was a gentle hand on her face, and the second voice said soothingly, "You can sleep, Emilia. You don't have to try to make sense of this." The hand left her face, and the second voice added, "Henry woke her up at five this morning."

"Henry woke her up? She didn't say. That must have been jarring."

"She did well," the second person said proudly.

Emilia tried to open her eyes again, but everything was still blurry. Her head pounded painfully as she tried to make sense of it all. She was having trouble making out the voices now. The person holding her stopped walking, and she felt herself being passed to someone else. This new person smelled really good. Like leaves and the fresh mountain air. The other one had smelled like wood and dirt.

The voices mumbled something to each other, but she couldn't make out the words and just snuggled closer to whoever was holding her. Tips for writing contracts were running through her head along with images of driving, a cabin covered in snow, August's face twisted in fear, a blinding light, an older looking Owen, a toddler in pajamas, Eric with facial hair—

Eric. There was something she needed to tell him.

She was struck by a blast of cold air and hugged the warm person holding her tighter. The chill didn't last long. She was warm again, then being lowered into a bed and tucked in. Someone whispered in her ear, "Hey, Emilia. It's Eric. I can tell you're fighting to stay awake but that never works. Just stop. It's time to sleep. I'll be in the room with you when you wake up."

"I need to tell Eric—it's important," she murmured, the words slurring on the way out of her mouth.

"What is it?"

Her eyes fluttered open, and she saw a blurry version of Eric in front of her. She figured it was her mind conjuring up the image of the person she needed to see. "That I love him," she whispered. "He needs to know. In case something happens, he needs to know."

She closed her eyes again and felt the person place a soft kiss on her forehead. "Don't worry, Emilia," he whispered right before she finally lost consciousness, "he knows."

* 19 *

Emilia woke up in what looked like the cabin she used to stay in at Camp Ouray. But she wasn't a counselor anymore. She'd given that up after graduating from college. She was in law school now. She must be dreaming.

Eric was sitting up in a bed on the other side of the cabin, looking much too old for camp, and reading a newspaper. What was he doing in a girls' cabin? How bizarre. He smiled when he saw her looking at him.

"Eric?"

"Hey."

"What's happening? This is a dream, right?"

He shook his head and put the paper down, then got up and walked over to her, stopping next to the bed. She looked around the room and saw she was lying in her old bed, but that the top bunk had been lifted off. It was sitting on the side of the room. What was going on? What was she doing here? And why was Eric here with her? Where was August?

August! She looked frantically around the room, half expecting to see him. Where was he? Was he okay?

She pulled herself to a sitting position and looked over at Eric, who was smiling at her as his eyes scanned her face. "There's a letter that explains everything going on or I can just tell you. Which do you prefer?"

"You," she said quickly.

He smiled. "Can I sit next to you?"

"Of course." Emilia shifted to the side of the bed as Eric climbed in. She was completely confused and couldn't imagine what was going on, but as soon as she laid her head on his shoulder, she felt better.

"Okay, here we go," Eric began.

* * *

Emilia had a bounce in her step as she walked along the snowy paths from the mess hall after lunch. She'd had a lovely morning with Eric and Owen spent snowshoeing, of all activities, but it was fun. She stayed at the back, so she could walk on the makeshift path created by Eric and Owen, making it way easier. It was a nice way to explore the surrounding forest, which looked completely different blanketed in snow.

After that, she and Eric helped Owen cut firewood. Actually, Emilia stacked the wood and let the boys handle the ax wielding. She had already lost her memory and didn't want to lose a hand, on top of that. Then they'd had lunch with Pam.

Emilia stayed back to talk to her old boss and help her clean up after lunch while the boys went to cover the pile of firewood they'd created, so it wouldn't be ruined as soon as it snowed again.

As she walked to the other side of the camp, where she'd agreed to meet up with the boys, she spotted the backs of their heads through the window of the main lodge. They were sitting on the sofa facing the fireplace, both with their legs propped on the coffee table. She let herself into the large cabin and heard Owen say, "Pam's lucky she has Emilia. Those contracts were a mess. Even I could tell."

Contracts? Emilia frowned. She had no idea what Owen was talking about. *What contracts?* Eric hadn't mentioned anything about that. And neither had Pam.

"Emilia's lucky she has Pam," Eric replied. "We all are."

"Yeah. True. She has this ability to see into people, you know? Like even though Emilia was crap in the outdoors and had no experience with kids, Pam just knew she'd be great. That's why she still does the hiring. I wouldn't have let Emilia past the phone interview."

Eric let out a laugh while Emilia rolled her eyes. "I'm glad you weren't in charge of interviews. We never would have met her otherwise." Something about the way Eric said that made her pause. She leaned against the wall behind her and smiled.

"That would have been a tragedy," Owen agreed.

Emilia's smile widened.

Eric hummed and Emilia was about to announce herself when Owen asked, "So what are you really doing today?"

Emilia frowned. *"Really doing today?"* Why had he said it like that?

Eric stretched his arms over his head and let out a groan. "I am planning to stop by the Pearsons'. I've missed the last few lunches, so should probably go say hi. Then I need to run a few errands before my date."

"Ahh. Another setup?" Owen asked.

"Yeah. This one is from August."

Emilia perked up at that. August had set him up? Why couldn't Eric find his own dates? He was handsome and funny and nice and clever and, and, and easy to talk to—certainly the sort of man who was capable of finding himself a date.

"How does August choose which women he's going to date and which ones he's going to set aside for you?" Owen joked. "And how does he even find them when he lives four hours away?"

Eric laughed. "I don't want to know."

"I don't know why you agreed to this," Owen continued in a low voice.

Eric just sighed. "Whatever. Tonight won't be so bad. Just dinner. Worst case, she's awful but I'll still get to eat some good food."

"Best case, you find 'the one'?" Owen quipped.

"Yeah right," Eric muttered darkly.

"You do realize it's Valentine's Day today, don't you?"

"I—what? Shit. I didn't."

Owen let out a low whistle while Eric moaned and looked up at the ceiling.

Emilia felt sick. She stepped back until she collided with the door. She'd gotten the impression that she and Eric had grown very close since her accident, but apparently he was keeping things from her. He'd mentioned going to the Pearsons' and having to take care of a few errands, but he'd left out the part about going on a date. Something he had no problem sharing with Owen.

She wiped away a few tears that were threatening to fall, took a deep breath, then opened the door behind her and closed it loudly. Both boys turned as she marched into the room.

"Hey," Owen said, standing up. "Good chat with Pam?"

"Yeah. Uh. It was good." She tried to act casual but her voice came out high-pitched. She swallowed and plastered a smile on her face as she avoided Eric's gaze. "She said something about me helping with contracts? Can you—can you tell me what that's about?"

"Yeah. Probably easier for me to just show you, so you can read through all the notes you left yourself."

Emilia nodded. "Okay. Yeah."

"That's my cue to leave," Eric announced. He got up from the chair and stretched again.

"You have errands to run, right?" Emilia asked as casually as she could manage.

"Yeah. I'll be back tonight."

"You don't have to drive all the way up here just to drive

back home tomorrow. That seems excessive. I'm sure Owen can drive me back."

She turned to Owen, who was rubbing the back of his neck and looking uncomfortable. "Uh, yeah," he said. "Of course I can."

"But then Owen will have to drive all the way back here," Eric countered. "I really don't mind."

She crossed her arms over her chest. "Okay. Fine. Whatever works best for you."

Eric looked at her oddly. "Are you okay?"

She waved him away. "I'm fine."

He looked unconvinced. "Okay. Well, I'll see you later. I should be back before it's time for you to go to sleep. Maybe we can go to the ridge and look at the stars; it's supposed to be a clear night."

Isn't that something you'd rather do with your date? It took all her willpower to keep those words in her mouth. "Okay," she forced herself to say instead.

"Are you?" he asked, taking a step closer to her, "Okay, that is?"

"I'm fine. I hope you have a wonderful rest of the day, Eric." The words felt insincere coming out of her mouth, but she couldn't pinpoint why.

* * *

Owen led Emilia to Pam's office, where there was a desk covered in notes, draft contracts and waivers, and a few legal textbooks she recognized from school. She tried to busy herself as best she could, but there wasn't much to do. Her past self had taken care of everything. All that was left was to have a lawyer read over contracts and waivers she'd drafted. Her past self had even made a note to bring these with her when she went to Beth's office on Monday.

She set to organizing Pam's desk, which was incredibly messy, just for something to do. But her mind kept drifting back to Eric. Why had he kept his date from her?

Or, better question, why did the thought of Eric on a date make her feel sick? It couldn't be jealousy. Could it? No, of course not. She'd never been jealous of Eric dating June, so why would she be jealous of him dating other women?

After she tidied the desktop and shelves, she dove into the drawers, which were stuffed with files from receipts, to Christmas cards, to employment contracts from over ten years ago. After investigating for a few moments and determining that there was no organization system, Emilia emptied the entire contents of all three drawers and placed them on the ground.

She took a seat next to them and started organizing them into neat piles. As she worked, images of Eric swirled through her mind. She saw herself laughing with him in bed this morning as they made dark jokes about her injury. Then she was hiking behind him in the snow as he tossed tips for making the snowshoeing easier over his shoulder.

She saw them visiting the ridge together, leaning back against the large tree up there as they looked out at the stars. Then they walked arm and arm back to the cabins, fingers laced together as he wrapped a strong arm around her waist and pulled her closer.

Wait—had they done that? Or was she imagining that?

As Emilia brought the image to the forefront again, she saw Eric with a faceless blonde woman instead of her. He was walking with his arm around the woman as they turned away from the main path toward the cabin Emilia and Eric had slept in last night. Eric led the blonde inside and pulled her into a kiss as the door closed behind them.

It wasn't until a tear fell and smudged a spot on one of the papers she was holding that Emilia realized she was crying. What was wrong with her?

She rose and paced the room, weaving through the neat piles she'd created. She rubbed at her eyes fiercely, willing the tears to stop, but something had taken hold of her. Something that wouldn't let go until it was properly acknowledged. She was at the end of the room, in the middle of a pivot, when she put it all together.

The date. How she felt about it. The inexplicable crying. Eric's lie.

"Oh, shit," she whispered. The answer was painfully obvious. Like, physically painful. She could feel it as a tightness in her chest.

Emilia had become attached to Eric. All day today, she'd felt calmer when she was close to him and had been on edge ever since he'd left. And the thought of him moving on with his life, finding another girlfriend, bringing her to his favorite places, falling in love. It didn't make Emilia happy, like it should. It made her sick to her stomach.

Eric must know about this unhealthy … attachment? … dependence? That was why he'd hidden the date, so he wouldn't upset her.

Emilia's tears began to fall faster. She'd thought her life was good earlier today, but as she viewed it through this lens, she saw that it was actually pathetic. She'd come to visit Owen this weekend and instead of staying home and enjoying his time alone, what had Eric done? He'd packed his bag and spent the night here with her, when it would have been so much easier to stay home, especially since he had plans tonight. But he'd driven up here anyway, just so he could help his crazy friend start her day off okay.

Poor Eric. He was probably desperate to move on, but at a loss for how to extricate himself from her. He'd never been good at letting hopeless causes go. He'd devoted himself to his family growing up: first his dying mother, then his sisters, then his nephew. But his sisters had moved on. Henry had been adopted by his aunt and uncle. It was finally time for Eric to focus on himself.

Then Emilia had her accident. It probably wasn't a coincidence that his life had fallen apart since then. He was no longer with June, no longer in the MD-PhD program. She had a suspicion it was because he was focusing all his energy on her. And she was in no position to tell him no. As soon as the idea formed in her mind, she probably forgot it.

Emilia continued to cry, but forced herself to sit down and keep organizing the files. She couldn't leave the office in greater disarray than she found it. As she worked, her mind turned over this newly-discovered Eric problem. And just like it always did when faced with a problem, her brain began working on a solution.

* 20 *

Emilia had a plan. It was rough, but she guessed most of her plans these days were rough. It's not like she had days and days to turn them over in her mind. But she figured it was better than nothing.

Once the reorganization of Pam's files was complete, she wrote herself a letter for what she had to do once she was back in Aspen Grove. She needed to call June and Viola. Eric couldn't be trusted with this. And according to her summary, August felt guilty for what had happened to her. Owen was too nice, but Viola and June were both blunt and not afraid to call things like they were.

She'd tell them everything she'd realized: how she was overly reliant on Eric and maybe even in love with him (something that had been very hard to write, but she'd forced herself to do it anyway). She'd tell them that she needed to find somewhere else to live and see if any of them could help with that.

Having Viola and June together would be a good balance. Her sister would look out for her and June would look out for Eric. At least, she hoped so. Her summary said June and Eric were still on good terms. Honestly, a large part of this plan would involve winging it, but she trusted her future self to figure it out, now that she had all the facts.

She read over the letter again. It wasn't great, but enough. She placed it in the folder on top of the contracts, where she'd be sure to see it. Then she left in search of Owen, or anything else to distract her from her thoughts.

Emilia spent the rest of the afternoon reading in the lodge with Owen. He was studying for one of his classes, and she kept him company while rereading her favorite chapters in one of the books she'd found on the shelf.

Dinner with Pam was uneventful. Emilia peppered the older woman with questions about the camp to keep her mind from drifting to another dinner at a nice restaurant in Aspen Grove, with Eric smiling across a low-lit table, probably wearing something nice, like a blue button-down shirt that matched his eyes.

He'd tell a joke and the girl would laugh, because why wouldn't she? Eric had a great sense of humor. Then maybe she'd say something to make him laugh. He'd reach across the table and take her hand, or whatever people did on dates. She'd only ever dated August, who she'd been friends with for nearly four years before they got together, so she didn't know how dates with strangers went.

Pam had stopped talking. She was looking at her oddly. Oops. Emilia forced her attention back to the conversation. Eric's date wasn't her business. She needed to let it go.

After dinner, Pam cornered her and said she wanted to talk to Emilia in her office. Uh oh. Had she read the waivers? Did she hate them?

"I know the wording on those contracts is harsh," she said as she followed Pam into the office, "but that's how legal documents are. You need to be clear and leave no room for—"

"I don't care about the contracts," Pam said, taking a seat behind her desk and motioning for Emilia to sit in the chair across from her. "I trust your judgment. Just tell me where to sign. It's this I have a problem with." She opened the folder and handed Emilia the letter she'd written to herself.

"Oh," Emilia breathed. Suddenly, she was nineteen again, sitting in front of this force of a woman as she interviewed for a job for which she was comprehensively unqualified.

"I didn't mean to snoop, but you know me. I can't help

myself when I see someone in need and you, my dear, are in need."

Emilia had no idea what to say. She just closed her mouth, which was hanging open, and nodded.

"You know I love that boy like he was mine. I have since he was ten years old, sportin' the nicest gear money could buy, with impeccable manners, and no earthly idea how to be a kid."

Emilia nodded again. "Yeah."

"He deserves the world," Pam continued harshly. "Not to have his heart torn out and thrown in a dumpster."

Emilia grimaced. "That's not—"

"That's what this will do." Pam was clutching the letter so tightly, it was crumpling in her hand.

A knot formed in Emilia's throat. She wanted to run away. She hated this. She never upset her superiors. She always followed the rules, sometimes to unhealthy extremes, so she could avoid landing herself in situations like this. "I just want what's best for him," she said, voice shaking. "I want him to move on, to—"

Pam held a hand up to silence her. Emilia cut off immediately.

"Do you remember the first time we met?" Pam asked. "You were sittin' right there."

"Yes. You said you thought I'd be a shitty counselor, but that your gut was telling you to hire me anyway."

It had been a terrible interview and afterward, Emilia told herself she could never work for such a rude woman. But she hadn't been able to resist the offer when it came. It paid about the same as all the jobs around town, but unlike those, it offered free room and board for the summer. She accepted without a second thought, figuring she could keep her interactions with

Pam to a minimum. She never expected the woman would become like a second mother to her.

"You were a shitty counselor," Pam said gruffly, drawing Emilia's attention back to the conversation. "And by the end of that first summer—"

"I was better?" Emilia provided.

"No. Still shitty."

Emilia's brow creased. "But you let me come back."

"I know. Why do you think I did that?"

"I have no idea. You liked me?"

"No. Not particularly. I like you now." She tapped the folder with the draft waivers. "You grew into a lovely young lady and a good friend. But back then, you were just an uptight, shitty counselor. There were a lot better people out there I could have hired, but I invited you back anyway."

"Why?"

Pam looked down at the letter and a lock of her dark gray hair fell into her face. She pushed it back forcefully, then glared up at Emilia, her green eyes flashing with irritation. Emilia resisted the urge to lean away from her.

"I saw what you were to him," Pam finally replied. "Even then, I could see it. He shined when you were around. For the first time since I'd known him, he was himself for longer than a fleeting moment. He was himself for days, weeks, all summer. You brought it out of him."

"Oh. I—I didn't know that."

"I know. I never told you."

Pam had let her work here for Eric? But they were just friends. They'd only ever been friends. Close friends, though. Closer than anyone. They understood each other, even during that first summer. And there was a truth to Pam's words. They'd always had this knack for drawing out the other's true self.

Emilia felt like she'd stepped into a patch of sunlight, only to be violently shoved into the shadows the next moment. She shivered and wrapped her arms around herself, but it did nothing to combat the cold feeling in her chest.

It was the feeling of loving someone so much it hurt. Of reaching that point where the countless reasons you love them are no longer a comfort. Because all you can think of is of the terror of losing them—of how thoroughly destroyed you'd be if they were gone.

Maybe it was possible to love someone too much. To be too drawn to them, too attached. To get to the point where things didn't make sense without them. Where all the reasons you have for loving them have twisted into all the reasons you can never be with them.

Pam watched her critically as she continued to hold herself. "Do you know what he wants more than anything?" Pam asked.

"To have his mom back and his family all together?"

Pam snorted. "Well, yeah. But that's not happenin', so what's the next best thing?"

Emilia thought about it for a moment before answering. "A family of his own." An image of Eric holding a baby Henry as he paced his apartment popped into her mind—Eric using one hand to pat his nephew gently on the back while the other held a large textbook open.

She took a moment to blink back tears, then looked up at Pam. "Eric deserves a family," she said, her voice even again. "He deserves someone who can give him a family. A huge one, like the Pearsons, if he wants."

Emilia met Pam's defiant gaze with one of her own. Pam wasn't the only strong woman in the room and not the only one who would do anything for Eric.

She expected Pam to look stern, to scold her again, but it was the opposite. Her tone was gentle as she said, "He already has a family."

"Oh. Yeah. I guess. You and Owen, and Henry, and—"

"No. You. You're his family, Emilia. I've seen enough in this world to know that blood doesn't make family. Look at what my stupid cousin did to poor Owen, or how Eric's ass of a daddy treated him. Sometimes you find your family later, but once you do, you know it.

"That was you and him. You both knew it from the start and haven't left each other's side since that first summer you spent here. You stayed together through school, then this accident of yours—you've made a life together. And if you think Eric's going to give that up without a fight, you're not as smart as you think you are."

"But—but Eric needs to get a real family one day," Emilia argued. "He needs to marry someone, have kids, and I—I can't be his roommate forever."

"I rarely say this, but it seems I need to be more blunt. Listen to me, and listen good, okay?" She paused to lean over her desk. "That young man is head over heels in love with you."

Emilia inhaled sharply. For a brief moment, she let herself believe Pam. She let herself believe that Eric hadn't told her about his date because it meant nothing to him. That there was a good reason for it, and she'd laugh when he explained it. She let herself imagine that she hadn't grown dependent on Eric, but was upset about being away from him because she was in love with him.

She let herself think that Eric had driven up here last night not because he'd felt he had to, but because he wanted to see her, because he missed her. She imagined him walking along the path to the ridge, but this time, the woman he had an arm around was her. And when he brought her back to his house in Aspen Grove, he didn't do it out of necessity or a sense of duty, but because he wanted her there as much as she wanted to be there.

It was certainly a better lens to look at her life through. But she had a sinking feeling it was just a desperate hope and not reality. Perhaps Pam was just reading more into their close friendship than was actually there. It wouldn't be the first time someone had done that.

"You're mistaken," Emilia said, her tone firm. "He's on a date right now with someone August Pearson set him up with."

She expected Pam to balk, or at the very least, blink, but she just continued to watch Emilia with that stern expression. "Your interpretation of the situation is based on a few hours of observation and some limited information about a supposed date. My assessment is based on years of watching the two of you, a lot of which you don't remember. So if I were a bettin' woman, I'd go with me."

Emilia had nothing to say to that. Pam settled back in her chair, looking smug. She took the letter Emilia had written and balled it in her fist. "I'm going to toss this. This isn't what's best for Eric. This is a dumb idea born from a place of fear and uncertainty and lack of understanding. If you're gonna make it through this, Emilia, you need to learn to listen to your intuition and ignore the insecurities from your past. They aren't servin' you no more."

"That's a lot easier said than done," Emilia said brusquely.

Pam's lips curved up. "I'm pretty sure Eric is willing to help you with that. You just need to let him."

* * *

Emilia was a wreck after her meeting with Pam. When she

returned to the lodge, Owen was gone, which was fine, since she was in no state to be with other people. She picked up the book she'd been reading earlier but kept getting distracted by thoughts of Eric. Pam said he loved her, and Pam was a sharp lady. But if he loved her, why was he with someone else?

Her eyes kept drifting to the clock on the wall, and she tried to guess what Eric was doing. It was 7:30. Would they still be at dinner? That depended on when the date had started. When did dates normally start? 6:30? 7:00?

Emilia tried to focus back on her book. She told herself that even if Eric did start dating someone else, he wasn't just going to be out of her life. That part of what Pam had said was right. They were like family. There would always be a spot for her in his life.

She managed to distract herself until 8:00. They must be finished with dinner by now, right? Or at least eating dessert. Where would they go next? Would he take her somewhere for drinks? Emilia rubbed her temples and was glad that in a few hours, she was going to forget this madness.

8:30. Dinner was definitely over by now. Perhaps they were even finished with drinks. Was it time to say goodnight? Were they standing outside the girl's door? Was Eric going to lean in and kiss her? Or would she invite Eric inside? Emilia shook her head, trying to clear it of that last thought. Her stomach turned, and she wished she'd skipped dinner tonight.

Emilia sighed. She needed to stop this. She got up and scanned the shelves, then pulled down a jigsaw puzzle she'd done a hundred times before and began spreading the pieces on the oversized coffee table.

9:00 passed and still, no Eric. Maybe he was driving up here. Or maybe he was making out with his date. She bit the inside of her cheek and focused on the puzzle. She had all the pieces turned over and was almost finished with the border. She forced her mind away from Eric and back on the pieces.

9:30. Yes, he was definitely having sex. If it was just some innocent dinner, it would have been over hours ago and he'd be here by now. Pam was delusional. He didn't love her. Or maybe he did but had come to terms with the fact that they could never be together, because she was brain damaged and unable to give him the life he deserved. Emilia hoped the new girl was nice, that she'd be able to make Eric happy, and that she wouldn't mind having Emilia over to visit every so often.

She had to stop to wipe her tears at that point. She couldn't see the puzzle pieces anymore. She had shoved her fists in her eyes and was rubbing furiously when she heard the door open. She looked up and saw Eric there, standing just inside the door and knocking snow off his boots.

"Hey, sorry I'm late, I—" He paused when he saw her. "What's wrong? Are you crying?"

"Eric," she whispered, stumbling to her feet. What was he doing here? He was supposed to be having sex with some blonde girl right now.

He kicked his boots off and walked into the large room. He looked good. He had on a pale gray button-down shirt with dark jeans. His hair was less messy than usual and his eyes were bright and smiling. His date must have been impressed.

"What happened?" he repeated when he was standing in front of her.

"You're ... here." It wasn't much of a response to his question, but she needed to say the words out loud. She wasn't sure if this was real, or if she'd officially gone insane and was just seeing what she wanted to see.

"I am," Eric confirmed.

She reached out and brushed his arm. It was solid, which was a good sign. She hadn't gone completely insane. Well, not yet. "You're not home?"

"No. Sorry I'm late. There's a storm coming tonight and I needed to get your damn cat inside. But he wasn't having it." He held up his hand, which had a long scratch down the back. Emilia took his hand and examined it. The scratch looked new.

"Bartholomew did this?"

"Yeah. Are you surprised?"

"No. I … so you're late because of Bartholomew?"

He nodded, then swiped at her wet cheeks with the back of his hand. "Is that why you're upset? Because I'm late? I'm sorry you were worrying."

She forced herself to smile. "It's fine. You're here now."

"Yeah, that's been well established. How was the rest of your day?" Eric sat on the sofa and stretched his legs out in front of him.

Emilia took a tentative seat next to him, moving her book from earlier out of the way. "I organized Pam's office. It was boring. Your turn. How was your day?" She tried not to sound too eager when she asked the question.

"It was fine. Saw the Pearsons, they all say hi. Took care of some chores around the house, like finally replacing some flickering light bulbs. Oh, and I installed shelves in the garage. You'll see when we're back; we needed something. Our shoes were just in a pile near the door."

Emilia nodded. She didn't care about shelves. She wanted to hear about the next part of the evening. "Okay. Then, um, what did you do after that?"

None of your business! a stern voice screamed in her mind. She ignored it.

"Then I went out to eat."

"Oh, nice. Where?"

"This small little Italian place at the edge of town. It's new, so you wouldn't remember it."

A small place near the edge of town. How quaint. So his date wasn't the type of person who needed to be taken to one of the large, fancy restaurants on Center Street. That was exactly Eric's type. "Italian. Nice. Sounds romantic too. Good for Valentine's Day," Emilia said with a forced smile. "What did your date think of it?"

Eric's face fell. "Did Owen tell you I had a date?"

"No. I overheard you two talking."

"Oh."

"You could have told me. I don't know why it was some big secret. You should go on dates. You're young, single, handsome, a very eligible bachelor and all that."

He grabbed both of her hands. "This is why I didn't tell you. I didn't want you to get the wrong impression."

Emilia kept her eyes down and focused on their hands, not wanting him to see the tears collecting in her eyes. "What impression?"

"That I think there's any other woman for me."

Her head snapped up. Was Pam right after all? Was Eric saying what she thought he was? "I don't understand," she said carefully. "If you've already found someone, why are you going on dates with other women?"

He gave her a small, apologetic smile. "It's hard to explain, but these dates mean nothing to me. They all end the same, as quickly as possible and with nothing more than a handshake. Then, I race back to the person I really want to be spending my time with."

Emilia looked back down at their hands again. Was this real? Or maybe she was imagining this entire conversation. She wasn't sure anymore. But if this was fake, she wasn't going to let it go without doing one more thing.

She leaned into Eric, stopping when her lips were just a breath away from his. She pulled her hands out of his grip and placed one on his face and the other on his chest, just over his heart. "Are you talking about me?" she breathed.

Eric laughed, and she felt it against her lips. "So smart, yet so stupid sometimes."

That was the only confirmation she needed. She closed the distance between them, pressing her lips into his.

Their movements from there were frantic. They each seemed to be trying to get as close to the other as possible. Eric buried his hands in Emilia's hair while she dug her fingernails into his back, pulling him closer.

What did this mean? Did they like each other? *Love* each other? She was sure by now she loved him, but how was it possible he felt the same way about her? And this kiss, it was so perfect and so… familiar. Had this happened before? This was a bit aggressive for a first kiss, but she loved every minute of it. She loved the feeling that Eric wanted her, *now,* and that he couldn't seem to get enough of her.

It took Emilia a moment to register that they weren't kissing anymore. Eric pulled a hand out of her hair and tapped her temple. "You need to turn this off."

"I have no idea how to do that."

He smirked, then leaned in and whispered in her ear, "I think I can help you." He nibbled on her earlobe and added, "Focus on how this feels."

Emilia nodded as shivers ran down her spine. He nipped her

earlobe again, which felt divine, then licked a line along the sensitive scar on her neck. He grazed his teeth against her collarbone, then placed a soft kiss on the hollow of her throat.

Her mind was completely focused on the feeling of his teeth, then tongue, then lips as she tried to guess what he was going to do next. He moved to the other side of her neck. "Do you like how this feels?"

The only response she managed was a large exhale. She grabbed his chin and pulled his face up so it was level with hers.

"Eric we've—we've done this before."

"Yeah."

"How many times?"

"More than is probably wise given… everything, but not as much as I'd like."

Emilia beamed. "I like that answer."

"Noted." Eric placed a kiss on one side of her mouth, then the other. "I'll use it the next time you ask me this question. Now please, shut up."

Emilia, more than happy to oblige his request, pulled him back into a long, deep kiss.

* 21 *

As Emilia kissed Eric on the sofa in Camp Ouray's lodge (of all places), a thrum of anxiety hovered at the edges of her consciousness. It was the jumble of dread and uncertainty that had plagued her all day. But the longer she clung to Eric—moving her mouth with his and pressing against him—the easier it became to ignore, as the mess of concerns was replaced by an all-consuming want.

They were engaged in a sort of dance, which she seemed to be leading. He waited for her to press her tongue past his lips before tilting her head up and entwining his tongue with hers. When she moved her hands up his shirt and trailed her fingers over his bare chest, he took it as an invitation to reach under her shirt, holding her sides and rubbing his thumbs along her ribs.

Once she figured out he was waiting for her before progressing to each new step, she pushed for more. That's how she ended up on his lap, grinding her hips into him until he let out a small moan, which she captured with her mouth. Emilia smiled inwardly. She wanted to get him to make that sound again. She reached down and felt he was hard, then stroked him a few times through his jeans. He stopped kissing her and leaned back, locking his eyes with hers.

There was an unmistakable question there. Before Emilia could overthink it and let the thrum of anxiety take over, she reached for the hem of her shirt and pulled it off. She took her bra off next, then leaned forward and began unbuttoning Eric's shirt, propelled forward by her overwhelming desire for him.

When they were both shirtless, Emilia pressed herself against him and kissed his neck, savoring the feel of his warm skin against her chest and the taste of him on her tongue. Every nerve in her body was screaming *yes, yes yes!* but still, she wanted more.

She climbed off his lap, and before she let herself consider it, began undoing his belt. Her hands were moving on their own while Eric watched her, eyes dark and filled with desire. She pulled his jeans and boxers down. He was fully hard and standing eagerly at attention.

Holy shit, Eric was naked. Eric Shaffer. Her best friend, who she'd never even kissed (well, not that she remembered). Damn, he was hot. She could sit there and look at him for hours, but the haze of desire pushed her forward.

She wrapped her hand around him and began to pump her fist, smiling at his immediate reaction. He leaned his head back with a groan and closed his fists around the edge of the sofa cushion. "Fuck," he murmured, the word barely intelligible through his clenched teeth.

As she stroked him, Emilia grazed her teeth along the column of his neck, causing him to swear again. She was on her way up, toward his mouth, when he caught her chin and held her face in front of his. His eyes were like endless pools, and she had a fleeting thought that maybe, if she stared in them long enough, she'd rediscover all the moments she'd lost.

The spell broke when Eric looked down and linked his fingers into the band of her jeans. "It's not fair that I'm the only one who's naked."

Emilia nodded, and Eric began undoing her jeans, moving slowly, probably to give her a chance to stop him. She expected to be shaking with nerves but instead, she pushed her jeans down and walked out of them quickly, then resumed her spot on his lap without hesitation.

And now she was sitting on Eric, naked, as his erection pressed into her stomach. Oh shit. Her brain was shocked back into action. This had progressed alarmingly quickly for someone who had never had sex before. Or had she? None of this felt scary, or foreign, or new. The truth hit her then.

"We've done this before. Not just the kissing but—but this."

Eric, who had been watching her carefully, nodded. "But that doesn't mean we have to do it now."

"I want to," she said insistently.

Eric leaned forward and kissed one of her bare shoulders, then the other. "Are you sure?"

"Yes," she breathed. The feeling of his beard against her skin was causing goosebumps to raise on her arms and nape of her neck. That need for him was back, pushing the rest of her thoughts to the back of her mind.

Eric moved his lips down to the top of each of her breasts before taking one of the peaks in his mouth. She let out a low moan and stroked his length as he continued to kiss her breasts. This felt incredible, but she wanted to be closer to him. She knew what she had to do, obviously knew the mechanics of it all, but she was suddenly scared.

"Eric," she whispered.

He pulled away quickly. "Do you want to stop?"

She shook her head. "I want to—I want to keep going, but I … I'm nervous."

She squeezed his erection, so her meaning was clear, and he gave her a small smile as he scanned her face again, probably for any signs of doubt. "Are you sure you want to do this?"

She nodded. *That* she was sure of. Everything else, not so much.

"Okay." He grabbed her hip to stabilize her, then reached down for his jeans, which he'd kicked off earlier. She watched curiously as he pulled his wallet out of the back pocket. What was he looking for? A condom. Duh. Why didn't she think of that?

"You're one of those creeps who keeps condoms in their wallet now? Was that in case your date went better than expected?" She tried to keep her tone light, but inside she was shattering.

Eric kissed the tip of her nose. "No, you dork. I keep a condom in my wallet on the off chance you rediscover your feelings for me and decide you want to do this. This creepy condom is mostly for your benefit," he added with a wink.

"Congratulations on saying the creepiest thing you could have at that moment."

"Are you done with me? Want me to go? Those sounds you were making earlier said otherwise."

"Smart ass."

He kissed her, running his hands down her sides. He stopped at the scar on her ribs and ran a finger along the sensitive skin there, which drew forth memories of the accident and everything she didn't remember. She placed a hand on his chest and pushed back.

Oh God, what was she doing? Was she about to have sex with Eric? The confidence that had carried her here was gone, leaving her drowning, trapped in those deep pools in his eyes. Which, admittedly, wasn't the worst place to be trapped.

"Emilia?" He was scanning her face again. "We can stop. We don't have to do—"

She cut him off with a kiss, worried if she let him keep talking, he'd change his mind about this. "I want to," she said honestly.

They kissed for a long while, long enough for the doubt that had gripped Emilia to subside, replaced entirely by her need for him, settling like an ache in her core. She reached for him and felt the condom. When had he put that on? She grinned against his mouth. He was clearly just as eager for this as she was.

"Can I touch you?" he whispered in her ear.

She nodded, then spoke her assent, so there wouldn't be any doubt.

Eric pushed a finger inside her. Emilia dropped her head against his shoulder and let out a long moan. Then he placed a second finger in and pumped his hand. She instinctively rocked her hips against him and gasped when he hooked his fingers. "Shit," she groaned into the crook of his neck.

He circled his thumb around that sensitive spot between her legs, and she swore again, bucking her hips harder into him. Suddenly, he pulled his hand away, and she nearly growled in frustration as that ache between her legs intensified. "You're ready," he whispered. "Just lift up for a second."

Eric helped guide himself inside her, and she slowly lowered down, relishing the feeling of him filling her up. It didn't hurt like she expected, and she figured that was because this wasn't her first time. This was so bizarre.

When she was sitting back down, her body took over. She placed her hands on his shoulders and rocked her hips back and forth, while Eric let out occasional groans. She loved watching him like this, on the brink of losing all control. His head was back on the sofa, and he was biting his lip. One of his hands gripped her hip while the other cupped her breast, his thumb flicking across the nipple and sending small jolts of pleasure through her.

He seemed completely consumed by this, by her, and kept looking at her like she was the most beautiful thing he'd ever seen. She couldn't remember a time when she'd felt so desirable.

"Oh, fuck," he muttered. "You need to slow down."

She stopped abruptly. "Sorry. Did I hurt you?"

He let out a small laugh. "Ah, no. Just sit there for a second and let me get you closer."

That didn't take long. He knew exactly how to touch her to set her body on fire. Every time she cried out he smiled to himself, which just drove her further to the edge. It wasn't long before the tension that had been building at her core finally released, causing her to let out a surprised gasp.

Eric moved his hands to her hips and continued to guide her back and forth as he pushed into her. After several more thrusts, he dipped his head into her neck and grunted out her name before going slack.

They held each other as they both recovered. She dropped her head against his shoulder and breathed in his scent while he traced lazy patterns across her back. "Fuck," he murmured into her hair.

Emilia leaned back and smiled at him. "That was incredible," she agreed. "'Or, well, it was for me. Was it, uh, okay for you?"

He smiled and pushed a lock of hair behind her ear. "All those grunts and incoherent moans, that was me enjoying it."

"Noted. Is it always like that?"

He nodded. "We're really good together."

She smiled and began to fix his hair, which was a mess. Then, she rubbed his jaw as she stared into his startling blue eyes.

This whole experience hadn't been what she was expecting. From hearing others talk about it, she'd assumed sex was all about chasing some earth-shattering orgasm, but it hadn't been like that at all. The orgasm was wonderful, naturally, but it was the whole part leading up to it she liked best. It was the small waves of pleasure passing through her as she shared something so intimate with the person she cared about most in the world.

She could not believe that out of all the women out there, he was here with her. She got to see him naked, and vulnerable, and got to hear his little groans of pleasure. And when he'd finished, he'd said *her* name. It was perfect, and then she realized she was going to forget it all.

A tear fell down her face at the thought. Eric wiped it away with his thumb. "What's wrong?"

"All this. It's going to be lost."

Eric leaned forward and placed a soft kiss on her lips. "It won't be completely lost. I'll remember. I've never forgotten a single moment I've shared with you."

She smiled sadly. "So, we've done that, um, a few times?"

"Yeah."

"When was the last time?"

"My birthday."

Emilia counted in her head. About two weeks ago. "And the first time?"

"Last summer."

"And that was my first time?"

"Yeah." Eric pushed her hair behind her shoulder and kissed her jaw.

But not his first time. He'd been with June before her accident. She remembered the awkward conversation when he'd told her about it, then begged her not to tell August. Then there had been a similar conversation with June, later that same day. Shit, this was weird. She cringed as Eric dipped his head and placed kisses along her neck.

"Was I awful?" she asked.

"No. You have never been awful."

That was a relief. She wouldn't have been completely out of her depth, so there was that. But as he continued to kiss her neck, she thought of how sad it was that she didn't remember her first time with him. Or even her last time with him. And in a few hours, she was going to forget this, too. Well, if it was going to end, she wanted to enjoy it as much as possible. She pushed him up.

"Hey," she said with a smile. "Do you have another condom? I—I don't know if I savored it as much as I should have. I know I'm going to forget but I want—uh—more time with you like this. Before it all goes away."

Eric beamed at her. "I do have another condom, but it's back in the cabin, in my bag. We should probably move, anyway."

She blushed as she looked around the empty lodge. Thank God no one had walked in on them. "Yeah. We should move."

Eric helped her up, then pulled off the condom and went to toss it in the bathroom. They put their clothes back on, pausing every few seconds to smile giddily at each other. Once outside, they laughed and stumbled down the path, tripping over each other's legs as they clung to each other for warmth.

When they reached the cabin, she pushed him playfully through the door. "So, we haven't had sex in the lodge before?"

Eric made quick work of his clothes, then turned his attention to removing hers. "No. We've never had sex in the lodge."

Once her clothes were off again, he pulled her in for a kiss, and she lost herself for a bit. "And here?" she asked after several moments. "Have we had sex in here?"

He led her to her bed and gently pushed her back, so she was sitting on the edge. "No. This is our first time having sex at Camp Ouray. Though, in my opinion, long overdue."

"Why is the top bunk taken off, if not for this?" she asked as he sucked on her neck.

Eric laughed, his beard tickling her skin. "So you don't bang your head when you wake up in an unfamiliar place. But you're right, it's convenient, having it gone. Having sex on a bunk bed would suck."

Emilia grinned, then shifted to the top of the bed, lying her head on the pillow as Eric climbed on top of her. "So, you want to savor this?" he asked, his tone almost dangerous.

She nodded as her heart beat hard in agreement.

"I love that idea." He kissed her cheek, then slowly made his way down to her neck, her collarbone, her chest, her breasts, her stomach, and further down to the inside of her thigh.

Emilia shook with nerves as she thought of him going *there*. He seemed to know what she was thinking. He winked at her, placed one quick kiss between her legs, then continued a path down her leg to her ankle, which he nipped with his teeth before switching to her other leg.

On his way back up, he showed her just how well he knew her body, pausing to give attention to every sensitive spot before stopping back at her chest. He paused for a moment to look at her, and she was about to demand he keep going when he slid two fingers inside her and began devouring her breasts. She threw her head back and let out a long moan.

Eric spent ages completely unraveling her until she was begging him to end it. He kept getting her close, then stopping abruptly, and it was driving her crazy. Her hands twisted in the sheets, and her back arched as she cried out his name and demanded he get inside her, now!

Eric cocked his head at her and gave her a wicked smile that nearly stopped her heart. "I thought you wanted to savor this."

"I'm done savoring. I want you. Please. Now."

He smiled again but thankfully, listened to her this time. He settled over her and slowly lowered himself until he was filling her up again. It didn't take long after that. When Emilia finally reached the edge, she cried out and pulled Eric down into a hard, passionate kiss.

A few moments later, Eric tensed up and groaned into her mouth. He bit her bottom lip, muttered something incoherent, and collapsed on top of her. Emilia wrapped her arms and legs around him. She loved the feeling of being completely engulfed by him.

"Can you breathe?" he mumbled after a minute of panting on top of her.

"No. But I don't care."

Eric kissed her, then rolled off her and gathered her in his arms, pulling her against his chest. His heart pounded against her back as she wrapped her arms around his and waited for both of their heart rates to slow. He moved her hair out of the way and placed soft kisses along her shoulder and neck. Emilia's body was still sensitive, and each touch seemed to travel all the way to her fingertips and toes.

"In case it wasn't already clear," he whispered in her ear, "I love you."

"Yeah, that came through. Especially that second time, even though you weren't listening to me." She felt him laugh softly against her, then shifted in his arms so she was facing him. "I love you too. I was sort of agonizing over it all day. There are feelings there, much stronger than I remembered from before, and I was trying to figure out if they meant I was in love with you or had just developed an unhealthy attachment to you because of my condition. Maybe it's both."

"No," he said quickly. "It's just the former. Or maybe we've both developed unhealthy attachments toward each other. I think that's just love, though. I think it feels like that sometimes, painful and dangerous—potentially fatal."

"Dramatic," she teased.

Eric moved his hands to her backside and pulled her close. "You have no idea."

"Why wasn't this in my summary about you?" she asked, resting her forehead on his chest.

He sighed. "It's a long story that I don't want to go into right now."

Emilia opened her mouth to protest but decided to let it go. It wasn't worth pressing. She was going to forget it all in an hour or so, anyway. Her chest clenched at the thought. "What happens in the morning?" she whispered.

"You'll forget here," he touched her head, "but not here." He placed a hand on the spot over her heart.

"Then let me write it down. Let me—"

He pressed his fingers to her lips. "I don't want to do the back and forth tonight. No broken promises, no poems pushed under the door. Just lie here with me. Can you do that?"

Emilia nodded and turned back around. He scooped her into his arms and resumed kissing her neck and shoulder. Occasionally, he took breaks to tell her how much he loved her and why. She told him the same. She never wanted this moment to end and tried to keep her eyes from closing for as long as possible but soon, sleep won out.

* * *

She awoke to Eric putting clothes on her. What was going on? She seemed to be in one of the cabins at Camp Ouray, but there was something wrong with the bunk.

"Eric?"

"Lift your hips," he instructed as he pulled her underwear on.

Why was she naked? "We need to get clothes on you, then I need to go back to my bed."

"No." She shook her head. "I want you to stay here with me." Why was he leaving? Had she done something wrong? "Please, Eric. I want to wake up with you every day. Please."

He kissed her cheek. "I want that too, more than anything, but I can't trust you when you're loopy."

"Loopy?" Emilia struggled to make sense of the word. She imagined a roller coaster looping around. That can't be what he meant.

"Owen calls it the in-between, when your brain is resetting itself," he explained.

That made no sense. "I don't care. I want to sleep with you. I know what I'm saying, let's just sleep here together." Emilia didn't know what she was doing in bed with Eric or why she was naked, but she was sure that she desperately wanted him to stay.

Eric gently pushed her down on the bed, then pulled the covers over her. "Okay, Miss I'm-Not-Loopy, tell me something." He crouched down next to her and pushed her hair behind her ear. "Where are we and how did we get here?"

She looked around and took in the scene. A cozy log cabin, Eric's face hovering nearby, a pleasant ache between her legs, and the taste of his kiss still on her lips. "Easy," she declared. "We're in a dream and we got here by falling asleep."

Emilia turned her head on the pillow toward Eric and saw tears welling in his eyes. She reached her hand out and wiped at his bottom lashes with her fingertips. His face felt warm and wet, oddly realistic for a dream.

Eric grabbed her hand and placed a kiss on her fingers. "This is what I dream about too, Emilia."

* * *

"That last summer, I was constantly thinking how I never wanted to grow up," Emilia announced as they drove back home to Aspen Grove. "I wanted Peter Pan to come and sprinkle fairy dust on us and keep us the same age forever, so we'd never have to give up our camp summers."

"I don't think that's how it works," Eric cut in. "The fairy dust makes you fly, but being in Neverland is what keeps you young."

Emilia was playing with the seat belt, folding and unfolding it in her hand, but stopped messing with it to look at Eric, who had his eyes trained on the road.

"Oh. Really? I guess I only saw that movie once. But I did think about it—all the time. I remember wanting it so badly, that if some magician showed up and gave me a wish, I was worried I might not use it correctly. The right thing to do would be to wish for world peace or the end of hunger, but I'd have probably blown and it just wished for that summer to never end."

"It's genies that give wishes, not magicians. And you'd have three, so you'd have been able to cover all that."

"You know I'm really bad at fairy tales. I never—" She cut off when she saw him. He was still watching the road, but his eyes were wet with tears. "Eric?"

He swiped at his eyes with the back of his hand. Was he about to cry? Eric never cried. "It's a good dream," he said, the words forced. He took a deep breath before adding, "It's too bad it was just that."

"Are you okay?"

He didn't respond. He just tapped on the steering wheel and kept his eyes forward, away from her. He was quiet for a long while. The only sound around them was the swishing of the highway and Eric's tapping.

Emilia just watched him as she waited for him to speak. When it was clear he had no intention of doing so, she said, "Eric, tell me what's wrong."

He shook his head and sighed. "I used to think if you worked hard enough and were patient, you could get what you want—accomplish your dreams. You know, the real ones that don't involve Peter Pan and genies."

"You don't think that anymore?"

"I don't know. It seems like it works for everyone except me."

"Why do you say that?"

She played through the day in her mind. She'd woken up in the cabin at Camp Ouray with Eric sleeping in the next bed. They'd had breakfast with Owen and Pam, relived some of their favorite moments from camp, then headed back home.

While driving, she'd asked about her parents, then his dad and sisters. She supposed that was depressing, since his family had all moved away, and he barely saw them anymore, but he hadn't seemed overly sad at the time. He'd even said nice things about his dad, explaining how he'd managed to make an unselfish decision for once.

Over a year ago, when Eric said he wanted to move into their family's old house, his dad had kicked out the current tenants, written the house over to Eric, and even paid it off so Eric wouldn't have to worry about a mortgage. No, Eric wasn't upset about any of that. This was something else.

"Eric?" she pressed.

"Tell me at least one will work out. That at least one of the hopes I have for my life will come to fruition. Do I get that, Emilia?" He turned to look at her, his blue eyes intense. "Tell me I get that."

Her heart was skipping against her chest. It felt like it was trying to tell her something, tapping out a code, just as Eric had been tapping the steering wheel. But she didn't know morse code, or whatever language her heart and Eric were trying to speak.

He looked back at the road. "Or maybe I was some terrible dictator in my last life and this is my punishment—getting really, really close to the things I want, then losing them."

"You'll get them," she said quickly, putting as much confidence in her tone as she could draw up. "One thousand percent, Eric. I know it."

He looked at her again, holding her gaze for several tense seconds before turning back to the road.

"Do you want to talk about it?" she asked tentatively.

"No."

She ran through her limited memories again, but there was nothing. Dammit. She wanted to scream in frustration. She had always been the best at cheering him up when he got down like this but now, she was at a complete loss.

"I want to help you, but I don't know how," she admitted.

Eric bit his lip, then reached over and took her hand. "Just be here."

She turned her palm up and wove their fingers together. "Done."

Part 6: August Pearson

He is still as loyal a friend to both you and Eric as ever.

* 22 *

"Emilia."

Emilia's eyes shot open. August was crouched on the side of her bed. She sat up quickly and looked around the room. Where was she? She spotted Eric leaning against the doorframe. When he saw her looking at him, he gave her a small wave.

"Eric?" She shook her head and looked at him again. He looked a lot different than the last time she'd seen him. She focused back on August, who was smiling at her. He looked different too.

August cocked his head back toward Eric. "Ignore him. He's just being his usual overbearing self. That's a new thing these days. Eric has taken over your role as mother hen."

Eric rolled his eyes as August climbed into the bed next to Emilia, stretching his legs out in front of him. "You can go, mother hen," August teased. "I've got this. I've done this a ton of times."

Eric crossed his arms. "I'm not sure why you're doing it at all."

"I told you, I prefer going through it all in person."

"So do I," Eric replied, "but she mentioned several months ago she preferred starting the day alone, and we really should respect her—"

"Stop!" Emilia cut in. "One of you needs to tell me what's going on. Because I have no idea what I'm doing here, and it seems like I live here now—wherever this is—and you two look older than I remember, and I need answers, not you two talking over me like I'm a child who can't understand you."

Both boys looked ashamed. "Sorry," Eric muttered.

"Yeah, sorry." August wrapped an arm around Emilia and pulled her into his side. "I'll tell you everything, then we'll go downstairs and get breakfast. Maybe, if you ask Eric nicely, he'll make pancakes."

"Fine," Eric sighed. He walked into the room and crouched next to the side of the bed where Emilia was sitting. He placed a hand on her shoulder and fixed her with a weighty stare. "Emilia, you're safe and healthy, your life is incredible, varied, and fulfilling, and I love you—we all do. I'll see you downstairs."

Emilia reached out and touched his cheek. Real. How strange. She didn't know which was more out of place on his face, the facial hair or the stern expression. August was joking and carefree while Eric looked upset. What was going on?

Eric stood up and sighed, then left the room, closing the door behind him. She looked back at August. "What's wrong with Eric?"

"He's just jealous he's not the one sitting here right now." August tightened his grip on her.

Emilia bit her lip as she considered this explanation. No. There was something else. She looked over at August. "Eric seems to have taken my job as mother hen *and* the serious one in whatever strange world this is. Now tell me, how did we get here and when do we get to go home?"

August let out a laugh. "Take two deep breaths and I'll tell you."

* * *

Emilia's tears splashed onto August's shirt while he explained about her accident. After he was done, he spent a long time rubbing circles into her back and assuring her everything would be okay, until her tears were spent. Once she sat up, he pointed out the notes on her desk. She went to review the items there, which included a large calendar and a letter she'd written about a challenge for the month of February.

Her eye was caught by a note she'd pinned up. She read it aloud, *"No matter what happens, I'm going to keep living with Eric. I made a promise to him, and I don't intend to break it."* She turned to August. "What's that about?"

"It sounds like you made a promise to Eric that you wouldn't move out. I don't know," he shrugged. But there was something forced about the casualness of the gesture. "See that stack of papers? Grab that and bring it over here."

Emilia did as he said but not before filing his weirdness about the note away for later. She read through the summaries quickly, skipping over August's so she could review that one last.

"Read mine out loud," he instructed. He was lying back on her pillow with his hands behind his head, looking up at the ceiling.

"Okay." She began to read. *"You and August are no longer together. You broke up shortly after your accident."*

Emilia looked up from the page. "Why?" She immediately regretted the question. It was obvious why. Her brain damage.

"I didn't break up with you because of your accident, if that's what you're thinking. You broke up with *me* because of your accident."

"I did?"

"Yeah," he sighed. "You had this whole list of reasons—said it wasn't fair for me. You were wrong, by the way. But I was having a hard time back then, trying to survive my clerkship while struggling with what had happened to you. I was relieved, honestly, but I should have fought you on it."

August sat up and grabbed her hand. "I'm sorry about that. About not fighting—not trying to convince you that you *can* have a boyfriend in the middle of this. That you get a good life, too. That this injury doesn't suddenly make you unworthy of that."

Emilia looked down. A knot had appeared in her chest, and she felt like she was going to cry. "It's okay," she whispered.

August nodded out of her periphery. "I think it worked out, though. I don't think we were the right people for each other. We're better as friends."

Emilia let the idea settle for a moment. August was her first real boyfriend, the first guy she'd ever loved. He wasn't hers anymore. It seemed … okay. She'd known they weren't in it for the long-haul. They were so fundamentally different. But they'd had fun together while it lasted. At least she remembered that.

"You okay?"

Emilia nodded as she looked up at him. She wasn't going to sit here and mourn him. He was still here, and besides, that was years ago. She was sure she had shed plenty of tears for him already. Enough was enough. She grasped his hand. "I'm good. I'm going to keep reading."

Emilia turned back to the page and started at the beginning. *"You and August are no longer together. You broke up shortly after your accident. He has dated a number of women since and is currently in between girlfriends."* She looked up at him and cocked an eyebrow in question.

"A number of women," he murmured. "What does that even mean? That could be any number from 2 to 200."

"Which is closer?"

He just smirked back at her, causing her to roll her eyes. She was happy to note that she wasn't feeling any jealousy as she thought of August with "a number of women." She continued reading.

"*August is officially a doctor! He's doing his surgical residency in Boise (of course he chose somewhere where he could still ski) but he says it will be awhile before he's a real surgeon and that he sometimes wishes he'd picked an easier specialty.*" Emilia looked up again. "Impressive. Congratulations, Dr. Pearson."

"Thanks. But you can change that note about my specialty—I actually like it. I just like to complain, you know me." He paused to wink, then sat back on his hands. "Besides, I don't know what else I'd do. I'm not fun enough for Peds, I could never keep up with the ER doctors, Anesthesiologists are boring, and Psychiatrists are, ironically, crazy.

"Nah. I'll take surgery. I know everyone says we're rude and arrogant, but it requires all this skill. You have to be so delicate and precise. You need to plan, then respond appropriately when nothing goes to plan. I like it, and I'm not bad at it. It's cool, being able to do something so few people can."

Emilia nudged him with her foot. "They weren't kidding when they said surgeons were arrogant."

He laughed. "No, that stereotype is true."

"I'm glad you're happy, August. You look happy."

"I am. Now we just need to get you there."

She perked up at that. "I'm not happy?"

"No, you are. I just meant—shit, this is why Eric doesn't want me doing this." He leaned forward and took her face in his hand. "Please don't dwell on this all day. You're happy, Em. Eric was right before. Your life is full and great and varied and… I forgot the rest of it. But you get the gist. I just want you to be *more* happy, that's all."

"How?"

August shook his head. "Don't worry about it. Let's just keep reading."

When it was clear he wasn't going to say more, she dropped her eyes and continued reading the page. *"August lives in a nice apartment in downtown Boise with another surgical resident named Jones. He still skis a ton, is still way too good at chess, still has an insatiable appetite, and is still as loyal of a friend to both you and Eric as ever. He also blames himself for falling asleep the night of your accident, and you try your best to reassure him every time you see him that it wasn't his fault."*

"August." Emilia placed a hand on his leg as she set the paper aside. He was looking down, all the laughter from before absent from his expression.

"I didn't know you had that in your summary," he said roughly. "I guess that explains why you're always telling me it wasn't my fault."

"It wasn't," she insisted. "Believe me, that memory is fresher in my mind. I shouldn't have kept driving. You pushed me to stop but I wasn't hearing it. That accident was *my* fault, not yours."

August placed his hand on hers and looked up at her. "Yeah. Okay."

Her eyes dropped to his summary. "What about the rest of it? All true?"

"Yep. I do live in Boise, my roommate is Paul Jones, a weird dude, I do still ski, probably more than I should, I am still a very good friend, and I am also hungry all the time."

They both shared a smile, then August climbed out of the bed and set the stack of summaries back on her desk. "Speaking of hunger, let's go see if Eric made any breakfast or is just sulking."

"What's he upset about?"

"He's fine. He's just—how do I put this? He's a fierce

protector of your wishes and free will and insists we follow the instructions your past self has set, even if they don't make sense. He doesn't want you to feel like you're not in control of your life."

Emilia nodded, eyes focused on the desk. It would be easy for anyone to come along and change her notes, which would effectively change her entire understanding of her life. Her worry must have shown on her face because August grabbed her shoulders and said reassuringly, "I know this no memory thing makes you vulnerable, a feeling you hate, but believe me, with Eric looking out for you, you can be sure no one is going to take advantage of the situation."

"But I still don't understand. Why is he upset?"

"Oh. You told him a while back you want to wake up and read through all this alone. I'm guessing because you didn't want to feel like you were putting any sort of burden on the rest of us—which you never were. But I insisted on doing it in person today, since it always puts you in a better mood, and today is special."

"It is? Why?" She hadn't seen anything on the calendar. Then again, the calendar was alarmingly blank. It seemed to be part of the challenge she'd set for herself this month.

"Come on. I'll tell you over breakfast."

When Emilia arrived in the kitchen, Eric pulled her into a strong embrace. She wrapped her arms around him as she breathed in his scent. It was ... familiar. How comforting. Eric leaned back, but she didn't release her grip on him. He tilted her chin up and studied her face. "You look good. Do you feel good?"

Emilia nodded and finally pulled her arms back. They stared at each other for several seconds, then Eric dropped his hand from her chin. She rested her forehead against his chest, not yet ready to move away. Eric felt like an anchor. She hadn't realized she'd been drifting until she hugged him and suddenly felt secure—a feeling she didn't want to let slip away.

It was Eric who stepped back first, saying something about flipping the pancakes. But he seemed to sense that she wasn't ready to let go of him and pulled her to the stove by the hand. He flipped the pancakes with one hand as his other held hers.

Emilia glanced over at August. She expected to see him looking disapproving, or even jealous, but he just watched them, looking like he was cataloging their closeness for later use. "Do you want coffee?" Eric asked.

She nodded, and he pulled his hand out of hers and poured her coffee, then gave her a warm mug. She stayed at his side, sipping on the mug as he finished cooking the pancakes. Their bodies were much closer than was probably normal, though he didn't seem to mind. He seemed okay with the fact that she apparently needed to constantly be touching him.

Was it like this all the time? Maybe not. Maybe she was just uneasy in the mornings. August had said something like that. But why hadn't she been obsessed with being close to August? She decided not to overthink it and just enjoy the feeling of Eric's warmth.

When they were at the table later eating pancakes, August turned to Emilia and asked, "Are you ready to hear what we're doing today?"

She nodded as she finished chewing her current bite. "Skiing."

Emilia scowled and turned to Eric, who nodded in confirmation. "We're skiing? But I don't know how."

"I taught you how. I know that's in my summary," Eric said.

"I thought it was a joke," she grumbled.

"You're not so bad, Em," August said. "Plus, that's only half the surprise."

"What's the other half?" Emilia looked over at Eric, who just shrugged.

"I don't know the other half. August planned that one on his own. Though it seems like everyone knows what it is except me."

"And me," Emilia chimed in. "I know nothing."

Eric gave her a warm smile. "I like when you joke this early in the morning."

"I wonder if it's because she had one of her best friends waking her up," August said thoughtfully.

Eric gave him a dark look, and Emilia could tell by August's wince that Eric had kicked him under the table.

* * *

Emilia had been holding out hope that the surprise would be that the whole ski trip thing was a joke, but no such luck. The real surprise was that August had secured a condo for them at one of the nearby swanky ski towns, thanks to one of the attendings at his hospital.

And now she was at the top of the mountain, staring down at the snowy slope with two planks of wood strapped to her feet. She was going to die. Or at least get seriously injured. Maybe she'd hit her head and get her memory back. When she told that joke to the boys on the lift, August patted her head and told her they'd heard that one before, which hadn't done much to improve her mood. How did her friends stand her?

"Emilia." Eric's voice cut into her thoughts. "You can stare the mountain down all you want, but the only way to get down is to just … go. You can do this. I promise you can. You'll see when you get going."

"I don't want to get going. I hate this. I could barely make it from the lift to here. I don't know why I let you drag me up here. I wish I were back at the condo, curled up with a book while you two risk breaking your necks without me. This is a stupid sport, by the way, and what happened to you being a fierce protector of my free will?"

"What?"

"August said that this morning. He said—"

"Emilia." Eric passed his poles to August, then grabbed her hands. "Come on. The more you stand up here thinking about it, the worse it's going to get."

He tugged her forward and because she was standing on two useless sticks and unable to dig her heels in, she began to slide downhill. "Eric! Wait! Are you going to give me tips or—or anything? Or some of those poles so I can stop myself?"

"The poles would just distract you and if you used them to try to stop, you'd probably hurt yourself. You don't need any tips, they'll just clutter your brain. Trust yourself. You know how to do this."

"I don't," she whined. He continued to pull her forward. "Eric, wait! Can we—?"

"Shh. Look at me. Just keep your eyes on me and try to clear your mind."

"But I'm going to fall."

He shrugged. "So? Snow is soft. Come on." He pulled harder, and they began sliding in earnest. Her heart jolted and started beating hard in protest. Eric squeezed her hands. "Just look at me, okay? Focus on me and trust your body. It knows what it's doing."

Emilia thought Eric was insane, but she was at his mercy. She was going forward now, with no idea how to stop, and could feel the panic rising in her chest. She tried to focus on Eric, counting all the different colors of blue in his eyes, brighter than usual in the brilliant sun. Holy shit, they were going to hit the trees! They were going straight for the trees! Shit, shit, shit!

Eric began to turn and pulled her along. Then, miraculously, she turned with him. Oh God. She was doing it! She was turning! They were skiing in the other direction now, cutting a horizontal path across the run, while Eric continued to pull her along. She tried to focus on him and not her skis, worried if she began overthinking things, she'd go tumbling to the ground.

"So you—you can ski backwards?"

He grinned. "Skiing backwards isn't that hard. It's holding my legs wide while doing it that's tricky. I fell so many times the first time we skied together. You loved it, said it was karma for forcing you on the mountain."

"Sounds about right," she quipped as they reached the next turn. Again, her body took over. Eric was right, this wasn't bad. It was pretty much just bending her knees, then shifting weight from one foot to the next at each turn. He let go of her hands and turned around, but stayed close to her, keeping a hand on her arm as they turned two more times.

"So this is skiing? Just turning back and forth?"

"More or less. When you get more of a feel for it, you can try to go faster, but you don't have to. Just enjoy the view, the nice day, and the pride of having learned something new."

She turned to smile at him, then something happened to her ski and it whipped out from under her. She fell, grabbing Eric's arm at the last moment and taking him down with her. "AH! Shit! What was that?!"

Eric was sitting next to her and rubbing his hip. His skis were still attached to his boots, but one of hers had slid a few feet away from her. He crawled over and grabbed it. "I think you caught an edge."

"What does that mean?"

"You probably hit a patch of ice. It's fine. Happens to me sometimes, too."

"A patch of ice?" She turned, looking for the obstruction. "What is ice doing here? It's just supposed to be snow, which is not soft, by the way. You said snow was soft."

"It is when it's powder, but not this snow." He was up and offering his hand.

"Liar," she grumbled as she let him pull her up.

"You're fine. Here." He bent down and placed her unattached ski next to her boot, then stood and told her how to push the boot back in. There was a satisfying click, then they were just standing there, him with his hands on her hips while she held onto his shoulders.

"I can't believe I skied," she whispered. "Me—the least athletic person in existence. I can barely run. Or have you gotten me into running, too?"

Eric pushed her hair out of her face. "No running. But we hike. And snowshoe. You're also pretty good at cross-country skiing. You're more athletic than you think."

"I—what? No."

"Yes."

Her body was still buzzing from the thrill of skiing on her own. That feeling of tapping into some type of latent memory was intoxicating. And if it had been up to her, she'd be back at the condo, missing it.

"Thank you, Eric," she said, putting as much feeling into the words as she could.

"Not a problem." He dropped his hand, which had been absently stroking the side of her face, and continued to fix her with an arresting gaze.

She leaned in without thinking, on her way to kiss him, but at the last moment, he turned his head and gave her a quick peck on the cheek. Emilia leaned back, embarrassed. "Sorry, I don't—"

"It's fine," he said with a kind smile. "Let's keep going."

He continued down the run as Emilia just stood there, trying to comprehend what had just happened. August arrived at her side the next moment, spraying her with snow as he stopped.

"Hey!" she cried, wiping the snow off her clothes.

August shrugged. "It's just snow. You did great, but why did you fall?"

"Eric said I caught an edge, whatever that means."

August nodded knowingly. "Pretty cool, right? Just because you don't remember everything doesn't mean you don't remember anything."

"Yeah," Emilia said absently. She was watching Eric, who had stopped twenty feet down and was waving them over. She'd almost kissed him. Why? It had seemed like the most natural thing to do at the moment, just like turning on her skis. Was this something else her body was remembering from her forgotten past? Her eyes darted to August. "Um, Eric and I ... is there, uh, something there?"

"I don't know. Is there?"

"I'm asking you."

"How would I know? Ask him. Or better yet, ask yourself. We just proved you don't forget everything." August winked, then turned and raced toward Eric. "Come on!" he called over his shoulder.

"Are you okay?" Eric called up the hill. "Do you want me to come back up there?"

Emilia took a deep breath, then shook her head. "No!" she yelled back. "I've got this!" She pointed her skis downhill, toward Eric, and let her body take over.

* 23 *

The next morning, Emilia and August were sitting on the porch of the condo, wrapped in a large blanket. They sipped on oversized mugs of hot coffee, watching the mountains in front of them grow brighter as the sun rose.

August had woken her up this morning and led her outside, then explained to her where they were, and why, and also why she had no memories of the past two years. After that, he'd handed her a stack of papers and instructed her to read the summaries she'd written about all her friends.

They'd been sitting in silence for several moments as Emilia let the thoughts sink in. She had one hand wrapped around her warm mug and the other one linked with August's, while they huddled next to each other for warmth under the blanket.

She felt August squeeze her hand and turned to find him looking uncharacteristically morose. "Don't tell me there's more," she whispered, wondering how much worse it could get.

He gave her a sad smile, then wrapped his arm around her. He motioned down toward the pile of papers on her lap. "I should tell you, that summary there, it's incomplete."

Emilia looked down at the page with details about Eric. "What? What's missing?"

He sighed and bent to place his mug on the ground, then resumed his spot at her side. "You and Eric are in love with each other."

That was not what she'd been expecting him to say. She'd just made peace with the fact that she wasn't with August anymore, and now he was saying she was with *Eric?!* Wow, she really got around. She looked down at the paper, which had betrayed her. That giant piece of information should have been listed there.

"Are you sure?" she asked, pulling out of August's arms and turning to face him. "Maybe you're wrong." It wouldn't be the first time someone had misconstrued Eric and Emilia's close friendship for something romantic.

"Emilia, it's real. You've slept together. Like, more than once."

"What?!" Emilia put the stack of papers and her mug down. She pulled her knees up to her chest and wrapped her arms around them as August tucked the blanket back around her. She couldn't decide which was weirder: hearing that she'd had sex with someone but forgotten about it, finding out it had been with Eric, or having August be the one to tell her.

"I don't, that's, uh, wait. Did *we* ever…?"

August shook his head.

She sighed and dropped her forehead against her knees. This was a lot to take in. She was in love with Eric. He was in love with her. She'd had sex with Eric, apparently "more than once." But she hadn't put it in her summary about him. And August had told her early in the morning, outside, while Eric was still sleeping, acting like it was some big secret.

August placed a hand on her arm. "I know it's hard to imagine out here alone with me. But believe me, the second you see him, you'll feel it. And, um, there's more."

"Okay," she mumbled into her knees. "What is it?"

"It's a really toxic relationship. You have this—back and forth and it's—well, honestly, it's tearing Eric apart."

She snapped her head up. "What?"

He squeezed her arm gently. "Emilia, you're hurting him. You love him and he loves you, that's clear, but you're stuck in this terrible cycle of self-sacrifice that you two can't seem to break out of. You keep stepping away, convinced he deserves better than you and the life you can give him, and he keeps letting you, obsessed with putting your desires ahead of his own."

His eyes were wet, and Emilia's own eyes filled with tears at the sight of them. He was obviously speaking from a place of pain. Had she really been hurting Eric? It must be true. August wouldn't lie about that.

She thought about what he'd said, about her stepping away, convinced Eric couldn't be happy with her. That made sense. Who wanted to be with someone who forgot their life every day? Someone who didn't even remember their first time together. Someone who had to be retaught their history every twenty-four hours. How exhausting.

Surely Eric could see the reasoning there. Even if he'd developed some feelings towards her, he couldn't possibly want that life for himself. Could he? Emilia dropped her head again.

"I think you're trying to do what's best for him," August continued, "but it's not working. It's getting harder and harder for you to deny your feelings for him. Just yesterday, you figured it out before lunch."

"What happens when I figure it out?" she said into her knees.

"It's different every time. Sometimes you just puzzle over it for the rest of the day and try to convince yourself it's nothing—that's what happened yesterday. Sometimes you two redeclare your love for each other and sleep together, and I'm sure there are a lot of variations in between. But each time, without fail, you let yourself forget. And it breaks him every time."

"Why are you telling me this?" she asked, looking up at him as tears rolled down her face. "What do you want me to do?"

"I need you to fix it, Em," he pleaded. "Just—I don't know—be with him. I know you think it's going to be awful for him to deal with your condition but believe me, dealing with this rejection is a million times worse."

She had no idea what to say. This was a lot of information to take in at once, made more confusing by the torrent of emotions swirling around as she tried to come to terms with her accident. She didn't even know what Eric looked like these days. Had he changed? She was picturing him from the last memory she had of him, when they'd fought about Henry and she'd said a lot of things she wished she could take back.

"So you don't care that I like Eric?" Emilia asked August after a while.

He let out a small laugh. "No, Em. You and Eric are perfect together. There's no use denying that. June doesn't care either, for the record. We're actually two of your biggest fans."

"Yeah?"

"Yeah. We got Eric to agree to date other women to try to force you two together faster."

"That makes no sense."

"I know, except it sort of works. He only agreed because June threatened to start pressing you about this whole thing, and he was trying to protect you. But June and I never really wanted him to find someone else and move on—I think that's impossible, at this point. It was just meant to shock the system—you know?"

"No. I don't."

"Owen and Viola are convinced that if we leave you alone, you'll figure it out. But June and I know you two better than that. You're both too self-sacrificing and if left alone, I don't think you'll ever resolve this. So, June had this idea that if we could throw you off balance, force you two to face this—maybe, I don't know, maybe get you to confront it instead of hiding from it."

"That sounds incredibly manipulative."

He shrugged. "Yeah. Maybe, but we mean well. And there's something different about this month. Maybe the dates and June's little disturbances, like proposing you move in with her, are finally working. Maybe it's your sister's challenge, or maybe time has finally caught up with both of you. But you're closer somehow… but still too far apart," he added after a pause.

Emilia tried to sort through everything he'd told her, but she was more confused now than she'd been at the start of the conversation. "You don't usually tell me this, do you?" She looked up at him for confirmation.

"Correct."

"But you told me now, first thing in the morning, so I could spend the day fixing it?"

He nodded and squeezed her hand. "It's not very complicated, Em. Just give this thing with Eric a shot. Stop quitting before you even start. Turn this off—" he pulled his hand out of hers and tapped her head, "—and try to stop sorting through all the implications. Stop worrying about what's best for Eric and just follow this." He moved his hand down to her heart.

They watched each other for a few moments, their breath visible in the frigid air. August leaned forward and picked up their mugs, then handed Emilia hers before draping his arm around her again.

Emilia looked out at the sky as tears stung her eyes. "I don't know what to do, August."

"You don't need to solve it now. You have all day. Let's just finish our coffee."

"Okay."

* * *

An hour later, Emilia was sitting in the same spot, wrapped in a blanket, and listening to the boys yelling at each other inside.

Eric knew within two minutes of seeing her that something was wrong. Maybe it was because she tensed when he hugged her. He grabbed her chin and studied her face, then looked over her shoulder at August and growled, "You told her."

August shrugged, then Eric had crossed the room and punched him. Emilia, at a complete loss for what to do, had retreated and left them alone to sort it out, figuring she'd just make everything worse by being there.

She knew she should probably close the door all the way and give them privacy, but she was too curious to find out why Eric was so upset. Why didn't he want Emilia to know about his feelings for her? Maybe they weren't real. Maybe August had made it all up. But why would he do that? She had no idea what to believe any more.

First, there was some back and forth as the boys argued about what was best for Emilia. Both boys made good points and she honestly had no idea whose side she was on.

"You cannot do that to her! You cannot take away her free will! She trusts us," Eric was saying again.

But Emilia wasn't so sure that by telling her this truth, August had been stealing her free will. It was just that—a truth. And apparently, everyone around them knew, including her sister, June, and even Owen, so why shouldn't she know? It was the same as hiding from her that the sky was blue—which was a point August had made previously.

"I can't stand here and watch this anymore!" August shouted back. "You gave up everything for her, then just gave up! Why?! You fight for everyone around you, Eric, but never yourself! Fight for this! Fight for her! Every. Fucking. Day. Tell her how you feel until she finally changes her mind."

"It's not that simple. You don't—"

"It is! You're making it overly complicated because I think deep down, you don't think you deserve this. You had a messed-up childhood and somewhere along the way you convinced yourself that you don't get a happy ending. But you do! You do, Eric."

Emilia teared up at that. That was heartbreaking, and she desperately hoped it wasn't true. But she could see Eric believing that. She hated that she wasn't in a position to assess the situation for herself.

"It doesn't matter what I want," Eric bit back. "This is about her, and she clearly doesn't want to pursue this. She's had over twenty chances to pick me and has chosen to forget every time." His voice broke at the end, and a few tears fell from Emilia's eyes. She'd rejected him over twenty times? Oh, Eric.

"But out of all those times, how many times has she had all the facts?" August countered. "And the feelings are there! They're not going away. They're just getting stronger. I know you see that."

Eric mumbled something Emilia couldn't make out. She craned her neck so she could hear better.

"I know," August replied in a low voice. "You're looking out for her, which is fine, but who's looking out for you? I know she thinks she is, but she's doing a shitty job. This morning—telling her—I did that for you, not her."

Eric mumbled something and August said something back that Emilia didn't catch. Then, louder, he said, "Okay. I'll go."

A few minutes later, August walked onto the porch holding a half-open duffle bag in one hand and a bloody wad of paper towels up to his face with the other.

When he spotted Emilia, he pulled the paper towels away and gave her an apologetic smile. "I'm so sorry, August. I know this is all about me. Can I help with this? I mean, you're way better qualified than I am to do anything but I—I feel awful."

"Don't. I'll be fine. It just looks bad because of the blood. He didn't hit me that hard." It seemed like he'd hit August pretty hard from where she was standing, but she let it go. There wasn't anything she could do about it, besides make sure August's efforts weren't in vain.

They stood across from each other, each unsure what to say. Eventually, August leaned forward and kissed her cheek. "I'm really sorry, Em. We all want the same thing here—you, me, Eric, all of our friends. We want you two to figure out how to be happy together. We just have differing opinions on how to get there."

"I understand. Thank you for telling me."

"Okay. I'm going to go." August gave her shoulder a comforting squeeze. "Have a good day."

Once August was gone, Emilia returned to her spot on the bench, pulling the blanket around her again. A few minutes later, Eric appeared and handed her a plate of eggs and toast, which she wasn't hungry for, but took anyway.

He sat next to her, and she wordlessly opened the blanket for him. He took the offered end of the blanket without hesitation and leaned against her side. "You heard all of that?"

"Yeah."

They sat in silence while Emilia took a few bites of toast, mostly because it was there and she had nothing else to do. She tried to access these supposed feelings for Eric as she chewed. She wanted to look over at him but thought that would be too awkward so instead, she focused on the warm feeling of his arm resting against hers.

It was nice, and solid, and while she didn't get much clarity from thinking about his arm, it was better than the other thoughts swirling around in her brain. Once the toast was gone, Eric turned to look at her. She kept her eyes forward.

"Can you forget it? Well ... before tonight?"

"Okay."

"Let's just have a good day."

Emilia turned her head toward him. When their eyes met, she knew. The Eric from before her accident had never looked at her like this, with such raw emotion. He liked her. *Loved* her, she corrected.

And she loved him. The fluttering of her heart was proof enough of that. All caused by something as simple as eye contact and a brush of the arm. This wasn't just an idea August had planted in her head, either. She felt it deep in her gut. But she tried to ignore it, since that's what Eric seemed to want. "Yeah. Let's have a good day."

* 24 *

Later that night, Eric and Emilia were sitting on the sofa in the condo, watching the fire flicker in the hearth. Emilia took a sip from the mug in her hand as Eric watched her expectantly. "Well?" he asked.

"Good," she said, coughing slightly as the bourbon in the hot chocolate hit the back of her throat.

Earlier, after dinner, she'd been complaining that she was still cold. Even wrapped in blankets on the couch, she claimed she could feel a chill deep in her bones. Eric had frowned at her, then tossed her a coat and announced they were going outside.

That seemed counter-intuitive, but she followed him anyway. He explained as they walked that what she needed was a warm drink. She asked if he was going to make spiked hot chocolate, remembering him doing so a few times back in college.

He shook his head and explained how alcohol only gave you a false sense of warmth when really, it caused people to radiate heat faster, and said that he'd been planning to pick up a pack of tea. She lobbied for the spiked hot chocolate, they had a staring contest over it, and she won, though she suspected he'd let her win.

"I feel so much warmer," she sighed.

"I know you *feel* warmer, but you're not."

"All I wanted was to feel warmer," she argued.

He stuck his tongue out at her and took a big gulp from his mug. They were quiet for the next few minutes as the hot chocolate and bourbon continued to warm her insides (while also causing her to rapidly lose body heat, but she didn't care).

"The lady at the liquor store," Eric said, cutting into Emilia's thoughts. "She looked like the Pearsons, don't you think?"

Emilia nodded as she conjured up the image of the woman who had checked them out. Blonde hair, angular features, light blue eyes. "Yeah," she agreed. "She could be a Pearson."

"Did you see her nametag?"

Emilia shook her head.

"May."

She laughed. "Named after a month. Well now she *has* to be a Pearson. God, I hope she's some long-lost sibling. We should go back tomorrow and take a picture of her. We should—"

Emilia cut off. She wouldn't remember this tomorrow. She kept doing this, committing to future plans, then remembering that tomorrow, everything would start fresh. Damn, she wanted to cry. She took another drink instead.

"I can remind you," Eric said softly. He knew exactly what she was thinking. Of course he did. He had spent the entire day catering to her every wish, but not in a creepy way. Just an, "I love you and am happier when you're happy" way.

"Okay." They both turned back to the fire. This time, Emilia broke the silence. "It really is too bad that they broke the 'naming kids after months' tradition with the twins. If you're going to have a theme, you need to stick with it. My parents had one, but I guess they didn't have to keep it going for five kids."

"They had a theme? What was it?"

"Shakespeare. I was named after Emilia from *Othello* and Viola is from *Twelfth Night*."

Tears stung her eyes as she thought of her parents. How they'd ended up getting divorced, and she didn't even remember it. According to her summary, they were barely in her life because they found it too difficult to be around her.

Eric tucked her into a space at his side that seemed like it was made for her as the tears she'd been blinking back finally fell. He set his mug on the table, then hers, and she buried her head in his chest.

"I know you don't like talking about them, but they're fine. Viola says they're a lot happier than they were before. They're okay, really."

Emilia nodded and wrapped an arm around his torso. It was like a treat, getting to be so close to him. Eric had kept his distance from her all day but the few times they'd touched, she'd felt immediately at ease.

"I didn't know that about you," he continued, "about who you were named after. Now I have to read *Othello*." He was combing his fingers through her hair. "I don't know who I was named after. I just assumed my parents liked how the name sounded."

"Eric Shaffer," Emilia said slowly. "It does sound very nice."

"Smart ass."

Eric smiled down at her just as she tilted her head up to look at him. Her heart fluttered. It had been doing that all day. Then, before she could talk herself out of it, she placed a soft kiss on his lips. "I think we need to talk about it now," she whispered as she pulled away.

Eric stroked her cheek and nodded, then pulled her back in for another, longer kiss. It was tender, and slow, and … everything. Emilia's heart felt like it was going to burst. Why hadn't they been doing this all day?

Instead, they'd been doing an excellent job of avoiding the topic August had tried to force them to confront. They had a long breakfast on the porch, watching the sun rise over the mountain as she asked him benign questions about their friends. They skied, had lunch at the lodge, skied some more, then came back to get showered and changed before dinner.

August had booked a reservation at the restaurant on the roof of the building, which they realized when they got there was just for two people. "That asshole planned to leave the whole time," Eric murmured to himself, then went back to pretending August didn't exist.

They continued to avoid the topic as they ate and enjoyed a gorgeous view of the sun setting on the horizon, coloring the mountains in swaths of orange and purple. But the truth they were avoiding clouded the air between them.

Emilia had been trying to figure out how she was supposed to "fix it," as August had said, but she was at a complete loss, mostly because she didn't know exactly what was going on. All she knew was that sitting here, with her body slotted with Eric's, felt perfect.

Eric spoke before she came up with anything to say. "What questions do you have?"

She took a deep breath, then said in a rush, "First, before any questions, I want to tell you that I love you. I'm not sure of much, but I'm sure of that. I—I always loved you, even before, I don't know if you know that. There was already a space in my heart for those deep feelings for you and today—when I tried to find them again, they were stronger—like, really, really strong. I don't know what the point of all this rambling is just, um," she paused to sigh, then laid her head on his chest again. "I guess I just want you to know how much I love you since I can see how because of my condition, I might not tell you enough."

Eric kissed the top of her head. "Thank you. I love you too. Like, a lot."

Emilia thought she could hear tears in his voice and almost looked up, but held back and kept her eyes on the fire. If she saw him crying, she'd completely lose it, and she wanted to keep her head.

"Okay, uh, questions," she began tentatively.

"Yeah."

"We love each other, we've established that, but we've never tried to pursue a relationship?"

"No. I wanted to," he said. "I still do. But you, uh, don't."

Emilia's chest clenched. August had told her this but hearing it from Eric finally made it feel real. It was her fault they weren't together. She was the one causing the pain she could hear in Eric's voice. And she was pretty sure she knew why she kept holding back. The long list of reasons why they couldn't have a proper future together had been running through her mind all day. She wasn't sure if she'd ever told him all her reasons, so asked, "Do you know why?"

Eric was silent for several moments. When he spoke again, his response surprised her. "You think you're the moon and I'm the sun and that because of our circumstances, we'd never be able to make it work, despite how desperately we love each other."

"How poetic."

"Yes. You were inspired by a book of poems. Certainly not by science. The moon and sun see each other all the damn time." His tone had turned quickly from sad to bitter.

She snaked an arm around his middle and held him closer, eager to savor this closeness before he pushed her away. "What happened, Eric? What's our story?" *Where did all this pain come from? What did I do? And most importantly, is it too late to fix it?*

Eric wrapped both of his arms around her and hugged her tightly. "I don't think I've ever told you everything. You've learned bits here and there but … never all of it."

"Will you tell me now?"

"Yeah."

But he didn't say anything. She waited patiently as her head bobbed with the rise and fall of his chest.

"It started two summers ago, when June and I broke up," he began. "She ended it because she was convinced I was in love with you. You were considering moving, but I was desperate for you to stay, so I cut back my hours at the lab and spent most of that summer with you at Ouray. By the end of the summer, I had dropped out of school altogether and asked you to move in with me. June thought all that meant I was in love with you. I didn't agree. I thought she was being immature and jealous but, well, she was right. Though it took me a lot longer to figure it out."

"How much longer?" Emilia asked, tracing patterns on Eric's arm.

"Not until the following winter, when you'd gone home for Christmas for a few days."

"What happened? You missed me?"

"So much it hurt."

She looked up at him and smiled, then kissed the underside of his jaw before returning her head to its spot on his chest.

"Anyway, I realized I'd fallen in love with you, then kind of sat on it for two months until one night, I think it was February by then, I cracked and just blurted it out. It wasn't a special day or anything, we were just watching TV when I turned to you and said, 'I'm in love with you.'"

"What did I say?" she asked, unsure if she wanted to know the response.

"You were quiet, eerily so. You kept your eyes on the screen and I was thinking, 'Damn. Did she hear me? Should I say it again?' But before I could work up the courage to say something else, you turned to me and kissed me. It was … incredible."

"Yeah?"

"Yes. A very good first kiss."

"Did I know it was our first kiss at the time?"

"You didn't know when you leaned in and kissed me, but I told you right after. And that whole night while I was lying in bed, I felt so giddy I could barely sleep. That next morning I woke up at five, eager to see you, and sat in the kitchen bouncing in my chair, waiting for you. And then ... you didn't remember."

"I didn't write it down?"

"No."

"I'm so sorry."

Eric propped his chin on her head and sighed. "Yeah. I was confused, more than anything, and that's when I started to second-guess myself. Not my feelings, I knew those were real, but I started thinking of all these reasons why it wouldn't work."

"Like what?" She wondered how many of his reasons overlapped with hers.

"First, I thought it would be impossible for you to fall in love with me the same way I'd fallen for you: gradually, over the course of several months. I still thought you mostly reset every day, even though your sister was insistent you were remembering things subconsciously. But around that time, Henry started staying over more and I watched you grow more comfortable with him, and saw that you'd come to love him. So, that disproved that theory.

"And then I got this other thought in my head; it came from Claire's wedding. Someone said in a toast that marriage was as simple as choosing to stay with your partner every day. Some days would be harder than others, but you just had to continue to choose them. I dwelled on that idea for weeks, thinking, 'Emilia can't do that. She has these systems setup that she relies on each morning when she's deciding what to do that day, and so much of it depends on her trusting the decisions her past self has made.'

"I thought, 'If Emilia chooses me, she'll just do so once, then continue to go along with it even if her heart isn't in it anymore. She wouldn't be choosing me every day, and how is that fair?'"

"That's a good point," she said as a lump formed in her throat. "I hadn't thought of that."

Eric sighed and shook his head. "Yeah, it was logical, but wrong. Because that whole spring, while I was trying to keep my distance and not blurt out that I loved you, you kept seeking me out. You were choosing me, over and over. Sometimes we kissed and sometimes we just talked and it occurred to me that I had been using that 'choose once' thing as an excuse because I was scared.

"You were a lot more intuitive than I'd originally given you credit for, and I was sure that if one day, you found yourself in a relationship with me and didn't want it, you'd just end it. You obviously didn't have any qualms about rejecting me—since you continued to do it every time you realized how we felt about each other."

"I just kept letting myself forget?"

"Yeah."

"And I never said why?"

Eric sighed. "No."

Emilia could tell this was leading up to something. "But then, something changed?"

"Yeah. Something changed. That was in June, when I'd figured out my reasons for staying away from you were unfounded. That first weekend—I even remember the day, June 21st—I decided to tell you I loved you in the morning so you'd have all day to think about it. I thought the problem before was that you didn't learn about it until later in the day, so you only had a few hours to consider everything before falling asleep."

"Did that work? What happened that day?"

"I made you breakfast, I told you I loved you, then kissed you—because I'd learned by then that your body knew we were in love long before your mind figured it out. You were wary at first, though I could tell you were feeling something, and as the day went on you got a lot more comfortable and—" he paused and gripped her tighter.

"It was a perfect day," he continued. "That night was the first time we slept together. It was wonderful, not awful, even though it was your first time. You always seem to worry about that." He leaned down and kissed the top of her head again. She couldn't help but smile, since she had been wondering that very thing. "Then after, we lay in bed for hours, talking about how we could make a relationship work with the memory loss. Then—" he cut off.

Emilia looked up while Eric kept his face forward. "What happened?" she asked, though she knew. August had told her. She'd left and broken his heart.

"You snuck out of my room when I was asleep," he confirmed. "And the next morning, you'd forgotten everything."

"Oh."

"Yeah. Oh," he sighed.

"That pattern continued for several months. Sometimes I admitted I loved you, sometimes you admitted it. Sometimes I kissed you first, other times it was you who started it. Sometimes we had sex, and every time, you forgot. I started to think that maybe you were putting off your decision until the end of the month. I know it's hard for you to make decisions without all the information, so I came to expect you to forget in the middle of the month, but thought surely once you reached your month-end review, you'd say *something*. Especially when you saw all the times we'd been together in your notes."

"I never came to talk to you during my month-end reviews?"

Eric shook his head. "I waited for you to seek me out. But months went by, and nothing. By January, last month, I was getting restless, and August and June were pushing me to confront you. They said that sitting alone in your room surrounded by papers was one thing, but that if you were forced to face me and talk through everything, you wouldn't be able to be so…so..."

"Cold?" Emilia provided.

"Yeah."

Her heart clenched. "Okay," she said tentatively. "Was January different?"

"Yeah. January was different. You made me a big breakfast for my birthday, then I went skiing to give you time to review your notes alone. When I got back around mid-afternoon, I checked on you. That's when I figured out why you hadn't sought me out during those previous month-end reviews."

"Why?"

"You hadn't written anything down about us. During all those reviews, you had no idea about our history, like I thought."

"So you finally told me everything?"

"Yeah. Most of it."

He was quiet, and Emilia knew whatever he was going to say next was going to be bad.

"I told you about us, even gave you the dates of all the times we'd been together—since I *had* written them down. You cried and apologized, and we talked, then made out, then slept together. After, when you were lying in my arms, you agreed that it was stupid to try to stay away from each other, since it clearly wasn't working, and that we should give it a shot.

"Then I got a call from a few guys at work, reminding me I'd agreed to go out to drinks with them—remember, it was my birthday. I didn't want to leave, but you insisted I go and told me you'd work on changing all your letters and summaries while I was gone, so that the next day, you'd know we were together. So I went."

Emilia waited for him to continue talking, but he stayed quiet. She could feel him taking slow, deep breaths. "What happened?"

"I don't know. Viola stopped by the house. She said later you were spiraling, but she won't give me any details about it. I assume you were talking yourself out of it or realizing you'd made promises to me that didn't match what you truly wanted. I should have been there. I shouldn't have left you alone. Anyway, you—" He paused to take a deep breath.

"You stayed in your room for the rest of the night. Earlier you said you'd come to my room and when you didn't, I went to check on you, but the door was locked. I knocked, and you didn't answer. I thought maybe you'd just decided to take some time to yourself to rewrite everything and left you alone."

"And then I forgot again?"

"You didn't just forget," he said, his voice shaking, "you erased me. You took everything I'd made for you, everything that made you feel better about yourself and your life and locked it away. You decided you'd rather be sad and uncomfortable than see any hint of me in the morning. I'm surprised you didn't throw my summary away too."

His voice broke at the end. Emilia hugged him, at a loss for what else to do. August's voice echoed in her mind. *"It's a really toxic relationship ... It's tearing Eric apart."*

She was about to apologize but she couldn't bring herself to speak. All the words she could think to say felt too hollow.

"Emilia, I need a favor."

"Anything," she said immediately.

"I can't do it anymore, the back and forth. I need you to write down everything I just told you and this weekend, when you do your next month-end review, you need to make a final decision. Choose me, or not, but I can't do the in-between anymore. If you don't choose me, no more kissing, or sex, or declarations of love. Just … friends."

"Okay."

"I can't say no to you. I've tried. I've told myself no more coupley stuff until we're actually, well, a couple. And then you'll kiss me and I … I'm yours. I can't … with you … it's just …" He pushed out a shaky breath. "Please, just don't forget anymore. Not after this month, okay? Every time you do it hurts less. I think it's because you're taking a piece of me each time. And I—I don't have much more to give."

It's tearing Eric apart

Tears streamed down Emilia's face, hot and stinging, making a wet spot on his shirt. She should shift away from him. She didn't deserve his comfort. But she couldn't make herself move. "I understand," she said through her tears as her grip on him tightened. "I promise. I won't forget."

* 25 *

A few hours later, Emilia was standing outside Eric's room, trying to work up the courage to do what she should have done months ago. But in her defense, she didn't have the context she did now. All those other times, she hadn't heard August describe her relationship with Eric as toxic, hadn't seen the tears in Eric's eyes or heard his voice break as he talked about all the times she'd given him hope, then stolen it away and let herself forget him.

After a few more minutes of just standing there, shifting her weight from one leg to the other, she managed to force herself to knock.

"Hi," he said as he opened the door.

She took a deep breath. "I came to say that, um, I wrote it all down, everything you told me. I wrote a letter and sealed it in an envelope and wrote in thick marker, 'Do Not Open Until February 28th.' So when I'm doing my month-end review, I'll read it and, um, I'll know and I'll—I'll decide…"

"Okay. Thank you." His voice was flat, devoid of all emotion, and she thought again of the thing he'd said that had broken her heart the most.

"You can't forget. Every time you do, it hurts less, and I think it's because you're taking a piece of me each time."

Emilia's eyes filled with tears and she dropped her head. *Say it! Tell him what you decided. You owe him that much.*

Eric placed a hand under her chin and pulled her face up. "What's wrong?"

A few tears rolled down her cheeks. She wiped them away quickly and stepped back, out of his grasp. "Eric. Um. I wanted to tell you that I already know what I'm going to decide. I wrote it in the letter. I've been thinking about it since we talked, well, all day, actually and, and—"

She cut off and looked back down at the floor. *Tell him! You're not a coward; you owe him this.* Emilia looked up at him, but couldn't hold his gaze. She closed her eyes and whispered, "I can't do this."

He waited for her to open her eyes before replying. "You can't do *this*? What does that mean?"

"Us."

His gaze hardened and he crossed his arms. "Why not?"

Emilia hesitated. She was struggling to put the hours she'd spent agonizing into words. The reason she couldn't be with Eric felt more like dread, than anything else. A sickening feeling when she pictured him getting upset when she didn't remember, repeating the same words day in and day out, sighing and rolling his eyes as his life became more tedious with each passing day. The jealousy he'd try to hide when August finally finished his training. The look of disappointment when all their friends started having children, and they couldn't.

"It's not because I don't love you, Eric," she said in a soft voice. "I want nothing more than to be with you, but you deserve better than me—than this whole situation. You deserve someone who remembers the first time she kissed you, the first time she made love to you, who remembers enough to know when she's hurting you. That alone—the fact that I was able to hurt you so thoroughly, without even realizing, is reason enough. You deserve—"

"—to have what I want," he finished for her. "Which is you. And that's my decision to make, not yours. Is that why you've been forgetting this whole time?! To protect me?!"

"I—I have no idea. I don't remember anything!" she cried.

She knew she shouldn't shout at him, but he was shouting, and it felt good to release the tension that had been building in her chest.

"Fine. But now, that's your reason? Because you think you know better than me what's best for me? I'm sure you haven't forgotten the promise you had me make that last night at camp."

Her insides went cold. Yes. She had forgotten. Not in the same way she forgot everything else, since it was something that had happened before her accident. But while she'd been thinking of what to do with Eric, she hadn't considered their promise.

"I know you remember," he pressed.

She stayed quiet.

"Are you fucking kidding me?" he asked in a low, cold tone. Emilia remained silent, at a complete loss for words.

"At the beginning of the month you sent me this note that completely gutted me. It said something like: *'The only thing I wanted more than you was your happiness.'* This whole time I've been obsessively defending your right to choose what you wanted for your life, but that note made it seem like you were deciding for me, not you."

He paused and looked at her expectantly, but she stayed quiet. "I let it go," he continued. "August kept pushing, insisting that this was the reason you kept rejecting me, but I argued. I told him you were drunk that night and probably didn't mean it because you, of all people, would never do that to me."

He paused again, obviously waiting for Emilia to speak, but she had no memory of leaving that note. He had to know that.

"I told August how you made me promise you that after camp, which you said officially marked the end of us being young, I'd give up on the hope that everyone around me would figure things out if I only kept trying to pull them together, and bending over backward for them. That I'd start living for myself, and find a way not to feel guilty about it. I'd been struggling all through college—through most of my life—with no clear reason why, but you figured it out. You diagnosed it, you found the solution, and you pushed me to stick to it. Do you remember that?"

"Of course I remember," she whispered.

"And I kept it. I left my sisters alone. I placed boundaries with Sarah when it came to Henry—as much as I could. I focused on school, and it was better. *I* was better, because of you."

She nodded as tears continued to fall down her face.

"Then I told August how we fought over Henry just before your accident, because you thought I was breaking that promise. I told him how you knew better than anyone how important it was for me to live my own life, and that you would *never* take my right to choose what I wanted away from me."

Emilia dropped her head, no longer able to look into his penetrating stare. He was right. How had she missed this?

"You did just that!" he continued. "I've been miserable—we've both been miserable, and it's all because you went and made a decision that wasn't yours to make!"

A sob escaped Emilia's lips as she continued to cry. She dipped her head and saw several tears fall onto the floor. Eric sighed and placed his hands on her shoulders. "Look at me," he said softly.

She took a deep breath and lifted her head. "I don't need you to look out for me, Emilia. I know you did that in the past, but I don't need it anymore. And this memory loss, it's not an issue for me. Yes, you need help every morning and yes, you forget the little details and yes, I spend time repeating things, but it doesn't bother me because I'd rather be with you, than anyone else."

Eric brushed her tears away with the back of his hand. "I want you—no—I *need* you because you are the best thing for me, always have been. I only feel like me when I'm with you and all the rest of it—I really, really, don't care."

The way he was talking about her condition, like it was inconsequential, caused something in Emilia to snap. "Well, good for you, Eric. But I *do* care, okay?!" She pushed his arms away.

"I don't want this! I don't want the guilt! I don't want the not knowing! I don't want to forget! I don't want to do this anymore! I don't want to be like this! We promised each other we'd live our own lives when we grew up but I'm never going to grow up! Sure, my body might, but I'm going to wake up and think it's 1984 for the rest of my life!

"I'm never going to be a lawyer! I was so damn close, just months away, and now it's never going to happen. I'm never going to achieve any of the goals I've been fighting my entire life for! Do you know how hard it is?! To battle every day to sort through references I don't understand and come to terms with this awful diagnosis? It's hard and I'm tired and yeah, I don't even remember it all, but I know I'm tired and it's not fair. I've always done everything right, I tried to be a good person, I worked my ass off, then this happened and it's not fair!"

She broke into sobs. Before she could drop her head into her hands, Eric stepped forward and pulled her into his chest.

"I know," he murmured in her ear. "You don't deserve this, and I know you hate it and I know you're tired, but it's not normally this bad. It's that fucking challenge. You stopped accepting help and you tried to do it all alone, but you don't have to do that. Let me help you. Please."

She had no idea if what he was saying was true. Had it been

better before this month? If that were true, why had she done the challenge in the first place? She was supposed to trust her past self, but the more she learned about that Emilia, the less confident in her she felt. She didn't know what to believe anymore, and she hated it.

"August was right," Eric said after a while. "I haven't fought for you before now. I thought that was the right thing, but it wasn't." He leaned back and lifted her chin. "You can't decide for me, Emilia. If you don't want this because *you* don't want it, then that's one thing—but I won't let you decide for me. I need you to add that to your letter."

Emilia nodded. They stood there watching each other in the doorway to Eric's room for a long while. Long enough for her tears to finally cease their race downward. She knew she should say something, especially after everything Eric had accused her of, but she was completely spent.

She'd taken in so much information today and weathered a whirlwind of emotions. At this point, she had no idea what she was doing for herself or what she was doing for Eric anymore. She was just tired.

She laid her forehead against his sternum and wrapped her arms around him. "You said earlier I told you that you were the sun and I was the moon. I think that's true because I know I need to go now. I need to go back to my room, write this down, and let this day be forgotten. But I can't pull myself away from you. There's a gravitational pull keeping me right here."

He was quiet for a very long time, then ran his fingers through her hair and said softly, "There was no moon tonight. Did you notice? After the sun set, everyone was saying how bright the stars were. That's why."

She tilted her head up and cocked an eyebrow in question.

He grabbed her chin and kissed her. Emilia melted into him, linking her hands behind his neck and entwining her tongue with his. The meaning of his earlier statement became clear when he walked backward into his room, pulling her with him.

Even the sun and the moon, who were destined to spend their whole lives apart, met up on occasion. "I can't stay the night, Eric. I–"

She was cut off by another kiss. She moaned into his mouth, giving over completely to the feeling of his body pressed against hers. How right it felt, like she'd been lost all day and had finally found where she was supposed to be.

Maybe she had been onto something when she said they were the sun and moon, because their collision had caused the world to stop, the whirl of thoughts in her head to pause, and the dread she'd been feeling all night to disappear.

"I can't let you decide without knowing," he murmured against her lips.

"Knowing what?"

"What it's like. What we're like. How it feels when we're together." He kissed under her ear and her body sang with multiple notes of desire.

Eric moved his hands under her shirt and slowly began lifting it up. Before pulling it over her head he asked, "Do you want this?"

"Yes," she breathed.

He tossed her shirt to the side, then pulled off his own shirt in one swift motion. "Okay. Then just be here with me. We can figure out the rest later."

Later

The word echoed in her mind, harmonizing with the rest of the notes there as Eric pulled her further into his room.

Later, she'd go back to her room.
Later, she'd write down everything Eric had just said.
Later, she'd fall asleep and forget.
Later, she'd read the letter she'd written herself tonight and know to never kiss Eric again. To never let him take her shirt off. To never run her hands along the planes of his chest, or press herself against him, no matter how perfect the sound of the notes they created together.

But that was later. For now, she was determined to enjoy their eclipse.

Part 7: Henry McCoy

Eric never adopted him; his aunt did instead. Yay!

* 26 *

Yellow tennis balls arced through the air, creating a blurry circle as Emilia's hands deftly tossed them aloft. Apparently she could juggle. She had committed to learning the skill a few months ago to entertain Henry. Though she needed to be careful not to think about it too much, since that caused the balls to tumble to the ground.

Eric and Henry began throwing numbers into the air alongside the balls.

"One!"

"Two!"

"Free!"

Emilia grinned at Eric, who was watching her admiringly. Her heart skipped and she fumbled, but recovered before the balls fell. He wasn't admiring her, she reminded herself, but her juggling. It was cool that she'd learned a new skill with her brain injury. He was probably just impressed by the medical science behind it or something.

She'd been misinterpreting looks like this from him all day. What was wrong with her? Was she lonely? Maybe she missed having a boyfriend, and it was causing her to see innocent gestures from her best friend, who happened to be a very charming and attractive guy, as romantic. How pathetic.

"Five!" Henry cried.

After five, which seemed to be the highest number Henry could count to in order, the counting became erratic.

"Nine!" Henry said next.

"Thirteen!" Eric provided.

"Eleventeen!" Henry shouted back.

Eric and Emilia snorted at the same time while Henry looked

confused, then laughed too, clearly wanting to be in on the joke.

"Twentyteen!" Eric said.

"Twoteen!"

"Threeteen!"

"SEVENTEEN!" Henry yelled, twice as loud as he had the rest of the numbers.

Eric burst into laughter, and Henry took the opportunity while he was distracted to climb on top of him and start jumping on his stomach. "Seventeen! Seventeen!" Henry cried out as Eric continued to laugh.

"That's actually a real number," Eric grunted as he tried to pull the small boy off of him.

Just then, the balls finally fell out of the air, bouncing all around the room. One of them collided with a tower of blocks they'd made earlier, sending them crashing to the ground. Everyone went silent, and Henry's eyes grew wide as his lip began to quiver.

Emilia looked up at Eric and mouthed apologetically, *"I'm sorry."*

"Twenty!" Eric declared as he got to his feet. "We said we'd watch Emilia juggle twenty times before bedtime, and she did! Time for stories!"

Before Henry could figure out if he was happy or sad about the abrupt end to the game, Eric scooped him up and tossed him over his shoulder, causing Henry to laugh at the inelegant way he was being marched out of the room.

When the boys were gone, Emilia started clearing the mess of blocks. Bartholomew poked his head in as she was finishing up, and she tried to entice him onto her lap, but he just stopped inside the doorway to lick his butt. Several minutes later, he left the room, giving her a lovely view of his newly-cleaned backside on his way out. She smiled to herself, in spite of the rejection. Tonight was fun. Much more fun than she'd thought when she read on her calendar that Henry would be spending the night.

Emilia sighed and lay back on the rug, pulling a throw pillow under her head as she looked up at the ceiling. The molding around the room was lovely. Actually, the entire room was lovely. Eric told her earlier that she'd designed the library, and she could see her style clearly: neat, clean, but also comfortable, the latter of which was necessary for a library. She turned her head to look at the bookshelves, and her eye was caught by a large book on the bottom shelf.

She crawled over and saw a note taped to the front in her handwriting: *Only read when you're in a good mood! I mean it, Emilia.*

Now she had to know what was inside. She moved to the sofa and pulled the book onto her lap as she wondered whether that note ever worked to deter her. She was in a good mood now, so it seemed like an okay time to open the book. But even if she was feeling off, she couldn't imagine herself seeing that note and not at least peeking inside.

She flipped through the book and realized quickly why the note was there. It was research on the meaning of life which was heavy, even for someone who wasn't suffering from debilitating memory loss. She stopped at a random theory and began to read the page.

Theory Two: To love and improve the lives of others
Relevant Philosophies:
Enlightenment—meaningful existence = social order
Mohism—the purpose of life is universal, impartial love

Emilia turned back to the front of the book and found a long list of all the philosophies she'd researched. She was impressed by how detailed her notes were and how they were cross-referenced with a deeper dive into each philosophy. She turned back to theory two, then moved to the next page. Her eyes were drawn to a quote, which she'd circled.

Loving others and being loved is the point of it all. And yet, love is such a complicated experience, and something few people understand.

Under the quote she'd written a few notes. The first one made her smile: *Complicated is right. Whoever said this had no idea.*

The second note was sadder: *Can I continue to build love with this condition? Or am I just relying on the love I'd built up before my accident? How would I know? How do you measure love? I feel like some people love me deeper than I can love them, and it kills me.*

"Hey." Emilia looked up and saw Eric leaning in the doorway.

"Oh, hi." She slammed the book closed and discreetly wiped her eyes, realizing just then they were wet. "How's Henry?"

"Asleep." Eric crossed the room and sat on the couch, then motioned toward the book on her lap. "Which section were you reading?"

"The one about love."

"Ah. What made you cry?"

She smiled. So much for trying to hide her tears. "You know me too well."

"Only as well as you know me."

"Still?" How was it possible for her to know him well these days, given her condition?

"Yes, still," he insisted. "I'm the same person I always was."

"But people change, Eric. As you grow, you'll change, and I won't know you anymore. I'll still see you as the person you were. So—how can I love you properly?" She motioned back toward the book.

"It's not as mental as you think, love. It lives in your heart, and your heart does not reset each night."

"Is that the medical explanation?" she teased.

He grinned. "I'm not trying to be a doctor anymore, so I can talk about the heart as more than just an organ that pumps blood." He shifted closer to her and took her hand in both of his. "I thought the same as you in the beginning, that you wouldn't be able to fall in love with someone new. They'd obviously fall in love with you—but if you didn't love them at the time of your accident, you wouldn't be able to develop the feelings over time. But that's not true. And if you want the medical explanation, it's because those deep feelings are created in your amygdala and the pathways between your amygdala and your hippocampus have recovered since your accident."

"Really? How are you so sure?"

"Henry."

"Hen—oh…" She smiled as she looked at the spot where they'd been playing. "You think I love him?"

"You tell me. You've spent all day with him. How does it feel? Do you love him?"

"I don't…" Emilia cut off and tried to assess her feelings for the small boy. She liked how it felt to hold him, and she really liked making him laugh. And earlier, when he'd tripped while running through the hall, her chest had clenched at the sight of his tears. But he was a very cute toddler. Maybe she was reacting to him because of some latent maternal instincts. "I don't know," she concluded.

"You do love him. I've seen your affection towards him build over time. In the beginning, you resented him and, well, you remember why."

They were quiet, and she knew they were thinking about the same thing, their fight just before her accident. Sarah, Henry's mom, had taken off, leaving Henry for Eric to care for. Emilia had been so worried Eric would just take on that new responsibility, without complaint, but the fear had ended up being unfounded. Eric's aunt had adopted Henry so that Eric could stay in medical school.

For years, Emilia had been worried someone in his family would do something to take away his dream of being a doctor. In the end, ironically, it had been her who had done that. At least, as far as she could tell. Though she knew if she asked Eric about why he'd quit medical school, he would invent some excuse that would make it seem like it hadn't been her fault at all.

The sound of Eric's voice snapped Emilia out of her thoughts. "I'm sorry I wasn't there." He was looking down at their hands, which were still clasped.

"It wouldn't have changed anything."

"I would feel less guilty now," he said with a small smile.

Emilia leaned into him. "I'm sorry for what I said that night. I was just upset about my parents and taking it out on you. I was sad you weren't coming with me, but I was being selfish. You were where you needed to be, and I'm glad everything with Henry worked out. I'm glad you're not having to watch him full-time, yet still have him in your life. He clearly adores you and you, him, and I—I'm happy for you both."

"You do love him," Eric repeated. "You can love people, Emilia. And that love can grow. You've told yourself you don't deserve love, that it's not possible, but you're wrong. You can have it. You just need to choose it."

The way he was staring at her made it clear there was more behind his words. Something she almost knew, but couldn't quite wrap her thoughts around. "You're talking about something besides Henry now," she whispered.

"*Someone* besides Henry."

"Who?"

His lips turned up slightly. "Who do you think?"

A rush of emotions hit Emilia as the answer to his question occurred to her. "Us," she whispered. She'd thought those strange, almost affectionate moments between them had all been in her head, but had they been real? Did Eric feel them too? The longing in his eyes said yes.

He lifted her hand up to his lips and kissed it. "I love you." Well, there was her answer. It *had* been real. He loved her. Wow. She stayed quiet, unsure what to say.

"I've resolved to tell you every day until the end of the month," he continued.

"What happens at the end of the month?"

"You're going to pick me and we're going to live happily ever after," he said simply.

She had a million questions, chief of which were, *Pick you? What does that mean? What's the alternative?*

Before she could open her mouth to ask her questions, Eric cut her off. "Don't worry about it now. And don't try to sort out the implication of being in a relationship with me. I'm not asking you to do anything, or decide anything, not today. I just wanted you to know."

"Okay," she said as a smile crept across her face. "So—um—what now?"

Eric sidled next to her and wrapped an arm around her. "Well, if it's like yesterday, you'll think about it for a few hours, realize you love me back, tentatively lean into me, hold my hand, or link your arm with mine for the rest of the day—just to test the feeling of being close to me. Then, by the end of the night, we'll be making out on the couch."

She blushed. "You're kidding, right?"

"I am not," he said matter-of-factly.

Emilia had no idea what to say to that. Eric's tone made it sound like this was some big joke, but she got the sense there was more significance behind it. What was she supposed to do with this information? "I don't—I'm—I'm at a loss. I don't know if it's a joke or—"

"Not a joke," he said quickly. "I love you, but you don't have to do anything. Let's just sit here and talk."

"Okay."

"Maybe work up to some kissing."

She hit him playfully on the chest. "This is so weird. I've never seen you like this. I don't know what to do with this."

He gave her a breathtaking smile that sent her heart straight up to her throat. "Let's play GHOST and see where things go from there."

He held an arm out and she snuggled into his side, winding an arm around his waist, just to see how it felt. The idea of being with Eric romantically was weird but this—being in his arms, feeling his chest expand with each breath, breathing in his scent—this wasn't weird at all. Rather, she felt like she was home.

* * *

"Best part of the day?" Emilia read aloud as she wrote in her notebook. *Making out with Eric after he told me he loved me.* Am I allowed to say that?" She smiled to herself as she remembered the scene in question. She couldn't bear to let that time with Eric just disappear. "I'm leaving it," she announced to the empty room.

She answered the other two questions easily, but paused on the last one. *What do you want most?* She started and stopped her answer three times before eventually writing, *To be useful*, ignoring the ache in her heart as her pencil scratched across the page.

* 27 *

The next day, Emilia was sitting at the desk in her room, reviewing the summary about Henry while he played with blocks at her feet. She'd spent the last few hours watching him while Eric had been working late, then taken a phone call in the office almost immediately after arriving home. Hanging out with Henry had been fun, but exhausting. He seemed to have an endless amount of energy.

Now, she was reviewing his summary to see if she needed to make any updates. Unlike the summaries about her friends, Henry's was a tactical, bulleted list of his likes and dislikes along with tips on how to care for him.

At the bottom, she'd written a note to herself that said, *Review and correct this list every time you watch him, since his preferences change week to week.* She scanned the paper as they waited for Eric to finish up with his call.

Henry McCoy

Note: Henry Shaffer is now Henry McCoy. Eric never adopted him; his aunt did instead. Yay!

Food: This child will eat all day if you let him. His standard meals are breakfast, mid-morning snack, lunch, afternoon snack, and dinner. If he's hungry in-between meals, he's only allowed cut-up vegetables.

Following that was a list of the types of foods he liked. Emilia reviewed it and put a line through "and meatballs" from the "Spaghetti and meatballs" note. She tried that for dinner, and Henry had been highly offended by the presence of the "gwoss balls" on his plate.

Sleep: Henry takes one nap a day after lunch for 2-3 hours. All you have to do to get him down is rub his back while you sing to him.

Emilia added, "He really likes the Beatles," at the end, a fact she'd discovered during bathtime. She liked singing the songs too, as they reminded her of her parents in a pleasant, nostalgic sort of way and not the devastating way memories of her parents hit her when she recalled the events leading up to her accident.

At night, it's harder to get Henry to sleep. He'll seem wired and you'll think, 'there is no way this kid is ever going to wind down,' then, suddenly, he'll pass out. Just keep at it.

Emilia smiled as she continued to read, checking that she didn't need to add anything to the "Play" or "Miscellaneous" sections.

Her attention was drawn away from the paper when she heard Henry say Eric's name. Eric was standing in the doorway, looking stressed. Emilia knew instantly he needed to speak to an adult. She looked back at the "Play" section.

If you ever need to distract Henry for a solid half-hour (like when preparing dinner) you can set him up with a movie. The video tapes are in the drawer just under the TV.

Emilia turned back towards Eric. "Bad day?"

"Yes," he said with a heavy sigh.

"How about I put a movie on for Henry and you can tell me about it? You can eat, too. I made spaghetti, like the meal plan said."

"Yeah, okay," he said distantly. "I need to get him back home before bed, but we still have an hour."

As Henry watched a movie in the sitting room, Emilia and Eric sat in the kitchen. He moved food around his plate while she waited for him to explain what was wrong. What could have upset him this much? She thought his work wasn't very stressful, so maybe it was the phone call. Was it his dad? Or one of his sisters? Or maybe something else entirely. She hated not knowing more about his life and wondered how much help she would be once they finally started talking.

"Sarah called," Eric began.

Emilia scowled. She should have guessed. Sarah Shaffer, one of her least favorite people. Eric's older sister was always making messes, then calling Eric to come clean them up. Like in high school, when she would call him in the middle of the night and make him pick her up from random houses. Or those times in college, when she'd show up at his dorm and ask to stay for a week or two, then steal his cash on her way out.

After Henry was born, she'd bring him to Eric's apartment and leave him, sometimes for days at a time, because she "needed a break from it all." It never occurred to her that Eric, who was in medical school, might not have time to take care of her baby. Then, one night, she'd dropped Henry off for good. Eric didn't find out until two days later when Sarah called from the East Coast and told him she was done. Before he could ask what he was supposed to do with her son, she hung up.

"I know you hate her," he sighed.

"Has she gotten better?" Emilia snapped.

He sighed and dropped his head in his hands. "I don't know. This is the first time I've talked to her since she left me with Henry. She—she says she's better."

Emilia summoned what little stores of patience she had. As much as she wanted to rail against his sister, he didn't need that right now. She placed a hand on his arm and said softly, "Tell me what she said."

He explained their conversation. How Sarah had said she wanted to be in Henry's life. How she'd reached out to their dad first, knowing he was the least likely to yell at her, and he'd told her that his sister had adopted Henry. Emilia wanted to stop and talk about how insane it was that until now, Sarah didn't even know who was caring for her son, but bit her tongue.

Then Sarah had called her aunt, who said quite bluntly that there was no place in Henry's life for her. That's when she'd decided to call Eric and make her plea. "She wants to come visit while I'm watching him."

"No," Emilia said immediately.

"I'll still be the one—"

"No! Eric, listen." She shifted closer to him and grabbed his shoulders. "You are not Henry's guardian. You don't get to make these decisions. The last thing you want is to lose your aunt's trust and with that, the ability to see him whenever you want."

Eric winced, but she pressed on, since she knew he needed to hear it. "This is between Sarah and your aunt. Your sister's just trying to manipulate you because she knows you, and knows you have a soft spot for her, and—and she probably said something about how a mom should be with her son, didn't she?"

He didn't need to answer. She saw it in his eyes, waves of anguish rocking in an endless sea. Emilia continued to hold his shoulders as she stroked his neck with her thumbs.

"You are so nice, Eric. You have such a big heart, and you want to fix everything. But this isn't your place. Legally, it's not your place, but even beyond that. Sarah gave up her rights to Henry when she left and didn't call for over two years. If she wants him back, she's going to have to work harder than a few phone calls."

"Yeah," he said, voice hoarse. "You're right. I was stupid to listen to her."

"You're not stupid. She might not be lying. She might turn things around. She might come out here and get a job. Maybe even keep the same address for longer than a month. Then once she proves she's serious, I'm sure your aunt will reconsider."

He looked past her, his eyes distant. "That's a good idea," he finally said. "We can give her a list of conditions. It's not a hard no, but something she can work towards."

Emilia's heart clenched. This man was the best person on the planet. After everything his sister had put him through, he felt bad for her. He wanted to give her hope and still believed she could change. Emilia did not believe Sarah would turn things around, but she forced herself to nod anyway. "She might. But it's not *your* list of conditions, okay?"

"Yeah. I hear you, I do." He grabbed her hands, which were still on his neck, and pulled them down. "This is my aunt's deal, and I'm not going to get in the way. Don't worry, I'm not going to break the promise, especially not after I bit your head off for breaking it for me a few days ago."

"I—what? What did I do?"

He shook his head. "The argument's over. No need to rehash it."

"I guess we don't have arguments that last over a day, do we?"

"We don't. We could, if you wanted to write something down to remember to pick up the next day, but you've never done that. Not with me, at least." He sounded a little sad. Before she could ask him about it, he squeezed her hand. "Thank you. I was sort of spiraling there."

Emilia smiled. When she had followed Eric into the kitchen, she was worried she wouldn't be able to help him, since she was missing the context from the past two years, but she'd done okay. It felt good to be useful, even with her handicap.

"I'm going to take Henry home now. Then I can talk to my aunt and see what she thinks about this idea of setting conditions for Sarah to see him." He was halfway out of his chair when she pulled him back into his seat. "You should eat. Is fifteen minutes really going to make a difference?"

Eric frowned at his plate, then nodded. "Yeah. Okay." He loaded up his fork with pasta but before taking a bite, smiled at her. His eyes were a clearer blue now, nearly back to normal, though there was still a hint of sadness floating in their depths. "I don't know what I'd do without you."

She returned his smile. "I'd be pretty lost without you too."

* * *

While Eric drove Henry home, Emilia tidied the house. She'd tried to keep up with Henry's messes as they'd been playing earlier, but there were still several toys she'd missed. She returned them all to Henry's room and on her way back downstairs, noticed one last mess in Eric's bedroom.

When had he done that? It must have been during the five minutes she'd gone to pee. Henry had taken all the contents out of one of Eric's nightstands and tossed them onto his bed. She shook her head and started putting everything back when she noticed several pieces of paper with her handwriting on them. Scrawled at the bottom of each note, in Eric's writing, were dates.

The most recent one was from earlier in the month. *The only thing in this world I wanted more than you, was your happiness. 07-Feb-1987.*

Emilia sat on the bed and gathered up the notes in a pile. There were about ten, dating all the way back to June of last year. *But if we could have been together, what would there be to dream of? 21-Jun-1986.*

Some were short and seemed like snippets from poems while some were longer, like the one from September.

To my dearest love, my brilliant Sun, the world has decided we can no longer be one. So you take the day and I'll take the night. You with your warm, happy glow. Me with my cold, lonely light.

It must be this way, always and forever, they say we can no longer share the sky together. But my nights will follow your brilliant days, I am right behind you and I will love you always. 16-Sep-1986.

Emilia shook her head as she read and reread the notes. They were love poems, but incredibly sad love poems. The words felt familiar and ignited a dark melancholy deep in her chest. What did these mean? Why had she written them out? Why did Eric have them? Did that mean they were for him?

"It's rude to go through people's things."

She jumped and looked up to find Eric standing at the door. She opened her mouth to defend herself, but no words came out.

"Henry?" he asked as he walked into the room.

She nodded. "How was—? How was your aunt?"

"Good. She liked the idea. We're going to meet for dinner next week to talk it through."

He stopped in front of her, and she placed the pile of notes onto his outstretched palm. "Rejection letters," he said in a flat voice, then put them in the open drawer. He added a few other items that were scattered on the bed: a small notebook, a few skiing magazines, and a pen. After closing the drawer, he took a seat next to her and let out a long sigh.

"We were together?" she asked.

Eric nodded slowly. "Sort of. I won't go into it all now, but I guess you could say it's been an 'on again, off again' thing. You can't commit because you believe, incorrectly, that the circumstances standing in our way are insurmountable."

"Like the sun and the moon."

"Yes." Eric sighed and pinched the bridge of his nose under his glasses. Emilia could feel the weight of his pain in his heavy exhale, and see its depth in the lines of his brow.

She stood and walked to the window, suddenly eager to put distance between them. As if separating him from the source of his agony would make things easier for him. She focused on the moon through the window, which sparkled innocently in the night sky—unaware it was being discussed.

Once upon a time, the Moon loved the Sun. Until ... The End.

How depressing. She wound her arms around herself as a chill spread through her. Was that really how her love story with Eric had gone? *Would* go? Since it still seemed to be playing out. How else could it end, given her condition? She was crying now, surprised at how quickly her night had changed. Not long ago she'd been laughing and playing with Henry.

Eric got up and crossed the room, stopping behind her. He placed soft hands on her arms. Through his reflection in the glass, she saw that his gaze was up, toward the moon. "The book of poems where you got all those lines, I've seen it," he said.

"Who was the poet?"

"Ranata Suzuki."

She had expected to hear a familiar name, since the poems had felt so familiar, but she didn't recognize the poet. "I don't know that name."

"It was published after your accident," he explained. "A gift from Viola, I think. Anyway, the book opens naturally to the part about the sun and the moon but there are other poems. I've circled a few that sum up my feelings, but I don't think you've seen them. I don't think you ever get past the sun and moon part."

Emilia turned around to face him. "Where's the book? I want to see them."

He gave her a small, heartbreaking smile. "I have a few of the lines memorized."

"Can I hear them?"

He nodded as he raised his hand and lightly traced the side of her face. "One of them starts with something like, 'I would do absolutely anything in this world for you. Just name it and it's yours. Anything at all. Anything... just please, not nothing.'"

Eric took a deep breath before leaning forward and resting his forehead on hers. "'The hardest thing I have ever had to do for you, was nothing,'" he continued, his voice shaking now. "'There was nothing more soul destroying than watching you walk away when all I wanted to do was beg you not to go.'"

"I did that," she whispered. "I hurt you. I walked away."

"But you kept coming back. You never left for good. And tomorrow..." He paused to sigh. "Tomorrow is a big deal. During your month-end review, you're going to decide, once and for all, whether or not you want to be with me."

Emilia was quiet as she stood there, her forehead still resting on his as his warm breath tickled her lips. She had no idea what to say. There was something here, something wonderful, but there was also pain. There were a thousand reasons this wouldn't work and as she listed them, more and more popped into her head.

Her mind stopped whirling when she felt his lips on her cheek. Eric leaned back and grabbed her hands. "I can see you thinking hard, but you don't have to. It's easy, Emilia. Pick me. Pick us. Just say the word and I'm yours."

His eyes bored into hers so intensely, she could feel it, like a searing heat. Why shouldn't she listen to him? Eric was incredible. She loved him; she could feel it in her heart. Hell, she could feel it in her elbows and forehead and the backs of her knees. Every inch of her loved him, and he clearly loved her back—the way he was looking at her was proof enough. She should be with him, and they could sort the rest out later.

Later. The word held some significance. Something hard to

pinpoint, a mix of comfort, and apprehension, and fear, and want. Something that propelled her forward.

Emilia kissed him. He let out a sigh of relief, which she captured with another kiss. She moved her hands to his nape and deepened their kiss, but as her lips moved in time with his, as if on instinct, her mind brought forth all the reasons this would be too difficult.

"Eric," she breathed, pulling away. "It would be so hard. You have to see that."

"It can't be harder than the past few months," he argued. "Believe me. Just—take a chance on us, and we'll deal with the complications as they come. Together."

"One day at a time?" she asked, recalling the name of her challenge.

He let out a dark laugh. "I hate that phrase."

Emilia shook her head. "Why are you telling me this? You know I'm going to forget soon. Am I supposed to write it down or—"

"No," he said quickly. "I mean, yes, obviously, that's what I want, but I know you won't. And regardless, you won't forget. You never do. Not completely."

Eric had mentioned this a few times today, pointing out instances when she'd seemed to know instinctively how to respond to Henry, or where to find an item in the house. And the way her entire body was nearly trembling with desire for him—that was new. She hadn't developed this profound level of attraction to him in just a day.

"So what happens now?" she asked.

Eric looked over at the clock on the wall, then took a deep breath and turned toward the window. She could see the moon reflecting off the lenses of his glasses. "Now you go back to your room," he said sadly. "I don't want you to," he added in a rush. "I want you to stay here and never leave, but if I invite you to stay, you'll sneak away." He gestured toward the nightstand and added with a humorless laugh, "Sometimes you even leave a poem behind."

"I'm so sorry."

He closed the distance between them and placed a soft kiss on her lips. "I know. But we're going to fix this. Tomorrow. For the first time since we got together, I'm going to fight for you."

He locked his eyes on hers, and his gaze was fierce, like he was about to march into a real battle. "I hope you win," she breathed.

He gave her one last kiss before finally pulling away. "I intend to."

Part 8: Eric Shaffer

He has this eerie ability to know exactly what you're thinking and feeling.

* 28 *

It was the last day of the month, and Emilia was sitting at the desk in her bedroom. She'd just woken up, read a letter from herself explaining why she didn't remember the last two years, read through the summaries about her friends and parents, then read a note from Eric.

Emilia,

I planned to be there when you woke up, but something came up. There's some family drama I need to deal with (shocker, I know). As you've probably already noticed, it's the last day of the month, and that means it's time for your month-end review. Everything you need is in the small trunk on your bookshelf. You like to do your reviews in the library (which is downstairs) so you can spread everything out.

I'm sorry I couldn't be there to make you breakfast before you started. As soon as I can break away, I will. Good luck and I love you.

-Eric

Emilia's eyes kept drifting back to the last line. *I love you.* It was so casual, the way he'd written it, but there was weight to the words—something she felt, but couldn't explain. Were they the sort of friends who said 'I love you' now? They had obviously loved each other before her accident, but only said so in extreme circumstances. What had changed? Emilia looked back at Eric's summary, which was on top of the pile.

You've been living in Aspen Grove with Eric, in the house he grew up in, since August 1985. He is the most understanding of your condition and has this eerie ability to know exactly what you're thinking and feeling—I suspect it's because a lot of your interactions are repetitive, though he claims that's not true.

He works in the medical field, still skis all winter and mountain bikes all summer, and has insisted on teaching you how to do these things as well—despite countless protestations.

He rarely sees his dad, who lives in California now (good riddance!). He still helps a lot with Henry—though he never adopted him, thank God. Sarah is no longer in touch, but Claire is. She lives in San Francisco with her husband (that same boyfriend you met a few times before the accident), and Eric visits her a few times a year.

You should know that he blames himself for not being there to prevent your accident (classic Eric). He's also not on a path to become a doctor anymore. He says he prefers the calmer, more flexible career path he's chosen, but doesn't like to talk about it.

Emilia sighed when she was finished reading. She'd been expecting more, but she couldn't pinpoint why. The phone rang, drawing her attention away from the page. She ignored it and followed a sign in the hall to the bathroom. As she was washing her face, the phone rang again.

Was she supposed to get that? It seemed weird to answer Eric's phone. Then again, it could be Eric trying to get a hold of her. Her eyes landed on a note Eric had written on the mirror, which answered the question for her. *This house is yours too; help yourself to anything.*

She decided to find the source of the ringing when she saw the bottom note, written in Eric's handwriting, like the rest: *I love you.*

There it was again. *I love you.* Why did he tell her that so much? If she didn't know any better, she'd guess they were together. But that would have been in Eric's summary, so there must be some other explanation.

Her thoughts cut off when she finally found the ringing phone in a room that looked like a home office, but it stopped ringing as soon as she picked it up. She flopped down on the chair as her mind drifted back to Eric. There was something there, a truth that was tantalizingly near but impossible to grasp, like trying to close her hands around the wind. She'd just have to ask him when he was back, though she wasn't sure how she'd go about wording that question.

The phone rang again. This time, Emilia didn't hesitate before picking it up, hoping it was Eric and that she could just ask him about all the *I love you*s. "Hello?"

"Hey, Em! You finally picked up."

It wasn't Eric. It was August. The *I love you* mystery would have to remain unsolved for a little longer. "Hey, August."

"Happy last day of the month! I'm glad I caught you before my shift. How are you?"

"Um, okay? I've only been awake for about an hour, so I don't have much to report. But I've read all my letters and learned that today is sort of a big day, since I get to read all about my past, so that seems cool."

"Yeah, it is. A little overwhelming, but good. This monthly thing was your sister's idea, and it's pretty smart. Before, you were doing this every day, and it took forever. Anyway, um, do you want to hear about what's going on on my end?"

"Yeah. Of course."

She leaned back in the chair and twirled the phone cord around her finger as she listened to August give her a painfully thorough account of his week. The mundanity of the conversation didn't match the initial urgency in his tone. Was this normal? Did he call her every Saturday and walk her through his past week in this level of detail? It seemed like something she'd have put in her summary about him.

"*Um, sorry,*" she wanted to say, "*but I need to go and catch up on the last two years of my life. I also have an 'I love you' mystery to solve. Besides, this isn't interesting and I don't understand half the words you just said. What the fuck is excoriation?*"

"August," she said, cutting him off. "I think I should go. All the notes I've read so far say this review takes a long time and—"

"Oh yeah, yeah," his voice replied through the receiver. "What's it been...? Fifteen minutes? Yeah, that should do."

"Do for what?"

She heard a nervous laugh from his end. "Don't worry about it, Em. Just follow your heart, okay? And try to ignore that giant brain of yours. Oh! And I apologize in advance for June, but she means well. I need to go before I'm late. See you!"

The line went dead. Emilia just stared at the phone in her hand for several moments, as if expecting it to explain August's weird behavior. Why had he mentioned June? Was she coming over today? She didn't remember seeing anything about it on the calendar. She walked to her room to check. She needed to get the large box that contained her whole history anyway and find the key to the lock.

"Oh!" Emilia jumped at the sight of June in her room. She was sitting on the bed with the box on her lap and a pile of papers stacked neatly at her side.

"June. Hi. Um, did I miss the doorbell?"

"Emilia," she said sternly. Emilia was caught off guard by her friend's harsh tone.

She carefully stepped into the room as she took in June's altered appearance. "You look, uh, really cool."

"Thank you," June replied quickly. "So do you. Okay. Pleasantries over, let's cut to the chase."

Emilia was about to point out that when people exchanged pleasantries, they typically smiled, something June hadn't done yet. But she stayed quiet. It was clear June wasn't in the mood for jokes.

"You are incredibly strong," June stated, "so I'm not going to baby you."

"Okay," Emilia said warily.

June sighed and tapped the top of the box. "I came over here to break into this box, read all your notes to see how much you've really been hiding from yourself, and fill in any gaps for you. But before I got a chance, I found a letter right at the top which you wrote that says everything I would have told you. Can I read it to you?"

Emilia shrugged. She didn't see the harm in that. If June weren't here, that letter would have probably been the first thing she read.

"*Emilia, You love Eric and he loves you,*" June began. She stopped and glared at Emilia.

Emilia didn't know what to say. Was June jealous? Is that why she looked upset? No, according to her summary, June and Eric had had a mutual breakup, and she was dating someone else. June returned her eyes to the page and opened her mouth to continue, but Emilia stopped her.

"Is that true? Does Eric really love me?" It explained all the *I love you*s from this morning. But he'd never shown any interest in her before.

June watched her for several seconds before answering, still wearing a stern expression. "He gets jittery when he's away from you, especially if it's the morning and he hasn't seen you yet. He hates when random guys flirt with you—balls his fists up and stomps around like a kid. He can't keep his eyes off you, like if he looks away you might smile or laugh, and he can't bear to miss it. He—*fuck*—he renovated an entire house for you, making it exactly like you wanted it, mostly by hand, and you know him, he's not handy. He trained that terror you call a cat to sleep here each night, so you'd always know where he was. *Yes,* Emilia. He loves you. Now shut up and let me read this."

She turned back to the letter. "*You love Eric and he loves you. But before you let that fact fill your heart with joy, you should know that you don't deserve his love. You have been a coward for the past several months, hiding this truth from yourself instead of facing it and because of that, you have been tearing Eric apart. But today, that's all going to stop.*"

June stopped again. "I couldn't have said it better myself."

"What?" Emilia had a million questions, but no idea which one to voice first.

"I'll keep reading," June said in response to the confused look on Emilia's face.

"*About a year ago, Eric told you he loved you and you kissed and talked and agreed to give dating a shot, then you forgot. He told you again and again over the course of the year, and you kept forgetting. Things continued to escalate: you gave him hope, you made promises, you even had sex with him. But every time, you left him, failed to explain why, and broke his heart. Eric told me tonight that every time you left, it hurt a little less. He thinks it's because when you go, you take a piece of him with you, so there's less of him left to feel the pain.*"

June stopped to take a deep breath. Her sky-blue eyes were wet, which for June, meant a lot. Before Emilia could cut in and ask if it was really this bad, June continued reading.

"*Eric is without question the most important person in your life. He loves you more than anything and fiercely defends your right to choose how you want to live. He believes you can have a fulfilling life with your memory loss and will do anything to make that happen for you, and look at how you've treated him in return.*"

"Okay. I get it!" Emilia exclaimed. She sank down until she was sitting on the floor, pulled her feet up under her, and dropped her head onto her knees. Tears were falling onto her pajama bottoms. How could she have been so cruel?

"These are your words. Not mine," June said from her spot above her.

Emilia wrapped her arms around her legs. "Message received. Okay?" she snapped back. "The knife is in. No need to twist it all around."

June's expression softened, and she patted the spot next to her. "Come here. It gets a little nicer."

Emilia stayed in place. "It does?"

"Well, there was nowhere to go but up." June patted the bed again. "Come on. I won't bite."

Emilia rose and slowly crossed the room. "This is why you're mad at me? Because I hurt Eric?"

June nodded and shook the letter. "To be fair, you seemed pretty mad at yourself, too."

Emilia let out a small laugh. "Yeah. No kidding." When she sat next to June, June wrapped an arm around her. "Does it really get better?" Emilia asked.

June nodded and continued reading. "*In your defense, without someone giving you all the context—as August and Eric have done today—it would have been impossible for you to know how much you were hurting him. I think you were doing what you thought was best. You were trying to protect him from the pain of having to be with someone who would forget him each night. But now that you know—you need to fix it. Here's how:*"

June stopped reading again. "For the record, I don't agree with any of this next part, but I'm going to read it anyway." She sighed and turned back to the letter.

"*End it. There is no world where you and Eric can live happily ever after. Putting aside the complications of a relationship where one person remembers nothing (from first kisses, to fights, to the fact that they are no longer a virgin). And putting aside the fact that Eric deserves a family (and that would be impossible with your condition), the events of the past several months are proof enough that this cannot continue.*

"Eric is broken, bleeding, and hurting, and you did that. And even worse, he let you. August described your relationship as toxic and he's right. This circumstance can't be repeated and although you love each other, the obstacles standing between you are too large. Love isn't going to be enough.

"But this time, instead of walking away in silence, you need to confront Eric and tell him no. You owe him an explanation and after you talk to him, you need to write it down and read it every day. No more kissing, definitely no more sleeping together, and when Eric finally moves on, you need to let him. You can do this. You've done hard things before. Remember, this is what's best for Eric."

June stopped. Emilia was crying again and nodding along. "It makes sense."

June rolled her eyes. "After I finished reading this, I started thinking about how I was going to slap you, then dismissed that and decided to punch you instead, since slapping seemed too mild."

Emilia leaned away from June.

"Luckily for you, there's more to the letter," June continued. "So I'm not going to hit you."

"There's more?"

"Yeah. Listen to this." June turned the last page over and continued reading. "*Disregard the last few paragraphs. That's just you keeping Eric from living the life he wants. Do you really want to do that to him? You remember the promise you had him make the last night at Camp Ouray. He's a grown man, incredibly smart and strong and kind and he deserves to choose for himself what he wants and he wants you, flaws and all.*

"So don't make your decision for Eric—let him do that. Instead, decide for yourself. What do you want, Emilia? Can you handle a relationship with your condition? Can you handle the uncertainty? Can you put almost limitless trust in another person? It will be uncomfortable and every day you'll feel guilty and unsure and scared. And if you'd prefer to be alone, that's okay. But once you decide, whether you choose Eric or not, you need to go all in. No waffling. There's been enough of that.

"I wish I could help you but right now, I'm completely spent. It's been a draining day, and I barely know which way is up. All I know for certain is that I love Eric more profoundly than I've ever loved another person in my life and that he deserves for me to give this topic a full day of measured, reasoned consideration. That, Emilia, is your task for the day. Trust your heart, trust your mind, trust your soul. You can do this. Lots of love, your past self."

They were both silent for several moments. June folded the letter and put it on the stack of papers on the bed, then turned to Emilia. "What do you think?"

"What do I think? What do I think?!" The question seemed absurd. What didn't she think, might have been more appropriate. Emilia stood up and began pacing the room.

"What am I supposed to think?!" Emilia cried. "This is impossible! 'Oh, just figure out what you want, Emilia,'" she mocked. "'You have no idea what's going on, but it's very critical that you make a permanent decision about your future with Eric—someone you supposedly love more than you've ever loved anyone, someone you've supposedly *slept with*—which is a whole separate thing—someone whose heart you've apparently broken on a number of occasions—Oh, and if that wasn't hard enough, let's not forget, you haven't even seen him today and the last memory you have of him is over two years old!'"

June was leaning back on her hands and smirking at her, which made Emilia want to punch her. "You think this is funny?" Emilia said menacingly. "If you find my life so amusing, I'd be happy to switch places. Just say the word!"

June's grin widened. "You want to ski professionally and date women?"

"No. But I would have fun pissing off your mom." They shared a smile, then Emilia sighed and went to sit back on the bed. She dropped her head in her hands and took several shaky breaths as she tried to keep back the tears stinging behind her eyes. "Help me," she pleaded.

"Okay. I can do that."

"You can?"

"Of course. That's why I'm here."

"I thought you were here to yell at me and maybe hit me."

"Yeah, but then you did a really good job of yelling at yourself."

"Yeah."

"Do you know about your 'one day at a time' challenge?" June asked.

Emilia nodded. "There was a letter about it. It was Viola's idea. I started every day from scratch so I could—" Emilia stopped talking as realization hit her. "Oh."

"Yeah."

"You think I started that challenge for Eric?"

"Of course. Why else? I don't know any of the details—Viola won't tell anyone—but apparently you were supposed to take the month to figure out what you really wanted. That's got 'you trying to figure out what to do about Eric' written all over it."

"Huh." Emilia got up and retrieved the letter she'd written explaining the challenge from her desk. She scanned it quickly.

You're supposed to start each day fresh, without any external distractions, and see how it goes. Then you reflect at the end in your notebook. Whatever you write goes in the box, so you can start the next day with another clean slate.

I have no idea what this is about, but I do know Eric doesn't like talking about it. Apparently a lot of those "external distractions" you removed from your life were tools he made to make things easier for you.

Emilia looked back up at June. It fit. She noticed the pile of torn out pages sitting on the bed next to June and wondered if those were all the entries she'd written in her notebook for the month. She crossed the room and picked them up, checking the dates on the top of the pages. Yes. These were all from the month of February.

"Okay. I'm going to leave you alone," June announced. She got up from the bed and picked up the miniature trunk.

"Wait. What? You're leaving? And you can't take that. I need it. That's where my whole history is stored!"

June sighed and pulled the box back, out of Emilia's reach. "You don't need to review history today. Do it next month. Do it tomorrow, even. You need to spend today figuring out what to do about Eric. No distractions. I already pulled out all the pages you wrote in February, so you have everything you need."

"You say that like it's so easy, but again, I haven't even seen Eric today! And you're taking away a huge source of information that might be useful in—"

"Emilia! The way I see it, you've already done a lot of thinking. You don't need to repeat all that. All you need to do is answer that one question you set for yourself at the end of the letter. What. Do. You. Want?"

"But how am I supposed to start when—?"

"Hey! Stop. You're getting too worked up. All the answers are on those pages." She gestured toward the pile of papers in Emilia's hands. "For a solid month, you started each day without anything influencing you towards Eric. Then, you reflected each night. Now use that analytical brain of yours to delve into the research and finally answer, once and for all, what does Emilia Rhodes want? Don't worry so much about the past. Just sift through data, look for patterns—I don't know, do your thing. Logic it out."

"I—I can do that. That doesn't seem so bad," Emilia allowed.

"Okay. Good." June reset her grip on the box and walked to the door.

"But what do I do when I see Eric?" Emilia asked before June disappeared into the hall.

"I don't know. Try your best to get as far as you can with this and when he shows up, just talk to him. You two have become awful at talking to each other. I think you both assume you know what the other is thinking, and you're mostly right but lately, you've been missing the mark. Just remember that Eric is your best friend and loves you more than he loves anyone. You can trust him."

June walked to the bed and gave Emilia a half-hug before going back to the door.

"What if I choose wrong?" Emilia whispered.

"You won't. If I thought it would help, I'd stay, but you need to do this one alone. Good luck."

Emilia just sat there for several minutes, staring at the stack of papers on the bed. She could do this. June was right, she didn't have to make any big decisions. All she had to do was look at the available data and answer the question about what she wanted. She'd focus on that small piece of the puzzle first. Once she had that, she could worry about the next issue.

This was the same way she had got her head around complicated cases in school. She could do this. But first, she should probably get ready. *Then*, when she smelled better and was wearing real clothes, she'd figure this out.

* 29 *

A few hours later, Emilia was in the library, lying on the sofa and absently looking up at the wood-trimmed ceiling when she heard someone clear their throat.

She jumped and tried to get to her feet so quickly, she lost her balance and stumbled on her way up. When she straightened, she looked toward the hall and saw Eric smirking at her. Of course he'd noticed her almost-fall. It didn't matter. What mattered was that he was here, just a few feet away.

She closed the distance with alacrity and reached for his arm. It was solid. That was the only confirmation she needed before placing a hand behind his neck and pulling him into a kiss. She'd been thinking about him nonstop and after a while, had begun to suspect he might be made up, as though turning his name over and over in her head had stretched its sounds and syllables all out of proportion. But as she kissed him, she decided that he was undoubtedly real. His mouth was real too—warm lips, wet tongue, all real. The thought sent her backwards, out of his arms.

"Sorry," she said as a blush warmed her cheeks. "Um—" Shit. She wasn't supposed to kiss him. She promised herself she wouldn't kiss him.

Eric grabbed her by the waist and pulled her into another sublime collision. She knew she should stop this, but her body was in no mood to listen to her brain. Her hands moved to his nape and played with his hair while he wrapped strong arms around her and worked at pressing away every bit of space between them.

As they kissed, she was overcome with an overwhelming sense of déjà vu. She knew how his mouth fit with hers, the feel of his thick hair through her fingers, and just where to turn her head to avoid hitting his glasses. She felt like she'd done this a hundred times, then realized that she probably had.

When they paused for breath, Eric was grinning, his blue eyes bright. He still kept a firm grip on her waist, like he wasn't ready to let the distance he'd worked to eradicate creep back in. "Hey."

"Oh. Yeah. Hi. I guess I probably should have led with that. I just, um, got in my head that maybe you weren't real and everything I'd read was some fantasy I'd made up to make myself feel better and—and maybe I shouldn't just blurt out every thought that pops into my mind."

Eric bent down and kissed her cheek. "You're cute when you're nervous."

She released a small laugh. "Then I must be really cute right now. I feel so… out of my depth. And after all the notes I read I was, um, expecting something different?"

"Yeah?"

She nodded. "I thought you'd be angry, or upset or, or—"

"Crying?" he quipped.

"Sort of."

He smiled as he kissed the other side of her face. "Yes, you've made me cry before. Lucky for me, you forgot it, since it's not very manly."

Emilia didn't know what to say. She was still pressed against him as they casually talked about how much pain she'd caused him—pain she could not remember. She moved her hands down to his shoulders and let out a long sigh. Her mind was reaching around for words, any words, and landed on, "How was your morning? Hopefully the family stuff is better."

He sighed and finally let go of her. "Exhausting," he groaned, running his hand along the hair on his jaw. "It was Sarah. She showed up for the first time in over two years and demanded to see

Henry."

"What? She stayed away this whole time?"

Eric nodded and waved her away. "It's a whole thing, but I can catch you up later. She ran away again when my aunt threatened to call the police, and Henry never found out about all the drama, so that's good. Anyway, what's been going on here? Honestly, this wasn't what I was expecting either."

Emilia blushed. "Me attacking you first thing?"

"That sort of attack is always welcome—though only from you. I meant, where are all your things? I thought you'd be surrounded by papers and much more ... stressed."

"Oh, right. The box. This morning August called and told me all about his week. Now I know it was just a ploy to distract me so June could sneak in and go through my things. She took the box and only left me with those." Emilia motioned toward the pile of papers on the table next to the sofa.

Eric had already turned back to the hall. "Those two can't stop meddling. I'll go get the box back," he tossed the words angrily over his shoulder.

"You don't have to. I don't need it today."

He turned around and studied her, then looked at the stack of paper on the table. "How much do you know? What did June tell you?"

That was a loaded question. She chewed her lip for a few seconds before answering. "I know about us, obviously. I know how bad it's become. I know today is the day I have to make a final decision about everything." She dropped his gaze, which had become too heavy to hold. "June didn't tell me anything. I left a letter for myself. One I wrote this past weekend."

Eric came back into the room and stopped in front of her. Even with her eyes on the carpet, she could feel his gaze. "It's okay that June took that box because it gave me time to focus on my task, which was to look through my notes from the past month and answer one simple question: what do I want?" She took a fortifying breath and looked up at him. "I did it. It was easy, actually."

"You're done?"

Emilia nodded.

"But, no. Before you decide anything, you need to let me—"

"I want you," she said quickly, cutting him off.

"Wait. What?"

She nodded and carefully stepped toward him. "I want to be with you," she repeated, resting her hands on his shoulders.

"But—"

"No. Can you just stop there? You want to be with me. Period. No buts."

"It's not that easy, Eric."

"Why not?"

He stared at her intently, and she forced herself to hold his gaze this time, even as tears welled in her eyes. "Maybe I should just ... show you what I found," she whispered.

"Okay."

Emilia sat on the sofa and picked up the stack of papers as Eric took a seat next to her. "Do you know about the questions I was supposed to answer each night as part of my 'one day at a time' challenge?"

Eric shook his head.

"There were four: *What was the best part of today? What was the worst? What are you most afraid of right now? What do you want most?*"

Emilia looked back up at Eric. "After I read the letter my past self had written, I was really overwhelmed, since I had to make this big decision and had no idea where to start. But at the end, the letter said that all I had to do was answer one question: What do I want? It was June who helped me simplify it all down to that, so I'm glad she was here."

Eric nodded, and she could tell he was impatient for her to get to the point, but something told her it was important to explain herself thoroughly.

"June said that my challenge for the month was aimed at helping me answer that exact question and pointed out that I had all the information I needed in these pages—the notes I took for the month of February. Then she left, and I thought I had this huge task ahead of me of sifting through countless notes while trying to find patterns and similarities and reconciling conflicting information. But it wasn't like that."

"It wasn't?"

Emilia shook her head. "It was incredibly easy. It took me fifteen minutes to find the answer. Look here, question one: *What was the best part of today?*"

She flipped through the pages and read the various answers out loud. "Talking to Eric. Playing GHOST with Eric. Mocking the Seavers with Eric." She looked up and saw him smiling at her. "I have no idea what that means," she admitted.

His smile widened, and she watched him for several seconds before returning her attention to the papers. "Cooking with Eric, playing GHOST with Eric,—again—*skiing* with Eric—that one was surprising, but not as surprising as, making out with Eric after he told me he loved me."

"You finally wrote one of those down?"

"There was more than one?"

He nodded, and that alluring look in his eyes caused her to blush. If the heady mix of sensations that had just taken over her body were any clue, they'd probably done more than make out on one of those days.

"Oh," she breathed, then crossed her legs and placed the stack on her lap. "So, um, in conclusion, every note included you. Even on days that I could tell I didn't spend with you, I picked out a short moment from the morning or night when I was with you and listed it as my favorite."

"It's the same for me. My favorite moments are the ones I spend with you."

Her heart skipped a beat. She gave him another smile and picked the papers up again. "Next question: *What was the worst part of the day?* These were more about my condition: Not knowing. Not remembering. Feeling lost. Feeling sad. Not knowing—a second time. There were a few about you, though. Missing Eric at the Pearsons', fighting with Eric, not knowing how to make Eric feel better."

A tear fell down Emilia's face and she wiped it away swiftly. "Third question: *What are you most afraid of?* I expected to see things about my condition again, things like: never healing from this. But like the first question, everything I wrote was about you."

Eric shifted forward and rested a hand on her knee. She placed her hand on top of his before starting to read. "That I'm a burden to Eric. That Eric is constantly annoyed with me and is just hiding it well. That Eric was lying when he said he needs me as much as I need him. That I'm holding Eric back. That I'm the reason he quit medical school. That I can't give Eric the same support he gives me. That Eric won't move on."

Tears were falling again, and this time Eric wiped them away before she got a chance. He leaned forward and kissed the top of her head. "None of that is true."

She just leaned back and nodded. "Ready for the last one? This was telling."

"Yeah. Go for it."

"*What do you want most?*" She paused for a few seconds before reading her replies. "To be happy. To enjoy life. To be useful. To help others. To leave the world better than I found it." Emilia looked up and saw Eric cocking his head in confusion. "They're all canned responses," she concluded.

"Yeah." He sounded disappointed.

Emilia put the pages aside and grabbed his hand. "If I had really written out what I wanted, I would have been suspicious that it hadn't actually been me writing those. It's just like me to hold back when answering a question like that. But I can see what's not written almost as clearly as I can see what is."

"I don't understand."

"Here." Emilia picked up the papers and flipped to a random page. "On this day, my favorite moment was mocking the Seavers with you. My worst moment was not recalling the memory behind a picture you showed me where we were smiling and having fun. What I feared most was that you would never find your happy ending. And what I wanted most? To live a fulfilling life." Emilia looked up at Eric and cocked an eyebrow at him. "It doesn't really fit, does it?"

She flipped to another page. "Best moment: Playing GHOST with Eric (he lost, but just barely). Worst moment: It was clear you were hurting and wouldn't tell me why. Biggest fear: That I can't support you as much as you can me. What do I want? To be happy."

Emilia put the papers aside and turned to face Eric. "I can feel the lie behind those answers. And I know why I did it. Because it's terrifying, the thought of being with you, and if I think about it for too long—my mind starts to go crazy and my breathing quickens and it's almost like I'm heading for a panic attack. But I keep trying to remind myself that the task I set for myself today was to answer one question. What do I want?"

Emilia took a breath and looked down at their clasped hands. "You, Eric," she whispered. "But it's not that simple. Because wanting you and wanting to live with this condition with you aren't exactly the same."

"Yeah they are."

"No. I'm not explaining well. Here, let me read this. This was from that letter I wrote myself last weekend. I told myself in this letter to walk away, that that's what was best for you." She turned the letter over to the few paragraphs she'd written at the end. "Then, I came back later and added this: *Don't make your decision for Eric—let him do that. Instead, decide for yourself. What do you want? Can you handle a relationship with your condition? Can you handle the uncertainty? Can you put almost limitless trust in another person? It will be uncomfortable and every day you'll feel guilty and unsure and scared. And if you'd prefer to be alone, that's okay. But once you decide, whether you choose Eric or not, you need to go all in. No waffling. There's been enough of that.*"

Emilia folded the letter and put it back on the table, swallowing past a hard lump in her throat. "That's the part I can't do, Eric. I know I want to be with you. I know it intellectually and I feel it in my heart but—but I'm not sure it's the right thing. I still have a thousand doubts and I don't think I'll ever reach a place of certainty. I'll always worry it's wrong, wonder if I'm really okay with it. I'll always be waffling, and that's not fair to you. I don't want to hurt you again."

Eric just watched her, face unreadable, though she could see the pain in his eyes. She shouldn't have kissed him. That was stupid. She gave him hope, then took it away. And all that rambling about how much she loved him, that didn't help. But she needed him to understand, she needed him to know it wasn't him. *He* was perfect. She was the damaged one.

"So that's it?" he said, pulling her thoughts back to him. "That's your objection? You love me, you want to be with me, but you just have too many doubts?"

"Yeah."

"So you're saying no."

"I—" She couldn't make herself say the word, so just nodded instead.

She tried to look away, but he took her face and turned it back to him. "You're saying no because you're not sure enough."

"I can't go into this doubting everything, Eric. It's not fair—"

"But it's not me you're doubting," he said, cutting her off. "It's just a relationship in general. Is that right?"

"Yes," she breathed.

He continued to watch her, then nodded. "Okay. I can work with that." Eric stood up and held his hand out for her. "Let's go for a walk."

She couldn't help but smile. "Why? Because going outside is your solution to all problems?"

He shrugged. "Maybe."

She gestured toward the window. "It's snowing."

"We'll dress warm. Come on. You can tell me about every doubt and we'll just—talk through it all. Okay? Something we should have done months ago."

Emilia looked at his outstretched palm for a long while, then placed her hand in his. "Okay."

* 30 *

They bundled up and ventured into the snow, with Eric tucking Emilia under his arm as soon as they were on the sidewalk. "Where to?" she asked.

"Let's go to the park."

They walked in silence to the end of the block, the entire world around them muted by the snowfall. It was so quiet she could almost hear the snowflakes falling onto the ground and the sound of her heart thumping in her chest.

When Eric spoke next, his voice was a whisper, like he didn't want to disturb the peace they'd found. "You told me once that when two people are arguing, it's best for them to go on a walk. That way, they're facing in the same direction as they work through the issue."

"I said that?"

"You'd read it somewhere."

"I like that. But I don't want this to be an argument."

"You love arguing," he pointed out.

"Not with you. Not about … this."

"Okay. Let's just talk then." Eric looked down at her and smiled. Her heart fluttered. He was very handsome. Had he always been this handsome?

Emilia tightened her grip on his waist. "Okay."

"Tell me what's making you unsure about us."

"It's a long list," she warned.

"I have nowhere to be."

She started with the small concerns, listing them off as they walked. Eric had an answer for each one. He'd clearly been thinking about this for a long time. They were crossing into the park as he finished explaining a process they could use for managing arguments. Eric took a deep breath and led them to a path that wound around a small lake, which was frozen over and covered with a light layer of snow.

"Okay," she allowed. "You're right, it's not impossible. It would just require a lot of trust."

"Are you worried about that?"

"No," she said quickly. "I trust you implicitly."

Eric leaned into her. "Ditto. What other concerns do you have?"

Emilia gulped. She was embarrassed about the next topic, but knew they needed to address it. "That covers all the logistical concerns. I guess my next area of concern is—um—sex."

"What about it?"

She could feel Eric's eyes on her, but she kept her gaze on the path. "I know we've done it. I don't know how many times. But, uh–" She stopped on the path. She was worried when she looked over at Eric he'd be smirking, but he was watching her seriously.

"What?" he pressed.

"Is it boring? Do I just fumble around like it's my first time? Couples need a healthy sex life, and if you feel like you're having sex with a virgin every time, I don't see how—"

Eric cut her off with a kiss. But unlike the kiss they'd shared back at his house, this one was… intense. He pushed her back until she collided with a tree trunk and pressed his body into hers. His mouth moved insistently, and when she parted her lips, he wasted no time before sliding his tongue past them.

He had one of his hands on her rib cage and the other in her hair, but she had no idea what to do with her hands. She was just trying to breathe and keep the mix of sensations from overwhelming her: the taste of Eric's tongue against hers, his hands pulling slightly at her hair, the scratching of his beard against her lips, his thumb resting just under one of her breasts, the icy air contrasting with his warm breath, the cold snow from the tree against her back.

When she finally stopped fighting the rush of feelings and gave into them, her body took over, moving on its own accord. She pushed her hands under his coat and pulled him closer by his shirt, then turned her head and caught his bottom lip in her mouth. She bit down gently, causing him to let out a low, perfect moan.

Her next kiss was so eager, their teeth clicked. He laughed, which she swallowed before running her tongue along his bottom lip. Damn his mouth was perfect. Why hadn't they done this before her accident? Then she'd remember it forever. God, she wanted more. She ground her hips into him and felt his—

A gasp escaped her lips and she pulled back.

Eric let out a laugh and placed a soft kiss on her neck before leaning back. He smiled at her, then propped his hands on the tree trunk and whispered in her ear, "Sex with you is never boring." He kissed her cheek, then her jaw, then her neck, sending shivers down her spine. "This feels familiar, doesn't it?"

Emilia nodded, unable to speak.

"When we're together, your instincts take over, and you know exactly what to do. This concern of yours—that we'd have a boring sex life. Believe me, it's a non-issue."

He gave her a final, chaste kiss on the lips before moving off the tree.

Emilia took a moment to catch her breath as she patted her hair, which was wet with snow. She looked around them but the park was empty. Most people tended to stay inside when it was snowing. But most people weren't Eric. The thought made her smile.

He stood on the path, watching her with a wolfish grin. "If you still don't believe me, I'd be willing to have sex with you as soon as we get back to the house—just to remove any lingering doubts."

Emilia laughed outwardly while inwardly, heat pooled in her lower abdomen. "Thank you," she said sarcastically, "that's very generous of you." She slotted herself back into her place at his side, and they continued walking around the lake while Emilia tried to work up the courage for the next topic.

"I know you have more," he said. "I'm waiting for one concern in particular, and I wonder if you're thinking about it right now, since it sort of relates to sex."

She was reminded of a line from the summary she'd read about him this morning. *He has this eerie ability to know exactly what you're thinking and feeling.* "Yeah," she sighed, but couldn't bring herself to say anything more.

"Kids," Eric provided.

Emilia nodded while he hummed. They continued walking, each facing forward while she clutched his arm and sorted through what she wanted to say. When she was ready, she stopped on the path and turned to face him. The snow fall had calmed, as if it was also waiting to hear what she was about to say.

"So much for facing in the same direction," he quipped.

She smiled. "I need to see your face when we talk about this, so I can see if you're lying."

"I'd never lie to you."

"Good. So you're not going to stand there and tell me you don't want kids, because I *know* you do. We've talked about it. You want at least two kids, since you liked growing up with siblings and want your kids to have that same experience. You want to teach them how to ski, and camp, and bike. You want to tuck them in each night and play with them every day. You want to be there, to learn who they are as people, to really pay attention and support them along the way. To give them that simple pleasure of having an engaged, supportive parent that you were denied."

Emilia crossed her arms and waited for Eric's rebuttal. He fixed her with a stern glare that mirrored her own expression, then said simply, "I remember that conversation. You also want at least two kids, since you also enjoyed growing up with a sibling. You want to read to them all the time and make sure they have a solid understanding of how our government works, and the role they play in it. You want to travel and show them other cultures. You want them to be more athletic than you were, and so you'll probably send them over to my house for those skiing and biking lessons."

Emilia wiped away a tear that had rolled down her face before hardening her gaze.

"I don't think your kids will have to go very far for those lessons," he said gently, wiping away the wet track the tear had made with his thumb.

"I changed my mind," she whispered. "Something awful happened and I changed my mind. It happens. But don't stand there and tell me you changed yours too, because then you'd be lying."

He placed his hands on her arms. "I didn't change my mind and neither did you. You *can* have kids, Emilia. It will be hard, yes, but I've seen you with Henry. You've grown to love him and that's just after seeing him a few times a week. I know with your own kids, those feelings will be even deeper."

"I won't remember them! I won't know their names! I won't

know their birthdays, their friends, what games they like. I won't remember their little stories or even what their voices sound like. It would be a disaster, and they'd hate me."

"You'd write it down, and I'd fill in the rest. And they would understand your limitations, just as everyone else in your life does. People say parenting is so complicated but it's not. It's hard, that's for sure, but not complicated. All you have to do is love your children and be willing to give them your whole heart. You'd be amazing at that part."

Emilia closed her eyes and shook her head. But before she could argue again, Eric continued talking.

"But I understand if you ultimately decide you don't want children. Really, I do. And I would honestly be okay with that. I know it's a different dream from the one I had for myself a few years ago, but all I really wanted was a family of my own, and who says a family can't have just two people in it?"

"But I can't take that away from you. I can't—"

"You're not allowed to make decisions for me, remember? We don't have to solve this now—but can we agree it's not allowed to be a dealbreaker? Because your only concern here is that you're taking something away from me, and that's my decision, not yours."

Emilia let out a long sigh. When did Eric get so good at arguing? She placed a hand on his cheek and gave him a small smile. "I hear what you're saying, but I don't want you to go into this thinking you'll change my mind. I may never agree to have children, and if you're thinking you're going to be able to convince me to do so later and I never do, then you'll resent me and we'll fall apart."

Eric regarded her for several moments, then turned his head and kissed the inside of her glove. "Okay. I understand and I wasn't lying before—I'd be fine if it was just you and me. I'd rather be childless with you than surrounded by five children with any other woman."

"Really?"

"Really."

Emilia leaned forward and studied his eyes closely. "You don't appear to be lying."

"Because I'm not."

"Okay."

Eric hugged her, then put her arm in his and continued down the path. "So, we're striking that off the list?"

"Yes."

He let out a large sigh of relief. "That's good news. I think that was the biggest one."

Emilia waited until they'd completed the loop around the lake before turning to him and saying, "That wasn't the biggest one. I saved the biggest one for last."

"Bigger than the kids concern? Wow. Maybe we should sit for this one." He motioned toward a nearby bench, and Emilia clutched his arm tightly as they made their way to it.

Eric swept the snow away, then sat down. Once they were both seated, he wrapped his arm around her and linked his gloved hand with one of hers. "Okay, still facing the same direction, so that's good."

She nodded and smiled as she looked out at the lake. It was gorgeous. Usually, this park was nothing special. It was the mountains in the distance that commanded everyone's attention. But snow and ice had the power to make the mundane look majestic.

The bare branches in the trees no longer looked dead when elegantly frosted with serenity. The brown grass was covered in a thick, white blanket. And the ice around the lampposts and street signs made them sparkle like diamonds.

She imagined it was similar to the effect Eric had on her life. Transforming it from the depressing scene of a lonely girl with no memories, who was forced to say goodbye to her dreams, to someone who sparkled and shimmered with peace. An enchanted story of two best friends who battled against the circumstances standing between them and fell in love. Who chose each other every morning and resolved together to make the most out of their days.

"What's your final concern?" His breath tickled her cheek, warming it for a few seconds before the chilly air took over, making the skin feel even colder than it had before.

It took her a while to get all the words together in her mind, but Eric waited for her to sort it out. She was reminded of how patient he was. He'd certainly need that if he was going to share a life with her.

"Eric, I know I hurt you very badly and that it got worse and worse over time, but I couldn't see it. That's what scares me most about getting into a relationship with you. The fact that I could cause such damage and not know. What's to stop that from happening again?"

Eric was quiet for a long time and now it was Emilia's turn to be patient. When she turned to look at him, his brow was furrowed and his eyes were a stormy gray-blue. "I let you do that," he said eventually, "cause all that damage, as you put it. You didn't do that alone."

"Why?"

"August told me this last weekend that because of my messed-up childhood I'd convinced myself that I don't deserve a happy ending," he said, eyes trained on the frozen lake in front of them.

"He said that was why I wasn't fighting for you. Or—more specifically, why I wasn't fighting for my own happiness."

He stopped talking and after several moments of silence, Emilia asked, "Was he right?"

Eric shook his head. "Not exactly. I was thinking about it all week and part of what he said was right, I wasn't fighting for us. I let you walk away over and over and never intervened, when I should have, but it wasn't because I don't think I deserve a happy ending."

He finally turned to face her and the look in his eyes was so intense, she almost leaned back. "I don't think I deserve a happy ending with *you*. Or, I didn't."

"What? Why?"

Eric wrapped both of his arms around Emilia and placed his chin on her head. When he spoke again his voice was shaky. "I never put you first. I was so caught up in my own stuff and rarely stopped to check on you. I was a good friend, I think, but nothing special. But you… you were incredible. You were always there. Like that time you dropped everything to take care of Henry when I had that exam. Or when you drove all the way out to the mountains to pick me up after my car had broken down, even though you'd pulled an all-nighter the day before.

"I can't think of any stories like that where I went out of my way for you. All I can remember was you asking me to come to Nebraska because your sister had called you in tears, and your dad had had an affair, and your mom had locked herself in her room and you didn't think you could do it alone. And I said no."

Eric shifted and turned to her, then took her face in his hand. "I am so sorry, but I got better. I almost lost you, then finally realized what I had in you, but it was too late. And what kills me, more than anything, is that the last memory you have of me before your accident is me choosing Henry over you. Every morning when you first think of me, that's the first thing that comes to your mind."

A few tears had fallen onto his face and Emilia started wiping them away with her sleeve. "I knew you weren't choosing Henry over me. It was a terrible situation. Sarah's fault, really. Not yours. I shouldn't have shouted at you. I was just taking out my frustrations on you because you were there, but I knew you couldn't leave. Please stop beating yourself up over it."

She wound her arms around Eric's neck and hugged him tightly. "That's why I let this painful back and forth go on for so long," he whispered. "Deep down, I thought it was adequate punishment for not noticing you for so long and taking you for granted. I was waiting for you to give me permission to love you, but, well, like you said—you couldn't see what was happening."

She pulled back and stared intently at him. "I'm giving you permission now. And if we do this, you have to promise me you won't do that again."

"I promise."

"And what you said," she continued, "about me remembering that fight before my accident first thing in the morning; that's not true. When I saw your letter, my main thought was: 'Why did he say "I love you" at the end? What's that about?'"

Eric let out a small laugh.

"And when I first saw you in person, I was thinking, 'Oh good, he's real. I didn't make it all up. He's different. He has a beard now. And I want to kiss him.'"

He laughed again. "It's funny you say that, since that was sort of the point of this." He was rubbing a hand along his jaw.

"The beard?"

He nodded. "At first it was just a stupid thing. Me and a few guys from work grew beards for a month for this fundraiser. I never meant to keep it, but you saw me one day and said, 'Oh, Eric. It's you. For a second I thought you were a different person.' That's when I decided to keep it. Because I wanted you to think that every time you saw me. I wanted you to know that I'm a different person now."

Eric placed his hands on either side of her face. "I'm not that clueless boy who was a subpar friend to you. I've grown into someone who loves you and sees so clearly how remarkable you are. Someone who wants to spend every moment he can with you and will never take advantage of you again. And, apparently, that man has a beard," he added with a smile.

Emilia smiled back, then leaned forward and kissed said beard before moving her lips to meet his. "I love you. I should have said that earlier. I love you so, so much."

He grinned. "I love you too."

Emilia dropped her head into the crook of his neck and took a deep breath. He smelled good, familiar, and he was so warm. She sat there enjoying the sensation for several moments. "That was it," she said after a while. "Those were all my concerns."

"Yeah?"

She nodded into his shoulder. "Yeah."

Eric gently pushed her up to a sitting position. "So now what? Do you—do you want this? Me? Us? Are you finally sure?"

"I ... yeah. I think so. I mean ... yes. I'm sure."

He gave her a beaming smile that nearly took her breath away. A smile better than any closing argument she'd ever studied—undeniable proof that she'd chosen correctly. Things would be hard between them, but for the first time that day, she felt hope when she thought of a future with him.

"What now?" he asked.

As if in answer to his question, Emilia's stomach roared loudly, causing them both to laugh. "How about lunch?" she suggested.

Eric stood up from the bench, then helped her up. "There's this Mexican Restaurant at the edge of town. They make great mole. How does that sound?"

"I don't think I've ever had mole."

"Not that you remember."

"That's true," she said as she grabbed his arm. "We agreed that if we did this, I'd have to trust you, so I guess I'll start now. Yes, let's have mole and you can order because I'll have no idea what anything is but I trust you know what I like."

"Actually, you know what you like. You choose the same thing every time. I'll show you."

Emilia smiled up at him. "Does this count as our first date?"

"You know, I think it does. But if it goes badly, we can just have another one tomorrow."

* * *

After a late lunch, Eric and Emilia walked aimlessly around the streets of the town. The snow had stopped so there were other people out on the sidewalks with them, also enjoying the newly frosted landscape. They just talked, mostly about the time Emilia couldn't remember. Eric was finishing up his explanation about how he'd managed to "train" Bartholomew as they entered a different park. They sat on a bench and Emilia laid her head on his shoulder as they watched a group of kids sledding down a large hill.

After that, they went to a café for some tea and dessert. It was late by the time they were finished but Eric didn't seem to want to return home. He'd dragged out their visit to the café to two whole hours, and now she suspected he was going to suggest they walk some more.

"You seem to be avoiding the house," Emilia said once they left the café and stepped onto the sidewalk.

Eric sighed, then pulled her close to him by her scarf and kissed her cheek. "That was the scene of the repeated 'Emilia declares her love for me, then changes her mind and disappears into the night' crime," he explained.

Her chest clenched. "I'm not going to disappear into the night. And we can't walk around forever. We're going to have to go back home eventually, unless you're suggesting we sleep on a park bench like we're homeless, then freeze to death. The shortest love story of all time."

"Probably not a great end to our first date."

Emilia shook her head in agreement. "Let's go home, okay? I need to edit my summary about you, right? Make this real?"

Eric nodded but his eyes looked haunted. She'd made this promise to him before but had never followed through.

When they returned to the house, they removed their wet outerwear, then went straight to her bedroom. Emilia was still rubbing her hands together, trying to get warm, as she sat at her desk, while Eric took a seat behind her on the bed. She looked over her shoulder and smiled at him, then couldn't force herself to turn back around. Eric cocked his head toward the desk and raised an eyebrow in question.

"I don't want to do this," she admitted.

His face fell, and she rushed to reassure him, taking a seat at his side. "I'm not changing my mind. I'm just exhausted and my brain is all muddled. I've done so much thinking today and even more walking and all I want to do is warm up in a hot bath, then go to bed. Both with, um, you," she added with a shy smile.

"That's ... hard to say no to. But ..." He paused, jaw tight. He waved back toward the papers on her desk. "When are you going to do this? If you don't do it tonight, you'll just forget."

"You can tell me tomorrow."

Eric was quiet and she could tell by his expression that he hated the suggestion.

"We'll sleep in here, so I can't leave in the middle of the night," she said in a rush. "And tomorrow, when my mind is fresh, we'll rewrite all the letters. But tonight, let's just focus on us. Please?"

Eric placed his hands on hers, which were still cold, and said. "I'm very scared you're going to change your mind and then all this will be gone. I really feel like we should get something in writing."

She waited for him to look at her before responding. "We already said that for this to work, I'm going to need to trust you implicitly. You need to trust me too."

Eric's eyes were swimming with pain. She knew he was remembering all those times she'd made promises to him, then broken them while he was asleep. But she meant what she said. He needed to trust her. And for that to happen, she needed to start building back the trust she'd lost. "I know you have a lot of reasons to doubt me, but I'm telling the truth, Eric. I'm not going to leave you tonight."

He exhaled heavily, then leaned forward and rested his forehead against hers. "I'm giving you everything, Emilia. My whole heart. Please don't break it."

"I won't."

Part 9: Emilia Rhodes

Emilia thinks the biggest tragedy of her life is that she can't remember things, but it's not.

* 31 *

Emilia woke up slowly the next morning. She could see a soft light through her eyelids, but she lacked the energy to force her eyes open. She felt warm, and as she flexed and unflexed her muscles, her limbs felt tired and heavy but in a pleasant, lazy sort of way. That's when she realized she wasn't alone.

Her eyes fluttered open to reveal a man in the bed with her. He was lying on his side, facing her, with one hand draped lazily over her bare stomach. She looked down. The bedspread shrouded the bottom half of their bodies, but Emilia could see the edge of her panties and the man's boxers. She let out a sigh of relief. They weren't completely naked; they just didn't have shirts on.

She slowly pulled up the sheet to cover her chest before looking back at the man. Now that her vision had cleared of its initial fogginess, she recognized him. It was Eric. But it was a different Eric from the one she knew in real life. He wasn't wearing glasses, and he had facial hair. She was in bed with Eric. How surreal.

She reached out and pushed away a lock of hair that had fallen over one eye. Once it was out of the way, he looked closer to the Eric she knew. The unfamiliar room was blanketed in a faint light, making everything look rosy and a bit fuzzy.

Emilia smiled as her hazy thoughts finally put it together. This was a dream. She felt so blissfully warm and couldn't think of a time in real life when she'd ever felt this content. She was fine to just lie here and revel in the illusion until she woke up.

After what seemed like a few minutes, Emilia felt Eric's hand move to her waist, then tighten its grip on her. This fantasy felt like reality, and she gave kudos to her brain for having the ability to create such realistic sensations. Eric's eyelids moved and eventually opened. When his eyes focused on her, his lips turned up.

He pulled his hand away from her waist and traced the edge of her face. "You are so beautiful," he whispered, sounding awed. "I've never woken up with you before."

Emilia grabbed his hand and kissed it, then noticed that his eyes were shimmering with tears. She watched as one floated down to the pillow. Emilia shifted closer to him and wiped his eyes with the edge of the sheet. "Why are you crying?"

He leaned forward and pressed his lips against her forehead. "Sorry. I'm very weepy lately, but nothing's wrong. I promise. I'm still very manly."

Emilia felt his lips moving against her forehead and his warm breath on her skin. She was beginning to suspect this wasn't a dream. It felt too real. Moving on instinct, she buried her head in the crook of his neck and linked her hands behind his head. The feeling of his thick hair between her fingers, the warmth of his skin, his scent—there was no way she could have imagined all of this. She wasn't dreaming. This was real.

And even though she had no idea where she was or how she got here, why Eric was here, or why they were half-naked, she felt safe. Her mind was beginning to run wild as it emerged from the sluggishness of sleep, but her body was calm. Emilia pressed herself against Eric and focused on her heart, which was beating steadily, almost in perfect time with his.

He wrapped an arm around her back and pulled her close. "I know you're probably scared and confused about where you are and why you're with me, but you can relax. You're safe. I promise."

Emilia still couldn't make sense of anything, but she could

feel the truth in his words. He began tracing his fingertips over the top of her back, which sent shudders of warmth through her body. She snuggled closer to him and focused on the feeling of her chest rising and falling against his.

She was safe. She was confused and had no idea where she was, but she was in Eric's arms, and she was safe. He seemed to know what was going on. She had no idea what it could be but for now, knowing Eric knew and didn't seem concerned was good enough. After a few minutes, she managed to peel herself away from him. She leaned back slightly, so she could see his face, then blushed and repositioned the sheet over her chest. "What's happening, Eric?"

With a small smile, he reached behind him and picked up a scrap of paper from the nightstand. He handed it to her, and she flipped it open and read a few lines written in her own handwriting.

You love Eric and he loves you. You can trust him. Everything's okay. You don't have to do it all alone.

-E

She looked back up at Eric, who was watching her expectantly. "Um, thanks, but I'd already gathered all of this on my own."

He let out a low rumble of a laugh. "I insisted you write something down last night, and you insisted you wouldn't need it, but did so anyway, just to make me feel better. I should have known better than to go against someone who's always right."

"I wrote this last night?"

Eric nodded and took one of her hands. "You were in a car accident and almost died when you were on your way to Nebraska with August. You sustained some lasting brain damage and now, only form memories for a day, then everything resets each night. It's March 1st, 1987 today."

"What happened to August?"

"He's okay. He broke his arm, but it healed fine. He's a doctor now, doing his first year as a surgical intern in Boise."

"And my parents?"

"They got divorced. They live in Nebraska still, but in different cities. Viola lives here, though, just a few miles away.

"A few miles from where? Where are we?"

"Aspen Grove. This is the house I grew up in. You visited here a few times before the accident, but I doubt you'd recognize it. We've renovated most of it since we moved in."

She looked around the room. There were a few familiar pieces: a lamp she remembered from her apartment, a teddy bear on the shelf from when she was a kid, but most of the room was new. Sometime in the past two years she'd helped Eric redecorate an entire house. She'd filled those bookshelves, picked out the bedding and curtains, maybe even the paint color. But no matter how hard she tried, she couldn't recall any of those moments.

Two years. Two whole years (plus a few months), with no memories. With her parents getting divorced, Viola leaving New York, August becoming a doctor, and she'd missed it. Maybe she hadn't technically missed it, but she may as well have. Emilia's thoughts were spiraling. She crawled back into Eric's arms and tried to find that serenity from before.

"You have a good life," he told her. "You've achieved so much and are still managing to put your mark on the world. You have a lot of friends who love you, you laugh, and have fun—all of it. Even with this limitation."

Emilia nodded as he held her close. It seemed impossible that she could be happy with this life, but she could sense the truth of his words somewhere deep inside. That feeling when she'd woken up—that contentment—she'd felt that at her core.

Apparently, she had a good life. With Eric ... She just couldn't remember it.

As Emilia lay in Eric's arms, taking slow, deliberate breaths, she began to recapture a bit of the calm from earlier. Eric ran his hands through her hair and whispered reassurances every few moments in her ear. Things like, "I love you," "You're okay," and "I'm here. You're not alone."

Everything's okay. You don't have to do it all alone.

"We're together," she said after a while. It wasn't a question; she was just testing the words on her tongue.

He took in a ragged breath, then repeated in a wavering voice, "We're together."

Emilia leaned her head back and saw he had tears in his eyes again. "That makes you sad?"

He let out a small laugh and shook his head as the tears splashed onto his cheeks. "Like I said earlier, I'm just very weepy. I'll get over it soon."

She reached up and wiped his tears away. "Why are you so weepy?"

"This," he said with a heavy sigh, "waking up next to you. I was starting to think we'd never get here. I was sure you were going to scream when you woke up and saw me here. I tried to get you to put your clothes back on, but you insisted you'd know. And you do, don't you?"

"Know what?" Emilia recalled the note again. "That I love you and you love me?"

He nodded.

"Yes. I know. I feel it. But I don't understand," she said carefully. "Do we not go through this every morning?"

"No. This is day two of our relationship, and the first time we've woken up together."

"What?" This thing between them, it seemed to run deep. It was hard to believe it was so new.

"Yeah," he smiled. "And apparently, I'm an emotional wreck now." He paused to take a large, shaky breath. "This is what you've reduced me to. You're to blame for all these tears, but I can assure you that they are very happy tears." He smiled again, then grabbed her chin and kissed the side of her mouth.

He tried to pull away, but Emilia didn't let him. She moved her hands to the back of his head and kissed him fully. She moved tentatively at first but soon, the achingly soft kiss wasn't enough for her. She pulled his bottom lip into her mouth and nibbled it lightly, then pressed her tongue against his. As she intensified their kiss, Eric met each of her actions; every lick, every nibble, every caress.

He grabbed her by the hips and pulled her close, and she could feel his erection pressing into her leg. She gasped and pulled away, fighting for breath as her cheeks colored. She felt embarrassed by her passionate response to what had started as an innocent kiss. She dropped her head against his chest as she caught her breath.

"Are you okay?"

Emilia nodded and looked back up at him. His eyes were swimming with concern as they darted across her face. "I'm great. But, um, I know this is probably a stupid question, because of that kiss and our state of undress, but, um, did we have sex last night?"

"Yes," he said simply. "We also took a bath together."

"Oh. And that was my, um, first time?"

Eric shook his head. "No. I think it was like our fifteenth or sixteenth time. Yesterday was our first official day as a couple but we'd been together before. It's a long story."

Emilia could see the pain in his eyes as he spoke. He'd said he hadn't expected her to be here this morning, which meant there were other mornings when she hadn't been. What had happened? Had they slept together, agreed to start a relationship, and then gone to sleep, just to have her steal away in the night and forget everything? How awful. She couldn't see herself doing that to him.

She'd have to ask him more about that later, but for now, she just wanted to make that pain in his eyes go away. She shifted closer to him and ran her fingers along the hair on his chest. It was strange, touching Eric like this, but it didn't feel wrong. It felt familiar, like she was watching a movie she'd seen years ago, but had mostly forgotten.

Emilia pressed her lips to one of his collarbones, then slowly kissed a path up his neck. She seemed to instinctively know just where to suck, a spot right under his ear, to elicit a low groan. She nipped his earlobe and whispered, "Can we do it again? Maybe go for round sixteen or seventeen?"

Emilia had no idea where this bout of sexy confidence had come from, but it seemed to be working. When she looked up at Eric, his blue eyes were dark with desire. She could tell her own body wanted this and resolved to just let it take over, since it seemed to know what it was doing.

She moved her hand down his chest, over his stomach, and stopped at the edge of his boxers. She slipped a finger under the elastic of his waistband and whispered, "I'm waiting for some sort of confirmation here. Consent is very important to me."

Eric let out a low laugh, then flipped her over onto her back, making her squeal. He pulled his boxers down and kicked them off before climbing on top of her. "Is this enough confirmation for you?" he growled in her ear.

She pressed her hips against him in answer, then pushed him up by the shoulders so she could see him. Her eyes scanned his body. "You're really handsome."

Eric smiled. "And you're beautiful."

"Also, um, I have no idea what I'm doing."

He bent down and kissed her cheek. "You say that every time, and you're wrong every time."

Eric moved off her and linked a finger into the elastic of her underwear. He cocked an eyebrow at her and said with a roguish smile, "May I take these off? Consent is very important to me too."

She nodded, and as he slowly peeled off her underwear, her heart started pounding so loudly, it was all her mind could focus on. He was back on top of her, watching her, seemingly waiting for something, and she guessed her nerves were showing on her face. She forced a smile there and reminded herself this wasn't her first time before pulling Eric into a kiss.

He moved his hand down and gently slipped one finger inside of her. "Oh," she gasped, clenching around him.

"Relax," he murmured in her ear, then began moving his hand expertly, just further proof this wasn't new for them. When he slid in a second finger and began rubbing her clit with his palm, she forgot to be nervous.

"That feels incredible," she panted after several moments, digging her nails into his shoulders.

He kissed her cheek, then lifted his head. "I need to get a condom. Don't go anywhere."

"Yeah, okay," she breathed, feeling instantly bereft once he left her side. Luckily, he wasn't gone long, and it gave her a chance to look at him, all of him, which was... she had no words. Just, *damn ... abs ... penis ... erect penis ... right there ... hot.* Yeah, her dirty talk needed work. The thought made her blush. She hid her face in her hands as Eric climbed back into bed.

There was the sound of tearing paper, then some shifting. She opened her fingers and peeked through them. He was holding his own erection. Holy shit, that was hot. Too hot. Too much. She closed the space in her fingers as heat pooled in her belly.

"Why are you hiding?"

"I'm—I don't—this is—a—a lot."

"We don't have to do this," he said gently, trailing a finger down her side. Every nerve ending he touched burned with want for him, as did the millions of others he hadn't touched.

"I want this," she said, slowly lowering her hands. "I promise."

Eric shifted slightly, then lifted one of her legs and linked it over his shoulder. He stopped just above her, holding himself at her entrance, and raised an eyebrow in question. She nodded again, and he lowered himself down. They both let out a collective sigh once he was inside of her.

He began to move and the feeling was … not what Emilia had been expecting. She'd expected a bit of pain followed by mind-blowing pleasure—if the gossip from her roommates in college was to be believed. But this was subtler than that. It felt good, being filled up by him, and at the end of each of his thrusts she was hit by small shudders of pleasure, but it wasn't as acute as when he'd been touching her before.

The experience was more emotional than physical. She was with Eric, locking eyes with him as he moved inside her. Panting in time with him and grinning with pride when he released an occasional grunt or whispered her name. This was intimacy, something she'd never shared with August or her high school boyfriends, and that knowledge hit her so much more intensely than any of the bodily sensations.

As if he could read her thoughts and had taken them as a challenge, Eric began rubbing between her legs, causing her to retract her earlier thought. This *was* mind-blowing. The combination of all the ways he was touching her was sublime. His length hitting her at a perfect angle, his fingers rubbing her clit while his other hand caressed her breast. She was struggling to think, even taking in air was difficult, but she had a fleeting thought about doing something to make him feel just as good.

She lifted up and sucked on that spot on his neck she'd found earlier. Eric let out a long moan, and she felt it vibrate against her lips. Then she reached down and fondled his balls. He swore and pulled back, then gave her a wicked grin. "I thought you didn't know what you were doing."

She just smiled, not trusting her ability to form words, then reached down and touched him again. It wasn't much longer before he finished, tensing up and groaning into her neck. He took several deep breaths, told her he loved her again, then pulled out and continued pleasuring her with his hand as he peppered kisses along her breasts and neck. She cried out as the tension in her core finally snapped. She nearly saw stars behind her eyes as the jolts of pleasure worked their way through her.

"Mind-blowing indeed." At least, that's what she'd meant to say. It came out sounding more like, "Mndblodeed."

"What?"

Emilia just hummed.

She lay there for a few moments as she tried to decide which parts of sex she liked best, the physical pleasure or the feeling of being so close to Eric. She hadn't come to a conclusion by the time she opened her eyes and saw him propped up on his elbow, beaming down at her.

"That was amazing," she whispered.

"Agreed." He lay down next to her and wrapped an arm around her middle. "Usually I call it a good day if you're smiling and joking within the first hour of waking up. Morning sex; that's a whole new bar you've just set."

"We've never had sex in the morning before?"

"No."

Emilia turned onto her side and saw his eyes were wet again. "More weeping? I think you have a serious condition."

"Happy tears," he said as he blinked rapidly. "I just never thought morning sex was something we'd ever get to enjoy."

She assumed he was referring to her condition, but she didn't want to think about that right now. "I liked it, morning sex," she said matter-of-factly. "Or, well, just sex in general. We should do it again."

Eric smiled and placed a quick kiss on her lips. "Deal. But first, we have a big day ahead of us. I need to catch you up on everything we decided on yesterday, we have to slog through all your notes and letters and add in the new, 'Eric's my boyfriend' information, we need to eat because I'm starving, and somewhere in there I need to go to June's to get the box she stole from you. Then, we'll have sex. At least one more time. Probably twice."

She caught the finger he'd been trailing along her jawline and kissed it. "That sounds like a big day. Do we really have to do all of that?"

"Yes," Eric said simply, shoving his glasses on and sitting up. He was clearly eager to get the day started. And she was curious to learn more about her life, like why Eric had said it took them so long to get here, why he'd thought she wouldn't be here in the morning, and perhaps why he was so weepy.

And his mention of June reminded her of her friends. She wanted to know what was going on in their lives. When had

Viola moved here? When had August moved away? Was he okay with her relationship with Eric? Was June? When had they all broken up?

She was distracted from her thoughts by the sight of Eric removing his condom and wrapping it in a few tissues he'd grabbed from her nightstand. "Thank you for, um, thinking of that," she said, feeling a little embarrassed. But her mom had always said if you couldn't talk about methods of contraception with your partner, you shouldn't be having sex with them, so she powered on.

"No problem."

"Maybe now that we're in a relationship I can take the pill. Or we can keep using condoms, if you want. As long as we always use something. Obviously, I can never have kids."

Eric bit his lip and frowned. "We've already had this argument. I'll catch you up later though, it's too heavy for a post-coital morning chat." He was at her side, holding his hand out to her. "Come on, let's go take a shower. And after that, breakfast."

Emilia placed her hand in his, and he pulled her to her feet, then wrapped an arm around her. The modesty that Emilia had been too distracted to remember during sex was back now. She felt exposed and had to keep reminding herself that she'd been naked with Eric before.

Eric didn't seem phased by it. Rather, he couldn't seem to stop smiling. And there was an unmistakable bounce in his step. He was giddy. She allowed that while this was weird, walking naked with Eric through an unfamiliar house, it was also sort of wonderful.

"Are you going to tell me what topics of conversation *are* appropriate for post-coital morning chats?" she asked when they arrived in a bedroom she assumed was his.

"Yes, of course. I have a list in the nightstand. I'm an expert on this topic."

"Oh yeah? I thought this was our first time having morning sex. But—oh. You're talking about other girlfriends? Or… June? I just assumed—"

"We broke up a while ago. There have been no other girlfriends. I was kidding. Come on, give me more credit. You're the only woman for me. That's why June broke up with me by the way, she knew it even before I did."

Emilia just nodded as Eric guided them toward a closed door. "I have no way to know if you're kidding," she said. "You could be cheating on me and I'd have no idea. And if I did ever find out, I'd just forget the next day."

Eric turned to her and tilted her chin up. When he spoke, his blue eyes were intense. "You *do* have a way to know. It's me, and I would never do that. There are a thousand ways for me to take advantage of your memory loss and I will never, *ever* use any of them."

"I know," she said immediately. The words spilled out of her mouth automatically, forced out by an almost overwhelming wave of trust.

"Good." He kissed her cheek and opened the door to the bathroom, then let go of her and stepped inside. "Also, infidelity is not on the list of approved topics. Pick something else."

"You're naked," Emilia blurted out. He was standing several feet away, and she had taken the opportunity to admire his body again. It was nice. *Really* nice. But now she was embarrassed for having drawn attention to it.

"Are you just now noticing? I thought you were supposed to be smart."

"I'm brain damaged now," she quipped as she followed him into the bathroom.

"Ah—you've stumbled on two approved topics," Eric said as he started the shower, "us being nude and jokes about your condition."

He put his glasses on the counter and walked into the shower. Emilia stood in place. Maybe this *was* a dream. She was naked, joking with Eric (who she'd just had sex with), and now they were going to take a shower together. This couldn't be real. But … it was. Her heart swelled at that last thought.

"Get in here, girlfriend, I can't reach my back," he called.

"What do you usually do?"

"Never wash it. It hasn't seen soap in years."

Emilia smiled and stepped into the shower. "It's a good thing you have me."

Eric grabbed her chin and kissed her. "Yes," he said when he pulled away, eyes shining so brightly, she wondered if the sun was hiding behind them. "Yes, it is."

✻ 32 ✻

Later, Eric and Emilia were at the stove, cooking pancakes. Well, he was cooking while she watched, standing behind him with her arms wrapped around his middle and her chin propped on his shoulder. She kissed his neck and whispered in his ear, "Am I crowding you? Do you hate this?"

He smiled and pulled his free arm up to cover hers. "You are not crowding me and I don't hate this."

"Of course he doesn't hate this," a voice said behind them. "This is what he's been dreaming about for months. Probably even years."

Emilia jumped away from Eric and turned around to find June in the doorway, holding what looked like a miniature trunk. Her blonde hair was cut short, she had a nose ring and a tattoo on her forearm, and she looked more muscular than Emilia remembered. But the harshness of her new, more intimidating look was offset by a glowing smile.

"Well, what do we have here?" June smirked as she placed the box she was holding on the table. Emilia pulled down the hem of the shirt she was wearing, instantly regretting grabbing one of Eric's flannel shirts to wear after their shower instead of going back to her room to change.

"Thanks for bringing that back," Eric said over his shoulder. "I'm going to tell you off later for taking it in the first place."

"Tell me off?" June scoffed. "You should be thanking me. Because by the looks of it—based on Emilia's wet hair, that outfit, and her ever-increasing blush—you two had sex, then took a shower together and it's—" June looked down at her watch, "—not even nine."

Emilia buried her face in her hands. This was so awkward.

The next moment, June was hugging her. "You don't have to be embarrassed, Emilia. I don't care. Eric and I broke up over a year ago."

Emilia dropped her hands from her face. June didn't seem jealous at all. Just giddy, like Eric. Emilia was more curious than ever to learn about their history, but he said he wouldn't tell her anything until after breakfast.

June nudged Emilia's arm and said teasingly, "You're welcome, by the way. I'm the one who taught Eric his way around a woma—"

June was cut off by Eric slapping a hand over her mouth. "Okay, that's enough. Time for you to go." Eric took June by the shoulders and marched her toward the hall. "Thanks for bringing the box back, we'll see you in a few days."

"Wait! You didn't even confirm. Are you two together?"

Eric dropped June's shoulders and raked his hand through his hair, like he did when he was nervous.

"Yes. We are," Emilia chimed in. He looked back at her and gave her a warm smile. Again, he seemed surprised that this relationship was real, which was odd, since it felt so natural to her.

"Yay!" June clapped. "We need to celebrate. How about a party?"

"No," Eric said while Emilia said at the same time, "Okay."

"Hah! Emilia said 'okay.'"

Eric groaned. "Fine. But it has to be small. Only the people she has summaries on."

"Yeah, small. Of course. We'll do it here at seven, that way you can't escape. Just the summary people, and Ruby, of course. Maybe Viola's roommate, too. I'll set it up." June started walking backward toward the front door. "I'm going to run off before you get a chance to change your mind or put any other constraints on it. Congratulations and I'll see both of you tonight!"

Emilia heard the door slam shut, then Eric gave Emilia an exasperated look. She frowned. "Sorry. A party sounded fun."

Eric shook his head. "As soon as she got that idea in her head, there was no stopping it. You're right, a party will be fun."

"Who are the 'summary people'?"

"Ah. It's part of what we need to work on after breakfast." Eric focused back on the plate of pancakes. He set them on the table and grabbed two clean plates from the cabinet. "You usually start the day by reading all these summaries about your friends, so you generally know what to expect when you see them."

"Oh. That's smart. Where do I keep those?"

"On your desk. I probably should have shown you but I was distracted." Eric grinned at her, and she blushed as she returned his smile.

"Anyway," he continued, "the summary people are June, August, Owen, and Viola."

"Oh. That is a small party. Good. And who is Ruby?"

"Ruby is June's girlfriend."

"Oh. Right. She's bisexual. She told us that."

Eric nodded as he finished his bite of pancake.

Emilia sipped on a mug of tea as she tried to reconcile this new, edgy, June who dated women with her friend from college. "What did you think when you found out she was with a woman?" she asked carefully.

Eric shrugged. "I was fine. The only person who had a problem with it was Mrs. Pearson. That's when June started changing her look, mostly to piss her off, but I like it. It fits her. Anyway, when June told me she was with a girl, my main thought was that I must have been a really shitty boyfriend to turn her off men. And she's only dated women since we broke up, so I may have been right."

"I'm sure you weren't a bad boyfriend."

"Oh, I was, because I was in love with someone else."

Emilia was chewing and smiled at him, then realized she may have just made an inaccurate assumption. "Were you talking about me?" she asked as soon as her mouth was empty.

Eric rolled his eyes. "Yes. You really are brain damaged."

She kicked him under the table. These offhand comments about how much he loved her were going to take some getting used to. But she'd never get used to them, would she? How awful.

"What's wrong?" Eric had noticed the abrupt change in her demeanor.

"It just makes me sad that I'm going to forget all this."

"I'll remember, if that makes you feel any better."

"It does." She sighed and took a large gulp of coffee. "What about August?"

"What about him?"

"June's obviously supportive of the two of us. Is August?"

"Yeah. You broke up with him shortly after your accident, and he hasn't had a serious girlfriend since. He likes his status of eligible bachelor." Eric turned and looked toward the hall. "Speaking of August, I'm actually surprised he hasn't called. I was sure June was going to call him as soon as—"

A phone rang from another room, causing Eric to smile. "There he is."

They both rose and walked toward the source of the ringing, a phone in what looked like a home office. As soon as Eric picked up the receiver, Emilia could hear August's voice on the other end, "Are you two really together?!"

"Yeah. Can you stop yelling?"

"Oh, fuck! Speaking of fuck, did you two…? You know. June said she was wearing your shirt and not much else." Eric groaned and pinched the bridge of his nose, but August continued anyway. "It's still the morning! How long after you woke up did it happen? How did you—?"

"Hey, August!" Emilia cut in, taking the phone from Eric. "Can you stop asking inappropriate questions about Eric's and my personal life?"

"Hey, Em! You'll tell me. What happened between you two? Are you finally together?"

"Yeah," she said, smiling at Eric. "We are."

"And you'll be together tomorrow and the next day, too? Is this real?"

"Yes, absolutely," she said immediately, watching Eric as she spoke, so he could see she meant it.

"Thank God. Okay, I need to run. The nurses are looking at me weird. Thank you for fixing this, thank you for not overthinking it, you made the right decision, okay? So no doubting or taking it back."

"Yeah, okay."

"And, Em?"

"Yeah?"

He lowered his voice, probably so he wouldn't be heard through the receiver. "Don't hurt him again."

Her eyes flooded with tears, and she dropped them, but not before Eric noticed. He stepped closer to her as Emilia said a final goodbye and hung up the phone.

"What did he say at the end there?" Eric asked.

"Not to hurt you again."

He hummed.

"What happened, Eric?"

"We should—"

The phone rang again, causing both of them to jump. Eric answered, then promptly handed it to Emilia. "It's your sister."

"Viola?" She didn't know why she'd phrased it as a question. It's not like she had another sister.

"Hey, Emilia! How was the challenge?"

"Um, good?"

"What did you decide?"

Emilia frowned at Eric, who shrugged, probably because he couldn't hear Viola, who wasn't as loud as August.

"I'm with Eric. Does that answer the question?"

Viola unleashed a very girly, very uncharacteristic squeal, and Emilia had to hold the phone away from her ear until she was done.

"Oh my God! Finally! So the challenge worked?! That's amazing. I'm coming over."

"No! Um, not now. Eric and I need to talk. Maybe, um, later? June is throwing a party tonight."

"Tonight? I should be allowed to see you sooner," she whined. "How about lunch?"

"Oh. Okay. Lunch sounds good."

Eric frowned as she said that, but Emilia just lifted her shoulders and gave him a look that said, *What was I supposed to say?*

"Perfect. Now hand the phone to Eric."

Emilia did as instructed and watched Eric listen to her sister. His face was unreadable during the conversation, though he'd occasionally lift his eyes to her and smile. Viola seemed to be going on and on while Eric just answered in clipped responses, like, "Yeah," and "I get it."

At the end, he began speaking in full sentences again. "Yeah, you should come here, so we don't waste much time. How about 12:30?"

Viola asked something and he replied with, "Abby's bakery, can you pick that up? She likes the number three and I like number five. Okay. See you then."

"What was that about?" Emilia asked as he hung up the phone.

He sighed and rubbed the back of his neck. "Lots of 'I told you so's, a little advice, and an 'if you hurt her I'll kill you' threat thrown in."

Emilia snorted. "Does she think she's scary?"

"No idea," he grinned, then pulled her into a kiss. "I love getting to do that whenever I want." He nuzzled his face in her neck, causing her to squeal as he tickled her with his beard. "Am I crowding you?" he teased. "Do you hate this?"

She was still laughing when she managed to free herself from the attack. "No. Never."

Eric took her hand and pulled her back into the hall. "Good. Let's finish eating, then get to work."

* 33 *

An hour later, Eric was sitting at Emilia's desk, holding a pen above a blank piece of paper and laughing at Emilia, who was trying very hard to hold her tongue.

"Are you literally biting your tongue?"

"Mmm-mph," she replied as she shook her head, making Eric laugh louder.

She *was* biting her tongue and bit down harder as Eric started to write. He'd just explained the method they'd agreed to for writing down the outcome of their arguments so they wouldn't keep having the same fight over and over. Anytime one of the topics came up, he would let her know they'd already discussed it and inform her of the outcome, or refer her to the argument log they were about to create.

The system made sense. It wasn't fair for Eric to have to keep having the same conversations again and again, but in practice, it was agonizing. All she was given was the topic and the resolution they'd come to, with none of the context that had gotten them there. That was why she was biting her tongue, because it was difficult for her not to fight back or point out arguments she may or may not have brought up before.

It also didn't help that Eric had chosen to start with the most contentious topic, but she figured he'd done that on purpose to get it out of the way.

"Topic," Eric said aloud as he wrote. "Whether or not you should have kids."

"Status: Not resolved," Emilia added quickly.

"Not resolved," he repeated. "Interim conclusion: This is not allowed to be a dealbreaker for us being together. Emilia is adamant she'll never want to have kids. Eric disagrees but knows it's a possibility and wants to be with her anyway. Families are allowed to exist with just two people."

"Did I point out—?"

"Yes," he cut her off.

"But—"

"Ah, ah, ah," he motioned back to the paper.

"It's not resolved, though, so we *will* have this argument again."

"True. But not now. We have years to sort this out. Okay, next topic." He added a blank piece of paper to the stack and began to write again. "Can we have a healthy sex life?"

"We talked about that?"

Eric nodded. "You had a very long list of reasons why you thought we couldn't be together and this was one of them. Status: Resolved. Final conclusion: …" He turned to her and cocked his head. "Any guesses?"

Emilia rolled her eyes. "No need to be so smug about it."

He wrote *YES* in all caps as he chuckled to himself.

They continued like that for the next hour as Eric filled her in on all the arguments they'd had and whether or not they were resolved. Emilia had to resist the urge to argue more, but it got easier as they went. She was just glad for the lighter conversation. Earlier, Eric explained their past and showed her a letter she'd written herself last weekend. She'd struggled to keep from crying as her heart broke for him.

"Was it really this bad?" she'd asked once she was finished reading her harsh words.

Eric sighed and looked away. After a few moments, she pressed him and he said, "I'm torn between not wanting to lie to you and not wanting to make you feel bad." And that was answer enough. No wonder he was so weepy this morning.

When she asked him why he'd let it get so bad, he admitted to the guilt he'd been holding on to about how he'd taken her for granted when they were younger, and how he hadn't gone with her to Nebraska. Emilia made a mental note to get that argument down on the log too. It would be important for her to know that Eric thought deep down that he didn't deserve her in case he tried to pull away from her again.

She could also see him conveniently forgetting to log that argument. But it should be in the front and its final conclusion: *Eric does deserve Emilia and has more than made up for any past indiscretions*, needed to be written in indelible ink.

After they finished their argument log, Emilia rewrote her summary about Eric since the original one was woefully inadequate. Once she was done, she stretched her hands over her head. "Are we finished?"

"Almost." Eric left the room and returned with the box June had brought by this morning. She'd almost forgotten about that.

"What's in there?"

"I don't know for sure, but I have a suspicion." He looked down at his watch. "Viola will be here in about an hour. We can wait until after lunch to go through this."

Emilia shook her head. "No, let's get it over with." She was already emotionally drained from all the information she'd taken in so far, and she knew if she stepped away, she might not have the energy to come back to it.

"I should have known that given the option of working more and taking a break, you'd pick working."

"Yes, you should have known. Aren't you supposed to have an uncanny ability to guess my thoughts and feelings?" she asked with a smirk. That was one of the few telling things she'd recorded in his previous summary. She was glad that the summary she had on him now accurately reflected the depth and complexity of their relationship.

Eric leaned forward and kissed her. He'd been doing that a lot today, but she still wasn't used to it. She thought again of how she'd probably never get used to it, but this time, the thought didn't upset her. She'd be lucky enough to forever experience the thrill of a new relationship—when even the smallest touches made her heart race.

"How bad is it going to be?" she whispered as Eric pulled away.

He shrugged and took a spot on the bed next to the miniature trunk. "I don't think it will be too bad," he repeated, "but before we find out, we need to find the key."

"You don't know where it is?"

"No," he frowned. "I assume somewhere over there." She followed his gaze to her desk, then got up and started searching. It didn't take her long to find it, hidden behind a picture of her and Eric. She couldn't describe how, but she'd just known when she saw the photo that there was more to it.

"I can't believe there was ever a question that I loved you," she told him as she put the frame back together, then took the key over to the bed.

He let out a laugh as he sat down on the other side of the small trunk and watched her open it. There was a folded stack of papers on top, tied with a thin blue ribbon. She untied the ribbon and saw there were two letters, one small one, taking up half the page, and a longer letter that went across several pages. She read the shorter note first.

Emilia,

I'm sure you've already figured out the point of the 'one day at a time' challenge. As soon as you realized you'd acted out of the ordinary, you probably set a goal to find out why. But in case you don't know, the point of it was to figure out what you want. More specifically—whether you want a relationship with Eric.

You spent an entire month starting each morning fresh, with nothing influencing you toward him, and now it's time to review what happened. How often did you mention him in your notes? How many times did you make your way back to him? Do you truly love him? If the answer is yes, decide next if you can handle the inevitable difficulties that would come from having a relationship with your condition.

Whatever you decide, you have to be sure. No more waffling. I know this is a lot to ask, but you've strung Eric along for too long and he deserves a final decision. You can do this. You <u>have</u> to do this. Good luck!

-Emilia from January 31, 1987

When she finished reading, about to summarize the note for Eric, she saw him looking at the longer, folded up letter on the bed. She followed his eyes and saw *For Eric* written on the outside. Emilia picked it up and handed it to him.

He just held it in his hand, looking reluctant to open it. "No matter what it says, nothing here is going to change," she said softly. "You don't even need to read it if you don't want to." Though she hoped he would, since she was curious to learn what was inside.

Eric nodded and shifted closer to her, so she could read alongside him.

Eric,

I owe you an explanation for why I never went back to your room the night of your birthday. For why I hid away the album, the notes, and the summary you wrote about me, and for why I broke the promises I made you earlier today. So here it is.

After you left, doubt crept in as I thought of us being together. My mind went through everything: little inconveniences like you losing an hour every morning to help me get settled to large ones, like never having children, and a hundred things in between.

I was pacing the house, driving myself crazy, when I ended up in my bedroom. I scanned the bookshelf for something to read, anything to take my mind off its current thoughts, when I saw a small book of poems. I began flipping through it and my eye was caught by writing on a few of the pages. I sat on the floor and read the pages you'd marked up, crying the whole time.

Then, I did something I've never done in my life (and still feel queasy about) and tore my favorite page out of the book. I began pacing the house again with the page in my hands but this time, instead of concerns and worries floating through my brain, it was your words. And when I reached my bedroom again, it hit me—I can't make this decision for you. All my doubts are thoughts and worries for you, not me. I love you and want to be with you, and if you want the same, who am I to get in the way?

I returned to the library and repacked the box, then a poisonous thought seeped into my mind (for the record, I've officially concluded that I think too much). The thought was: "Of course you're going to be with Eric. You owe him after everything he's done for you." Then, I began to lose it.

I began to wonder if I truly loved you or if I just thought I loved you because I'd become reliant on you. I was pretty sure it was real, but I was worried, because I wasn't sure. I don't have the history to draw on, just countless notes—many of which were written by you.

This is when Viola found me. I asked her if it was real, because if I was going to go through with this, it had to be real. She said only I could answer that. I cried again and the longer I thought about it, the more confused I became. That's when the idea for living one day at a time came about.

ONE DAY AT A TIME

I know this past month was probably hard for you, and I know that on February 1st, you probably felt betrayed, but I want you to know I did it for you. At the end of this month, I'm going to make a final decision. And I need to know for certain that I'm all in, because I'm going to write it in my notes and commit to it every day.

It's like you told me earlier; most people choose their partners every day but me, I choose once, write it down, and follow my notes. I just need one month to see what I choose when I start the days fresh. If I choose you, we'll both know definitively that it's real. If I don't choose you, I'm so sorry, but it will be for the best. Otherwise, I'll probably change my mind later and restart this awful back and forth and that can't continue.

I've considered walking across the hall and telling you all this right now, but I can't. I know you. You'll fight me on it, and I know me; I'll cave, because I've always put your happiness ahead of everything else. So I'm trying hard to stay here on the bed. I'm trying to forget that it's your birthday and not think of how devastated you're going to be tomorrow.

This is for you, Eric. For us. I hope you understand and can find it in your heart to forgive me. And now, it's time for present day Emilia to tell you what she decided. Even if she didn't choose you, know that I love you and wish you every happiness.

-Emilia from January 31, 1987

Eric sighed and put the letter down, then took his glasses off and pressed his fingers into his eyes. While he did this, Emilia saw a page from a book fall out of the letter. She grabbed it and recognized what must have been the page she'd torn from the book of poems.

"I wouldn't have fought you," he said, voice strained. "I would have let you go about your challenge. You should have told me. We could have avoided a lot of unnecessary heart ache."

"I'm sorry. I do overthink things. And I tend to make them more complicated than they need to be."

Eric let out a small laugh and put his glasses back on. "No kidding. But it's done and like we said, this changes nothing." He reached over and placed a hand on top of hers, then noticed the page she was holding. "Oh. The poems."

"Yeah." Emilia looked down at the page, where there were two poems, followed by some writing. "Do you mind if I read them?" Eric shook his head, and she began to read the first poem.

Please, don't forget about me. Please, don't stop loving me or change your mind about how you feel about me. Because I need you in my life—even if it's just a little bit. I need you to be able to be me. You are the only place I can be me and that's okay.

When she looked up at Eric, he was watching her sadly. "This is beautiful, but really sad," she whispered.

"Yeah. Beautiful and sad. That pretty much sums up our story. The second one is sadder, but just as true as the first."

Emilia looked back at the page and read the second poem.

You can't always be somebody's 'forever'. Sometimes you're just their 'summer' or their 'little while' ... Sometimes not even that.

Sometimes the closest you'll get is their 'almost' or their 'maybe'. And when they leave, the best you can hope for is to be their 'what if' or 'remember when'. Because you can't always be somebody's 'forever' ... even if they were yours.

Underneath the poems, Eric had written a few lines of his own.

Maybe I'm not your 'forever'. Perhaps I'm just your 'almost, if things were different' or your 'in another life, maybe.' But regardless, don't send me away. I need you, and I'll take any part of you you're willing to give. The poem said it better than I ever could: "You are the only place I can be me and that's okay."

Emilia was crying by the time she reached the last line. Her heart ripped itself into tatters as she imagined Eric writing these lines. How had he found the book? What had made him stop to read the poems? How long had he waited for her to find the lines and seek him out?

This page made Eric's anguish clearer than anything else she'd seen or heard today. No wonder June and August had been so happy for them this morning. They'd been forced to watch Emilia hurt Eric for months without realizing what she was doing. But now she'd know. It was in her summary and in their argument log, and maybe she'd frame this, too, as a reminder of where their relationship began—a dark place of misunderstandings and a yearning to be somewhere neither of them knew how to find.

Eric was watching her warily, as if *he* was concerned for *her*. Emilia set the page to the side and crawled closer to him. "Eric, I'm sorry. The words don't seem adequate, but I am. And I understand if you haven't forgiven me yet and need more time."

"There's nothing to forgive. You were trying your best to do what was right for both of us, given your limitations. I played a part in this too, remember? But now we're together and can begin to put all this pain behind us."

He pressed a kiss to her forehead, then turned to the box and began rifling through the contents. His lips turned up as he pulled out a large book. "Here, look at this. This will make you feel better."

He pushed the box to the side and wrapped an arm around her as he showed her a photo album he'd made filled with pictures and notes from the time she couldn't remember. Every picture had a small caption and a date, written in Eric's writing. Occasionally he'd written longer notes, further describing the event or scene.

Emilia loved getting to see herself laughing with her friends. She imagined that looking through this every morning had helped her come to terms with her memory loss quicker. This was proof that she was still able to live a good, happy life.

She also noticed why her past self had seen this album as something that had predisposed her toward Eric. Not only were all the notes written by him, but anytime they were in a photo together, she was right next to him, usually touching him. Hugging him, resting her head on his shoulder, grabbing his arm, or just holding his hand.

When she reached the end of the album, she started back at the beginning, wanting to go through it more slowly the second time. She was looking at a photo of June, August, and her at their parents' house, before June had cut her hair, when Eric's voice cut into her thoughts.

"Ah. Here it is." He pulled a piece of paper out of the box. "This is the summary I wrote about you. You used to read it every day, right after you looked through that photo album. Do you want to hear it?"

She nodded, and he began to read.

"*In 1984, Emilia had an accident. She thinks it's her most defining characteristic, but she's wrong. On a long list of the most important things to know about Emilia, her memory loss doesn't even rank in the top one hundred.*

"*She is kind, brilliant, funny, strong, and beautiful, with an infectious smile, and an even more engaging laugh. She loves everyone with her whole heart and is determined to leave the world better than she found it. (See a list of accomplishments below for proof of how much work she does for others.)*

"*But before you start to think that Emilia is a bore who works all the time, let me set the record straight. She enjoys a number of leisure* activities, such as skiing, heckling the Seavers, winning the spelling game, GHOST, and losing at chess. She likes hiking (yes, you really do) and loves to read, especially snuggled up with her cat, Bartholomew.

"Emilia thinks the biggest tragedy of her life is that she can't remember things, but it's not. The biggest tragedy is that she doesn't have a proper view of herself. She thinks she's plain and boring, overly bossy at times, and a burden to her friends. But she couldn't be more wrong. She improves the lives of everyone around her, and I count myself lucky to be one of her closest friends."

Eric handed the page to Emilia when he was finished reading. Written below the summary was a long list of things she had accomplished in the time she couldn't remember, along with dates. She shook her head as she read through the list, wiping her eyes when she reached the end. "I read that every morning and didn't know immediately that you loved me?"

"In your defense, I didn't know I loved you when I first wrote that." He took the page from her and placed it back in the box, then put the photo album and the rest of the scattered papers back inside before placing the box on the ground.

"We were both really stupid."

He shifted toward her, closing the distance between them. "Agreed."

Eric kissed her and Emilia responded eagerly. He pressed her onto the bed and their kisses turned fierce, almost aggressive, as the emotions from the past few hours poured out of her and into their embrace. He had a hand under her shirt and was gripping her waist, running his thumb along the sensitive scar on her ribs. She fumbled with the hem of his shirt and—

"Hello?!" Viola called from downstairs.

Eric let out a frustrated sigh and rolled off her. Emilia sat up next to him and wrapped her arms around his neck, not yet ready for their separation.

"Where are you two?" Viola called from below. "Can you put your clothes back on and come down here? Your food is getting cold!"

Eric rolled his eyes, then kissed Emilia's burning cheek before getting to his feet and pulling her up after him. "I'd just like to point out that it's your fault she's here."

"What was I supposed to say?" she hissed. "She's my sister."

"You're allowed to say no to her," he replied as they approached the stairs. "But she knows you never will. She looks sweet, but that Viola is manipulative. And today, I'm sure she's going to be … smug."

Viola was finally in view, smiling sweetly at them from the bottom of the stairs. "Of course I'm smug," she grinned. "It was my challenge that brought you together, wasn't it?"

"I really need to stop giving everyone keys to the house," Eric sighed. "We have a doorbell. Feel free to use it."

Viola shrugged. She reached out for Emilia, who had just landed at the bottom of the stairs, and pulled her into a firm hug. "You did it!" Viola said into her hair. "You silenced your thoughts and followed your heart, and now you're going to live happily ever after."

"I don't think it's that simple," Emilia said as she pulled away.

"It is," her sister insisted.

Emilia turned to Eric, who gave her a lopsided grin that said, *Why not?*

Emilia stepped into her place at his side. "Okay then. I guess it is that simple."

"Works for me," Eric beamed, then bent to kiss the top of her head.

Part 10: The Shaffers
Ten years later

* 34 *

Emilia was dreaming that she was married to Eric. Nothing much was happening in the dream. She was just lying in bed with him, holding his hand and rubbing her thumb over his wedding band while he slept.

As she watched the sky brighten from black to grey through a slit in the curtains, she imagined what their life was like in this dream world. He looked older, maybe somewhere in his late thirties, so they probably had kids. Two kids. That was a nice number.

Past that ... her mind didn't fill in any more details. Which was fine. She was enjoying the feelings embracing her and didn't need to know their source. She was wrapped in a warm quilt crafted from blissfulness, peace, and satisfaction, and she never wanted to wake up.

Eric's eyelashes fluttered, and she smiled into her pillow. She kissed his hand, and a sensation that was both cold (from his ring) and warm (from his fingers) touched her lips. What an impressively detailed fantasy.

An alarm went off. But instead of waking her up, it woke him. Eric groaned and turned to shut off the alarm. When he saw her watching him, he cupped her face in his hand. "Hey, how'd you sleep?" When she didn't answer, he added with a smile, "Good dreams?"

She lifted her hand and placed it over his, half worried if she pressed too hard, it would fade into nothing. But it was solid, just like his other hand had been. *He* was solid. Was this ...? Was this real?

Yes. It's real, Emilia, a voice said from somewhere deep in her mind. He pulled her into a firm embrace and she felt immediately at ease.

"You're okay," he murmured in her ear. His voice was thick with sleep, but still undeniably Eric's. "I love you, okay? And you're fine. I promise."

"I love you too," she whispered back. She knew it was true in this place, time, alternate reality—wherever they were—and she also knew it was important for her to tell him, as many chances as she got.

"Is this real?" she asked next. Something told her Eric would know what was going on, even though she had no idea.

"Yes."

"We're married?"

"Last I checked."

Emilia lifted her head and when her eyes met Eric's, he smiled at her and pushed her hair behind her ear. "Eric, I, um … I'm not sure how to put this but I—"

"Don't remember marrying me?"

His smile didn't fade. He shifted so he was lying on his back and motioned for Emilia to join him. She crept closer and rested her head on his chest as he wound an arm around her. She thought again how real this felt. Wow. She and Eric were married. In real life. Not just some fantasy world her mind had created. That meant all those feelings from before—the peace, the contentment—were also real.

Eric began to explain what was going on and the truth was much less exciting than some incredible leap to an alternate reality. He told her about her accident and gave her a brief overview of their life since. She'd initially moved in with August but they broke up after a few months. That's when she'd moved in with Eric, in the house he'd grown up in in Aspen Grove. It took them about two years after that to fall in love and start dating, and another two years to get married.

About a year ago, they'd moved out of Aspen Grove to a house closer to the city, so they could be closer to Eric's office. He wasn't a doctor, but a clinical study director at a medical device company. He told her he loved his job even more than he'd imagined, that he never regretted not becoming a doctor, and that she shouldn't either.

"What's the date?" Emilia asked when Eric was finished speaking.

"April 11, 1997."

Emilia stayed in Eric's arms as she processed the information. She reached out and grabbed his hand and began to turn his wedding ring around his finger. As she played with the band, a thought niggled at the back of her mind. There was something missing. She knew it, though she couldn't pinpoint how.

She looked up at Eric, who was playing with her hair with his eyes closed. "You left something out."

His lips turned up. "I did."

"Why?"

Eric ignored her question. He opened his eyes. His irises seemed more brilliant without his glasses, especially with the light from the lamp shining in them. "Tell me what I forgot, Emilia."

Her mind was racing now, reaching around for clues, but there wasn't information to draw from. She thought of the dream again, or what she had thought was a dream, and the one detail her mind had given her about the supposed fantasy. "Kids," she whispered. "We have kids."

"We do." Eric reached over and wiped away a tear that had fallen onto her cheek. She hadn't even realized it was there. Her mind was completely focused on these phantom children. The ones whose existence she could feel, but whose names and faces were a mystery to her.

"How many?"

"Two."

Exactly as she'd guessed. "Wow." She lay back down. It seemed wrong, being a mother with her condition, but it felt right. And she wasn't doing it alone. She had Eric, who she was sure was an amazing dad.

She suddenly wanted to know more. She wanted to know her kids' names, ages, genders. What they liked and disliked. What they looked liked. She wanted to meet them. They were in the house, they must be. But as she thought of meeting them and not knowing their names, her stomach rolled.

You're okay. Breathe

It was the voice again. It told her to slow her mind. To keep her thoughts short and simple. She was married to Eric. He loved her and she loved him. Things between them felt amazing. They lived just outside the city. They had two kids. Eric was a clinical study director. All the rest of the details she would fill in as the day progressed.

Another alarm went off, and Eric silenced it quickly. He patted her back and said softly, "The kids are going to be here in five minutes."

Emilia sat up on the bed, her eyes wide with alarm. She watched Eric grab a shirt from a nearby chair and pull it on, followed by his glasses. He reached past her to light the lamp on her nightstand, then got up and drew the curtains back, even though it was still mostly dark outside. When he returned to the spot at her side, he leaned in and kissed her cheek. "You're going to be fine. I promise."

Emilia nodded. She didn't feel very confident. But she didn't want to disappoint Eric, so she sat up taller and squared her shoulders. She could do this. "What are their names? How old are they? What are they like?"

He leaned back against the headboard and pulled her against his side. "They're both four—five in a few weeks. Twins, a boy and a girl. They are simultaneously annoying and wonderful, and you'll know their names when you see them."

"How is that possible?"

"I don't know, but you haven't been wrong yet."

Emilia wanted to argue, but she could tell by Eric's tone he wasn't going to budge on this. She hoped if she was flailing in the moment, he'd step in and help her. No, she *knew* he'd help her, if she needed it. She could feel deep in her heart the limitless trust she had in him. That's probably why she felt okay asking him, "Am I a terrible mom?"

"No. I promise. You don't forget them each night. Just now, I left them out of my summary and you knew they were missing."

"Yeah. I guess so." Emilia wrapped her arms around Eric and buried her head back into his chest. She was probably being overly clingy, but she felt safe here, in his arms. It was a welcome escape from the fear and turmoil of her thoughts.

"Who's watching them now? Or do we wake them up or—?" She looked toward the clock on the wall. It was early. They could be asleep. But didn't little kids wake up early? Shit. She was a mom who knew nothing about kids.

"Our nanny watches them," Eric said. He ran his fingers lightly along her back, and she focused on the soothing sound of his voice to keep her thoughts from spiraling. "Her name is Brianna. She comes over early to take care of the kids so you don't have to wake up to chaos while you're trying to reorient yourself."

"That's clever. Whose idea was that?"

"Yours, actually. And I agree. It was clever. They're really great kids, you'll see. But they're also ... a lot. Clever as hell, just like their mom. Funny, especially our daughter—she says the most hilarious things. And our son ... God, he's so caring. And affectionate. I think he got that from you, too."

Emilia smiled up at him. She could listen to Eric talk about their kids all day.

"Do they get along?" she asked.

"Yeah, actually. I think the opposite personalities help with–"

They were interrupted by a knock on the door. She tensed and sat up quickly.

Eric grabbed her chin and gave her a wonderful kiss, which she wished didn't have to end so quickly, then whispered in her ear, "You're going to be fine. And you're not alone." Louder, he said, "Come in!"

The door opened, and before Emilia could properly take in the appearance of the three figures on the other side, the smallest one rushed forward and jumped onto the bed, then hugged her so hard it nearly knocked the wind out of her.

"Mommy! Mommy! Did you think about it?! Did you decide?! Can we spend the summer with Pam and Owen and Greg?! Please? It'll be so fun! And we'll be on our best behavior! We won't get in trouble. Promise. And we can swim every day! And eat in the mess hall and sleep in the cabins and help on the farm. Pleeeaaase?!"

Emilia's mind was racing, trying to keep up with the small girl's words while also trying to guess at her name. "Um ... are you—uh—Camp Ouray?" she asked tentatively.

The girl nodded quickly. "Of course. Where else?!" Her blue eyes, which were exactly like Eric's, were large and pleading. "Please," she said in a softer voice.

Eric reached over and placed a hand on the girl's shoulder.

"You can't bombard your mom with requests first thing in the morning. You know that. Now, please take a deep breath, like we talked about, and give her a second to take in how lovely you are."

The girl let out a long, dramatic sigh. "Fine." But when she looked back at Emilia, she was smiling kindly. "Good morning, Mommy. You can guess my name if you want. Or I can just—"

"Let her guess," Eric cut in. "How about you count to ten in your head?"

The girl nodded, and Emilia could tell this was something she was asked to do often. Emilia took the moment of silence to study her. She was beautiful. When Emilia had first seen her, she'd thought she was a tiny female version of Eric, but she realized that it was just her coloring that was his: chestnut brown hair, brilliant blue eyes, and the same skin tone. But her features were more of a mix.

Her face shape and mouth were Emilia's. And her hair wasn't wavy, like Eric's, but thick and straight. She also had a few freckles peppered across her nose and cheeks. Those were from Emilia; Eric didn't have any freckles.

Emilia closed her eyes and pulled the girl close. The girl melted into her and as she wrapped her arms around Emilia, a name popped into her brain. "Rosalind," she whispered.

The girl nodded and pulled away. "But everyone calls me Rose. I'm only Rosalind when I'm in trouble."

Emilia smiled and reached out to touch Rose's hair. It was thick, but soft. "You really are lovely."

"Thanks. Can we spend the summer at Camp Ouray?"

"Oh. I don't know." Emilia looked to Eric for help.

She noticed a small boy had crawled onto the bed and was sitting at Eric's side. Emilia's eyes locked on his, and she forgot all about Camp Ouray. Eric picked Rose up and moved her onto his lap, then motioned for the boy to climb over to where Emilia was sitting.

"We can discuss this over breakfast," said Eric. "It's your brother's turn."

Rose pouted and crossed her arms over her chest as Eric gave Emilia a knowing smile. She remembered how he'd described them. *"Simultaneously annoying and wonderful."* He'd certainly gotten that description correct.

She focused on the boy who had stopped at her side. Besides having Rose's same color hair and complexion, he looked nothing like her. His eyes were closer to Emilia's shape and were brown, like hers. His face was long and thin, like Eric's had been when he was younger, and his mouth was full and reminded Emilia of pictures she'd seen of Eric's mom. But the biggest difference between the boy and Rose was his demeanor. He gave off an air of calm Emilia was sure Rose had never exhibited.

Emilia smiled at him and he leaned in and said softly, "Hi, Mommy. Bri said there are only seventeen days left 'til our birthday." He said it like it was some big secret that he didn't want to get out.

Emilia lifted a hand and stroked his cheek. "Is that so?" She looked up at Eric for confirmation, who nodded. "Bri's right," she added.

The boy's eyes widened in wonder. "That's not that many. Twenty is a lot but seventeen is less."

"Do you know how many less?" she asked immediately, then wondered if this was too advanced for an almost five-year-old. She didn't know anything about five-year-olds. She looked to Eric again, but he was distracted by Rose, who was whispering loudly in his ear.

Emilia looked back at the boy and saw him thinking hard, then he said, "Three," and held up his hand to show her three small, chubby fingers.

"Excellent."

He looked very pleased with himself.

Emilia tried to focus back on the boy's name. It was right there, hovering just out of reach. Something short, but also long. Something like Rosalind, because there had been a theme. That's when she got it. Emilia, Rosalind, *Benedict*. "Shakespeare," she said aloud.

Eric was watching her and gave her a beaming smile. "It's a family tradition," he whispered, and Emilia had to blink back tears.

She turned back to the boy. "And you're Benedict, but most people call you Ben, don't they?"

He nodded, then climbed into Emilia's lap and gave her a hug. Emilia folded herself around him. Rose had been wiggly in her lap but Ben was a solid, steady weight. Emilia could hold him forever. She guessed by the way he was clutching her that he wouldn't mind.

"Okay, kids." The nanny, Brianna, who had been leaning in the doorway watching the interchange, stepped into the room. She was a slight woman who looked like she'd just graduated college. She had dark hair and a shrewd expression, which Emilia thought was good for someone who spent time looking after a child like Rose.

"We need to give your parents time to get ready before work. We'll see them for breakfast in an hour." She clapped, and the kids jumped out of the bed and rejoined her side.

"And we get to talk about camp at breakfast. Daddy said!" Rose said insistently.

ONE DAY AT A TIME

"Yes, I heard," Brianna said with an exasperated smile. She had a strange metal book in her hand and gave it to Eric. "Here you go, Mr. Shaffer."

Eric shook his head as he took the item. "You can call me Eric, Bri. You're like a third parent to my kids and march them into my bedroom every morning. I don't think we need the formalities anymore."

She just shrugged and guided the kids out of the room. "Old habits. We'll see you two downstairs. Nice to see you, Mrs. Shaffer."

Brianna closed the door with a nod as her final words echoed in Emilia's mind. *Mrs. Shaffer.* That would take some getting used to. Then, Emilia realized she'd probably never get used to it. Her heart rate quickened, and her breathing became shallow as she remembered that she was going to forget everything that had just happened while she slept tonight.

Take a deep breath, the voice in her mind said. *You're okay.*

She did as instructed. When she looked up at Eric, he was watching her expectantly.

"They're beautiful," she said.

"Yeah," he grinned. "They're great. You'll see." He reached out and stroked her cheek. "I love watching you fall in love with them every day. Parents forget, I think, what a miracle their kids are. But you're always in awe of them. It's a good reminder for me. So thanks."

"Anytime," she smiled. "It's hard to believe their twins, though. They look alike, but everything else … they really are opposites."

"Yes," Eric laughed. "And we were lucky it was twins, since your pregnancy was a disaster. The sickness, the shock every time you woke up, and all those night-wakings near the end, you don't do well without a full-night's sleep. Your mind gets very confused. Anyway, it was lucky we had two kids in one go. I don't think we would have survived another nine months of that."

Emilia reached over and grabbed his hand. "You are a saint, Eric."

"Nah. Don't do that. This isn't hard for me, supporting you. Just like supporting me isn't hard for you. I'm not your caretaker," he said insistently, his eyes just as intense as Rose's had been when she'd been talking about Camp Ouray. "We're partners."

She smiled again. "Okay then, partner. What now?"

"You read the information you've left for yourself at your desk," he motioned to a desk at the other end of the room, under the window, "and I work." Eric took the black metal book thing Bri had handed him and opened it to reveal a keyboard, of all things. "I can go through everything with you, but you've told me you prefer to read through it alone, but with me in the room, in case you have any questions."

"What the hell is that?"

"This is a computer. Technology is weird now. You'll see. We both have portable phones that work from anywhere, which I'll show you downstairs. And the kids have these stupid beepy pet things that—well, that one's hard to explain. You'll see."

"O…kay. So you're… doing work on that thing?"

Eric already had the computer open on his lap and was clicking around on it. "I don't have to," he said, looking over the strange object at her.

"No. Go. Work. Of course. I can, um… read my notes."

Eric focused back on the small screen, and Emilia looked at the desk, but hesitated before walking over there. There was one more thing she wanted to do before she left Eric's side, but she didn't know how to ask for it.

Eric pushed the screen down a few inches. "What's wrong?"

She bit her lip and asked quickly, before she could talk herself out of it, "Can I kiss you?"

He let out a small laugh, and Emilia felt her cheeks redden, but stuck her chin out and tried to remain confident. Eric was her husband, so she should be allowed to kiss him whenever she wanted. Eric put the portable computer on the nightstand and crawled over to her. "I would *love* to kiss you."

He closed his eyes and tilted his head to the side, then leaned forward and placed a soft kiss on her lips. Emilia thought that was going to be it, and was a little disappointed, but then he pulled her bottom lip into his mouth and ran his tongue along it. Emilia buried her hands in his hair and deepened their kiss, pressing her tongue against his.

Their kiss was tender and unhurried as they explored each other's mouths, and it was exactly what Emilia had been hoping for. She wondered if maybe this whole morning *was* a dream, since parts of it—like the sight of her children, and this kiss—seemed too perfect to be real.

"I love you," Emilia whispered as she pulled back, remembering how earlier she'd resolved to tell him that as many times today as she could.

"I love you too." He gave her cheek a quick peck, then returned to his side of the bed and picked up the computer. Emilia gave him a final smile before walking over to take a seat at the desk.

✳ 35 ✳

Emilia was relieved, but not very surprised, to find everything on the desk neat and orderly. The various notebooks had clear titles and there was a legend that identified each item and when she was supposed to review it. The legend listed things like: *Argument Log - Review and update as needed, Planner - Read in the morning and reference throughout the day,* or *Summaries - Only read pages for the people you plan to see today (see names in red on calendar).*

There was a short note that described the information gathering process Emilia was supposed to follow each morning and the logging process she would go through each night. After she read that, she turned to the large calendar and found the spot for April 11th. She'd written: *Morning in the office, Lunch with Owen (1pm), Pickup kids (3:30pm), Henry coming for dinner (5:00pm).*

"I have a job?" she asked over her shoulder.

"Of course you have a job. Do you think I'd just let you sit around all day eating bon bons?"

She grinned. "What do I do? What *can* I do? Or, wait, I'm supposed to read about it, aren't I?"

"You can, but I don't mind telling you. You work at the newspaper, *Aspen Whispers.* You have an advice column and do most of the editing."

"Who would want advice from me?"

He smiled, looking like he'd been expecting the question. "Everyone, apparently. You wrote an article for the paper a few years ago and sort of became famous. This *Ask Emmy* column came out of it, which was all you had time for back then, since the kids were still young and absolute terrors. But last year you took on more. And before you ask, it's not charity, or pity, or anything like that. You are really good. When you get to your desk, you'll see tons of notes about what to do. It's sort of the perfect job, since newspapers run in 24 hour cycles, just like you."

"That is … so weird."

He smiled again before turning back to his computer. Emilia grabbed the binder filled with summaries, smiling yet again when she saw that the pages were color-coded. At the front were five pages in blue with a short note that said, *Read about the Shaffers (plus Bri, now an honorary Shaffer) every day.*

Emilia read about Eric, Rose, Ben, Brianna, and at the end, was surprised to find a page about herself. It was written by Eric and by the time she was finished reading, she was wiping away tears.

"What you wrote about me here is lovely, Eric."

He paused his typing. "Lovely, yes. Also true."

She smiled (she was doing so much of that this morning) and turned back to the binder. She found the pages for Owen and Henry and read them as well, since the calendar said she'd see them today.

Next, she was supposed to look through her daily planner. There was even more information in here about her family, but the notes were more tactical. Things like:

Ask Bri how her exam went yesterday

Ben's friend Wyatt King's mom is sick, send a card (address book is in the kitchen)

Rose needs to practice listening to others instead of trying to monopolize every conversation

When you're alone with Eric, make a joke about how you're older than him and will therefore die first

Emilia shook her head as she read the last line, but still resolved to try to fit it in sometime today. When she was finished reading through the notes for the week in the planner, she closed it and stretched her arms above her head.

She looked around the desk again and this time noticed two framed pictures near the back, under one of the bookshelves. She pulled them out and saw a framed article behind them and pulled that out too. The first photo was of Eric, Rose, Ben, and her standing in front of the Golden Gate Bridge. It looked recent, based on the kids' ages, and she guessed it was taken last summer.

Ben was hugging Emilia's leg while Rose was standing at Eric's side, making a face at the camera. The Emilia and Eric in the photo were just watching each other with matching expressions—a look that said, *Well… we got them here,* as well as, *Out of all the people I could be here with, I'm so glad it's you.*

Her heart fluttered and she put the photo back on the desk, moving it closer to the front so she wouldn't miss it tomorrow.

The next photo was of her, Eric, August, and an auburn-haired woman who looked about their age. They were all dressed up, and August had his arm lazily draped over the woman's shoulders. Emilia squinted but couldn't make out any rings on their fingers.

"Is this August's wife? Is he married?" Emilia asked, then realized she could just read his summary instead of bothering Eric, but he didn't seem to mind.

"Yeah. Christine. She's great. He was dating these awful women for years then one day, he showed up with Christine. We were all so shocked and began looking for something wrong with her but couldn't find anything. Then, the mystery became what she was doing with him."

Emilia laughed and looked back at the photo. August was married. They were all married. It was so strange. "How often do we see August?"

"Every few months. He lives in Denver now so it's a short flight, but a little too far to drive. We call him every weekend though."

"Did he ever become a surgeon?"

"He did. And Christine, she's a lawyer, ironically."

"Oh." Her heart thudded, giving way to a pang in her chest. But instead of trying to push it to the side, like she usually would, something told her to examine it. The ache was old, like the scar of a wound that had healed ages ago. Uncomfortable, but not painful.

"You okay?" Eric asked softly."

"I am," she said honestly as she put the photo down. "Sorry. I shouldn't be bothering you."

"You're not." He held her gaze for several seconds, as if to drive the point home, then looked over at the clock. "We have to start getting ready in about fifteen minutes. Are you almost done?"

"Yeah. I only need five minutes."

Eric smirked and muttered, "Overachiever," before turning back to his computer.

Emilia looked at the last frame she'd grabbed from the back of the desk. It was an article she'd written titled, *My Search for the Meaning of Life*. This must be the article Eric had mentioned. The one that had gotten her the column in the paper.

She shook her head. The meaning of life? She was a philosopher now? She skimmed the article and read about an elaborate research project she'd conducted over several years to figure out which theory about the meaning of life was correct. It included personal details, like, *My whole life I dreamed of becoming a lawyer but with my condition, achieving that was impossible. Sometimes you have to let old dreams go and make new ones instead.*

That ache in her chest was back, more acute than it had been before. She took a deep breath, counted to four, then let it out before skipping to the end, curious to see what she'd concluded.

Ultimately, it was my husband who ended up cracking the code. I asked him which of the theories he thought was right. He thought about it for three seconds (that's right, it took him just seconds to figure out what has taken me over seven years) and said, "All of them, none of them. Just live, Emilia, and try to be the best person you can. I don't think it's much more complicated than that."

So that's what I'm doing. Some days, I sit with my twins for hours and watch them sleep in my arms, accomplishing nothing for the day. Other days I try to challenge myself to learn a new skill. And on others, I spend the whole day crying over everything I've lost. It's all just life and like Eric said, you can try to meet all the theories simultaneously, or, even better, ignore them all.

And that's where I'm concluding my research. I've decided that instead of locking myself away in a library, trying to figure out what it all means, I'm just going to live.

Emilia carefully set the article back down on the desk, breathing heavily to ease the tightness in her chest.

"Beautiful. Isn't it?" She turned to see Eric sitting at the foot of the bed, watching her. The computer had been folded back up and was resting on his nightstand.

She nodded as she turned in her chair to face him. "I'm a lot different now. The old Emilia never would have written that."

"Well, you are twelve years older," he pointed out. "And, yes, you've grown. We all have."

He walked to the desk, then pulled her into a hug. "It was always a dream of mine to write an article and have it published," she said into his chest, "but I always thought it would be related to law or politics. Not … that."

When Eric pulled away, he wiped away a few tears that had fallen onto her cheeks. "I think you reached more people with this article. We got tons of mail afterward confirming it, saying by being so public with your struggles and lost dreams, you helped people come to terms with their own. You should be proud of yourself. I am."

She was proud. But everything felt ... bittersweet. That was the best way to describe the morning so far. She'd found herself in the middle of a wonderful life she couldn't remember building. And she was with Eric, the person she'd always loved and trusted most, but she couldn't remember their past.

Their first date, first kiss, first time sleeping together. The day he proposed, their wedding, the moment they found out they were going to be parents. She kept wondering if this was actually real. Could it be real if she didn't remember?

Eric seemed to know exactly what she was thinking. He leaned forward and kissed her cheek. "I remember," he whispered in her ear. "And deep down, so do you."

She was about to ask him if it was enough, but he beat her to it. "It's enough," he said as he pulled away from her. "I promise, it's more than enough."

"You're a mind reader now?"

"Only when it comes to you." Then, he unexpectedly smacked her butt and said with a playful grin, "Okay, enough of that. Let's go take a shower."

He crossed the room and opened a door she hadn't noticed before. "Uh, are we showering together?"

"Yes. It's more efficient that way," he said with a wink. He took his shirt off and threw it to the side before disappearing into the bathroom.

Emilia's heart quickened and her stomach quickly filled with butterflies. She took a deep breath. She could do this. Eric was her husband, and they'd obviously been together. They'd been married for eight years and had children. She steeled herself, peeled off her clothes, and followed him into the bathroom.

He was standing in front of the mirror, naked, and trimming

his beard with a pair of tiny scissors. She tried to keep her eyes off his body and focused instead on his face. "Hi," she said when she entered the room.

"Hi," he replied, keeping his eyes on the mirror.

Emilia turned to what she guessed was her sink and took a deep breath before looking at her reflection in the mirror. She frowned at what she saw there. Her hair was a mess, but that was typical in the morning, and her face looked about the same, a little older—something she'd noticed in the photos—but that was okay. She was older, and Eric looked older too. The biggest change was her body.

Her breasts looked deflated, a thick scar cut across her ribs, and her stomach was flabby with an odd texture. She looked down and saw the texture was from countless white stretch marks. She tried to suck it in, but no matter what she did, her belly continued to poke out. She placed her hands over it and was disappointed to find that it felt as flabby as it looked. Emilia could feel Eric's eyes on her, but was too embarrassed to look over at him so instead, she closed her eyes.

A moment later, he was behind her and hugging her against his chest. "You're beautiful."

"I was more beautiful before," she whined, keeping her eyes closed. She'd always hated her body when she was young, but now she wished she'd taken more time to appreciate it.

"I saw you before. You were younger and your stomach was flatter, but you weren't more beautiful." Eric turned her around and grabbed both of her hands. "You carried and nursed twins. That's an incredible thing your body did for our family."

Emilia crossed her arms over her saggy breasts. "Yeah, I guess," she sighed, scanning his appearance. He looked perfect. When she'd last seen him without a shirt on, he was thin and fit, with long, lean muscles. He was still fit, but a little more filled out, like he'd gained about ten pounds. She couldn't see the definition of his abs anymore, but his stomach was still flat—nothing close to her flabby mess. She raised her eyes and studied his face in the better light.

Damn, he was handsome. Even the added lines around his face were handsome. How was it fair that men got more attractive as they aged while women just got fat and wrinkly?

"I hate how handsome you are," she grumbled before going to start the shower.

When she had the water running, Eric placed his hands on her waist and turned her around, pulling her into a passionate kiss. He moved one hand to her backside and used the other to cup one of her breasts, flicking his thumb over her nipple. She let out a low moan and leaned her head back against the wall behind them. Eric moved his lips down her neck, then nibbled her earlobe before whispering, "I think you're gorgeous, and if we didn't have to be at work in an hour, I'd show you just how much I appreciate your body."

He gave her one last kiss before pulling away and stepping into the shower. Emilia stopped to catch her breath before joining him. When she got in, she wrapped her arms around his middle and gave his shoulder a soft bite. "Why don't we just call in sick so you can show me now?"

He turned around and smiled at her. "We did that just last month. I probably shouldn't do it again, especially with enrollment for my trial starting next week."

Emilia stepped back in surprise. "Wait, what? We called in sick just so we could stay home and have sex?"

"We did. It was your idea."

She laughed so fully that her flabby belly jiggled, though she wasn't paying attention anymore. "Wow. I really have changed."

"Yes, you have." Eric handed her the soap. "Can you wash my back? There's this spot I can never reach."

"What do you do when I'm not in here?"

He shrugged. "You're always in here."

Emilia couldn't help but smile at that.

* * *

Breakfast was a whirlwind. Emilia understood why they made sure there was always someone here to help with the kids, ensuring they had a quiet morning while she readjusted to her life. Waking up to this chaos would have given her a heart attack.

There was shouting. Not because anyone was angry, that just seemed to be the volume at which Rose spoke. And to be heard over her, everyone else had to shout. The radio was also playing, which didn't help with the noise, but Rose threw a fit anytime someone suggested turning it off. Eric gave in, muttering to Emilia, "We need to pick our battles with Rose."

The kids kept popping up out of their seats, reminding Emilia of the gophers she used to see back in Nebraska. Bri dutifully guided them back to the table for what must have totaled 30 or 40 times. Emilia thought she might have had better luck taming actual gophers.

When it was time for Eric and Emilia to leave, she was immediately scolded for trying to open the door to the garage. Apparently, she and Eric needed to be subjected to giant leap-hugs from each of the kids before leaving the house. Eric, who had just answered his portable phone, had to catch the kids one-armed while the other held the strange looking phone to his ear.

Once in the car, Emilia finally had a chance to hear herself think. "Holy shit," she said, exhaling heavily.

Knock. Knock. She jumped, then turned to find Eric standing outside the car, no longer holding the phone to his ear. Emilia looked around for the crank to lower the window and, finding none, just opened the door.

Eric reached into the car and pressed a button to lower the windows. "Oh. Power windows. How fancy," she remarked, closing the car door again.

"Almost all the cars have them now." He knelt down so he was at her level. "And before you ask, no, there's nothing fundamentally different about driving cars these days."

"You really are a mind reader," she grinned.

Eric leaned forward and pressed a kiss to her cheek. "Yes. Trying to guess your thoughts is one of my favorite hobbies. Speaking of which, I know you're nervous, but you're going to be fine. Hannah is the blonde woman who sits at the front. She'll show you to your office when you get in. Once there, you'll find everything you need: your computer, notes, another calendar, photos of your coworkers, all of it. And everyone knows about your memory and won't care that you don't know their names."

Emilia nodded as an unexpected feeling began to spread through her. Something cold and empty, at odds with the tone of the rest of the morning. The reason behind it wasn't hard to figure out.

Eric took her face in his hand, running his thumb over her cheek. "You okay?"

She swallowed back a lump that was forming in her throat and nodded. "I'm good. I'm just, um, going to miss you." The words came out much smaller than she'd meant them to. She mentally berated herself. She was a grown woman, middle-aged, actually. A *mom*. She was stronger than this.

His lips curved into a sad smile. "God. Same. But I'll be home by 5:30. I usually try to duck out early on Fridays, but with enrollment coming up—"

"—things are really busy at your work," she finished for him, recalling reading this in her planner. "I get it. I'm not trying to keep you from doing what you need to. I'm just—I'm fine." She forced a smile on her face as he gave her one last kiss before pulling away.

"I love you. I hope you have an incredible day. Call me if anything comes up. *Anything.* Even if it's dumb."

"Okay. Thanks."

Eric went to his car as Emilia used the switch to raise the window. She waited until he was sitting in the car, with his seatbelt fastened, to press the #1 speed dial button on her miniature phone. She watched Eric reach into his bag, then smile at the tiny screen.

"Hello?" he answered, grinning at her.

"You're hot."

She saw him laugh, then she heard it slightly delayed, through the phone. The sound was a little off, lacking the richness of Eric's laugh, but she knew it well enough to fill in the missing notes.

"You're my favorite person," he said to her.

She smiled, then hung up the phone. They just sat there in their cars, grinning at each other like stupid teenagers for a few moments, before Emilia finally turned the key to start the car. She turned and blew him a kiss through the windows separating them, then pulled away.

* * *

Emilia's morning went by so fast that she felt like she'd just sat at her desk when she looked up from the article she was revising and saw it was time to meet Owen for lunch. The work was a lot better than she'd been expecting when Eric had described it. She only had to respond to two questions a week for her advice column and found she actually had insightful things to say.

When she sat at her computer and began typing (something she was much better at than she remembered) the words that came out were a lovely mixture of wisdom, compassion, and humor. They were not words her 25-year-old self would have come up with. She thought they might belong to that voice in her head. The more mature, more self-assured 37-year-old Emilia who had lived with a debilitating condition for 12 years, but managed to build a wonderful life in spite of it.

Emilia liked that woman, and she wasn't surprised the people of Aspen Grove did too. Every time she reminded herself she *was* that woman, she was overcome with a weird, tingly feeling, like embarrassment mixed with pride.

Besides the advice column, she worked on editing articles. A note on her desk said Stewart, the head editor, wanted the articles to be stand-alone, so anyone could pick up the paper and know what was going on, even if they hadn't been following. Well, she was perfect for that. And she'd always been a good writer, able to communicate things clearly with as few words as possible.

If someone had asked her this morning if she could hold down a real job with her condition, she'd have said no. Yet here she was, working in an office, like millions of other, non-brain damaged people. And it wasn't dull work. By lunch, she felt productive and energized, and marveled again that she was somehow getting paid for this.

It was all so surreal. She was married to Eric, had two beautiful kids, and a flexible job she actually liked. How was this real? But the longer the day went on, the unreality of her current life began to feel less like a dream, and more like a memory.

* 36 *

Later that night, Emilia was sitting at her desk by the window. She looked up occasionally at the brightly shining moon while she prepared for the next day. She felt a bit like the moon herself, waxing and waning day after day—becoming more whole as the day went on, as she learned more about her life. Then losing it all at night, until she started the next day, new again.

Do you forget yourself too? she silently asked the moon. *Does it make you sad? You shine brightly, despite it. I think that's all we can do, really. Shine as much as we can, while we can.*

Just then, Eric entered the room. "The monsters are asleep," he announced. "Are you okay?"

"Yeah. Just … thinking." She turned to him and found him leaning in the doorframe, smiling at her. "Oh!" she said suddenly remembering what she'd wanted to ask him once they were alone again. The bomb her boss had dropped on her just as she was leaving work.

"I've been meaning to ask, something my boss brought up…" The rest of the words got lost in her throat.

Eric came into the room and took a seat on the edge of the bed. "Stewart? What did he say?"

She turned in her chair to face him, then hesitated. Eric got up from the bed and crouched in front of her, taking her hands in his. "What is it? What's wrong?"

"Nothing's wrong. I just—Well it's—" She cut off and started again. This was big. At least, it seemed big. But why hadn't Eric mentioned it? And why wasn't it in her notes? Was it okay to bring it up?

Trust Eric, said the voice that had been guiding her all day. She nodded and squeezed his hand. "He mentioned something about me going to the hospital to see a neurologist. Can you—can you tell me more about that?"

"Oh. Of course." Eric leaned back on his heels and looked up at the bookshelves above her desk. "Here." He stood up and grabbed what looked like a miniature trunk and placed it on the desk.

"This contains some of it, and there's more in the study, if you really want to dive in." He opened the trunk before stepping back. Emilia peered inside and saw a large stack of folders along with scattered post-it notes of various colors.

"I can give you an overview," Eric offered.

"Yes, please."

"Okay," he said, returning to the bed. "It's probably not worth getting into all the medical details this late at night, but the gist is, medical science and technology, just like normal technology, has progressed a lot in the past decade. What the doctors who worked on you back in 1984 thought impossible, might not be impossible anymore. And it's getting better every year."

"So I can—? There's a—?" She couldn't make herself say the word.

"Cure?" he provided. "Maybe. You were visiting with a neurologist about it. This new guy moved into town, Dr. Rolland, one of the best neurologists in the country—apparently drawn here by the teaching hospital, though I think it was the skiing. He goes more than me, but I don't know how he fits it in. Anyway, you met with him, and he loved you. Why wouldn't he? A beautiful, personable, intelligent woman with a very interesting form of brain damage. I think he knows if he can fix this, he won't just be published in every medical journal in the country, but interviewed on the news, by Oprah—"

"Oprah?"

Eric's lips turned up. "Yeah. She—how do I explain Oprah?" He waved dismissively. "It's not important. The point is, he took on your case. Very eagerly. Cleared his schedule for you, gathered a team, all of it. So you started spending your afternoons in the hospital about three times a week, working with him and his team to characterize the injury."

"What does that mean?"

"I'm no expert," he warned. "I know the basics of neurology from school, but nothing like Dr. Rolland. You've probably amassed more knowledge than I have by now," he said, tapping the edge of the box on her lap. "But I've been to a few of the appointments, so I saw some of the process. They strapped you up to all these sensors, then played videos of your past—times you've forgotten—then tracked how all the different areas of your brain reacted to the stimuli."

"Videos! I never even thought of that. Those giant video recorders that you'd put a tape into were new back in '84, but now, with technology, are they better? Do we have one?"

"No."

Her face immediately fell and he reached out and took it in his hand. "We did, but it broke recently. We do have videos, locked up in the safe in the closet. We usually watch some of them on the weekends. And I'm going to surprise you with a nice camcorder at the twins' birthday party in a few weeks, but don't write that down."

"I promise to act surprised," she deadpanned.

Eric laughed. "Good. Anyway, you were going to the hospital, then would come back home and summarize what you'd done and anything the team had learned. It was a lot, since you were working late trying to catch up on the work you'd missed while at the hospital, all while trying to keep up with errands and stuff, but you seemed really excited about it, and I was excited for you. That went on for about two months then, one day ... you stopped."

"Why?

"You've never told me why."

"But you know." She could see it in his eyes.

"I have a suspicion, but I don't want to influence you either way, Emilia." He took the box off her lap and set it on the floor, then picked up her hands. "If you want to throw yourself back into this project, go ahead. I'll support you. I'll get the babysitter back and call Dr. Rolland to set up your appointments. I know he'll be thrilled. But if you want to leave it alone, that's also fine." He lifted her hands to his lips.

Emilia furrowed her brow. She was trying to think why she would have abandoned her attempts to find a cure. "I think I want to look through my notes, if that's okay."

He pressed another kiss to her knuckles and returned her hands. "Go ahead. I have a mountain of emails to reply to anyway."

Eric grabbed his computer from a bag he'd placed on the chair as Emilia set the large box on her desk. She pulled the stack of files out and was trying to figure out where to start when she spotted a blue post-it note on top of one of the piles. Blue was the color she always used for notes related to her family. She picked it up and read the line written across it: *You may not have memories, but they do*

Tears stung her eyes as she carefully placed the blue post-it onto the top folder, then set the pile back in the box and closed the lid. She recalled the article she'd read this morning, the one she'd written, and reached for it and read the last line again.

I've decided that instead of locking myself away in a library, trying to figure out what it all means, I'm just going to live.

Emilia knew why she'd stopped the research. She was no expert in the medical field, but she'd listened to August and Eric enough to know that experimentation on this scale, especially into a subject as complicated as the human mind, could take years. Maybe even decades.

Did she really want to spend all her time holed away at the hospital, or at this desk, closed off from her friends and family? Even now, as she sat here, all she wanted to do was put everything away and snuggle up in bed with Eric.

Maybe in a few years, once the kids were in school all day, she could throw herself into this project. But even then, she'd want to limit it to just a few hours a day, since she didn't want to give up her job or stop helping around the house. Emilia stared at the box as she decided what she wanted to do.

She made a note to set aside a day next month to review everything in the box, then meet with Dr. Rolland and see if they could work on the project slowly, no more than once a week. She wouldn't mind chipping away at the problem, but didn't want it to take over her life.

She listed out the next steps in her planner and put the box back on the shelf. She'd deal with that later. Now, she was tired and wanted to spend time with her husband. Emilia grabbed a random book off the shelf and went to join Eric on the bed.

"Already done?" Eric asked absently. Emilia watched him click a button that looked like a flying envelope, which made a *whooshing* sound. That was cute.

"Yeah," she replied when he turned to look at her. "I changed my mind. I'm too tired to look through those right now, I made a note to go through it next month. I'd rather read here with you, if that's okay."

"Yeah, of course. Here, come on this side." Eric shifted over to her side of the bed and lifted his left arm up. Emilia snuggled into his side and he wrapped his arm around her, kissed the side of her head, then turned back to the computer on his lap.

Emilia opened the book and saw it was full of poems. She started to read, but the words were blurring together and she wasn't in the mood. She preferred to just lay her head on Eric's chest and watch him read emails. Every so often, he said something like, "Are you serious? You put that in an email? Talk about passive aggressive," or "Who taught you to spell, Martin?"

He got through a few more emails before looking down at her. "You're not reading."

She shrugged. "My eyes are tired. I think I'm getting old."

"No. Well, yes, we're all getting old, but your eyes are tired because you need glasses. I've been telling you this for months."

Emilia sat up and crossed her arms. "I don't need glasses, it's the old thing. You wouldn't understand, since I'm a lot older than you."

Eric smirked. "Is that so? Tell me, how much difference does eight months make? Do you even remember?" he teased.

Emilia swatted his arm. "It *is* different. And it's time you came to terms with the fact that I'm probably going to die first."

Eric paused, then laughed loudly. Emilia laughed too, just at the sight of him completely losing it. She obviously didn't know the joke. She'd just been following the instruction in her planner.

"Oh, God," Eric said when he finally recovered. He pulled her against his side again. "Your commitment to jokes across weeks and months, sometimes even years, is one of the many things I love about you."

"You do know that I have no idea what's going on."

"I know. That makes it better." Eric let out a final laugh, then put his computer on the nightstand and turned to her. "Would you like me to read to you? I have glasses, so I can actually see."

"Oh, no, you don't have to do that. You can finish working."

Eric shook his head and picked up the book she'd dropped. "I can read the rest of those tomorrow morning while you're reviewing your notes. Or maybe I'll just mark them all as read."

"You're not a very good employee," she said as she snuggled back against his chest. "Skipping work for sex, taking shortcuts when reviewing emails…"

"It's my wife who's to blame. She's very distracting." Eric opened the book to a random page in the middle, but she took it from him and set it on the nightstand.

"I don't want to read. I—I have another question. Just one more," she said.

"Ask as many as you want."

It took her a minute to find her words. While she searched, they stared into each other's eyes. Damn, she loved him—a love comprised of a million small moments over the years that her brain had forgotten and her heart had remembered.

She leaned forward and kissed him, since that seemed like the perfect thing to do when you realized how much you loved your husband. "You're happy?" she asked. "You're happy with me? With this life?"

"You ask me this every day, and my answer is always the same. I'm happier than I ever imagined possible."

"Do you want me to try to fix it? Commit to working with Dr. Rolland again?"

He kissed her, holding her close as he laid her onto the bed. "I love our life, and I don't need you to fix anything. I don't think anything is broken."

He took his glasses off and put them on top of the book of poems, then began kissing her neck.

"I love our life too," she breathed, burying her fingers in his hair.

Eric lifted on his hands and cocked an eyebrow at her. "Are we finished talking? I want to show you just how much I appreciate your body," he added with a lopsided grin.

"Yeah. We can talk more tomorrow, when we start everything over again."

"Perfect," he grinned. "I can't wait."

The End

Acknowledgment

Thank you to Jamie and Carol, who are truly awesome friends and were forced to read this story way too many times. It would not have been nearly as good without your help.

Thanks to my online supporters for encouraging me to keep writing.

And thanks to YOU for reading. If you enjoyed this story, please leave a review on Goodreads and/or Amazon.

About the Author

Tessa Alexandra

I live in the western part of the United States with three lovely kids and an even lovelier husband. I enjoy reading, wine, hiking, my day job, puzzles, and writing (shocker).

I've always had a vague dream about writing a book and having it published, but never thought it would actually happen. Then I sat down and simply started working on it one day. As Thoreau said, "If you have built castles in the air, your work need not be lost; that is where they should be. Now put the foundations under them."

Made in United States
Troutdale, OR
08/02/2023

11768498R00248